Ellen H. B. Mason

Civilizing Mountain Men

Sketches of mission work among the Karens

Ellen H. B. Mason

Civilizing Mountain Men
Sketches of mission work among the Karens

ISBN/EAN: 9783337288051

Printed in Europe, USA, Canada, Australia, Japan

Cover: Foto ©Andreas Hilbeck / pixelio.de

More available books at **www.hansebooks.com**

CIVILIZING MOUNTAIN MEN

OR

SKETCHES OF MISSION WORK AMONG
THE KARENS.

BY MRS. MASON

OF BURMAH.

EDITED BY L. N. R.

AUTHOR OF

" THE BOOK AND ITS STORY," " THE MISSING LINK," ETC.

LONDON :

JAMES NISBET & Co., 21, BERNERS STREET.

1862.

TO THE GOD OF ISRAEL

THIS RECORD IS HUMBLY OFFERED IN THANKSGIVING. MAY IT

PROVE A SILENT PLEADER FOR THE HEATHEN.

INTRODUCTION.

If the readers of this bright little book have as much
pleasure in its perusal as its English Editor has had,
they will have no reason to complain of the time they
bestow upon it. It is the ROBINSON CRUSOE of Missions, and is directed, as most readable little books are,
very chiefly to the world of children; but sensible,
grown-up people always like good children's books, and
we fairly confess that our sister from the green mountains of Vermont has so bewitched us, that amid many
toils and pressing duties, in a land of civilization, we
have found it a daily refreshment to turn with her into
the jungles, and listen to the mountain echoes. We
have followed her steps over crag and hill, and reposed
with her in gorge and glen; have gone out with her

Karens to fell timber for the Institute, or sat within listening to her lively and practical Bible lessons, luxuriating always in all her *tableaux vivans* of the matchless mountaineers, and truly, we are half sorry that our task is over.

Stern critics have bid us part with the first chapter : we can only say to the reader that when he has arrived at the end of the book, he will return to it as a natural Preface to the Mission work accomplished. For ourselves, we like to know when such a "teacheress" was "raised," as her countrymen would say. This work for the Karens must have been done. This loving leadership of the wild and untaught children of the hills must have been undertaken, and the native poetry of their peculiar history and character has found its record from the sympathizing heart of woman; of a woman made meet for the singular occasion.

Mrs. Mason fills her niche in the long line of America's noble sons and daughters, (how many turn now gathered " to the shining shore,") who seem to have had appointed to them by their Master's hand, and by consent of other Missionaries, the mighty privilege of seeking and carrying the word of salvation to the mysterious and scattered descendants of long exiled "ISRAEL,"—a privilege that bids us glory in the Anglo-Saxon origin and language of the successful explorers. For further details on this head, we must refer the reader to our concluding chapter, and in our Introduction confine ourselves to indicating what the rest of the book is about.

It is chiefly the history of the raising of SELF-SUP-PORTING FEMALE SCHOOLS among the Karens, in which shall be trained those village teachers and Bible-readers, who shall spread everywhere the knowledge of the Lord among a people prepared above all others by ancient associations to receive it.

Mrs. Mason remarks, that teachers, as *men*, have seldom the time and the patience to sit down on a low seat with the ignorant, and say one simple truth over and over, in varied ways.

If you would have Burmah redeemed to the Lord, she adds, send *woman to woman*, and let her teach the A B C of Christianity, which is mothers' work all the world over :—" Moung Shway Moung is like Mount

Meru, very high; he knows everything," say the women of Burmah, "but *he can't talk woman talk ; we don't understand ;"* therefore, if you want to teach heathen women, begin with them as girls.

Now, this is what Mrs. Mason has done, amid many "waitings, and watchings, and wearyings, and heart-achings." She has had the gift from God to stir up others to liberal donations and earnest labours in this department. She has persuaded wild chiefs to choose the cleverest girls of their clans, and bring them down from the mountains to be educated, supporting them and providing for their simple wants while undergoing the process. The capacity and docility of the pupils are amazing, and the result of their acquirements, as taught to others almost as soon as attained by them-selves, is not a little marvellous. The true elevation of woman by Christian education has been thus recognised as a duty by the chiefs of seven tribes in Tounghoo.

So few people read a Preface, that we have sometimes thought it is scarcely worth while to write one; we hasten, therefore, to dismiss our readers to their moun-tain rambles, believing that they will return from them most deeply interested in the hitherto despised and outcast KARENS, and willing to help in every way the disinterested workers in that now important Missionary field.

It may only be further necessary to remark, that the name of the nation is pronounced Ka-*rens*, the first syllable short; and the appellation "mama," so frequently used by the natives, is not pronounced as in English, but contrariwise—*mam*-ma, the accent on the first syllable.

L. N. R.

CONTENTS.

PART I.

PART II.

PART III.

PART I.

CHAPTER I.

WHEN a child eleven years old, my mother always gave me one hour a day for my own time. This was invariably spent by the side of a wild mountain brook, that came tumbling and dancing down through a grove of birch-trees. It was a most companionable little stream, clear as crystal, full of smooth white pebbles and little speckled trout.

My brother fitted me up a small leafy alcove, carpeted with scarlet lichens, close down to the margin, with my pet flowers, the wild violet and the forget-me-not, all around, and close by, a patch of those bright red winter-green berries that all New England children know. There the old family Bible was daily spread open at Solomon's Prayer. There, too, the woods often echoed with the "Sweet Bower of Prayer," while I dug gold thread and made little golden skeins for baby sister.*

There, with the brook and the trout, I planned many

---

* The fibrous yellow roots of the three-leaved Hellebore, which New England school children delight in.

B

a castle, which then seemed as much beyond my grasp
as the moon ; yet, somehow or other, almost every plan
has been realized. The reason may have been, that
every castle had a Bible and a Bower of Prayer.

I don't know why I liked Solomon's Prayer so much
better than Agur's ; but young Solomon, the brave
Daniel, the good Samaritan, and the poor Publican, were
my favourites among Bible men ; with Deborah and
Mary Magdalen among the women. There were other
companions too. These were the letters of Ann H.
Judson and Harriet Newel ; and often did I turn the
old brown and yellow birches into Burmese and Hindu
girls. Many a time have I talked till tears came to
these imaginary heathen women, and then sung to them
ever so much more.

I loved my Bible, and I loved nature. It seemed a
great deal easier to pray out in a grove among the
mountains. I never wondered that Jesus went on to
the mountain to pray, or that Daniel kept his window
open.

Even the great giant-looking larches of Canada had
a charm. They were real old Samsons, or Knights
Templars, all in their armour, as they lay so stiff, and
black, and awful, in the moonbeams, on the crusted
snow.

One time they were indeed awful to me. " Elder
Huntley," as everybody called my father,* was for more
than forty years a " Gospel Ranger " among the hills of
Vermont, New Hampshire, and Canada ; and as soon as

* Leland Huntley.

I was old enough, he took me into his cariole with him. One time he had been out to hold a "Protracted Meeting" in Lower Canada. We were returning home at midnight, through a tamarack swamp, winding leisurely along the well-trodden wood road, my father thinking of his sermons, and I covered head and eyes in the buffalo skins. Suddenly a strange sound : "Crazy Jane" pricks up her ears. Again, faint, low, fearful. Instantly Crazy Jane gave a bound that almost broke the traces. My father heard it, and, with an anxious look at me, he gave the startled creature the reins, when she flew over the road as if chased by lightning. On came the boding sound, nearer, nearer, clearer, clearer. A murmuring as of many waters, a clear bark, a tremendous howl of a whole pack of wolves! "Oh, God, save papa! Oh, God, I will, I will go!" This was the earnest cry of the moment, for I had no doubt but God was calling me to work for the heathen ; yet deep and painful had been the inward struggle, even at that early age, and I had always answered, "I cannot leave mamma."

Crazy Jane had just time to leap into the open village when the hungry wolves appeared on the skirts of the forest, thanks to the Hearer of prayer.

"Call upon me in the day of trouble, I will deliver thee." This was the promise that came to me as I nestled in the buffalo skins.

When but nine years old, there seemed to be some propelling power ever pushing me on to Burmah. "Get ready, I will call for thee," was for ever whispered in the air. How I should get ready, was the difficult question.

B 2

My father was a poor Baptist Minister; he could not
help me. He loved the cause of missions; but he was
poor, for he gave all his time and talents for others;
and so did my faithful, self-denying, and beautiful
mother.

The first effort toward my undertaking was made in
flowering oil-cloths, by which I bought myself a grammar, when thirteen years old. I had never had any
school books but a spelling book and "English Reader;"
but I had read, and thought, more than many children.
I borrowed a geography, and studied it open in the
window, while I rinsed the cups and saucers, standing
upon a stool beside the table. "Milton's Paradise Lost,"
"Young's Night Thoughts," "Pollok's Course of Time,"
"Thomson's Seasons," these were among the graver
books that had charmed me till midnight over my pine
torches—I could not afford candles—so my brother,
dear, kind little fellow that he was, would, every few
days, lay before me a votive offering of pitch pine-knots
from the plains; and it was by the light of these that I
read two thick volumes of moral philosophy, and studied
the fragments of a copy of Josephus, found on the shelf
of some old book store. After securing the grammar, I
obtained permission to leave home for a few months, as
companion to a doctor's wife. It was one evening while
with her, that I found a large volume of the "Arabian
Nights" in my bed-room. I had never seen it before,
and, of course, strained my eager eyes over it till the
long candle was burned to the socket. The next night
the "Arabian Nights" was gone, and a Missionary

Magazine lay there. I took it up, a little vexed to lose the stories; opened it, and the first thing that struck me was the "Journal of Francis Mason."

Next Saturday night I said, "Papa, I must go to Burmah." I had often spoken of going, but my father had never believed me serious, and always called it "El's wild scheme." Now he looked at me with the deepest earnestness of his grave eye, and uttered not a word. From that time he never opposed, never ridiculed; and my mother—my dear, fond mother—expected me to go some time.

It was very near where the Fairfax Literary Institution now stands that I first read that journal which threw a spell, a strange, drawing spell, over all my future.

With the money the doctor's wife gave for my little services, my bill was paid at a select school, where I made my first attempt at model letter-writing. I remember it perfectly, the old yellow page ruled down the side, leaving an inch margin, and beginning, as all models did, " I take my pen in hand," &c. I can see her now, that tall, straight schoolma'am, so shocked when I said, "Oh, Miss Sage, I can never get this right; please let me write my mother a real letter."

I wanted to tell her I had got her a new cap ribbon. It was the first thing I had ever earned for her with my own hands, and I was all on tip-toe to show her what I thought the daintiest little ribbon in the world. Miss Sage bade me write my copy, and learn propriety—a thing I have been trying to learn ever since.

I can't tell you, reader, half the things about getting

ready, graved in burning lines upon my own memory, but if you will glance at two or three dissolving views, they will fling a few faint lights over the shadowy past. I speak of these personal scenes only to show you that God does honour trust and works, and allows our best hopes to be realized.

———

Making way through drifted snows, boys shoveling the road, a young girl has prepared breakfast for five little brothers and sisters, has dressed them, put the house in order, and is on her way to the school-room, where she has a charge of some forty children, young men and young women. Her father and mother are on a mission to the Isles of Lake Champlain, and are ice-bound. They cannot know the load on their daughter's heart; they could not reach her if they did. She is sixteen years old—is striving for Burmah.

" Ye shall reap *if ye faint not.*"

It was among the lumber* men on Lake Champlain, close upon the romantic waters of Lake George, over which I have glided for hours in a little log boat, steered by lumber women, catching the yellow perch and trout which we could see through the lake clear to the bottom. It was a missionary undertaking, for they had no church, no tract visitors, no school of any kind within many miles. It was Sunday. I had called on all the mothers, and now they came dropping in, leading their little ones.

_____
* " Lumber: in America, timber sawed or split for use."— WEBSTER.

The room was fragrant with flowers, and Bible-pictures hung on the wall. We had just sung—

"There is a land of pure delight."

Who is that? A fine-looking man, the superintendent of the colony, appears, steps to the open door. "Miss Huntley, may—may we come in?" and eight or ten strong-souled men in their checked shirts are waiting admittance. A stammering "Yes, if you'll help us," was given, and I am sure no one can tell, but the angels, what delightful Bible readings we there enjoyed, amidst the log cabins, partitioned only with blankets, glazed with paper, and made habitable by huge altar-like pillars of stone in the middle for chimneys.

What is the matter? why does the young girl tremble so?

"Children, you may go home." And she sits an hour, helpless, shaking with ague, then recovers and creeps home. The next day tries again; but every other day these horrors return; so for two years she struggles on; thin, pale, weak, suffering as only one can suffer with the terrible lake fever and ague. It is the effect of the miasma of the lumber region.

At last the goal is reached,—a female seminary where she may quench her burning thirst for knowledge. Months pass: "Miss S——," she asks, one morning, in faltering tones, "may I go home? I have no more money, and I can't bear to give up now when the term is so near over." She had been living three months on a trifle over five dollars, boarding herself.

" Why do you go home ?"

" I have a dear brother ; possibly he may help me."

" How are you going ?"

" On foot."

" On foot !   How far is it ?"

" Twelve miles !"

" Twelve miles !   Why, child, you can't travel twelve miles.   You 'd better send for your brother."

" He cannot come.   Only say I may go."

A reluctant consent is given.   The young girl starts alone.

She draws her belt very tight, for she is hungry.   She has tasted no supper, no breakfast ; scarcely anything for a whole week but a loaf of bread.   Not a cent is left ; but she cannot beg.

" Good morning, Ellen.   Come back soon," says her preceptress.

" Good morning, Miss S——."   When you are hungry, may God feed you, she prays inwardly, and departs.

Longer and longer seems that weary way.   Now up a steep, hard hill, now stretching like a narrow line away over the plains.   She comes to a river ; the bridge is gone ; she enters in, is carried down, struggles, reaches the bank, walks on, comes to another, fords it.

What is the matter ?   She cannot see ; everything swims ; she falls, revives, and creeps up on to the steps of an old church—prays for strength, prays for Burmah.

At ten o'clock she sees the light glimmering from her mother's window, falls upon the steps, returns to consciousness, is lying in her own little room.   Her tender

mother is chafing her brows, the big tears chasing each
other down silently, while little hands are holding cups
of hot tea and gruel, murmuring out,—

" Sissy not die. God takes care of sister."

" For I say unto you, that their angels do always
behold the face of my Father which is in heaven."

There are other scenes behind. Higher and higher
swell the waters, keener and keener grows the anguish ;
but purer the longings, sweeter the peace.

See you that young girl's eye ? Mark you the pent-
up agony ? She holds a newspaper; the superscription is
her lover's ; she knows there are burning words within
that wrapper. The spirit longs, thirsts for their sweet
sympathy, for she is a stranger in a strange circle.

. " Must I leave it ?" she asks herself, pressing her
temples. Yes, her purse is empty, utterly empty. Those
rainbowed, precious words must go to the dead-letter
office. She lays it back—that dear, dear handwriting—
that *radiant* hand. She turns and leaves it there,
crushing down agony for heathen women.

What hand that upon the burning brow ? A letter.
It opens. Out falls a bank bill—the most beautiful,
shining bank bill ever made. Who sent it ? The Angel
of the Lord sent it. By whom ? Ask the loved teacher,
now Mrs. Nott, of Schenectady, and her Persis-like sister,
Miss C. Sheldon, of Philadelphia. The Lord told them
to send it. May He tell somebody to send them beautiful
bank bills if they ever need them !

Another scene. A school group—but not a white group. There are mountains, but not the old green mountains. There are trees, but not the birches, the beeches, the spruces of her childhood. There are flowers, but not the daisies and honeysuckles of her fatherland. Her pupils are black-eyed, bronze-coloured girls, boys, men, and women. The trees are the light bamboos arching over them, and each mountain has a spire, a tall beacon spire all alone—it is a Buddhist pagoda, and that land is Burmah.

When I first stepped upon the shore of India, it was at Maulmain. The Rev. Dr. Judson kindly met our large party at the quay, and, giving me his arm, led me through a long line of native Christians to his own door. My own emotions on reaching a heathen land were perfectly overpowering. I could not speak. I could do nothing but weep.

It was the remembrance of my childish yearnings, and of God's infinite goodness, that so overpowered me on reaching a pagan land. The letters, the journal, the old family Bible, the "gold thread," the wee sisters' eyes, all came back with the last, last kisses of a home, and the deep love of the tenderest of mothers that I was never to see again. Then I heard those strange old household names, Mah, Dokes, Menlas, and a host of others, all verily living beings before me! Dr. Judson's princely brow too! Was I indeed in the body or out of it?

It was truly a strange linking of circumstances, that the writings of Dr. Judson's wife should first have stirred my soul for Burmah, and then that his lips should have been the first to greet me, and his arm the first offered me to lean upon. It was strange that Mr. Mason should have united him with his loved Sarah, and then that Dr. Judson should have performed the same service for us at a day long after this. I had been married to Mr. Bullard some time before I left America.

Heat, bilge-water, destitution of milk, and of every comfort for my babe, in the six-foot cabin of a merchant ship for nearly five long months, had induced extreme weakness and inflammation in my eyes.

It was during these weeks of intense suffering, just after reaching Burmah, that I learned the real kind-heartedness and self-forgetting spirit of Dr. Judson. Full of anxious desire to speak to the women, it was hard to do nothing! I had not then learned to wait as now. Dr. Judson saw it, and seemed to give me a special corner in his warm heart, for after we left his house, which he would not allow for many days, about two o'clock daily I would hear his military-like step, and feel the sympathizing grasp of his dear hand as he drew me down beside him, and made me forget past sufferings and present agony in his inimitable manner, language, and stories. With him I lived over the whole past history of the mission, and much of its hidden life.

One day he was telling me of a lady who always greeted the native women with, "'Ma-a-lah—H-o-w-d-ye?' drawing it," he said, "clear across the room in her *everlasting rocking chair*." Another spent nearly

her whole time in making pills, smelling bottles, and
plasters for the natives! "What wonder," he would
ask, "that both gave up and went home?"

The proper medium line between indifference and un-
due anxiety in regard to the physical wants of the
heathen,—this was what Dr. Judson was endeavouring
to impress upon me, and what he never lost sight of. I
loved him ever after as my own father, for it was no
small self-denial for a man of his experience and his duties
to lay all aside and sit down daily to instruct an inexperienced Missionary woman. His exquisite tact, too, won
my most profound reverence, while his gay good humour
taught me the secret of good health in Burmah.

It was seventeen years ago that I sat there the won-
dering pupil of Adoniram Judson. Alas, the changes!
Then Sarah B. Judson was there, always so gentle and
loving in her pretty pink or white wrapper, and often
she would call me to accompany her when she took aside
the native Christians to settle their petty difficulties in
her prayer room. Then Fanny Forrester was struggling
upward in Utica. My husband, Mr. Bullard, was with
us, and Mr. Mason was with his little Maria and her
mother in Tavoy.

Now, where are we all? What a changing, painful
drama! Dr. Judson's Sarah on the rock of the sea,
himself in his ocean coffin; his Emily triumphant over
her sharp mission conflict; sweet Maria and her loved
mamma passed into heaven; Mr. Mason in a region then
unexplored, translating the Bible into a language then
unknown; Little "Enna" Judson, who used to come

in to rock " Baby Ella," now proclaiming the Gospel for his father; Baby Ella wandering over half the globe, a teacher to heathen women; while her adored father, who would have given his life for either of us, is calmly sleeping by the Salwen,* and I struggle on amidst innumerable hindrances for the same great work for which Anna H. Judson died, viz., the establishment of Woman's Mission in Heathen Lands.

* Mr. Bullard died at Maulmain, April 5th, 1847.

CHAPTER II.

HALTINGS AMONG THE CITIES AND WATERS OF MARTABAN.

"The Golden Waters! The Golden Waters!" all exclaimed in raptures, as the good ship *Charles* swept round into the Gulf of Martaban, and along its semi-circled shore of wild adventure and Christian toil. Four sun-lit streams roll their waters into this lovely scallop of the ocean. First, on the right, comes pouring the noble Salwen, with the city of Martaban on one side, and Maulmain on the other. Farther round, the Sittang, with the city of Sittang; then Pegu, with its antique ruins; and still beyond the Irrawaddy, with the cities of Rangoon and Bassein.

The first city of importance on this coast is Rangoon —Lord Dalhousie's enchanted garden—which, under Col. Phayre, is rapidly becoming one indeed. It resem- bles the modern portion of New York. I did not learn the number of streets, but saw one marked, I think, the fifty-third. The principal streets are parallel with each other, very broad, and nicely macadamized. Along these, in the business part of the town, stucco buildings are rapidly running up in simple Grecian style, with flat roofs and Ionic pillars. The officers and civilians erect beautiful teak bungalows in the environs, surrounded by tall forest trees.

To the north there is a romantic drive through a wide tract of woodland, out to old Kemendine. There the numerous clusters of snowy tents whitening the landscape, with the broad Irrawaddy pouring its silver spouts around, make it truly, to the artist's eye, enchanted ground. This drive to Kemendine also leads to what is intended to become the Binney College, just founded by three benevolent gentlemen in Philadelphia, Wm. Bucknell, Esq., W. C. Mackintosh, Esq., and David Jayne, M.D. Mr. Bucknell invited Dr. Binney to undertake this enterprise, and he with the other two have ever since sent him a personal support of 1,200 dollars, or £250, per annum. This is nobly done, and now, if the founders go on, endow the college and make it permanent, it will be an honour to the denomination, an honour to their country, and an inestimable blessing to the Karen tribes through all time. Both Dr. and Mrs. Binney possess a magic power over their pupils. There is also a Theological School in the same buildings, all under the patronage of the American Baptist Missionary Union.

There are two other schools of importance at this station, a Preparatory English and Vernacular School, aided much by Government, under Mrs. Vinton, a lady who has prepared many valuable books in Karen, and whose hymns will be chanted over the Karen hills when she shall be harping with the harpers. Another Normal School is in charge of the Rev. D. L. Brayton. This is for the Pwo Karens. It is taught in the vernacular, and

is dependent upon voluntary aid for support. Both Mr.
and Mrs. Brayton, and their daughter, Mrs. Rose, are
teachers of long experience, and their school really merits
sympathy and support.

Not far from this station is a most hopeful mission
under Mrs. Ingalls, widow of the late Rev. Lovell Ingalls. This is a mission to the Burmese as well as to
the Karens, and the very remarkable success of our lone
friend proves that woman's sympathy, patience, and quiet
perseverance may tell more upon the hearts of heathen
men than even public preaching. Mrs. Knap, also a
widow lady there, is another of our silent coral workers.
This friend greatly aided Mrs. Brandis, sister of Lady
Havelock, in establishing the Burmah Female School
Society, and a day school for girls in Rangoon.*

Seven children of the Burman Missionaries have entered upon the same service. How cheering it is to see
a mission receiving back its own sons and daughters to
stay up the hands of their parents! May the time come
when it will be understood that this is the duty of Missionaries' children, rather than to seek ease and civilized

---

* Messrs. Stevens and Dawson are in charge of the Burman Department of Rangoon, and Mr. Vinton, son of the late Missionary
Vinton, is a preacher in the Karen Department. Doctor and Mrs.
Wade are the oldest Missionaries on the coast. They are at Maulmain, working on with all their rich experience as earnestly as ever,
with Messrs. Bennett and Haswell, and J. Haswell, Jr.

There are also American Missionaries on all these rivers, except
Pegu : Messrs. Kincaid and Simons at Prome, Messrs. Thomas and
Crawley at Henthada, Messrs. Beecher and Vanmeter at Bassein, Mr.
Harris at Shwagyn, and Messrs. Mason, Cross, and Bixby, at Tounghoo.

comforts for themselves, while their fathers and mothers faint under their burdens alone.

In all, there are on the Burmah coast twenty-two American Missionary families, with about four hundred and fifty native preachers and schoolmasters, and some twenty-six thousand baptized converts. Of these, about five hundred and fifty are Burmese and Talaings, and twenty-two of them are preachers ; the others are mostly Karens. The population of Rangoon is about thirty thousand.

Now, reader, would you believe these Pegu waters and lands to be the veritable Ophir of the Ancients, and the real old Byssinga of the Alexandrian geographers ? My word-loving husband says so, and you will find some pretty strong proof of it in his book on Burmah.

I can almost see the strange old Phœnician craft and banner floating still before me ; King Solomon's boys chasing each other over the ridges after peacocks for Queen Belkis, and King Hiram's sailors plying up the rivers for Almug-trees. Yes, truly, I have to look round to see if these old Tyrians are not now washing out the gold for the basins, the tongs, and the pomegranates. Who knows but the Tyrian king did send a colony over to these rivers ? The Talaings look enough like the old Theban mummies to be their brothers. I saw mummy heads from Thebes in the Academy of Natural Sciences in Philadelphia, that in form were as near as possible like Talaings. They are known to be the oldest race on this coast, and Dr. Mason thinks them related to the Koles of Hindustan by their language. Evidently their first simple faith was rock-worship, like that of the Koles, the Santals of India, the ancient Peruvians, who set up an emerald as a goddess, and the Arabs.

Going over the mountains once, near Siam, we were passing a cairn like those of the Highland Scots, when I noticed that every Talaing with me stopped and threw a stone on to the pile.

" What is that for ?" I asked.

" Oh, nothing. A spirit lives here." This was all the explanation.

If it takes as long to Christianize Burmah as it did to turn it to Buddhism, it will be a task for the millennium. Twelve hundred years they had to work, according to their account, before Buddhism became the national religion of Burmah.

But for real enchanted ground we must go over to Maulmain. Here pagodas ! pagodas ! shooting up on every mountain peak, from twenty to three hundred and sixty feet high, like colonnades of gold, in burning, prismatic radiancy. And such foundations ! Terrace upon terrace. The highest plateau is eight hundred feet in circumference, and the lower more than one thousand eight hundred feet, tapering up so like old Belis' feet. Perchance some Layard may yet join them into international links. But just to think how tired these strict religionists must be to climb such long flights of steps to church—five hundred, seven hundred, and nine hundred steps ! The pagoda of the Aing Pass is said to have nine hundred and seventy stone steps.

Some of the pagodas are walled, others not. One in

Paghan was barricaded with a wall upheld by stuccoed elephants, after the style of that vestige of a ruin called the " Diamond Gate" in western India, indicating a relationship between the architects of the two countries.

There are two kinds of pagodas. The common one is a sacred structure; it is octagonal, and built of solid masonry, with a small gold or silver god and charmed scroll morticed up within. The other is a monument in honour of some prince. This is arched, generally of a quadrangular form, with four gateways, a dome in the centre, and vaulted galleries running round the interior. Syms tells of the ruins of a pagoda of the latter description in the northern part of Burmah, with walls and aisles of eighty feet in height. There is a .smaller one in Tounghoo, which, it is said, contains a royal urn ; but the royal god that graced the dome now sits in the Hartford Museum in Connecticut.

Look upon one of these illuminated zadees, as I have done, at evening. Listen to the soft breathing of the wind-bells on the *tee*, the umbrella of the top ; think of the mysterious scroll, the hidden god, the enchanted hieroglyphics. Watch the lights and shadows of the burnished spire, glimmering and mingling with those of the vaulted aisles, which come flashing out upon the glaring enamelled eyes of griffins and lions, lighting up the many-coloured scales of serpents and dragons, then vanishing in gloom, as the winds rush through the corridors, and you will not wonder that the natives are awed by the strange, dreamy effect.

c 2

Directly over Dr. Judson's house in Maulmain was
Mount Rama. This is the Pali name for Maulmain,
and the mountain is a lovely undulating line of slate and
sandstone, which divides the old and new town. On a
plateau, many hundred feet in circumference, rises Payah
Pu, the principal pagoda of Maulmain. Opening up to
this are four gateways, fifteen feet in width, guarded by
huge lions with enormous glass eyes.

Upon the north stands a Tomb temple, with an image
of Gaudama. It is crowned with Mosaic work representing an antique tiara or royal horn of magnificent eme-
ralds. His god-ship is lying upon a Mosaic catafalque,
his head resting upon twelve Mosaic pillows, over a large
lotus, held as sacred here as in Egypt. Around him six
crowned apostles, twelve feet high, standing on elevated
pedestals, like so many stylites all in gold, with the right
hand laid reverently upon the breast. Peering over the
feet is the sacred hydra, with its dilated hood, while the
immense coil of the serpent, glistening with enamelled
scales, serves as a pedestal for one of the statues.

In a niche at the entrance of this temple is a female
figure, in a sitting posture, and, Eve-like, covering her
person with her long black tresses.

Just under the shadow of the cliff stands another temple, with the Foot of Gaudama, which everybody knows.

The roof of this foot-shrine is a perfect forest of pinnacles, while over the low oriental portal stand two
supernatural warders, with terribly large searching eyes.
The vaulted ceiling has a representation of the zodiac,
which struck me as very like the pictures I had seen of

Dendera. The roof and cornices are, like the old Greek temples, adorned with tracery and vermillion, and the low pedestals are modelled into lilies, some of them lettered with the donors' names.

I have seen in a temple of Tavoy an oriental tableau of Gaudama, previous to his becoming a god. He is represented as prostrate on the ground, humbling himself into a flag stone, while Dobindea, the former Buddh, with his troop of begging boys, is walking over him. This act of deep humility was one of the principal deeds of merit that secured to him his divinity. There is another temple there, shaped precisely like the famed " Paradise" of Western India, and containing a statue of the last Buddh Dobindea.

Go up on to this plateau. A poem, a very poem, you exclaim at once, made up of natural stanzas, with the music all set. First comes Martaban, with the lofty Zingabat mountains, the classic vale of Thadung, the Dong Yahn fortress looming over its mourning river, wide forests and savannas, and the temple mountain of Damathat, shooting up in natural Gothic. Then come the Atteran, the Salwen, the Gayng, linking among the cliffs, and silvering the prairies ; far-stretching Thanee, all buried in half-tints ; while Maulmain lies in the foreground, forcing its way up the hills, amid groves of palms, cocoa-nuts, bananas, tamarinds, mangoes, citrons, papayas, and pumpalows ; and each face of the mountain is alive with convents, temples, pillars, turrets, altars, idols, and pagodaettes, as if multiplied by a Lysippus hand, bristling among ever-blooming avenues. Here and there, also, rises a guardian group of statues, or the hideous Belu, who, history states, were Gaudama's body-guard; and one can believe it, for they are for ever pre-sent—the real Scandinavian Memming, or the Beer-seeker of the Scalds.   Everywhere, winding up the mountain, are trains of priests, with their bald pates or tonsures, with here and there a priestess, in her floating white mantle, counting her rosary, gliding in at some monastery, or half concealing herself behind the lemon-trees.

It was the festival of the New Year, and the Pagoda Bath Day, which interested me particularly.   This fes-tival occurs annually, like the Grecian days for bathing the statues of Minerva.

The young men were clad in their long silk patsoes girded up over their tattoo-imitation pantaloons, or thrown gracefully over the shoulder, while their long hair, black and glossy, was neatly braided with white muslin fillets so as to pass for the eagle-plumed bonnet, and with their scarlet sandals, they seemed to look upon themselves as perfectly irresistible.

Each carried two small jars of clear water nicely covered with fresh plantain leaves, on which lay a small silver goblet.   A curious sight it was to see the whole city, men, women, and children, doing battle with the fierce ardor of Trojans, and all with the same dashing weapon —cold water.   The young women, I believe, had come off conquerors, and taken the young men prisoners, who were compelled into the service of the gods; and while they carried water, the maidens bore a web of sacred cloth, extending a quarter of a mile in length, like a line of golden cloud. They were going to drape the large pagoda, or give Payah Pu a new turban.

At night the whole city was magnificently illuminated. The great Pagoda was encircled with rings of little festal lamps from the base almost to the summit. Mount Rama was covered with colonnades of lights, every street bordered with flame, and illuminated arches rose before every door—for the same reason that the ancient Britons made bonfires on New Year's Day, to drive away evil spirits, as the Jews, Sabians, Vestals of Rome, and other nations have done.

These decorations continue fifteen days; but the grandest illumination follows the regattas in October, after the ninety days' Lent. Then, soon after sunset, cannons fire, serpents run through the air, coloured lanterns are wafted overhead, while innumerable tongues of flame are floated on bits of plantain stems down the rivers, quite covering their surface from China to the Indian Ocean, offerings to Shen Oboogoke, the Neptune of Burmah. It is doubtful if the old god received any grander honours from classic Athenians than the Talaings and Burmans give him here on their illuminated rivers.

Sometimes there comes sailing down a little pagoda fancifully lit up, constructed of delicate wicker-work; and once I saw passing, on the Sittang river, a sitting Gaudama, braided in the same manner, like the old wicker deities of the Druids, of life size or larger, with a beautiful tiara imitative of coloured gems, and holding

in his hand a wicker rice-pot, which shone in the dim-
ness like a great bowl of gold.

Shen Oboogoke is said to dwell in a leaden palace
under the sea. He receives special homage from the
Burmese and Talaings; and their sailors, when embark-
ing on a voyage, offer him a turtle. So, one season in
a time of drought in Tavoy, he was honoured with a
fountain and a pair of leaden fishes, at the side of the
court-house, where the people poured water daily, and
offered prayers for rain, sending up showers of cotton
flakes.

This grand water-festival is closed with entertain-
ments and music, when the wild, varied harmony of
their numerous instruments is blended with the crying,
thrilling kyzoup, with the glee-maidens clapping their
castanets; the screaming of the minstrels, the shrieking
of the trumpets, and the pounding of the drums, all
mingled in one tremendous detonation.

The Burmese call music the language of the gods, but
from the bubbling, shrieking, crashing sounds of their festivals, one would suppose it must be the language of the
Dii Inferni ; yet there are passages in their softer airs
melodious, pathetic, and subduing.

The Burmah maidens were certainly attractive on this
festival day, flitting amid festooned arches. Their graceful forms were set off by yellow silk robes of circling
stripes, with crimson cinctures and black lace jackets
fitting close to the bust, with rose satin scarves, and
exquisitely-wrought gold chains; just such, according
to antiquarians, as were once worn by the honourable

women of the British Isles in the days of the Druids.
They also wore gold ear knobs, bracelets, and bangles,
brocaded sandals, and their coal-black hair wreathed
with golden champac, rose-buds, or the delicate mimusops.
Altogether they presented a most picturesque *tableau
vivant.* Many had made free use of cosmetics, and
were chalk-white; others would rival the purest bronze
antiques, while in the fine chiseling of their features
some of them would lose little beside the classic models
of Greece.

It was in passing down from Mount Rama that I met
a coffin—a very little coffin—followed by a Christian
mother. Beyond were a group of heathen women also
burying an infant. I could but contrast the emotions
of the two mothers, the one believing her little one for
ever wandering in unrest, lost in dismal swamps, tired
and hungry, while the Christian mother could look up to
the pure blue sky. I could but ask, Who hath made them
to differ? But thought followed the little spirits upward, until there fell these low, tremulous murmurings
from the Infant Paradise. It was long before I could
catch the song, for it came only in snatches of the
faintest trillings upon the air.

AN INFANT TO ITS CHRISTIAN MOTHER AFTER ITS FIRST DAY IN HEAVEN.

What beautiful music is waving along !
It trances my senses, it bathes me in song ;
Now around me, now o'er me, again and again,
Does its low rolling cadence steal over the plain.

Is this the sweet tuning of seraphs who sing
While crowns are fast shower'd at the feet of their King?
Is this, mother, that heaven afar in the skies,
Where so oftentimes turn'd were your sweet, loving eyes?

Yes, yes, this is heaven I've enter'd to-day,
For the angels are singing wherever I stray;
It was only this morning I found I had wings,
Yet I've seen, oh I've seen, ma, such wonderful things!

My soul, when unfetter'd from that little clay
That now you are laying so gently away,
Oh, how it expanded! what speech too I knew
As with gladness and wonder far upward I flew!

Yes! long before reaching the deep azure sky,
A convoy of spirits appear'd from on high;
And "Hail, little brother!" cried one very bright,
As, embracing, he veil'd me in robes of pure white.

'Twas Calla, dear Calla, 'mid that smiling band,
With a wreath on his brow, and a harp in his hand;
Oh, that you, mother dear, could have seen his bright eyes
Look down on me so loving, like stars in the skies!

Quick speeding me onward, said he, "Come, behold,
High floating in blue, the great City of Gold,
With its walls of pure jasper, and all precious stones,
That around it lie blazing in radiant zones.

"And a throne of pure sapphire, on which sits above
The adorable Saviour, all shining in love;
Yet with manner more regal than mightiest king,
And oh, how the rainbows around Him do spring!"

Then open'd the portals, and up to the throne
The good angels bare me—I was not alone—
And He spake to me kindly, and welcomed me home,
Saying, "Yes, little spirit, yes, yes, you may come."

Now peal'd from the harpers a triumphing strain,
" All worthy the Lamb who for sinners was slain ! "
And now it rose softly from newly-born powers,
On a mount ever blooming, o'erwoven with flowers.

O sweet, they have told me, earth's murmuring shades,
And pure the still waters that silver its glades ;
Yet sweeter, far sweeter, these blest spirits say,
Are the zephyrs and streamlets here warbling away.

But hark ! mother, heard you the little ones' feet ?
'Tis the Saviour ! the Saviour ! they 're running to meet ;
I 'll go, then, and wait for you, sweet mother dear !
And you 'll come very quick, we 're so happy up here !

CHAPTER III.

THE DONG YAHN CONQUERORS. MY HUSBAND'S PEOPLE.

Looking from Mount Rama toward the north, we see shooting up a limestone peak, called by the English the Duke of York's Nose. I don't know how it came by this strange title, but the Talaings have not given it a better. They named it Zwagabang—the Boat Mooring, and tell tales of a time when the waters came up over that peak; that there was just one boat seen on the waters, and when they began to go down, the sailors tied it up there to this great nose.

This mountain is in Dong Yahn, on the Salwen river, twenty-five miles north of Maulmain, a place which became our home for four years. The country round is the Canaan of Pegu, one of the richest rice-growing valleys in Burmah, full of fruit-trees, encircled by charming hills, and covering a large extent of territory.

It was under the high rock-fortress of Dong Yahn that I took a sketch of Guapung, a noble Karen woman, a descendant of one of the Two princes who had invaded this region; she had an interesting niece, who bore, however, the frightful name "Halter." Halter's mother was taken captive by the Siamese in a skirmish which

took place, about the year 1811, between them and the
people of Khan Koming, when the enemy carried nearly
all into captivity. Her mother was corded by the neck
to another woman, as all the rest were, two and two;
their hands bound behind them, and the poor prisoners
goaded on without mercy. Seeing that this woman could
not possibly proceed, they left her upon the road, where,
a few minutes after, the infant Halter was born, and so
named to commemorate the dreadful scene. The little
brother, an only son, the mother beheld pricked on
by the robbers, the poor little fellow frantic with grief
and terror. She never saw him again. Indeed, there
was no end to the sufferings of these poor Karens, who
were always hunted by the Burmese, Talaings, and
Siamese, until the English, whom they call the "Sons
of God," gave them peace and protection.

There is a stirring tale connected with this wild home
of ours in the wilderness.

One day Guapung was in a shanty by the Salwen
river, when she saw a "Flying Ship" come up the river.
It was about the year 1827. She ran down to see the
"Flying Ship," when a tall, handsome, white foreigner
stepped on shore, and, coming right up to her, extended
his hand, asking in Burmese if she was well.

"Ma, th'kyen—well, my lord,"—she replied with
native grace. The stranger had only time to ask after
her business, and say, "Go in peace," when he returned
to the Flying Ship, and she stood gazing after him in
mute amazement.

Soon her brothers came, and she said :—

" I 've seen one of the sons of God!"

" Did he speak?"

" Yes, and he gave me his hand."

" Did you take the hand of a foreigner?"

" Yes, for he looked like an *A ing*" (angel).

" Would 'Worship-Face' had been here with his golden arrow!"

" Nay, but I 'm not ashamed," insisted Guapung— "Aunt or Lady Pung." The name indicates a notable housewife, as she was, and so were all her daughters after her.

The brothers took her home to A Wah—" White Patriarch"—the highest chief or king of Dong Yahn. He was a heathen, and though he adored his beautiful Guapung, his jealousy was aroused, and he beat her, as he often did in a fit of drunkenness. That night she was called to attend the ceremony of the "Dead Bone burial."

" No," said this modern Semiramis—for she was so, indeed, in majestic beauty, with the finest brow and richest eyes ever created—" no, ever since I was a child I have served Satan and Shen Gaudama, yet they have never stopped my husband from beating me once. This white man spoke to me kindly, and gave me his hand. His God must be *The* God. Hereafter I worship Him."

True to her purpose, she began that very night to pray to the Unknown God of the white foreigner, and this was her prayer:—

" Great Aing! Mighty Judge, Father God, Lord God, Uncle or Honourable God, the Righteous One!

In the heavens, in the earth, in the mountains, in the seas, in the north, in the south, in the east, in the west, pity me I pray! Show me thy glory, that I may know thee who thou art!"

This prayer, she told me, she prayed for several years, I think five years, never once again making offerings to idols or demons. After a long time, another white teacher visited her village, when she ran and sat down at his feet for nine days. Then a white woman appeared, that indefatigable American, Phœbe, Eleanor Macomber, whom Guapung hailed as almost divine, and escorted her home, as, she said, "their goddess, right from the heavens, come to deliver the women of Dong Yahn from their oppressive masters;" and indeed she did, under God, for the arrack pots were soon cast out, and the men, from being a whole village of bacchanalians, became a sober, God-fearing people.

Guapung, with Miss Macomber, was the means of raising up in Dong Yahn a flourishing Christian church, that became the parent of two other two churches which Mr. Bullard organized in that province. All this was the result of a little human sympathy towards woman. Guapung felt that, in her land, woman was regarded as a slave, fit only to bear burdens, and never walk beside her husband or brothers; and this was why the simple act of giving the hand left such an indelible impression. Verily, this was Dr. Judson's Great Sermon, for it was he who gave the hand; and if his ransomed soul could now speak down from the spirit land, would he not say to his brethren, "*Pity Heathen Women?*"

This Christian body in Dong Yahn was the first to build its own chapel, which was once or twice burned by the heathen. It was the first to support its own pastor, to send forth a Missionary, and the first to sustain a schoolmistress; indeed, the only district school reported in the Maulmain province for 1860 has been sustained all these years through the perseverance of Guapung. This remarkable woman, more than any other person, brought about my husband's plan.

It was the Rev. Edwin Bullard, then in charge of the Pwo Karen department of the Maulmain Mission, under the American Baptist Missionary Convention, who first introduced and established a self-sustaining Ministry among the Karens of Burmah, a plan which has already saved the Missionary Union more than a hundred thousand dollars.

The recommendation to support their own preachers was met by a shower of indignant reproaches, for at that time all pastors and preachers were being regularly paid by the mission,—in Maulmain, seven rupees the month; in Arracan, Rangoon, and Bassein, the same or more; and in Tavoy four, the lowest of all.

I well recollect the morning when this subject came up. Mr. Bullard had been preaching in Karen a very searching sermon on the subject of presenting their bodies a living sacrifice. The next morning good old Mong Chung came in, saying he could not sleep; he had thought all night about the sacrifice. We suggested to him that when the churches should come to understand that Scripture, they would no longer ask American

Christians to support their pastors; they would do as Christians did in other lands, support their own.

"Teacher," he said, with a look of extreme mortification, "Teacher, this would ruin the cause in Dong Yahn. The heathen would reproach, and ask if we didn't beg just like their priests. Teacher, would you make us Poongyees?"

It was a painful task to convince the old man that it would be right even to ask the Christians to support their own preachers. He was deeply grieved, and I am sure we sat there full two hours arguing the point, Mr. Bullard pointing out Scripture which favoured it, he reading it in Burmese and trying to turn it differently. At last the old patriarch seemed to get some idea of the history of the Church, and the sacrifices of Christians in America and England. He shut up the book, rose very solemnly, as if full of a mighty determination, and went out. The next day he and Guapung were all over the village, teaching the people their duty concerning a self-supporting ministry. It was decided to attempt it in Dong Yahn, and that church has ever since supported its own pastor, which is now the general practice among the Karens of Burmah. My dear husband lived only three years on heathen ground, but if he had accomplished nothing more than this one thing, this alone was enough to compensate for all expense of going, and acquiring the language. I will describe some of the scenery amid which we then dwelt.

One morning we had reached the shore of a small still lake at the base of a limestone cliff which loomed up

D

perpendicularly several hundred feet. Here an old ferry-man took us into a skiff, and we glided over to an aperture low and narrow, in the base of a mountain opposite. On we went right through the mountain, when there opened out a large rotunda with deep green waters lying still as the Sea of Sodom. Everywhere, above, before, behind, the huge black masses of rock rose up in misty, grim, colossal forms, just visible by the few streaks of light shooting in from the distant orifice. Just as we reached the middle in awed silence, my consamer or cook became restless, and nearly overturned us.

" I 'll hurl him over, Miger ! "—indeed ! shouted our old ferryman, leaping up, and darting a stick of sugar-cane at the fellow's head.

" Hurl him over, Miger ! " thundered the Genii of the cavern, as if close upon us, all around and underneath.

" Hurl him over, Miger ! " eagerly answered all the powers above, and it seemed as if they were responded to by ten thousand behind, and those by ten thousand more, until the whole cavern bellowed it out there in the darkness like charging artillery.

" They 'll swallow him up," said the steersman, with a wicked laugh. " Swallow him up—hi—hi—hi ! " gurgled up ten thousand hoarse voices from the regions below. " Swal—swal—low ! hi—hi—hi ! " laughed out all the furies in their upper halls. The poor Malabar, half dead with fright, cowered down flat on the bottom of the boat, and we paddled on in impatient silence, not daring to arouse the threatening Genii again. The angry Gin abated somewhat their wrath, but still kept on grumbling, and even when we had emerged from their haunted precincts, we still heard them growling after us, " S-w-a-1-1-o-w," and laughing with a malicious glee in their dark abodes. Very glad was I to return once more to the light of day.

Next we glided round to a cave temple, over slippery heights and dismal hollows, with torches and ladders. On, on, on ! the dark recesses resounding with ten thousand bats rushing, chasing, soaring, chattering, until we come to a halt, in a grand, pantheon-like chamber, with an arched, columnless portico, sixty feet in height. Here a curious, throne-like stalagmite shoots up fifteen or twenty feet, quite in the centre, with natural steps leading up to the top, as pulpit-like as possible. The audience, too, are provided with semi-circular seats, one above the other, and the rotunda lighted by an aperture right over the pulpit or throne-seat, while the roof is jewelled with pendant stalactites, some of them clear as crystal. The Talaings say Gaudama preached here, and consecrated the temple from this quaint, self-made pulpit. At any rate, it has been consecrated to GOD, for, at the request of the Karens, we called them to prayer there, and taking the seats the grotto-Builder had made for them, the whole cavern resounded with a hymn of praise to the Deity. This was in December, 1844. After singing, Kowong and Halter spread us a pic-nic in an enchanting little oriel under the portico, overhung with the greenest ferns and the sweetest air plants. Here the consamer fried us little fishes from the lake at our feet, roasted us rice in a bamboo joint, and spread tea on wild palm leaves. The Karens had their repast of sour leaves, red ant nests, and bamboo shoots, while Guapung amused us with tales of the Genii inhabitants of this cavern.

Amongst the Karens there are four regular orders of ghosts—the Tarataka, Taprai, Jah, and La. The first is a terribly malignant genus, the spirits of bad rulers, false prophets, and such like. The grasp of this demon is certain death, from which no mortal can deliver. This is the spirit which the Hindus think lives in the tiger, in the lightning, storm, &c.; the Dearga of the Gaels. The dress of the Tarataka is also green, like that of the old Dearga of Ben Ledi. The names, too, seem to be the same.

Next to this invisible they fear the Jah, which means the same and is the same word as the Saxon Gast, English Ghost. These are the restless spirits of drowned persons, infants, and all who have perished from contagious diseases. The Jahs live in the caverns, and, like gnomes, under the caverns. They have been denied the rites of burial, consequently each

> " Flits to some far uncomfortable coast,
> A naked, wandering, melancholy ghost."

They are heard, too, in the forest,

> " Faint, like broken spirits crying."

" Hark! don't you hear it?" asked Halter, and that moment the gigantic bamboos bowed their tall, hairy heads, and wailed out the most ghost-like tones that ever came from forestry. The moan of the bamboo is

more mournful than anything heard in Burmah, except
the wailing casuarinas upon the sea-shore, and they
would almost make one believe they were indeed haunted
by spirits.

The Taprai is a spirit, as tall, said Halter, looking
up, "as the teak-tree." It is seen stretching out its
long arms to clasp the belated traveller.

"But did you ever see a La?" I asked Halter's
mother.

"Oh yes, mama, once when going home from this
very cave."

Every Karen has his La, and so with all animated
nature. Some call it a So, which, with La, makes soul.
It has a little throne in the crown of the head, as the
Greeks thought. This is man's tutelar divinity, the
same, it would seem, as the Highland Scots had, for
they believed the shadow to be a sort of Banshi, or
guardian, and the Karens call the shadow by the same
name La, or the light of the body.

Sometimes the La goes wandering about, and gets
caught in a thorn bush. Then a great seven-headed
demon enters into the person, perhaps the same as the
"Seven other Spirits" mentioned in Scripture. The
Karens tell of one being whom they call Paba. It
seems to be Ceres. They make offerings to this goddess,
and build her a lilliputian house in their rice fields, in
which they put two cords for her to tie up the straying
La, if she catches them. In sickness the Karen soul has
either been tied up, or has gone on a visitation, so they
try to call it back. They deposit an offering in the

jungle for the truant soul, and knock upon their house-
doors to beseech it to return.

With the Burmese the spirit at death flies away in
the form of a butterfly, just as the Greeks believed.

With the Karens it forms a globule of life, and after a
time bursts, when the ethereal vapour (or gas, of course,
attendant upon the decomposition of bodies) falls upon
the opening flowers, thereby imparting to them the prin-
ciple of life.   Then whatever devours the flower imbibes
the soul.

It was Guapung who attempted to teach the women
of these Golden Waters *to make children good.*   For
three months, one season, I accompanied her over the
plains of Dong Yahn, mostly for this purpose.   So much
cruelty to children we saw, that my whole soul was
stirred.   Often my little boy has felt unable to remain
in the house, but has sometimes demanded the ratan, and
taken it from them.   I recollect going to one mother, after
enduring the scene long enough to have punished a
dozen Five Points children, and found she had a bundle
of ratans beside her, which she was still using upon the
naked body of her own little girl six years old!   I
never was so strongly tempted to use one myself.   The
poor child was covered with wales and cuts.   I saw a
mother, in a fit of weariness, fling her nursing babe from
her bosom out upon the bamboo floor, and that mother
a chief's wife, and among the best of them too.   The
little one died, I think, the next day, and I dressed it
in flowers for the grave with my own hands, for the
father was an excellent Christian man, and was incon-

solable. This woman was not naturally cruel, nor are the women generally, except when passion rules.

Guapung had great power with these Dong Yahn women. Indeed, she had with every one, for she was one who lived on the Word of God, and seemed to catch the tones of the " Better Land." Sometimes our way lay over Swiss-like bridges of slender bamboos or single logs, then over the prairies, where I could never have endured the heat, but for a turban dipped in cold water. Once we were lost upon the prairies, and followed a lone taper for three hours. We got into a wide morass, Mr. Bullard, myself, and babe, and all our party. Darkness came on, and no one could tell which was the way out. It is a dreadful thing—did you ever know it, friend ?— to be out in a prairie marsh in the black night, with only a few glimmering torches, sinking deeper and deeper at every step, turning and turning, and finding no solid foot of ground. I think the feeling that comes over one is about as horrifying as anything I ever experienced. For a long time we followed the wicked ignis fatui, but finally emerged from the fathomless bogs, and reached our home.

At another time our boatmen, who were strangers among the creeks, lost their way, and insisted on remaining out over night. The next day was the Sabbath, and we were going to meet the women of Dong Yahn. We had made no preparation for the damps of night, expecting to reach the village before dark ; but there was not any alternative ; my babe had to be wrapped in whatever could be found, and put to sleep on sweetened

water, while I stood all night upon deck to point out
the landmarks. Many a night, indeed, during these
wanderings, I was compelled to lay my little girl to sleep
on rice water, and hear her moan out in her unrest,
" Ma, mie, mie." It almost broke my heart, but not a
drop could be obtained at any price. After the first
year we learned to supply our boat with a goat, and
little Rasa had the pretty creature all to herself; but
for years after she would grasp her cup of milk, and sip
it for hours, holding it with all her strength, as if she
remembered—little thing—the sufferings of those dreadful nights.

Indeed, these labours were not prosecuted without
severe pain, weariness, and suffering, even to Guapung,
as well as to ourselves. There was one season when I
could obtain no vegetables of any kind whatever for six
weeks. The work was too urgent to be left. Mr. Bullard
had just called out a company of lay converts, and was
traversing all the plains, preaching to the heathen, while
Guapung and I were talking to the women from six
o'clock in the morning till ten in the evening, in the
bungalow, for they thronged us continually, so that,
although I remained with them four months at a time, I
never could command time to touch a needle, or take up
an English book ; and several times returned to the
city, so utterly exhausted, that the boatmen were obliged
to carry me from the landing to the house.

But then all weariness and pain were forgotten on
seeing those poor mothers seeking so earnestly for light.

" My husband loves me now."

" My boys bring me fire-wood now."

" My little girl don't run away now."

" There," exclaims a fourth, " you see that boy ? He was the worst child in the world : he would hold his breath till almost dead, and all my beatings did no good. Now see, I haven't struck him for a week, and he 's just as good as *chepoke*" (sugar cane).

Then others were thronging round, anxious to learn how to make home happy. One day a woman in great distress came some five miles to Guapung for a charm to cure her husband from running away. Guapung sat down, listened to her sad tale, then said,—" Yes, sister, I have a charm," and repeated to her the story of Christ, of His forbearance, His humility, and His love for His enemies.

" Now go," says Guapung, " and ask your husband home, and then don't scold him again, and see if he don't love you."

About three weeks after, a man came over from that woman's village to see " Guapung, the big teacheress, who had the charm;" for he understood that Jesus Christ's religion did not allow women to scold their husbands ! The unhappy woman, he said, was living quietly with her husband, and the men of the village were all anxious to have their wives join the Christians.

" Ah," said Guapung to me that night, " if Jesus Christ's women only make home happy, the men won't oppose them."

Was she not right ? Yet how sadly has this truth been forgotten !

Yes! if preachers and teachers are only sent to *men*, and *women* are left idolators, scolds, and gamblers, how slowly the work moves on!

In this department of mission labour, woman has yet a great work to do—woman in Christian lands and in pagan lands. Let our brothers marshal their forces of preachers and books, but we will be the coral-workers, out of sight, under ground. Mark that assembly of cultivated men and women under the impassioned elo-quence of some master spirit. What sympathy will be elicited, what indignation, what determination, when the voice rises and falls! Even so have I seen it in the Mother's Meetings at Dong Yahn, under the inspir-ing lessons of the Bible. Yes, the Missionary woman who has the native language, and the confidence of the people, wields a wand as magical as the orator of London or New York; so does the Bible woman of Christian lands. Nay, still mightier, for her instructions are not for the whirling, changing mass. She goes behind, and tones the secret springs that move the mass. It is no light thing, Christian sister, this lofty privilege, either in Heathen or Christian lands, to move the heart-wheel that is to roll and roll, and send out links doubling through eternity.

There was a lady, the editress of the "Mother's Journal," in New York, who often sent these Dong Yahn mothers a few sweet crumbs of strength and comfort.

*   *   *   *   *   *

*   *   *   *   *   *

But oh, it is dark—dark—dark! What is that gloomy

cavalcade ? Ah, do not ask—do not ask—silently—
silently we wind along. Oh, who—who can pity but
God? Who but the Almighty give strength ? Why does
the rain pelt so ? Oh God, the grave is full of water !
Will they put him there ?—the loved, the husband, the
father, the heathen's friend ! I cannot see—I cannot see!

Alone!—what a crushing burden is on the air, floating over the pillow, pressing upon the eyelids, and sinking upon the heart like the sound of the first turf upon
that coffin lid,—on awakening after an hour of feverish
sleep, in the arms of dear Mrs. Stevens. That moment
my little boy of six months nestled closer to my bosom,
looking up so pityingly. It was his father's blue eye—
a tear gathered under the silken lashes. I knew it—
accepted it—his father's glance of sympathy—and it
nerved the heart and hand for future struggles.

" Are we not to be like the angels ?" And are there
not " ministering spirits sent forth to minister to them
who shall be heirs of salvation ?" Did not Jacob see
the angels ascending and descending ? Do not " their
angels behold every day the face of my Father ?" and
did not the angel father inspire his darling girl, then four
years old, when she planted her tiny foot firm beside me,
and, with a faltering voice, yet with the determination
of age, said, " Don't cry, mamma, don't cry. I 'll be your
comforter !" wiping off my tears with her infant hand ?
Never shall I forget that voice—that glowing eye that
spoke so thrillingly of peace. It was the father's great
heart coming back through his little one. Blessed child !
They *were* inspired words—faithfully kept, thank Heaven,

Nobly my dear husband strove, nobly he died. May the father's mantle fall upon his boy!

Dong Yahn was the centre of Mr. Bullard's field of enterprise—our loved Jungle Home—where he laboured with an inspiration that inspired all Dong Yahn, and linked many a Karen heart to his for eternity.

Although my dear husband compressed the labours of a long life into three brief years in India, yet his ministry had been twenty-two years; for he was but twelve years old when a deacon of the Rutland church in Vermont sent for him twelve miles to come and preach in his own house, and he ever after bore the title in his childhood of "the beloved little John," for his peace-making gifts at school, gifts for which he was remarkable through life. He was always studious, and indefatigable in overcoming difficulties. He mastered the Pwo Karen language within a year; preached in it a thousand sermons, baptized thirty-eight Pwo Karens, taught nearly a year his Theological Class with great devotion, organized two churches, gave them their first discipline in their own language; left them a rich legacy in a Karen Missionary Sermon, and translated for them the Gospel of Matthew, with Explanations; besides ministering to them, from door to door, nearly all over the Pwo Karen territory of the Maulmain Province.

He carried up to his Master a crown of a hundred stars, his own dear converts, baptized by himself. He was ordained three years before going to Burmah, and two precious revivals followed his preaching in Massa-

chusetts; and how many converts he found above, or
meets coming up there now, no one here may tell.

He was, too, the tenderest of husbands—the fondest
of fathers.

The following lines were written on leaving this our
first home in the wilderness :—

FAREWELL TO DONG YAHN.

Kind forest-child, away, away !
Oh urge me not, I may not stay ;
But on your breast this tear-drop lay,
While now, with heart all torn, I say,
 Farewell, Dong Yahn !

Farewell, high rocks, and caverns gray !
Farewell, sweet flowers that smile so gay !
Farewell, my birds in bright silk clad,
Ye who have sung my lone heart glad,
 In sweet Dong Yahn !

And must I leave that Inga grove,
That bower of prayer we loved to rove ?
Ah, yes, sweet bowers, your drooping flowers
Sigh with me now o'er by-gone hours,
 In bright Dong Yahn.

Leave, too, that stream, that blessed stream,
O'er which a star now seems to beam,
Where ransom'd souls have lowly bow'd,
And, strong in God, have firmly vow'd
 To save Dong Yahn.

How oft on this secluded plain
We've smiled and wept o'er joy and pain !
How often angels hover'd near,
Over the penitential tear,
 Here in Dong Yahn !

And can I leave that temple there,
Where once your *Teacher* knelt in prayer,—
That Teacher who, with pitying eye,
Would ever soothe the mourner's cry,
    In our Dong Yahn?

And, more than all, my pupils kind,   .
Round whom the cords of love are twined,
Must I, then, never, never see
Those eyes that beam so tenderly
    In my Dong Yahn?

Entreat not, child, with that sad tear!
It pains my very soul to hear;
Oh look not up so grieved and pleading,
For my crush'd heart is also bleeding
    O'er lone Dong Yahn.

Dear ones, farewell! I go, I go!
Though sorrows brim and overflow;
God comfort thee in all thy woe,
And span thy hills with heaven's bow,
    My loved Dong Yahn!

After many months of grief, which I trust was sanctified, I turned to the Indo-Britons, a large and sadly neglected class in Maulmain.

A very pretty, intelligent Anglo-Indian young woman became my Bible Reader. Her name was Jessie. She visited more than a hundred and fifty Burmese women with me, besides many of her own people. Jessie had known sorrow, and was therefore fitted for the work. No person whose heart has not been bowed by grief is prepared for it. Lessons in sorrow are just as necessary to the Bible reader in heathen lands, and in Christian lands too, as discipline in language or arithmetic.

"Miss Jessie, have you brought your Jesus Book to-day?"

"Yes, Rabbi."

"Well, read, Miss, read. Don't speak. I'm sick, read."

It was Mr. ——, of Maulmain, who thus spoke. He was a Hebrew. Jessie understood the tone. She was much surprised at the command, for he had always forbade her opening her New Testament ; but she obeyed at once, asking no questions. Slowly, distinctly, she read on, the fifth chapter of Matthew, then the story of Nicodemus, then of the young lawyer, then the parable of the sower, the husbandman, and much more. The Hebrew had turned his face to the wall, and uttered not a word. His wife sat by and listened, swinging her infant. She, too, so silent, they could hear every drop of the pattering rain. Finally, Jessie closed her Jesus Book, pressed the sweet Jewess's hand, and went out.

It was soon after that I left Maulmain, and heard no more from my Hebrew friends. Jessie married, and we both had new cares.

It was in 1860, on my way to the States, that I again met Mr. —— in the steamer *Burmah*. He had with him his wife, a son and daughter, and a friend with servants. He was going up to Calcutta to take a wife for his son—the babe the Jewess was tending when Jessie was there. They were very happy, for the alliance was to be with a powerful family, one that had worked itself up as I suppose as they had done.

The Jews are the Yankees of the East, always managing to make their way upward if it is only one step a month, and they do it in the same manner as the "Song of the Shirt"—by work, work, work, morning, noon, and night—and by watching men's eyes.

When I first knew Mr. —— he was a poor man, just beginning as a small shop-keeper in Maulmain. Abraham, Isaac, and all the patriarchs had re-appeared in the bazaar there, and it was amusing to hear them : if you inquired of Mr. —— for an article not in his shop, he would go through all the bazaar calling up Samuels, Moshas, Daniels, and Davids, till you would begin to ask if his mother lived in Endor. But it did not matter what you thought; he would be sure to bring you the article desired, whether satins, nails, or pickles.

Now, Mr. —— was said to be worth twenty lacs of rupees, or about ten hundred thousand dollars.

The son was dressed on this wedding tour in blue silk pantaloons, with the finest linen—a long tunic of the richest blue silk brocade over a white linen robe, and a Fez cap with a rich heavy crimson tassel. He had a costly ruby upon his finger, but no other jewelry.

The sister was beautiful. Her dress generally was of silks, cut very much in the style of our present dresses. She wore no veil, but a delicate mantle of exquisite gauze, thrown gracefully over the head, and around the waist a chain of gold, with a heavy talisman or scroll of gold. She wore rich bracelets, and a Burman necklace of gold threads, with diamond earrings and rings. The Jewessess in Burmah do not veil themselves within doors

any more than Sarai did, but I have met them returning from the synagogue veiled in Persian style, showing
only their fine large black eyes.

The Hebrews of Maulmain are very light, almost
white, indeed. They have not the transparent rose and
white of Erin and the Norseland, but they are white
Asiatics. They are cultivated people, well read, and
very polite, except that —— and his lovely family
would not eat with us Gentiles. They kept their own
cook, and had their meals served by themselves on solid
silver.

Mr. —— was a fine singer, and I wanted him to
sing me a Hebrew Psalm, but he did not like to do it
there. This led to a long talk about the Scripture pro-
phecies. He seemed unwilling to hear them, but
digressed continually to the genealogies and histories of
the Israelites. He could silence me very quickly in the
genealogical line, for it is as much as I can do to remember who my grandfather was. I had to give up
that. I could trace Abraham's only to Terah the Gen-
tile. He did not like to touch on the hundred and
tenth Psalm, but could chant the whole of the hundred
and fifth. Finally, after indulging him and all his companions in a victorious laugh over my obstinate ignorance
of the Chronicles, I succeeded in getting him to read
attentively the twenty-ninth and fifty-third chapters of
Isaiah, when a pious, intelligent officer joined us, and I
left them. The discussion was prolonged until a very
late hour, and after all others had retired, I saw ——
standing with his friend Mr. Cohen, apparently preach-

E

ing to him Jesus, the Holy One of Israel, while Mr. Cohen's excited tone, eye, and manner, expressed all the scorn of the Pharisee. They were speaking in Arabic, but I could distinctly hear —— saying the " Mesheah," the " Mesheah," and pointing him to Isaiah. It was a moment of the deepest interest to me; and the officer told me that Mr. —— did acknowledge to him alone that he had a New Testament in his own house, and had read it twice through; [moreover, that he did sometimes doubt, and scarcely knew what to believe about their long-expected Messiah. But he added, " Suppose we believe this Book. What can we do ? We are dependent upon our business. If we confess Jesus to be the Christ, we shall surely be cast out of the Synagogue, and then not a Jew will do business with us."

Do people think what it was, and what it is now, to be put out of the synagogue ?

As I looked on my friend ——, in the saloon of the " Burmah," thought went back to Jessie and my Eurasian friends in Maulmain. One eye after another rose around the cabin, beaming with hope, love, and high resolve, till I laid my head down and wept for Jessie and my old Sunday-school. The pupils and teachers of this school were very dear to me, and Jessie was my principal helper. Thrilling scenes and discoveries did we make in our visitings among the Eurasian children and their heathen mothers in Maulmain.

One Burman woman insisted that she was married, that the white man ate pickled tea with her, which is the same as joining hands in English ; but a third, the mother of three little children, looked up and said, "My mother sold me when thirteen years old. The father of my babes will never marry me ; I am not his colour. I dare not ask it. He never promised it. What can I do ? If I leave him, my children die. Lady," and the big tears stood in that heathen woman's eye, " Lady, it was a Christian who bought me: will not the Christian's God pity me ? "

At another place we found a woman sitting upon the grass beating her bosom, and moaning most piteously. Her curly-headed, blue-eyed boy had been taken from her—stolen from her in the night—and sent across the ocean for an English education. She would never see him again, or if she did, only to be cursed by him. She was a maniac.

I was told of another poor creature, who went tearing her hair, rushing wildly up and down the streets calling for her two little girls. Their father had taken an English wife, a perfect stranger to the children and to their mother ; a dashing, working woman, just come out from Scotland. She would want help, so, to save other expense, the two sisters were taken by force from their mother, who idolized them, and put under this hard foreigner, with a father who only cared for gold. This was my Jessie and her little sister. Their poor mother, I think, never saw them again, and their sad story is too harrowing to relate. Many of these children inherit their father's high spirit, scorn their Burman relations, and are equally scorned by them. So that the condition of this class is truly pitiable. They need a real Yankee

school in their midst—that is, one giving them a sound
English education, mentally and physically, and one that
will teach them to scorn the oriental fear of work.

When I began teaching the Karens of Dong Yahn,
they refused to wash their own clothes, but insisted on
my hiring a washerman for them. I insisted on their
doing it themselves. Then they would not bring their
clothes at all; so I was obliged to go to the rooms of
each pupil, for I had then men, women, and children.
Finally, it occurred to me that they held it as degrading
because *we* hired a dhoby. So one Saturday I called all
together, placed the children to mind the fires and the
well, and took the mothers to the wash-tub; I got out
my children's clothes, and went into the soap suds in
earnest. "There," I said, "you see how book-women
can wash."

"Mama makes herself a *cooley*," said one of the
preachers, with unutterable scorn.

"And what, Bahme, did the Son of God make Himself?" I asked, when he walked away. The example
moved them all, and proved a decided success; so that
from that time no more washermen were called for my
school, and ever after I found they washed every week
regularly in the jungles. One had gone so far as to get
a flat-iron, and even ironed her husband's jackets.

Their subsequent habits of cleanliness seemed to
change them every way. One boy who was very lazy,
and who would sit down at play hours, after he began
to wash his turban, became all at once the most industrious fellow there; he subsequently learned the printing

business, and became so efficient, he was called for everywhere. He dated his conversion from that time; and
so did a fine little girl, now a preacher's wife, as her
pastor wrote me subsequently.

Another young girl had troubled me much with her
bad temper and language. Suddenly she changed, and,
from being hated by her companions, became a favourite.
One day I called her aside, and inquired how it was she
had kept from saying bad words so long. The tears
started.

"Mama," she said, "when my dress was dirty, my
heart was dirty. Now I want to keep my heart clean.
So when the bad words rise, I pray to God, then shut
my teeth tight, and choke them!"

Six of these young washerwomen became Bible readers
and teachers; one married the highest chief in the land,
and another the head teacher in the Theological School
in Maulmain.

Another time one of the women remained out of
school, because her child cried. I called for the child,
and found it all over eruption, from the crown of its
head to the soles of its feet. I ordered an ointment,
and gave her a cake of castile soap.

"Mama," she exclaimed, with all the disgust she
could express, "it smells!" And no persuasion could
induce that mother to put her delicate hands to the
ointment.

"Very well," I said, "give me the poor little thing,"
and dashed him into the water; then anointed the little
tubercle of humanity with my own hands. The next

day he was so much better, the mother was encouraged, and ventured to follow ; and from that time her children were the most cleanly in her village, and have risen up to honour their parents. These were Karens, but—

"Will Mrs. Bullard please send her servant?" asked a poor Eurasian young woman, who had applied to me for sewing. She was living with her Burman mother alone, down among the huts. I made her up a small roll, and handed it to her as we do at home; but she was the daughter of a baron, and a high military officer. It would degrade her to carry that little roll of cloth. This is orientalism, and one of the greatest hindrances to the education of eastern nations.

"No, Julia," I answered ; " I don't think I could send Sammy. He's gone to market, and he has no one to do the work for him. But I'll take it myself; I should like to see your mother."

Julia's eyes opened as they never did before: "Oh, no, madam ;" but I took the roll home. Julia never again asked for a servant.

Now, these Indo Britons need to be taught after the Yankee model, to put their hands to work, and to regard all work as honourable if honest. Then they would rise up and become the elevators of the heathen, and the strength of the Government.

CHAPTER IV.

BEGINNING OF THE TOUNGHOO MISSION, AND OUR
JOURNEY UP THE COUNTRY.

WILL you take a sail now in "the rains" down the Bay
to Monmogon, on the coast of Tavoy? It is an awful
kind of beauty that nature puts on here; but come, it
is inspiring.

Wild, sublime, and lovely as ocean, sky, rock, and
flower can be, is this Monmogon, our home by the sea;
especially when a storm broods over the islands, or draws
up in a line of water-spouts. At times I have seen a
long colonnade of these glorious water columns, now and
then lit up by a crossing sunbeam into prisms of indescribable grandeur. Indeed, the lover of marine scenery
always finds Monmogon enchanting ground.

The dark graceful avenues of feathery Casuarinas, the
two lonely mountains north and south, the frontage of
rocky isle and green sea, and the knowledge that there
is a village a mile behind in the mangoes, make it all
that the lover of romance can want in scenery. The
orchids are flowering in the woods, the creepers carpeting
the alluvial plain, and the darling little pink and white
shells embroidering the shingly beach. It is exciting,

too, when the fisher monkeys come scampering along the sand, digging out the shells, cracking them as boys would their nuts, and helping themselves to breakfast. It was exciting to see our boys chasing them, or tending their great baby monkey. One day a Burman brought them a young white eyelid monkey, of a pretty flesh colour, that did truly look like a little baby boy. They were glad to send it off to the woods again, for they had another pet monkey, and the moment the pet saw them touch the white one, it sprang at it, and would have killed it.

The boys amused themselves also by running after the sea cocoa-nut, along the beach, and watching the cunning scarlet-coloured crabs : but one time they came bounding into the door in breathless haste, and a few minutes after a barking deer leaped, almost flew past, through the jungle, and the children fully believed they could hear the hard breathing of the tiger over the imploring eyes of the pretty deer. There were tigers all around us we knew ; for they had devoured two men in the neighbourhood after we went there, and we sometimes heard their dismal " peo, peo," ranging round the mangroves.

It is in August, 1853 ; Mr. Mason lies on his cot in the centre of the bungalow, too weak to speak loud, or raise his hands.

" Husband, do get well, and we'll go to Tounghoo !" I say playfully. He looks up a moment earnestly, smiles, and drops into a calm sleep. Strange to say, from that very hour he begins to mend.

One week passes—a light cot of bamboo, covered and enclosed with thatch, stands at the door.

" Gently—gently—Moungyen," and they lift him in on to his little bed. He is nicely tucked up and covered from the rain.

" Who are to carry the Sahib ? "

" These, ma'am," pointing to six of the smallest men present.

" No, no, these men can take me, but the stoutest ones must be master's bearers. Stand up together. Let's see if you are the same height."

The natives think nothing about this, and generally put tall men on one side, and short ones on the other ; then go trotting on, regardless of the constant anxiety it gives the persons borne lest they should be tipped out.

Turning a bend in the path, I see my little daughter swinging over a slippery precipice, in a basket borne by two Burmans, on a bamboo. The poor little thing is drenched with the pouring rain, for her umbrella, like mine, had been smashed by the bearers. Beyond, on the verge of a high perpendicular cliff, are my two little boys astride of men's shoulders. One is on the neck of a tall, sleek Coringa, clinging with might and main to the fellow's long black hair, which was streaming Absalom-like, a part in the wind, and a part tangled in the jungle branches above.

" He is a votary of Kali," I think, as my eye glances down at the rapids beneath. But at that moment there appear half a dozen red, checked, and white turbans from below.

"Ho, ho! Stop, stop, Moungyen!" Useless halloo-
ing. They 're too far on to stop, and I hold my breath
as they cross, for the bearers are dangling my husband's
cot right over a deep gulf as black as night, and they
stand on a single log, thrown as a bridge across the
ravine.

"Now, Allay, these Burmans are not to do such a
daring thing again," and I leave my chair, and walk
before to watch the road, stopping now and then to
wet my husband's lips with wine, and say a word of
comfort—full of terror, lest he should expire on the road.
Nothing but a faint hope that he might live through
such a journey could have induced me to go at such a
time. But he was so nearly dying, I felt sure he could
survive but a few days if he remained. No physician
near—no white face.

On they go, tugging up the steep ascent, over toppling
crags, and through the dripping, pinched-up fissure
beyond. We had crossed the submerged, unreaped rice
field, with much effort descended the steep falling bank,
and crossed the Tavoy river. A stout Burman, with
only his patsoe trussed up, caught me in his arms, and
plunged at once knee deep into the mire, and kept
plunging to the top of the bank. These men have such
a way of walking, one feels quite safe ; and they never
dropped me, although they have carried me many a time
through swollen streams, and up steep precipices, clench-
ing their naked toes to the rocks like the mountain goat.

I have crossed these mountains in painful anxiety and
fear at midnight, by torch-light, almost fleeing before my

bearers, who plodded on with their empty chair, fearing lest we should be left in utter darkness with the tigers; but this time it was more fearful still, for the whole seemed like a funeral march.

Nothing was heard but the roar of some hidden torrent behind a crag, the scream of the peacock eagle as she plunged down the tiger-haunted abyss, the surge-like sounds of the hornbills' wings soaring around the splintered pinnacles, and the mournful requiem of the congregated wauwau monkeys, calling and answering from mountain to mountain, or hurling rocks right over our heads. The craggy precipices loomed up from five hundred to fifteen hundred feet on each side the gorge, almost shutting out the light; and not a blossom looked out to cheer us, except now and then the blue thunbergia, which I have loved ever since; but instead of flowers, immense creepers swung over the lonely ravines and along the cliffs like mourning weeds draping a cathedral.

In the same manner I had carried my husband to the sea-shore nearly two years before, and the change restored him for a time to health.

After nine miles travel in the heaviest rain, over rocks and crags, rivers and gulfs, we are glad enough to reach Tavoy.

" Husband, dear, are you still alive?"

" Please go quickly!" I entreat of the Missionary brethren, "and see if we can get passage to Maulmain in the steamer just ready to leave."

All shake their heads, and fingers are raised in token of warning.

"She's crazy," they say to themselves; but I put some wine to his lips and hasten out.

In the steamer—"Captain, captain! will you take my husband? Please do; he'll die here."

"The captain is not here, madam; can't engage."

"Oh, Sir, do take my husband. Say he may be brought."

The second officer has a human heart.

"Well, madam, I've no right. The captain may be displeased, but I'll venture. We leave in an hour though. You can't get him here?"

"Only say the word—we'll try."

In the streets; not a bearer left; hungry and wet, all have run away to their homes. No time to lose, I hasten over to our old Burman bazaar-woman. By a few words and more gestures make her comprehend. Out she goes, and in half an hour my husband's cot is alongside the steamer. Good, kind Mr. Gray lifts him up, cot and all, on to the deck.

There I knelt beside him, telling him earnestly he would not die, for he was called to Tounghoo, and all the time my own heart beating as if it would burst through. Thank heaven, he lived; and on arriving in Maulmain, the change of air, diet, and medicine set him in his chair again. We were much indebted here to Quarter-Master Craig, an officer then in Maulmain. This kind friend of Mr. Mason came in one day with a bottle of the best old port wine, and a paper of charred cork. He begged my husband to try it—a wine-glass of wine and a tea-spoonful of the cork together, three times a-day. He did try it, and it cured him of the most obstinate chronic illness, which had baffled the skill of all his physicians.

A week has passed—Mr. Mason is still very weak ; but he calls me beside him—

"Ellen," he says, "don't you think it may be duty for us to try and go to Tounghoo ?"

"Most certainly. Haven't a doubt of it."

"But you can't——." Before he could finish, I was gone.

In the streets of Maulmain. I call an extra servant.

"John, will you go with the Sahib to Tounghoo ?"

"Oh, no, mistress. Plenty robbers. Me very 'fraid."

At last, after three days a servant is engaged. But it was nearly a week that he and I traversed those streets, hour after hour, and day after day, in search of a boat and men who would dare to make the perilous attempt of going to Tounghoo. Pegu had been taken by the English, and the country was overrun with dacoits.

Finally, on Saturday, in answer to prayer, I am sure, a few volunteers appeared at our door. Among them a Karen boatman, a Christian, who could speak Pwo Karen, the language I was familiar with. Mr. Mason said, "Take him for your Tutauman, or interpreter." I did so, and wonderful indeed has been this man's career ever since.

After a few days we are on the way for that unknown land of song, old Tounghoo. Almost everybody then condemned the undertaking, or at least thought it a wild scheme, and a most perilous exposure of life.

Imagine us in a small Burman boat, with a queer, hood like cover of thatch over the centre; a corps of six native preachers in another boat, and rowing a few miles up the Salwen. I could not help wishing that our way led up as far as Trockla, for I do love trees, and this is the land of that queen of trees, the Amherstia. I have seen several in full bloom in Maulmain, but could only talk to its native glories in imagination.

It is something like an umbrella in form, with light drooping branches of lively green. Its blossoms are of brilliant red and yellow, which float down more than a yard in length. Doctor Wallich first discovered it, and named it after Lady Amherst, wife of the Governor-General of India. The tree is said to be worth fifty pounds in England.

About fifty miles north-west of Martaban Gulf, we passed in sight of a land I had many times visited. The last time I went in search of a pupil, whose mother had kept him away from school. The family lived quite alone on the skirts of a forest, and we had to walk some three miles over the paddy fields, with feet almost blistering, and fainting from the noon-day heat. A Karen girl carried my babe, and on reaching the ladder, I saw two women cutting up fish on the verandah. I called to them, but they gave me no answer. I ascended, but they gave me no mat. I took a stone for a seat with my babe, all of us utterly exhausted. Not the slightest attention was bestowed, nor any recognition of our presence. The house was quite full of young men and women; but one looked at the rice pot, another at the fishing net, another at the water bucket, and another played with the dog's tail, making him keep up a continual yelp. All seemed determined not to know us, and kept on their loud talking and jesting, both girls and boys.

Clack, clack, too, went the knives, and for a moment my heart sunk within me. Never before nor since did I receive so much rudeness, or see so much scorn in the countenances of heathen men and women.

Finally, my school girls, who had accompanied me, struck up a Karen hymn; clearly, slowly, sweetly they sung on about the Saviour, and as their plaintive notes floated round among the lime-trees and over the bananas, it seemed to fall upon the boisterous company like a gentle shower on tumultuous waves. For a moment there was a calm, and I began to explain the words of the hymn.

Clack, clack, faster and faster went the knives. Soon another loud contemptuous laugh.

We sung again. Another pause, and again we addressed them. So the scene continued, until at last, when we had sung nearly through the third hymn, they began to drop, one after another, as if mesmerized. All sat down but one, a tall, handsome, light-coloured maiden, whose rolling eyes and mischievous tricks greatly troubled us. She was the daughter of the mistress of the house, one of the choppers on the verandah. Gradually, just as we have seen the dawn opening, the surrounding eyes began to lose their wildness, and the lips their scorn; finally, the mouths all around began to open wider and wider, while the glance of the eyes grew sharper, steadier, more penetrating.

Clack, clack, went the knives.

Earnestly we entreated the Great Enlightener to descend, and I do believe He was there, wicked as the place was. Suddenly it occurred to me that I did not hear the knives. I looked round, and there lay the two women, the very personification of two great porpoises, stretched upon the floor behind, their chins propped up by their hands and elbows ; but their eyes were full of tears. Yes, those savage-mannered women had human hearts.

I found my pupil hidden behind a rice basket, where the chopping women had put him on seeing my approach. On questioning him about the Sabbath, he said he remembered the Sabbath day.

" And how do you spend it ? "

" I read this," he answered, taking out the Gospel of Matthew from under the basket. He had paid two annas for it. After Mr. Bullard had printed St. Matthew for the Pwos, he suggested to my school children that they should each pay sixpence a-piece for it. Books had always been given them before, and the idea of buying books was wholly new to them. " It hit their minds " though, as they said, and they came forward to purchase in great numbers, and went and covered them the first thing they did—which I had never seen them do with any book before.

It was in 1846 that I made this trip to the Prairie women. In 1850 I went to visit my old school. I was

passing round the room, feeling mournful that I could
not recognise any old familiar faces, when suddenly a
heavy hand was laid upon my shoulder, and I confronted
a large elderly woman, who gazed into my eyes with a
depth in her own I could not account for.

"Mama!" she exclaimed, "I 'm not as I was! Don't
you know me? I 'm not as I was;" seizing both my
hands in her brawny palms, and leading, rather hurrying,
me up to a desk—" My daughter, Mama! My daughter!" Both had been baptized.

Oh, did not the angels weep tears of joy with me that
morning? Did not their loved teacher in heaven look
down with unutterable delight upon that scene? Thanks
be to God who giveth us victory—" victory through our
Lord Jesus Christ."

As I thought of these scenes in passing the prairies,
my eyes peered toward the misty north, and the veiled
future; and I heard—yes, it seemed like a voice saying,
" Only believe."

Then the sun shone out brighter, the birds sang more
sweetly, our boat glided on, and we rejoiced over the
coming days of Tounghoo. It seemed as if everything
else rejoiced too with us, even the water fowl on the
way.

These prairies are the home of innumerable water
fowl:—adjutants nodding their floating marabout plumes
among the red lilies and crimson leaves of the nelum-
biums ; cormorants, teal, and thousands of snow-white
herons with black legs, mingling with the white lilies as
if blossoms themselves. In a cove here I saw a hun-

F

dred pelicans netting up the fish like skilled old fisher-
men. A hundred more swept through the air above,
with several magnificent cranes ; and down came from
a distant pinnacle the fisher-eagle ; while the wide plain
was flanked with many a herd of great black buffaloes, standing like lines of cavalry drawn up around
the horizon.

Then came the "Guiding Island" in the midst of
this desert. The canal here enters a small lake, encircled
by little lights glimmering among the morning shadows
as we float under the lime-trees, reminding us of what
children sing of

> "—One of those beautiful islands,
>   Away in the tropical seas,
> Where flow'rets blossom all winter,
> And oranges hang on the trees."

But right beside the oranges is a poor, woe-begone
peasant plying his skiff through the prairie—now up,
now down, while his wife keeps two small bamboos
working on the sides. They are gathering grass seeds
for their children's breakfast. In times of famine the
natives of India use grass seeds for rice.

Afterwards Sittang bursts upon us like a fairy-land,
lying in a tranquil mirror-like semicircle, a mile or more
in width. Rows of cottages and avenues of trees on
either side, with the dim battlements of the ancient city
in the distance ! These make the place so lovely, and
it looks so civilized, that one doubts for a moment if the
inhabitants can be heathen.

Old Sittang was founded about six hundred years ago, by the Talaing monarch of Pegu, about twenty miles west of this place. It was designed by nature for a stronghold, and such it has continued to be, passing through innumerable changes ; now sacked by the Shans, then by the Burmans, and by how many more nations I know not, but at last taken by the English in 1824 or 1825, given up again to the Burmans, and retaken by the British in 1852.

Modern Sittang has a very tolerable bazaar close to the river, which here flows round a crescent-shaped precipice, rising just behind the principal street, forming a natural rampart from one to two hundred feet high ; perpendicular, and covered with brilliant green shrubbery, it presents a very striking and beautiful background. On this hill the English have planted their cantonments. The place is garrisoned by a small force ; the town at present numbers only from one to two thousand inhabitants, mostly Burmans, and I believe all are heathen.

Passing up this river the boatmen tell us many tales— among them the following :—

While the British troops were on their march from Shwaygyn to Tounghoo, a party of horse one day galloped off some distance from the army, and came suddenly upon a skirmishing party of three or four hundred Burmese soldiers, armed ready for battle. As soon as they saw the Colahs, they all cowered down and *shekoed*, except one, who was dauntless enough to fire a musket. He had no sooner fired, than a sepoy leaped to his side and caught him by the hair, calling out :

F 2

"Who are you, you rascal?" Whereupon somebody who knew him muttered, "Rajah."

"Rajah!" shouted the sepoy. "Who? Where?"

"Hoga, Rajah! Rajah!" cried the caught man, pointing fiercely to a Burman who was galloping off at full speed.

"So, ho!" shouted the sepoy, starting with all fury after the flying rider, when, to his great chagrin, he learned that the man he had let go was the Rajah, the robber Governor of Martaban, and the one he was pursuing was his servant. In the mean time, the Rajah had run for his life.

So, you see, many scenes have been acted along these waters—many shockingly tragic, and some tragi comic.

"Saya, Saya!" came in subdued tones through our boat-curtains the morning after we had slept at Sittang.

"What—what is it, Kodote?" hurriedly questions the Missionary, rousing from his sleep, for it is scarcely dawn.

"*Thane nat! thane nat!*"

"Ha! What? Where are the guns?"

"Gone, Saya. The *demiahs* have got them both!"

It seems incredible, for the missing muskets are both loaded, and lie on each side of our head boatman under his curtains. But gone they are, and thankful are we that the dacoits have not turned them upon us as we lay helpless before them.

We have been repeatedly told that our way is infested by robbers, and that a notorious brigand has posted his followers not far from this place; but having an old soldier to lead us, and our boats being well armed, we have felt comparatively safe. We now see more than ever how weak is man, how strong is God.

Imagine one vast plain stretching to the west as far as the eye can reach, its banks fringed with luxuriant cucubine reeds and the long purple tassels of the saccharrine grass. Here and there, too, is a village, and then comes a green field of waving rice instead of the forever glaring yellow. The spirit is cheered, too, by human sounds which tell of a heart-tie. When travelling far among deep forests and burning plains, we forget nations, and feel so grateful to grasp any human hand or hear any human sound ; no matter what is said, even a curse would sometimes be thankfully received from a brother man.

Our right shore contrasts finely with the left in its magnificent precipices, which occasionally tower up all of a sudden from their level basements, overhanging the river with great boldness and beauty. On our right is a grand range of mountains, the same chain as seen at Martaban, which separates the Salwen and Sittang valleys, and extends far above Ava. And here we are at Shwaygyn, the City of Gold, one hundred and thirty-six miles from Maulmain.

'Tis an old town, and if you wish to know how it looks, you must think of two broad rivers meeting up here, a little way from the foot of these great mountains. At their junction lie two precipitous ledges of rock, like terraces, one above the other. On the highest of these hills, which presents a broad space of table-land, the

British troops are cantoned, mostly within the old Burman stockade.

The lower terrace of Shwaygyn presents the aspect of having been in its day one of the loveliest spots in India. The beautiful Abbey Hill here opens over a perpendicular precipice of forty or fifty feet, on the verge of which stands a line of fairy-like pagodas, and then a line of ancient abbeys. In Burmah, monasteries are perched on the cliffs, like the Romish Convents of the Levant. Below these hills are about a thousand houses, bordering each fork for about two miles, making the city some four or five miles long, and perhaps one mile in width. The houses are nearly all low huts of bamboo, or teak and matting; but the monasteries are principally of teak, strongly built, some of them richly carved, and with roofs of five gradations in height.

Shwaygyn excels in the grandeur and elaborate carving of its public buildings. But what a queer medley is Burman architecture! everywhere of a perfect chameleon order. Look at these huge sea-serpent spouts, which join the roofs, and you think they ought to have come from the Cyclopean or old Phenician land. Glance again at these fairy temple-spires, and the pointed arch, and you cry, " The Goth! the Goth!"

Look at these monastery domes, and the pavilion roofs, the relics of sun idolatry, and you say it is Chinese surely; but just then you glance at the arch turned into a horse-shoe amidst flowers, and vines, and mosaic, and you cry, "Arabian!" but another look, and you declare it is no Arabian, and nobody's order at all.

Symes tells us that the King of Paghan destroyed one thousand arched temples, and four thousand square ones, to obtain bricks and stones to build a contemplated wall of defence against the Chinese. From this we may conclude that the Burmese formerly built of stone. The most curious little temple perhaps in Burmah is the Peepul-Fane of Tavoy, where the branches of an old peepul have taken root close around the idol, and completely embower it. .

One of the monasteries which I visited was ornamented with paintings, among which were the four Buddhs who have already blessed the earth, three represented upon thrones, but Debendea, the third, as always pictured, sitting upon the sacred lotus. Three nuns were bowing before them, and when I begged of them not to worship, " I'll worship, worship, worship!" one repeated till I left.

Burmese painting seems to be all of one type. But there is a barbaric inspiration in it after all. Perspective, foreshortening, chiaro-scuro, graduating tints, and the softening outlines they have no idea of, yet they make eloquent pictures without them. Their figures are often struck out quite in proportion, with the boldness and freedom of a Correggio; yet they seldom know what to do with the feet, and pack them up as much out of the way as possible.

In Burmah, paintings of all kinds, good, bad, and indifferent, are valued according to the *size*—one rupee the cubit.

A Shan painter wanted me to sit to him for my

portrait, which to encourage the old man I did, but when he got to the eyes, he could not make them turn, so one morning I said, "Let me take the brush," which he did, but as soon as he saw the picture was looking at him, he gave a cry of terror as if it had been "an evil eye," dashed down his pallet, and fled. I never saw him again.

Burmah has a genius for painting as much as Italy, but this base valuing of art as chips and blocks suppresses any attempt at rising, and so they drudge on by the old monastic rules of Mount Athos. The wall paintings of the temples are usually the best. The most antique are monochromes executed in gold bronze on wood.

The Burmese always expend a great deal over their dead. I took pains one time to enumerate the articles borne to a grave. The deceased was only a carpenter's wife, yet there passed five maidens with flower pots, five with bamboos, two with harps, six with oil jars, eight with water jars, eight with pillows, six with mats, ten with jars, twelve with cocoa-nuts, ten with bananas, all followed by some three hundred people. The house was crowded with invited guests, all chatting in lively groups, and feasting. The young men were attending outside to two immense cauldrons of rice and curry; the old women were making confectionary, and the young women preparing loads of betel-leaves. The married men were the only class allowed to be idle, and they were looking on enjoying the scene. The festival cost the poor man many hundred rupees; but pillows, mats, &c., were borrowed from the Kyoungs and returned,—a common practice when one is unable to meet the expenses. After the burning, a sheet was held over the ashes by seven persons, who perambulated the pyre seven times, each- time elevating and lowering the sheet. The few small bones remaining were then deposited in an urn.

Anciently the Karens always buried their dead. They have the old Welsh custom of lighting tapers at the head and foot of the grave, and their wail-dirge sounds much like the coronach. The chiefs place small darts around their pyres to prevent the spirit from returning home. They also tie strings across the streams as bridges for the ghosts of the departed to get conveniently over to their graves.

At their funerals they engage in a game prefiguring the struggle of man with evil spirits, and then chant a dirge, recognising the truth that sin brought death.

In the plastic art the Burmese exhibit some degree of skill. Like the ancient Greeks, they colour and drape their figures, and frequently provide them with imitation eyes. Burman bronzes have some of them as delicate a green, and appear to be quite as skilfully cast, as the bronzes of Egyptian museums. Papier-mâché work is carried on in Tounghoo, and some of it is executed with taste and skill. They understand a coarse kind of mosaic in running vines, flowers, a lion, peacock, or other simple subject; but fine mosaic of Burmese execution I have never found. Painting on glass and ivory is done to perfection by the Mussulmans of Delhi, but not much understood by Burmese. Their chessmen, however, their ivory-hilted knives, and cocoa-nut-shell work, show a good degree of skill in delicate carving.

Among the beautiful trees on the Sittang river is the Nauclea Kadamba. It was Sunday, and Mr. Mason had just closed his services under the wide-spreading branches of this tree, when a little skiff came gliding along silent as a wavelet.

"Ho, brother! take mama into your skiff?" cried my boys.

The man is a highlander in his mountain tunic, who has never seen a white woman. Quite frightened, he pushes on faster and faster; then Shapau hails him, and finally succeeds in bringing him to shore. The skiff is only big enough for three to sit safely in. So, giving my Tutauman the bow, I take the centre. Shaupau reads to the boatman the Gospel of St. Matthew for an hour, steadily, carefully explaining every word until he comes to the account of Christ's healing the lunatic. Upon this the stranger stops, lays down the oar, and, taking up a small joint of bamboo very carefully deposited, he empties the whole contents deliberately into the river.

"There! brother, I have been twenty miles after this *Ootee*, or charmed water, and paid a rupee for it; but henceforth I worship this Yasu Krick who healed the crazy man!" Is it not "the Sword of the Spirit?"

There is, far inland, a hidden hamlet, a deep glen flanked with mountains. Here we find all the women like Ruth gleaning in the fields, and a high time these buccaneer brothers are having over their great fires on the shore of the creek, where they are drying their jerked deer, having just beat up a huge stag in the thickets, and killed him in their bamboo traps, made like a bow and arrow loosely covered from view. With great wonderment all dropped their work and stood gazing, as I stepped down the precipice right over their heads.

Both men and women listened with attention and astonishment to the message of a Saviour's love, and a few followed me down to our encampment, promising to learn to read. I have never seen them since, but on returning from America, two years after, we heard to our great joy that they had a flourishing little church in that place. "The Lord hath spoken."

Another Sunday morning we turned to the west, a mile over an unreaped rice-field full of water, to a hamlet of Pwo Karens. Not one would receive us. We sought shelter with a poor woman in a stable. Very reluctantly she consented to receive us; for she evidently feared some terrible calamity would befall her in consequence.

We talked and read to her about the poor in body and poor in spirit. She seemed interested, and I quite forgot that there were buffaloes beside us. Suddenly she screamed: "Flee! flee!" I had just time to glance round, and saw the buffaloes had stretched their noses on a straight line, as they always do when about to charge, and their eyes burned like coals of fire.

"Flee! flee!" cries the woman, snatching her babe; but just at that moment the leader breaks loose, and dashes past us so near, that his awful horns graze my hat.

"Thank God, we're safe!"

"Come in, friend! come in, friend!" shout all the women at once, and every heart is opened. Mats are spread, and they are now disposed to regard us as gods.

"Look here," says an old woman who passes for an eldress, after I have been telling her that God is always near :

"Why, the Elders told the Karens the same thing, and my grandmother used to say, Yuah was like this"— waving one hand just above the other. The Omnipresence of God known to this wild heathen woman!

Moored again farther up the Sittang. A woman appears on the shore with an eye that I cannot mistake ; I am sure that is a Pwo Karen, though she is dressed in the Talaing robe.

"Sister," I say, "have you any husband?"

"Lady! white lady! you speak Pwo?" Instantly she was at my feet, entreating me to go to her house, and could scarcely be restrained from bearing me away. On reaching her house, I commenced reading the Gospel of Matthew in her language. With the true Karen spirit she could not be content to receive so much pleasure alone.

"Teacheress, read! read!" she says to me eagerly, having assembled all the neighbours.

I read the Pwo ; she interprets into Talaing, for a whole hour, the Talaing women quite as much delighted as the Karens ; for they never before heard of Christ, and not one of them can read at all in any language.

Suddenly I stop, and strike up in Pwo—

"Alas, and did my Saviour bleed?"

The men, hearing the singing, throw aside their dahs and baskets, and assemble around the house, pressing up the ladder.

Hark! what's this? Crack! crack! and crash, we all go on to the ground!

"Read on! read on!" cries the Karen woman. "Light! light! give us light." So there I sit among the ruins, and read the stories of the crucifixion and resurrection, and certainly I never felt so near the unseen and eternal. We are in the middle of the account of Christ casting out devils:

"What's that? what's that, lady? Tell that devil story again. Yasu Kriek kill the devils?"

We read it again when the man—a fine-looking Karen of some thirty-five years—steps out:

"Lady! lady! You see this cord (the nat-cord worn on the wrist) there!" wrenching it off, "never again will I offer to any lord but Jesus Christ." This was really a very decided act, for usually the nat-cord is the last thing Karens will give up.

On our returning two years after, we learned that this man had been baptized, and was the leading deacon of a little Christian church in or near his own village.

CHAPTER V.

TOUNGHOO, AND WHAT WE FOUND THERE.

I HAPPENED to be the first white woman who ever entered either the city or the kingdom of Toonghoo, so that my poor face was as much of a curiosity as the mermaid a few years ago in America, and all the way up the villagers thronged us to see the wonder, and discuss its merits. The great point was whether it was a fair specimen of the race.

" Wa ! wa ! " exclaims one, " I thought them a great deal whiter—but then I dare say many are whiter than she is."

" No, I don't believe they are," joins in a prim young belle, sitting so as to look over the first one's shoulder. " I didn't think the colah woman very handsome."

" Hae ! " grumbles a matronly chaperon, as she sees some young men approaching : " you know nothing. They're not white like *jackets*. I dare say she's as white as any of 'em."

" Koungtha ! koungtha ! " cries a gay young fellow, jauntily flinging himself off after a furtive glance. " Anglaik very pretty—Burman woman *taemathe*"— (very black), with a teasing laugh at the ladies. And it really does seem to tease them to see fairer women than themselves.

As Mr. Mason was not ready to go up into the city, and wished to wait for the cool of evening, I attempted to proceed, thinking I would have time to prepare a comfortable place for his reception. A native of the city stepped forward, and very politely volunteered his services as guide to the house, which he professed to know all about.

I followed the man, as it was only about a mile, and on he went till he reached the principal street, when he began to inquire of everybody where the white lady's house was. This, with my being the first white woman ever there, attracted such a crowd, it was impossible to proceed.

"Don't you know the place, friend?" I questioned in dismay.

"Don't know Th'kyen," and vanished out of sight. Seeing a good road in front, I escaped from the crowd to that, and meeting a Madras servant who could speak English, I tried to make him understand my wants.

"Did some carts go there this morning with tin cans?" he asked.

"Yes."

"Oh, then, I'll find it in a minute. Missus, please come."

So again I walked on, on; and soon pale faces began to pass, one after another, all in the same style of dress— dark trousers, checked shirts, with military forage-caps loosely covered with white muslin havelocks. Immediately it occurred to me that we must be drawing near the cantonments. As quick as the thought flashed, I stopped short once more with—

"Boy, where *are* you going?" rather sharply.

"To master, missus. Master knows all about it."

"And who is your master, pray?"

"Major H——, of the Madras Fusileers. He lives close by—right here. Missus, *please* come."

"Oh, no, no," I replied; but before the words were half uttered, he had whipped out of sight behind an old kyoung that looked as if it might possibly have been changed into a bungalow. Not caring to meet a stranger just there, I instantly turned, and attempted to regain the wall. But at that moment my Burman servant took a fancy to leap off after the Madrasee, thinking he would find the house immediately. "Shwaho, Shwaho!" I called, but in vain. The last I saw of him was his yellow silk patsoe streaming on the air, as he flew, John Gilpin-like, up the street. Finally, I walked straight on, as if quite at home, back to the landing, and found Mr. Mason wickedly enjoying the sport, because he did not care to have me get into the city before him. He had called a Burman cart, and I concluded to patronize that, although I had rather any time walk two miles than ride one in this vehicle. Wearisomely it dragged its slow wheels along. The driver was a malicious-looking fellow, and was continually walking his bullocks up on to the bank; but at last we got safely over the gullies into the bazaar street, and turned off into a re-tired square, where we found an enclosure bounded by a bamboo trellis some fourteen feet high, and covered with blue flowered creepers. A huge double gate was flung open to receive us, and in front of a pleasant green plat stood the keep of the former Myusaya, or city recorder. This building was our home while we remained. It was a true native-built house, of teak, probably a hundred years old; sixty-seven feet long, set up seven feet from the ground, built in three separate portions, three roofs joined together by huge water-spouts of teak. The verandah was strongly barricaded, and behind the reception-rooms of the master and mistress was the donjon.

Now, imagine this old city on the Sittang, which has been shut up three hundred years from all the civilized world. Think of a wall five or six miles round, some twenty feet high, and thick enough, with the inner embankment, for a carriage drive. A large brick church now stands upon it, with dwelling-houses and palm-trees. The wall is constructed with bastions and battlements, and with four pagoda turrets, watch-houses for the guardians of the city.

Tounghoo must once have been very handsome, with its towers, and spires, and statues; with its broad, regular streets shaded with palms; its monasteries, temples, pagodas, and palace, all surrounded by palms; its many huge gates; its encircling flagged walk and carriage road, and its moat extending clear round the city. The moat was said to be sixty yards wide, and was filled at any moment by secret channels from a beautiful lake within the fort. Then the grand bridges

G

across the moat, adorned with statues, rich carvings, and the national peacock-emblem, mounted on pillars in every direction, sixty and eighty feet high ; with magnificent tanks, caravanserais, and rich rice-fields. I do not wonder that old Tounghoo in its glory excited the cupidity of European adventurers, as Burman history says it did. The Portuguese navigators made their way up to this city and took possession, but the governor lost his life in consequence. The Burmese then held it as a principality of Ava until it fell into the hands of the English in 1853.

When we entered Tounghoo, there might be two thousand palm-trees counted in and around the city; but Tounghoo history says that there were six thousand in ancient days. They yield a sweet wine in great abundance, that is much sought after. It is dealt out to the troops in daily rations, and much of it is used to make yeast for bread.

Most of these trees are planted by the priests, and are, of course, attached to monasteries, especially the corypha palm, which supplies the book leaf for the priests and schools. The corypha dies immediately after it has once blossomed ; but the Burmans affirm that it is always a hundred years old before it blossoms. The palmyra palm flowers annually after fifteen or twenty years. I saw in Tounghoo, in 1853, five or six hundred coryphas in blossom all at once, a sight seldom seen, and, of course, as the *Tanyaka* or "vintage of the palms" approached, there were grand times in the city. Every-where women and children were running, and men walking with business-like rapidity, tugging bamboos to secure their trees. Palm wine is not obtained like maple sap, from the trunk, but from the top of the palm. The tree is ascended by a ladder, and just as the fruit begins to form, the flower is cut off. The stem is then turned down into an earthen vessel, or into a bamboo, which is secured to the place by means of a slight frame around the tree. When the juice is drawn into an earthen vessel, it is sweet; but if drawn into a joint of bamboo, as frequently done, it almost immediately becomes intoxicating; and if it is not sufficiently spirituous, the strength is increased by dropping in a few broken areca-nuts, when one glass of the liquor will intoxicate.

It is curious to see these men and boys go up the tall palm-trees. The bamboo ladder is made about a foot wide. The climber has only a patsoe, or cloth, girt around his loins, to which is attached his knife, threads, ratans, and everything, with a dah, or short sword, thrust in behind, and two little earthen chatties. He begins to ascend by cording the ladder strongly to the trunk for a few feet up, then goes up and ties again, so continues tying on the ladder, and ascending at the same time. Of course, it is very slender, and looks most hazardous, but one ladder would hold up half a dozen boys.

Each palm yields about seventy-five quarts of sap in a season, valued at six rupees, or more, so that two thousand trees would yield a revenue of twelve thousand rupees. Now, many of the palms have been destroyed to make room for buildings. Indeed, whole avenues were burned down by the priests on the approach of the English. The palm-gardens are sold annually at auction, for, I think, ten thousand rupees.

Each tree yields about one hundred and fifty fruits, used mostly for sweetmeats ; but I have made tarts or pies of the pulpy part, quite as good as pumpkin pies. The leaf, of course, is highly valued for writing, especially the corypha ; and scrips of palm leaf, with Government orders, are common still among the native officers.

Modern Tounghoo is mostly built without the walls, extending some three miles along the river.

The residences of the officers are a kind of Anglo-alhambras, magically fascinating, as everybody says who comes to Tounghoo. Then the gardens are perfectly charming ; the drives, too, are very pleasant, and the ladies of the cantonment daily enjoy them with their Shan ponies.

Tounghoo is a famous mart for ponies, which are brought down in great numbers from Monay, a large Shan city, a month's journey to the north. They vary in price from twenty to five hundred rupees. I have seen very good ones bought for thirty rupees, and a pair of splended iron-greys for five hundred.

The officers keep a pleasure boat, and a moon-light sail up the Sittang is one of the pleasantest pastimes for the English gentlemen and ladies. Game is abundant in the region east of Tounghoo, and the officers often go out shooting, while the ladies spread pic-nics for them among the caravanserais of the celebrated Seven Pagodas.

Tounghoo is well fortified, and the place is strongly garrisoned, chiefly by English soldiers, so that an enemy could scarcely take it, except by stratagem, cutting off the commissariat boats in the river, or by coming in stealthily in disguise from the north.

This city is about two hundred and forty miles north of Rangoon, two hundred miles south of Ava, one hundred west of Siam, and eighty east of Prome. Tounghoo is the capital of a province about eight thousand miles square. History says the ancient city was founded six hundred years ago by the Karens, and even now the province is pretty nearly divided between Karens and Burmans. The population is estimated at 50,000, including Burmese and Talaings, and thirty thousand Karens, but there are two hundred thousand Karens adjoining these in a state of independence.

The Karens once occupied the plains of Tounghoo, but the Burmese, they say, having a knowledge of books, drove them back and took their lands.

Mr. Mason thus describes the climate of Tounghoo :

" We have a delightful climate here on the mountains. It is March, and the thermometer was to-day, at sunrise, 58°, the hottest part of the day 84° ; and while I write, 10 o'clock P.M., it is 65°. It has not been higher than 87° since my arrival, and with one exception the mornings and evenings have never been hotter. Then we have a fine thermal spring at the foot

of the hill, particularly good for liver complaints, good
for consumptives, good for people who have coughs, and
good for people who have no coughs ; 'good for fevers,
nervousness, erysipelas, impurity of the blood, inflammation, melancholy, sick headache, pains in the chest,
side, back, and limbs ; bilious affections, and all other
diseases !' What more attractive place for an invalid ?
Then for those who are not invalids, there are the
steepest mountains to scale that can be found in this
empire.

"After leaving the alluvial plain, near the river,
not an acre of level grass is to be found anywhere.
The whole coast is a pile of mountains rising to steep
ridges, at an average angle of 45°, oftener more than
less.   Sick or well, then, happy or melancholy, send
your patients to Tounghoo—the sanitarium of Burmah!"

Teak, rice, and betel-nut are the principal articles of
export in Tounghoo.   Silk is cultivated in some parts
by a tribe of wild men called Baings, among whom it
might be very desirable to introduce Christianity.   The
Karens bring in sesamum seed, cardamom, turmeric,
tobacco, beeswax, honey, swine, oranges, mats, baskets, ratans, and bamboo ; but the most valuable pro-
duction brought by them is betel-nut, the best in all
Burmah.

We had been in Tounghoo a short time, when two
Sgau Karens came in from the western hills.   One of
them wished to learn to read, and stopped with us.   His
name was Sau Kamoo.

It was only a few mornings afterwards that he came

up in great agitation, crying out, "They'll kill me! They'll kill me!"

"Who'll kill you?"

"The Myuthugyee, or city magistrate."

"Do right, Sau Kamoo, then trust in God."

"Oh, mama don't know these Burmans."

At last I made out his story. He had been waylaid by a Burman head-man, who inquired what he was doing at the foreigners.

"Learning books," he answered.

"A Karen dog learn books!" exclaimed the Burman with profound scorn. "See here, wretch. If I catch you round in the city after to-morrow, you see this!" brandishing his sword over the trembling Sgau.

Servant announces,—

"A peon, ma'am."

"A peon!" I go myself to meet the officer.

"What is it, peon?"

"The Karen."

"Well, what of the Karen?"

"The magistrate calls."

"Show your paper."

"Not here, Th'kyen."

"Then begone. Tell your master to bring his authority; but when the Karen goes to court, the white lady will go too."

I send off to the Commissioner, and acquaint him with this persecution.

"Have no fears, Mrs. Mason," he replies, and sends me the following note :—

" MY DEAR MRS. MASON,—

" If you find any slaves in my province, tell them
they are free to go where they please, and to learn what
they please.—E. O. RILFY,

             " *Commissioner of Tounghoo.*"

I transmit a copy to the magistrate, and hear no more
from him ; but, of course, if we had been under Burmese
rule, there would have been a very different ending of
the matter.

It is the boast of Burman slavery that it is only
debtor slavery ; but the shrewd Burmans know ways
enough of increasing the debt to any extent and making
it utterly unredeemable. So fraudulent and violent were
they in their dealings with the Karens, that the English
Commissioner, soon after taking Tounghoo, issued a
proclamation forbidding any Burmans to enter the hill
settlements without the permission of the head men,
and then to leave whenever he chose.

The governor and recorder had fifty or sixty slaves,
most of whom were driven off to the north when the
English were approaching. Some of them had heard
that the foreigners liberated slaves, and refused to go ;
but they were caught, and barbarously tortured by
cramping the hands until the pain was unendurable, and
so they were forced to flee into perpetual servitude.

A case occurred near the city soon after we reached
Tounghoo. A poor fatherless boy was passing through
a garden, and, being hungry, plucked an ear of corn and
ate it. The owner saw him, and thinking he would
make a good field-hand, immediately had him caught,

and taken before the head man of the district, and having slipped a bribe into the hands of the man's wife, the case was decided according to his own pleasure. The boy was fined twenty rupees, and as they knew he could not raise it, he was sold to the chief's son for the amount. On hearing of this cruelty, we immediately sent a note, saying that if the boy was not released within two days, he would be cited before the Commissioner. He was soon sent home.

These were our first pupils ; but not one had yet appeared from the eastern hills, the real Karen land. Time was passing, and Mr. Mason began to feel greatly solicitous about it. Finally, I told my tutauman to go and stand in the main bazaar road and watch, for I knew the Karens must come to the bazaar or market some time for salt. He went and watched all day with no success. Went again the second day, none appeared. Again the third day :

" Well, Shapau, none to-day ? ' Three times and out,' as we used to say when school-children."

" But I'm not out. Here they are though dreadfully afraid."

He had stood till he saw, on the third day, a small number coming with their bamboo spears, fierce, wild, and savage-looking. They approached very timidly, going round half a mile out of their way to avoid any of the English or sepoys.

" How do you do, brothers ? A white teacher has come—a Karen teacher," Shapau said, grasping their hands.

They saw he was a Karen, but they could not make much of him, for he spoke a dialect different from any they had ever heard. They understood a little Burmese, and he made them comprehend that a foreign teacher had come from the west.

"We know," they answered. "Did he come in a big boat?"

"Yes, a long way. He wants to see you."

"See us! We know. He wants slaves to put in the flying ship. No, no, we don't go. He'll carry us off where the sun goes down."

"But there's a white lady come, the teacher's wife. She won't let anybody carry you off. Brothers, come and see!"

"Oh no, no. Where are the flying ships?"

"Why, the ships are gone home again."

"Aye, gone?"

"Yes, brothers, don't fear. Come and see. You'll love the teachers."

At last he succeeded in coaxing along three, and there they sat, canine style, before the gate. I went out, and offered them my hand, but they had no idea what for. Finally, they ventured into the house, and how their eyes did open, when they saw the slave child learning to read, and Karen books too! They seemed like beings wild with delight, yet their emotions were visible only by their eyes and rapid talking one with another. They gazed at me as if I had just dropped down from the moon, and when I made them up each a little roll of salt, they quite forgot the flying ship.

We asked after their home, and they pointed to the distant hills. We inquired how many days it took them to come, and they counted three fingers.

We asked how many houses there were in their village, and they held up one finger.

We asked how many in the house, and they spread out all their fingers and toes, then clapped their hands twice, then held up all their fingers again. "*Knaza,* fifty," I said, in Burmese, when they nodded, much pleased that I comprehended them.

Suddenly, as they were about leaving, I felt impelled to send out the little book which Mr. Mason had prepared in Karen many years before—the "Sayings of the Elders." I told Shwa Moung to write on the fly-leaf in Burmese: "Yuah's Words come back to the Karens," and bade one of the young men go over the mountains and show it to all his countrymen. Mr. Mason stood by, smiling approval, but neither of us had much idea then of the results; and yet I felt a hidden assurance that God would bless it.

Days passed, however, and I believe weeks, and no Karens came again. Once or twice Mr. Mason rallied me about my "Faith book," but finally it was quite forgotten amid the deeply interesting scenes with the Burmese, who filled our house daily to overflowing, and kept Mr. Mason preaching from morning till evening.

Every Burman officer, great and small, from all the region around, came to pay his respects—not, however, until they heard of the proclamation given regarding the Karens, when they concluded that I was "the

Queen's sister!" (their expression for a favourite with the Government). This perhaps led the nobility to come; but the poor also flocked in, and we had reason to believe they came from a true desire to hear of the new religion. Some of my interviews with the women were thrilling, and excited me so that I could scarcely sleep or eat. One day I was talking to a house full of women, through my interpreter, for I could not speak Burmese, when a tall handsome man rose up from the door, where he had been sitting unnoticed in the crowd.

"Lady, lady, let me tell that," he exclaimed, and he began and narrated a history of the creation and fall, as perfectly as any Christian could.

Mr. Mason was deeply interested in this man. He stated that he was an officer in the last war with the English and Burmese; that his son was killed by a shell on the taking of Shwadagon. He was seeking for his dead boy on the battle-field, when he saw a white book on the ground. He clapped it into his bag, and after interring the remains of his son, he started back in his boat for Tounghoo. There, lonely and sad, the white book recurred to him. He took it out. It was the first paper book he had ever seen, and he was led to notice it on account of its whiteness, and its being there so like a spirit, he thought, beside his boy.

"Wonder if Moung can read this?" he said to himself. He throws aside the oar, flings his mat down on the bottom of the boat, and there, drifting on the river alone with his God, he read that Christian tract. It was "The Balance," by Dr. Judson. He reached home. His wife and daughter came, eagerly inquiring for the son.

"Gone—gone with the dead. The god let him die. Why should we worship?" and then he took out the book, and read to them. It comforted them too, and so whenever they felt distressed about their dear boy, they would take out the white book, which seemed almost to take his place in their affections.

To our great surprise and joy, this man's wife and a beautiful daughter, I should think of sixteen, came forward, and corroborated all the officer had stated; and he immediately said, like the Ethiopian officer,—"See, here is water : what doth hinder me to be baptized?" I have ever since wished that they had been received, but it was so sudden, and as Mr. Mason was just leaving, he counselled them to study the Scriptures, and defer the ordinance until he should return. The wife and daughter, too, came forward before our houseful of Burmese, and applied for baptism. The daughter had learned to read on purpose to read the white book herself, and I have no doubt is now a hidden Bible-reader in the interior of that dark empire.

On our return we found the family had gone,—had been driven away, without doubt, on account of their new faith ; for the magistrates well remembered the man, and spoke of him as that Yazu Kreik man.

We heard of him in Baumo trading, but he still had the tract, and went everywhere reading to the people, so that he was known as the "White Book Man."

I think it was some three weeks after I sent out the little Karen book, that we were assembled for prayer with the Burmese, when a company of Karens appeared. They came up at once to the verandah as if sent for, and seeing us at prayer, they bowed down with the rest. At the close, the leader, a white-haired, majestic chieftain, came forward very respectfully and laid before me a roll of plaintain leaves. Then, after gazing into my face very intently, he began slowly to unroll. Fold after fold was laid aside, and last he came to a dry leaf, out of which he took the identical little book that I had sent out !

" Will the lady explain ?" he asks, reaching forward,

" A real little dove !" Mr. Mason said, after his quiet, intense manner, his eyes brimming with emotion, while my own ran down with tears of joy and thankfulness. Mr. Mason immediately brought out the Karen Bible, and read to the chief the first chapter of Genesis ; and though it was a dialect somewhat different from his own, he understood that it was in Karen, and told their own traditions. He clasped the book to his heart, and bowed down before it three times, exclaiming,—

" It has a spirit ! It talks Karen ! It talks Karen !"

He then brought out a little roll of beeswax as an offering to the spirit of the book ; beeswax, or candles, being a most sacred offering to the gods.

This chief was an old Nat worshipper, and had been a kidnapper, but he returned to his village a preacher of righteousness. His people never again made offerings to the Nats, and the first Christian church organized in

Tounghoo was, I believe, in his village, where, and in the adjacent villages, there are now a thousand redeemed heathen sending up their anthems to Jehovah.

Of course, the tiny book had very little to do with the matter. It was an olive leaf, as Mr. Mason said, and no more; but God uses such a small thing, just as He did the clay and the spittle, to show forth more mightily His own power and Godhead.

" The Morning Star of Tounghoo!" Mr. Mason said with his quiet thoughtfulness again, as the chief departed.

We had gone up amidst great unbelief on the part of our friends, but still hearing the voice: " Go up. Ye shall not fear them, for the Lord your God He shall fight for you." And now, in this visit of the highlander, we recognised the bow and beheld the ANGEL OF THE COVENANT.

CHAPTER VI.

THE MINSTREL AND HIS BATTLE SONG.

THERE came in one day a tall, light-brown chieftain, with large melancholy eyes, and an uncommonly pleasing countenance, habited in a striped cotton tunic, girded around him like a Highland kilt. His costume and bearing were not very unlike that of a Highlander I once met on Loch Lomond. His long, black, shaggy hair was half confined by a narrow red turban, and a curious shaped basket was hung over his back. He carried a long bamboo spear, which served both for a weapon and a staff. Eight or ten swarthy six-foot mountaineers, attired like himself, accompanied him. These men had none of the ingeniousness visible in the leader; but their eyes were ever restless, as if on the alert for a foe.

"Has God's Son come down from heaven, lady? A man told us so on the mountains, and we've come to see him."

"Yes, brother, but—"

"Where is He?" interrupting with eager eyes. "Is He here? In Rangoon? In Bengala? Tell us quick, lady, for we've come to see Him!"

" He has come—sit down, brother—He has come, but He's not here. He's gone back to heaven, but—"

Instantly the tall chieftain turned and strode away with all his followers.

" Stop! stop, brother! He has left a letter for you," I called after him.

No answer—on he goes, and disappears. In about a week he returns.

" Lady! good lady!" he calls, putting his head in at the open door. This time he accepts a seat, and throwing off all reserve, tells me his country's history. There is something peculiarly striking and original in his words and manner. He is all soul and fire, mingled with the most persuasive grace and a handsome figure, with a very high brow.

As I sit listening to his painful romance, the palm shadows fall in colonnades around me, and the sky and earth meet and mingle in one deep golden glow. All is still, save the low, murmuring voice of the Highlander, and fancy throws together his romantic tales, uttered now in prose, and now in hurried rhymes in his own tongue.

SONG OF THE MOUNTAIN MINSTREL.

This Minstrel Chief had often known
The pain that waken'd sorrow's tone,
The pang that wrung the bitter groan,
The suffering deep, borne all alone,
   Yet borne it patiently.

" I've seen," he said, " my clansmen part
Driven in chains to the debtor's mart,
Beneath the lash to toil and smart,

Or droop and die of a broken heart,
　Yet strange, *I* did not die.

"One had a wife—a dark-eyed bride—
How did his heart beat by her side—
Or when she near would softly glide,
Spreading repast at eventide
　In her sweet, winning way !

"He saw her look, as she fondly smiled,
Suddenly changed to terrors wild ;
He saw her limbs with fetters piled—
Her arms outstretch'd for her infant child,
　Then snatch'd away.

"He saw it all—O God ! what pain
Upheaved, and burn'd his madden'd brain
Convulsive, fierce, he grasped her chain—
Vaunting, they flung him back again—
　He senseless lay.

" Deep sunk that wrong as a burning dart,
He could not from her image part ;
At midnight still he 'll often start,
And think to clasp her to his heart,
　But clasp the air.

" He 'll watch each form with features fair,
Each beauteous head of raven hair,
Then round on all will wildly stare,
Or his own dark locks with anguish tear,
　To find her never there.

" He 's sought her far, he 's sought her near,
Where tigers prowl he has has no fear—
Will stand for hours and list to hear
Aught that recals that voice so dear,
　Then sink in dumb despair.

"Time now has lull'd this cankering pain,
And reason calm'd his throbbing brain ;
But still hot tears will pour again,
Which a heart like his can ne'er restrain,
   Over his lonely prayer."

Again the Minstrel glanced his eye,
To mark if any Burman high
Should be behind, or drawing nigh,
To hear the tone, or note the sigh
   Of wrong and misery.

And finding none but friends around,
With an alter'd look and an alter'd sound,
   That spoke the Highland fire,
Boldly he pitch'd his voice again—
Boldly he sung of Shembuyen,
   Striking the martial lyre.

Kyouk Long!—dreaded name—how the echoes groan !
While the monk counts his beads in an under tone,
And if one ever dares the fiend's story to tell,
The abbess hides quick in her cloister cell.

They say—I don't know—'tis a horrible story,
That puts to the blush all our legends hoary,
How he called a fair maid from the fairest Shan daughters
To join him on Ava's soft, murmuring waters.

"Do you love me ?" he cried in a ruffian tone,
As she crouch'd at his feet there all alone ;
"Do you love me, maid ? speak quick and be free ;
For *I* am no lover of courtesy."

"Yes, my lord," she breath'd with a stifled sigh,
Though tears almost blinded her beautiful eye :

              H 2

"I will serve my lord if he bid till I die,"
She murmur'd so low and falteringly.

"Then up," quoth the Chief, "and come to my side,
I'll make thee my bride—my headsman bride—
We'll brim the red beaker, we'll brim it long,
And the Nats shall join in our nuptial song!"

Then opening a case in his low, thatch'd room,
There clanking with armour, and frowning with gloom,
He drew forth the bridals—strange suit for a maid—
Red turban, and jacket, and glittering blade!

"Don this, my maid; this never can hide
The lip of my bride—my warrior bride—"
Then his baldrick he snatch'd from the beam above,
Buckling it to her with, "Love, maid, love!"

His swarthy arm around her was thrown,
Her tresses fell back, and were loosely blown;
"Oh, Heaven!" she cried, as backward she shrunk,
And low at his feet in agony sunk.

"What? ho, slave, up! No tears with me,
We two are for foray and revelry;
Look to your weapon, nor heed ye a groan:
If ye blench at blood, it shall drink your own!"

*   *   *   *   *   *   *   *

Now hark! a moan, a moan!
Again, a stifled groan!
Five noble heads are on the ground,
Hot orphan-tears are bubbling round—
To Moung Kyouk Long a welcome sound:
The headsman bride is standing by,
Quivers on her lip the pleading sigh,
She dare not pray, she dare not cry,
Nor seek a pitying eye.

'Twas thus that pass'd this Ava chief,
Scathing the land past all belief,
Shooting, spearing, branding, flaying,
Every day some Burman slaying ;
And this poor girl, the headsman bride,
  Coop'd in his tiger den,
Was forced to travel by his side,
To sing, and dance, and wander wide,
  And slay her threescore men.

Moung Kyouk Long was the Commander-in-Chief
of the Burman forces on the Sittang river, east of the
Irrawaddy, during the last war between the English and
the Burmese. He was the Queen's brother, a most cruel
tyrant ; and the story related above is true. He did compel a Shan girl to follow him as executioner for noble-
men, so as to inflict upon them the shame of dying by
the hand of a woman. In Shwagyn the tyrant drove
many Burmans to despair, by taking from them their
young brides. One swore revenge, and attempted to
escape to Ava to report him to government. He was
brought back and flayed alive, and his body impaled by
the river, where the English found it on entering the
city. The wretch was subsequently thrown into prison
 at Ava, and, I believe, left to starve. The poor girl
was at last set free, but she was almost a maniac, she
had suffered so terribly.

THE FUTURE OF TOUNGHOO.

Now away, ye Natsoes!* ye wild Elfin stories,
Ye Poongyees and Zaidees, and all idol glories,
Meukaule is conquer'd, his banner is furl'd,
And God re-appearing, encircles the world!

The Christian has triumph'd, our nation is free!
Oh, hail it, ye brothers! hail, hail liberty!
Yes, liberty! liberty! sound it along!
Unfurl the new banner with trumpet and song!

No more shall we groan with our bondage and woe,
Or writhe in the grasp of our merciless foe;
No more shall the slave-fetter tarnish our name,
Or the "One God" prophet be branded with shame.

No, come now ye Wise Men and sing of salvation,
Redemption! redemption to every nation!
"The Book" is come back to us! clasp it for ever,
And bear it triumphant o'er jungle and river!

And I see—oh, I see, to this glorious fountain,
They run from the valley, they leap from the mountain!
They come—for a Saviour for sinners is bleeding!
They come—for a Saviour in mercy is pleading!

Light! light down the future is rapidly streaming!
The East and the West with its glory are beaming;
All nations are looking—all nations are bending,
And praise to Jehovah from all is ascending!

The Karens were enslaved by the Burmese, and t.
has been during all the Burman rule a perpetual struggle

* Natsoes—Demons. Poongyees and Zaidees—Priests and pagodas.
Meukaule—The Karen for Satan.

between them, the Burmese seeking, by every power, by craft, and by their superior knowledge of books, to bind them in servitude; the Karens, on the other hand, fighting for freedom, and struggling to maintain their own rights and lands, or fleeing from them to inaccessible glens and fastnesses in the mountains. There was no hope left for them, and nothing to excite them to rise, for as soon as one obtained any property, their sharp-eyed officials were down upon them, and nothing but ruinous bribes could secure to them a single comfort. They have ever had seers and wise men among them instructing them in their biblical traditions, and because of these traditions and these priests, they have often been made to suffer by their idolatrous rulers.

"The Book" of the Karens, the only one they seem to have any remembrance of, contained the words of Jehovah. Their wise men say there were seven brothers, and they, the younger, had God's word on skins. They were careless, laid it at the foot of a plaintain-tree, and the White Brother carried it off, and by it became the favourite son of God. This looks much like the story of Jacob and Esau. They fully believe the White Brother is to bring it back to them from north-western lands.

Of course, the minstrel did not utter all this exactly as it is here written. He told it to me mostly in prose, and through an interpreter, but with such poetic fire and inspiration, it moved me to pencil it down that very night, almost word for word, as I here give it.

This chieftain was son-in-law to the high chief of the

Mopaga tribe. He came to see me, I think, every week after this interview, and listened with intense interest to the Scriptures. He was soon afterwards baptized, and has since been one of the warmest advocates for female education. In 1859 he was made captain of one of the Karen companies in the Toughoo Military.

*CHAPTER VII.

FIRST CHRISTIAN SCHOOL IN TOUNGHOO.

" KARENS have books !" say the minstrel and his warriors. They hear the children reading. Wonderful! wonderful!

" Lady, lady, hear! We like this. It hits our hearts. Give us rice ; just one meal. We will keep your Holy Day and worship. We wish to hear, but we are poor men. Lady, hear ! Yonder on those mountains are our wives, our little ones. Lady, we cannot buy. If we buy and stay here idle, our wives and our little ones will die. Pity us, good lady. We have only mats, baskets, and seeds. Lady, hear ! Give us to eat just once, only once. We will fast the rest."

This pleading came from the lips of half a dozen tall, armed chieftains from the hills of Tounghoo. We had been telling them they should keep the Sabbath-day holy, and not return on that day.

What could I do? "May I give them rice ?" I questioned eagerly of my husband.

" You cannot. There is not a rupee in the treasury for any such purpose."

" Husband, God will send it.   Only say I may try,"
I plead again.

" It is certainly rash ; but if you must go to work on
faith, then go to work."

Oh, how my heart bounded !   How happy I was I
shall not try to tell you, reader ; but immediately I
bought a basket, five feet square, filled it with rice, and
bought also two dozen rice chatties or cooking pots.
Then I stood beside it, and saw it measured out, so
that each man had enough for one meal, with a little
fish and salt.   Each group of ten were provided with
cooking vessels.   Of course, they cooked for themselves,
and this first day cost me about ten dollars, or twenty-
one rupees.

So it continued for four weeks.   But, then, what was
gained ?   Just this.   Crowds of heathen men, some
heads of families and of villages, have listened four
Sabbath-days and nights to the Scriptures—listened,
too, as few heathens ever do listen, quietly and solemnly.

At night they strewed the floor all over every room
but our own bed-room, so that I was obliged to tell
them to pull up their heels to make a path for me to go
through, for they put heads together and heels together
as close as they could stow themselves.   The interest
manifested was intense—burning, past all description.
Our six native preachers were planted over the whole
area, one in each corner, their own arrangement, and
there they would lie and question, the assistants
answering, till it seemed as if they must be utterly
worn out.

" You say this wonderful man is God's Son. How do you know ? Did you ever see Him ? Did He come down in your country—in the Anglaik land, in Rangoon, or Bengal ? Did you ever see anybody that did see Him ? How do you know your book is true ? You tell us God's Spirit is like the wind, but which wind ? We have north wind, south wind, cold wind, hot wind— is God changing like the wind ?" All these, and a thousand other questions just as strange, were asked in rapid succession ; so that the last thing when I lay down at an hour past midnight, and the first when I awoke at five o'clock, would be these same wild but close questionings, showing that the Holy Spirit was doing His work on the earth.

Four Sundays have gone by—the most interesting, thrillingly interesting Sundays I ever knew, but my bill for rice has run up to many dollars. I cannot go on, small as the gift is ; so on Monday morning I begin speaking to every company that comes in, asking if they cannot help me to fill up the basket.

" It is so little," I say, " that I have supplied, I am ashamed to mention it ; but I have no more money."

What is it that has so touched those savage hearts ? Why do tears start under those sun-crisped locks ? Oh ! sympathy, that blessed angel, has descended, and now the image of God comes out. If there is anything left in the likeness of Christ upon earth, it is sympathy.

" I have no money," says one, " but would a mat do ?" he asked very timidly.

" Oh yes, give a mat ; anything will do."

" I can give a basket. Will the white lady accept a basket ?"

" Yes, brother, bring your basket."

" Brother, bring mama that honey," says a chief, pointing to a bamboo joint he had set up against the house.

" Here is a bit of beeswax," says a fourth, fumbling in his wallet.

So the flame catches, spreads, and soon the report flies over the hills : " Mama has got an eating-basket, and anybody can put in whatever he likes."

This showed just what the Karens wanted in Toung-ghoo—a head—a responsible leader to inspire them ; plan for them at first, and step by step raise them upwards.

It was not a very pleasant thing, indeed, to have our house full of such filthy, vermin-covered figures as the Karens of Tounghoo then presented. I recollect a lady in the States could not allow a trunk in her house that had come from Burmah, lest it should bring roaches into her rooms ; and it was hard at first for me to accustom myself to all the unpleasant sights and smells in our own house, and over our own *well*. But what are such little self-denials by the side of the Brook Kedron ?

Our four slave children were hard at their studies, attracting the gaze of every strange mountaineer that ventured to put his head in at the doorway.

Next comes the earnest entreaty :

" Mama, teach my son."

" And mine. Please pity us."

Again comes the trial of faith. "May I, dear husband, take a few ?"

" How can you ? There are no funds."

" It shall not cost the mission a cent,—a single cent, —only say yes."

" Well, yes. Try, if you will, what you can do."

" What is it, lady ?"

" You must promise to bring down the very best young men that you have, and let them become teachers."

Whispering—stammering—" Can't do that, good lady. Can't give my son for a Sahib."

" Nor I," joins another, and another.

I suggest to them to go and think till morning, for I can take them in no other way.

At early dawn half a dozen heads peer through the lattice.

" Lady, white lady, very good—very good."

Giving them a piece of chalk, I request them to mark out their country on the floor. They do so, amid much merriment, of course. Then, dividing it into twelve parts, I tell them they may bring twelve young men, one from each district, that is all I can take, and if they should bring slow learners, they won't do at all.

A few days pass, and the young mountain chivalry stalk up to the verandah with their short tunics, their long streaming hair, and their baskets strapped upon their foreheads. I have to put them immediately into quarantine, until they have taken one thorough lesson at the bath.

Taking up the soap, one of the party, a wild Bghai, bites it, then flings it spitefully into the hedge. Finally, Shapau succeeds, by setting the example himself, in persuading them to try the soap, which, in the end, perfectly delights the whole party.

The young men are hard at work, but how? I have to speak to them in Pwo. My interpreter tells them in Burmese, which is all Latin to them : then they learn the Sgau Bible, while they themselves are Pakus, Mopagas, and Bghais. But strange truth, and as encouraging as strange, in two months these young men can all read quite correctly, and with a good degree of understanding.

The whole cost of the twelve young men, and of the four Sunday feedings, I have assumed entirely myself, and without knowing the least where I shall find a penny. I ask for it, though, every day of One who I know has it in His treasury, and never for a moment doubt but it will come. "If ye abide in me, and my words abide in you, ye shall ask what ye will, and it shall be done unto you." This is my bank book.

A fortnight goes by. A Colonel calls with his Lieutenant. The younger officer hands me ten rupees, which calls forth this little answer :

" Lieut. J. P. Maud :

" My dear Sir,—Somebody says, ' Running streams are always clear.'

" I can readily see why you feel an interest in the

salvation of the heathen ; you have kept the sympathies of the heart clear by outgoing, and I am sure the hundred-fold reward will be yours, for nobody ever yet lost by investing in God's mission-bank.

"My husband has translated the Bible for the Karens, but it remains a sealed Word to them until they are taught to read it, and not one can yet read in all this Tounghoo province. I can but recognise in your thoughtful and kind donation the hand of an over-ruling Providence."

I then alluded to an incident in the life of one of the principal civilians then in Burmah, who took an orphan child, an East Indian, left to grow up in heathen ignorance, educated her, and thereby saved her from temporal and eternal ruin.

I believed it was one secret of that officer's success in life, which had been very remarkable.

What was my surprise to receive the following :—

"My dear Mrs. Mason,—Now that I know your work, I shall use every effort in my power to assist you myself, and get others to do the same. It is a sin to see a theatre springing up in Tounghoo, where no Christian temple has yet been raised to the God of our salvation. Many subscribe liberally to theatres and races from mere thoughtlessness, and need but a word to stimulate them to higher purposes. As I have a dear sister, perhaps you will kindly name the little slave girl after her, and I will send you every month ten rupees for her and the boys.—Believe me, dear Mrs. Mason, very sincerely yours, J. P. MAUD, 5th M.N.I."

Nor is it a sudden or idle start with this young officer. He sets to work, goes himself from kyoung to kyoung, for the officers then in Tounghoo all lived in kyoungs, raised a subscription, and relieved me of my pecuniary embarrassment. Thanks to God, and thanks to his kind heart! I have never seen him since we left Tounghoo, a month or two after, but I cannot think of his brave, unselfish spirit without remembering that to him belongs the honour, under God, of establishing the first Christian school in Tounghoo.

Mr. Mason was much struck with the reply of one of the young men in this school. The question arose as to where each should go to commence his teaching, when one, laying his hand firmly upon the Bible, said,—

" I know where I shall go. *I go where the Holy Book goes."* We had but one copy of the whole Karen Bible in Tounghoo. This man was a Bghai Karen, the first Bghai that had ever learned to read, and he did as he said, followed the Bible, and sat down beside it until he was baptized and sent to a foreign tribe ; and you will hear from him again by and by.

Until Mr. Mason went up to Tounghoo, only two clans of Karens were known. Red Karens had been heard of, but travellers thought them Shans. Kah Kyens had been heard of, but they too are still thought to be Shans. Books had been introduced among the only two clans known, Sgau and Pwo.

The Karen nation is broken into three great classes, each class comprising many clans and sub-clans. Two classes are called the Pwo, or " Mother Branch," and the other the Sgau or "Father Branch." The Pwo Class has more or less of the nasal sound in its language, while the Sgau Class has none. The Pwo Class embraces Pwos, Mopagas, Sanches, Hershoos, Gaykos, and all the mother Pwos above Tounghoo. The Sgau Class embraces Sgaus, Pakus, Mauniepagas, and Wewaus. The third, and largest class yet known, is the Bghai, embracing Tunic Bghais, Pant Bghais, and Red Karens, but it is probable that many more will yet appear as the country opens. The Kah Kyens are undoubtedly the chief Karens, as the name implies. The Kyens will, perhaps, be found to be an offshoot from this nation, and the Kemmes of Arracan another branch. These classes differ a good deal in their habits of life ; the Pwos claim to be the princes. They seek the plains and surrounding mountains, and are great hunters. They build mostly in separate houses, but in the Tenasserim mountains I found their houses built long enough for three families, divided into compartments, each division in tent-shape. This may have arisen from their old Syrian custom of demanding the services of the son-in-law three years for his wife.

The Pwos generally are better livers than the Sgaus, and bear in their figure, manner, physiognomy, and all about them the air of princes.

The Mopagas come next on the north in this class. They are a small clan, or part of a clan, so far as yet known, and they very closely resemble the Pwos in physiognomy and independent manners. They are not herdsmen, but a race of hunters, especially bee-hunters.

I

The other tribes of the Pwo class are as yet but little known. The Sgaus in their songs boast that

" As Sgaus have the words of Jehovah,
    Sgaus will pay no fine for killing a Pwo."

The Sgau-speaking class is docile, peaceable, and much given to husbandry. Karens of this class live in separate houses, with gardens attached. They cultivate oranges and betel-nuts in abundance, with yams, beans, and cotton. With a little encouragement and patience they would supply all Old and New England with cotton.

The Bghais are the most wild and singular of these clans. No stranger is admitted into their villages without a guide, and even then he has his quarters assigned him, and must remain there and eat of every dish set before him. It is the duty of every family in the village to carry him something as a mark of hospitality; to refuse it would be to declare war at once. Sick or well, hungry or satiated, it matters not, eat he must of every dish—dog-curries and all. If he refuses a single one, it is a slight to their hospitality, and he is a spy in the camp; but if he submits with grace to these feudal customs, he becomes their friend, and the honour of the whole village is concerned in his protection; a custom common, I believe, among the North American Indians. They had a place on the mountains where they brought blankets, betel-bags, mats, baskets, &c., to barter for handkerchiefs, turbans, coin, knives, sugar, and salt. The Burmans are particularly fond of using false weights and measures, but they never dared attempt it at this mountain bazaar. If they did, *death was the penalty without judge or jury.*

At this place the Bghais used to settle all disputes, and compel the Burmese to do them justice, like Rob Roy and the Lowlanders. I was reminded of the simi-larity of this custom to those of the ancient Scots. Once, on Loch Lomond, a Highlander pointed out to me Rob Roy's rock. "Here," said he, "Rob would take the Lowlanders, and say, 'An is it that ye'll gie me twenty black coos? An is it no that ye say? Then say y'r prayers quick, and be aff,' and over they went," said my informant—himself a Macgregor, in kilt and plaid and long stockings,—"over they went into the deep, black hole that ye see yonder." Many are the stories that the Burmans tell of the Rob Roy khans of their mountains, and there is certainly much in their bearing and feeling that reminds one of the old Scottish clans.

CHAPTER VIII.

THE Bghai Karens have some peculiarities of dress
not observed in the costume of the other clans. For a
head-ornament they wear a huge boar-tusk set in copper,
with bells of the same metal attached. This is secured
to a knot of hair, and worn on the crown of the head,
the horn upwards. It is worn only by men, and just as
white men adorn themselves with stars and ribbons to
show the world their bravery. They also wear little
bells attached to their pantaloons.

Bracelets and bangles are worn both by men and
women. These are usually manufactured of copper and
zinc, and one individual will sometimes wear several
pounds weight besides eight or ten chains of beads, and
forty or fifty rings of horse hair on the wrists and just
below the knee, like the old Welsh knee-bands. I have
seen Karen women with ear-knobs of ebony as large as a
silver dollar, so bright as to be used for mirrors; and I
saw a Siam Karen chief, in the mountains near Siam,
with cylinders in his ears as much as two inches long,
and I think an inch and a half in diameter.

The native Karen dress will, in a few years, become

almost extinct, like that of Scotland, for, like ourselves, they have a great love for foreign manufactures. With the Pwos it has been already superseded by the Burmese, but the tribes of Tounghoo are rapidly adopting a sort of Anglo-Shan costume, very comfortable and dignified.

As the Scottish chiefs had distinguishing plaids to mark their clans, so the Karens have clan emblems on their dress. The general costume of both the Pwos and the Sgaus is merely a loose tunic, reaching just below the knee, but often for chiefs made down to the ancles. These tunics are simply two breadths of cloth sewed together so as to leave holes for the head and arms, and are worn sometimes falling off one arm. They are, as nearly as possible, like the tunics figured on the bas-reliefs from Nineveh that I saw in the British Museum. The betel-box and purse are carried in a handsome wrought bag.

I am told that the Cosyahs of Upper India also wear the same style of dress; and Major Biddulf, of India, who had travelled among them, told me they were striped with red, blue, and white, and sometimes with red and blue, with fringes and tassels, like the Karens. I have wondered if the patterns on Karen dress were not hieroglyphical, a branch of the picture-writing of Egypt and Mexico.

The Mopaga tunic has very narrow perpendicular stripes of a brilliant red. The Bghai has a wider stripe of a duller red. The Sgaus and Pakus are plain, but the borders of each are their chief feature. The Mopaga

border is from two to four inches in depth, closely
wrought with silk in beautiful vines and characters.
The Mauniepagas weave theirs in narrow stripes, in a
great variety of patterns. The Sgaus sometimes weave
a border twelve or fifteen inches deep, of circular stripes
and laboured patterns, and again, others a foot and a
half deep, of entire scarlet silk floss. These are common
on the western hills of Tounghoo. The most delicate
little vine-patterns creep round the neck and arm-holes.

The Karen woman's dress consists of two garments, a
robe and jacket ; the Pwo robe is striped circularly, the
Mopaga perpendicularly. Their border is often of work
that would vie with almost anything in the looms of the
West. The Karen robe is whole, girt straight around
the waist, and tucked into one large fold. The jacket
is very pretty. The Pwos and Sgaus embroider over a
ground of blue, the Bghais over white. The Pwo jacket
is always wrought with brilliant silk floss, and a girl
will be a year in embroidering one. The work seems to
represent a sunrise, and the shading and blending are
most beautiful. Its usual price in Dong Yahn is ten
rupees. The Sgau jacket, on the contrary, seems to
represent evening, with all the stars coming out on the
deep blue sky. These stars are made very perfectly of
long white seeds, like rays. The Bghai woman's jacket
is woven, not wrought, with a nap of scarlet floss up to
the armpits, then a crescent and seven rays over the
bosom and down the back.

The Pant-Bghai men wear loose white pantaloons only
eighteen inches long, wrought with rich silk borders.

They certainly excel in the arts of dyeing and weaving, and they understand perfectly the use of mordants, so that they can make as brilliant and durable a purple as Lydia, or any of the dames of Tyre.

These relics of a higher state of the arts point to the north-west, and seem to prove that the Karens were once in a higher position than at present. So their bamboo work seems to point to a higher knowledge of weaving and architecture. They weave in this a great many patterns.

I once met a Chief on the Tenasserim river in Tavoy Province, with a robe like the Hebrew High Priest, all tasseled. This man had three wives, all of whom refused utterly to go to the Christian worship till he gave them a sound beating. Then they went to chapel, and one was converted! This was the old Chief who became a Christian, and had to give up two of his wives. One, the oldest, was sickly, and the youngest very pretty. He referred it to the church to say which he should keep, and they decided that he had a right to retain the youngest, so he concluded to do so. Then his conscience troubled him, and he finally resolved that as somebody else might be willing to take the young, pretty wife, but nobody would pity the feeble, sick one, he ought to keep the old one; so he did, and put away the younger.

The Karens, like all demon worshippers, believe in witchcraft. There was a poor childless Karen in Tavoy, who retired with his wife to the forest, and cultivated a small patch of land there alone. After awhile a man died in the neighbourhood of congestion of the liver. Dark suspicions began to be whispered that the old man of the jungle knew more than he ought to know of the matter. Soon he was openly pronounced a wizard, and his precincts enchanted ground. After this, whenever any singular death occurred in the neighbourhood, it was laid at his door. Finally, a child died of an unaccountable disease, and, lo, when its body was burned, a portion of the kidneys was found unconsumed. This to a Karen is proof positive. The neighbours, therefore, went up from all parts to the magistrate, clamorous for the old man's death. They found out that the English law would give no help, so three stout young men, arming themselves with axes and knives, hastened to the old man's hut, and there in broad day they *hewed* the wretched man to pieces as they would a log. When arraigned for trial, they at once confessed, producing the unburned kidneys as proof that they had acted only as public benefactors.

The Karen wizard is called by the Pwos "*Longch-erthe*—the can-in winder." This dreadful being bewitches by introducing noxious substances into the body, as bits of glass, flesh, leather, water, &c., which things are charmed by him into demons.

A man died in Tavoy of dropsy. He was killed, they said, by witchcraft. The civil surgeon determined on a post-mortem examination. The friends were called in the hope of convincing them of their error.

"Ah," they said, on seeing the quantity of water; "there it is! there it is!"

" There what is ? " questioned the surgeon.

" Why, the water-demon which the wizard cast into him. We thought he was turning him into *drink.*"

One mode of bewitching is by producing dumbness; this is done by modelling an image of the person from the earth of his foot-prints, and sticking it with cotton seeds. Here is certainly a relationship to the old Saxon witch that troubled England a few years ago.

Another wizard produces insanity with a hair suspended in a whirlpool. Others use a human skull concealed in the forest, with daily offerings before it. The skull is often used also to drive away evil spirits, such as the cholera demon and the small-pox demon. They tell wonderful tales, one about a family being turned into toads.

Burman witches have power over the sea. A sailor, on coming home in Tavoy, accused his wife of having been the cause of all his trouble at sea, and gave her a severe beating.

The Karens have various modes of detecting witches, among which is the water ordeal. When detected and alive, the witch or wizard is shaved, and set over a stream. The Burmese laws decree that if the person rises, she is guilty; if she sinks, she is innocent !

In Nicobari, witches are tied to a tree, and left to starve; and when sentence is once pronounced, not even a daughter would dare carry food to her mother.

" Who is this YUAH you tell of ? " I inquired of the Karen minstrel, when he repeated a stanza of poetry, which embodied their old traditions, saying, Yuah made the heavens, the earth, the sun, the moon. Yuah made man, and all things, just as we have it in Genesis. Passing strange this, for the minstrel had never before seen a Christian teacher, or heard of Karen books ; yet he had the very same traditions that we had found in Tavoy and Maulmain, two and four hundred miles distant ; and yet his dialect was so different from the Karen dialects of those regions, that he could not understand five words.

" Where did you learn this ?" I inquired.

" Oh, far back, anciently."

" Who taught you these things ?"

" The Fathers. Old people."

" And who taught them ?"

" The Mau."

" Who were the Mau ?"

" Don't know. Prophets ; good men, inspired by Yuah."

This was just what the Pwo Karens had told us everywhere. When I first met Guapung, she told me the same story, and a Pwo chief down in the Mergui jungles also.

Turning to a Paku, I asked, " Have you these same stories ?"

" Yes."

" And where did you get them ?"

" *A-poo-a-pee*—grandfathers and grandmothers."

" Where did they learn them ?"

" The Wie taught them."

Who the "Wie" were, or where they were, he could tell no more than the minstrel could of the "Man," but this is what all the Sgaus say, dating back to a very ancient time—it was the "Wie" who instructed them.

The Biblical traditions of the Karens are singularly clear and pure. The story of the first man and woman, of the temptation, of God having dwelt with man, and of salvation by the One God, they have handed down, they say, from that ancient skin book.

Who these Karens are, to what people they are allied, and from whence they obtained their glimmerings of truth, are inquiries of the deepest interest, for this reason : God seems to have planted His footsteps through the nations just as He has laid the foundations of the earth in strata. If we strike upon a stratum of real precious ore, we follow it. It seems as if He would teach Christians to do this in teaching the world. If they hit upon a tribe ready for the Gospel, then it would seem wiser to follow that stratum or dip of the languages, for we are sure, it appears to me, to find the same, or a similar, disposition in all allied tribes, however separated by other nations.

These terms, "Man" and "Wie," ought to help us somewhat in tracing the Karens ; and before we have done, it may be that we shall find them nearer to us than we think.

Of all the Karens near Tounghoo, the Bghais are the most warlike, and it was a question of a good deal of anxiety as to who should venture among them as a teacher of Christianity. Finally, I asked my Tutauman who should go.

" Don't know," he replied, and sat for some minutes in deep thought; then, looking up very sadly and timidly, he said :—

" I wish I knew enough to go to the Bghais."

" Perhaps you do, or if not, God can make you know enough," Mr. Mason answered.

This man, Shapau, had lost his wife and all his children but one. He looked sorrow-stricken ; that was all that was remarkable about him. When alone upon the sea-shore with my sick husband, I had written a few Karen letters to the preachers' wives, which were published in the Karen " Star." One of these gave a brief sketch of the Madagascar mission, and another exhorted them to stir up their husbands, and set off to the Red Karens.

Shapau said he had read this letter, and he felt a strong desire to work among them. This was why he came and offered his services for this journey to Tounghoo.*

We became much attached to Shapau, because he was always trying to improve himself, as well as to do good to others, so, when he made that reply, I felt sure God was calling him, and, therefore, sat down at once and began to catechise him in the Scriptures. He had studied but little, but had been a pupil of the Rev. Mr.

* Several preachers, and some women, came over to Monmogon, to talk about the possibility of a Red Karen mission, and four of them did subsequently labour in Tounghoo and Shwagyu.

Vinton. I think we sat two hours, when he looked up delighted.

"Why, mama, I didn't think I knew half so much!" he said as innocently as a child. Finally, I told him he could teach the Bghais, but asked if he could be willing to give up his child and home, and go and live with such kidnappers, and dog-eaters too.

"Don't know," he answered. Then, besides, I had to tell him that he knew the teacher paid him as his boatman fifteen rupees per month, but if he went to the Bghais, he could give him only four rupees.

"Would you go for that?" I asked, after giving him a sketch of the old Gospel Rangers in Britain and America. Shapau took his Testament and went out. He was absent some time; but when he appeared again, his face shone with unearthly radiance, at least it struck me so as he came in.

"Well, Shapau," Mr. Mason asked, for he had heard our conversation, "what is the decision? Can you go to the Bghais for four rupees the month?"

"No, teacher," very solemnly, "I could not go for four rupees the month—*but I can do it for Christ!*"

And he went. There was deep meaning in that eye, and in that grasp of the hand, when he said,—

"*I can do it for Christ.*"

That man has since been ordained, has baptized nearly a thousand Bghais, has established some forty churches, and has since gone on another foreign mission to the Red Karens. "For I say unto you, That unto every one *which hath shall be given*," saith the Faithful Promiser.

It was one day when the chiefs were in with us that a
letter arrived from Tavoy. It had been sent by the
Christian converts of that province to Mr. Mason, entreating him to pity his children there, and not call
away their teacher, San Quala.

"Read it, Shapau," Mr. Mason said to my Tutauman.
He did so, standing up in the centre of the group like a
Saul, for he was almost a head and shoulders above them
all. The scene was intensely exciting. They had no
idea they had any brothers in the south, and now to
find that they were numerous, had become Christians,
and had really and truly written that letter themselves !
Then the question arose—Would they take care of the
great Karen teacher if his people did consent to let him
come up to them ?

"Take care? Er, er! We'll feed him, we'll clothe
him, we'll build him a house. Tell them let him come,"
they answered in chorus; and then a strife arose as to
who should have him first, but one chief, elbowing his
way along through the crowd to me, said, with a great
deal of quiet determination,—

"Teacheress, take my name."

Much amused, I told Shapau to write it down.

"And my wife's name," again very slow and with
great dignity. We took his wife's name.

"And my sons' names," so down went the sons'
names, when all seemed to think he had gained the
victory. I believe this was the same chief who brought
in the little book.

Quala came up, and Mr. Mason determined to make

over the mission to his care entirely, during his absence at home, and see what a native could do in carrying on a mission alone.

Soon after this I started, under the protection of an English convoy, to go down for our children in Maulmain, as Mr. Mason thought he must remain in Tounghoo a year there before leaving. On the second night, about midnight, I was awakened with a violent trembling, and with the impression that my husband was sick. Something said to me, " Go back ! go back, or you will never see him again !"

I sat in dismay, meditating upon this strange revelation, some twenty minutes, when I determined to obey. So, writing a hasty note to the Commanding Officer, I asked my boatman to turn back. It was midnight, and they were greatly afraid of falling into the hands of dacoits. I told them not to fear ; that I would place my chair on the little deck, and I was sure no robber would shoot a white woman.

" Hoga ! hoga !—yes," they exclaimed, and started off with alacrity. Sitting out so was not very pleasant, for my garments were drenched with the heavy dews long before morning ; and, moreover, though I had re-assured the boatmen, I could not help every moment listening for the balls of the robbers. As we approached Tounghoo, we heard of them skirmishing on all sides of us, and of one or two most daring robberies just upon the shore ; but after four such nights we reached the city again unmolested.

Singularly enough, when I reached our bungalow, I

found Mr. Mason had really had another attack of his complaint, and was on the point of starting himself for Maulmain, so that my return was very providential, as I could be with him on the way down.

Having arranged this matter, the school was made over to Pwapau, one of Mr. Mason's old pupils from Tavoy. A cocoanut grove was purchased, the Sacred Oracles deposited, and then, amidst prayer and singing, Quala and I went out with the school and planted a Christian banner in Tounghoo, with these words inscribed :

"The Holy Book. Read—Hear."

Then came the pressing of hands, and the tearful goodbyes, in which the poor Shans from Monay came up and joined.

When we passed down, the tidal wave in the Sittang river rose fearfully, and the waters rushed past our little boat as if they would instantly sweep every vestige of us away. It was impossible to advance. The darkness of night enfolded us, and we sat under our slender cover listening with no small degree of agitation to the rush of waters. Just then the boat was lifted suddenly up, and shot away with a velocity past all description. I screamed to the boatmen, who were already screaming to one another, and to the accompanying boats for help. Our anchor had given way, and had not the men put forth every nerve to secure her to a larger boat, we should have been lost. No sooner had they fastened the rope, than the winds began to rise. Louder and louder they roared, until they really bellowed along the waters, which lashed themselves, rolling, tumbling, and growling around our boats with the greatest fury; weltering under us as if they would instantly suck us into the seething brine. For an hour we remained thus, the billows every moment threatening to engulf us. That was an hour for thought —tossed in darkness amid the yawning waves and howling winds; to think that our anchor gave way just then, when the tide came—when it was most needed— awakened the most solemn reflections. In such a place, one can imagine a little what the feeling must be should *the anchor of hope* fail when meeting death's dark tide. With thousands it undoubtedly will fail, and leave them to perish. Oh! what an agonizing moment will it be to feel *that* anchor giving way, and the soul sinking into eternity!

After the strength of the tide had come in, the men considered it safest to cut loose, and run before the wind, which, coming from the east, blew us with great violence farther and farther out to sea. We were in company with three or four other boats; but they were much larger, carried more sail, and, consequently, soon left us far in the rear. According to Burmese custom, they now and then threw out signal lights from their boats, and with what anxiety did I strain my eyes for those receding beacons! Now, as our skiff rode up on a mountain wave, we could just discern them far away, trembling for a moment, then disappearing; now another light rises, faintly flickering, fainter, fainter, and again all is darkness. Hark! a grinding sound! a ploughing of the boat! and the men instantly leaped into the waters. But it was of no use; she had struck upon the sands in

K

the midst of the sea, some eight or ten miles from land,
as near as we could make out. The tide was fast falling,
and it was impossible to move her. It was three o'clock.
The men had been toiling for seventeen hours without
food, and seeing nothing of our provision-boat, they all
but one left us to go in search of help. The man who
remained, wearied out, lay down and slept; but sleep
was far enough from me, though chilled through with
anxiety and cold; for I had stood three hours in the
water, baling out, during the fury of the tide.

Never but once did I experience so trying a moment
as this. Mr. Mason was too sick to make any plan,
or think of any proposed. He could neither walk nor
sit up; and I knew the tide would be in soon after
sunrise, when we should either be swamped, or driven
out to sea without anchor, provisions, or boatmen. Not
a craft, not a soul, was to be seen or heard, in all the
surrounding distance. For a moment death seemed
inevitable, and had I been alone, I do not know but I
should have yielded to the overpowering sensation; but
my husband lay helpless before me; and I knew my
little ones, whom I had not seen for nearly four long
months, were anxiously watching for father and mother.
I stepped out upon the sand, and looked up to the Eye
that ever watches over land and sea. The sun began
to rise, and no one had returned. But just then I
descried something like the mast of a vessel far in
the distance, across the wide sandbanks. It was just
discernible, but I instantly resolved to reach it. So,
rolling up a small bundle, I placed it upon the head of

a little Karen girl with us, and then tried to help my
dear husband to rise. He made the effort, but was too
weak ; and with feelings indescribable, I was compelled
to leave him. With swift feet Mary and I made our
way over the sands and waters which were beginning to
come in. When about half way over, we met the boatmen returning :

"We are all lost, mama!" they exclaimed. But
without stopping, I charged them to run and bring the
teacher, and hastened on. They did so, and soon we
had the inconceivable happiness of seeing him lifted
into a larger vessel, the master of which, not for love,
but for *rupees*, would take us in. The men had barely
time to secure a few clothes, and a handful of tea and
biscuit, when the breakers came dashing over the sands.
At that moment we discerned two objects apparently on the
horizon, so far away that it was impossible to tell if they
were masts or human beings. At last my little girl cried :

"Colahthu! Colahthu!" and we discovered that it
was indeed the *colahthu*, or cook, with the Burman
preacher in search of us. In their anxiety to find us,
they did not seem to see that the waters were at their
heels, and it was not without a multitude of gesticula-
tions and exclamations, that they were made to comprehend their own danger, and flee to their boat. The
craft we now occupied was a crazy old thing, destitute
of every comfort. It had not even ballast, and rocked
about among the breakers, as if it would surely go to
pieces, but it was a paradise to the other, because it was
comparatively safe.

The remainder of the way, I made tea in a bowl, which was all the sustenance I could get for my husband except a little dry bread, and the poor boatmen had not so much as that. For two days and two nights, I believe, they never tasted food, except a few dry rusks which I succeeded in tossing to their boat. It was then that I knew *why* I had been turned back to my husband in so singular a manner, for had not some friend been with him, he would probably have died in the river. No one can imagine what I felt as we rocked about in that old boat, while these words of my childhood came back to me : " You must go to Burmah, and help Mr. Mason." Truly, stranger than fiction is the story of one's own life.

PART II.

CHAPTER I.

GOING TO INDIA—NOT OVERLAND.

LIGHTS AND SHADOWS OF THE SEA.

AWAY! away! on the rolling sea,
   When the blue waves bound and curl ;
Let the mariner's song pour loud and free,
   And the canvas wide unfurl.

Away! away! where the Nereids sing
   With Arion's harp of old ;
Now toss'd on the foam with the petrel's wing,
   Now rock'd on billowy gold.

Away! away! o'er the glistening brine,
   When the soft air breathes of love,
When mellow tints o'er the waters shine,
   Crayon'd by heaven above.

And lightly float on the moonlight sea
   As beneath a silver dome,
While the sails are falling gracefully,
   And the dreamer dreams of *home*.

But the sun-light down—the night gods frown !
   Growling, they're battering the stern ;
Then hurl at the clouds o'er the shivering shrouds,
   While billows in darkness burn.

Now the surges boom 'mid the thickening gloom,
  Making all the canvas rattle ;
But the bow drives low, and charges the foe,
  The ship and the storm doing battle !

Loud thunders roll, red lightnings fly,
  And earthquakes vault'in the waves,
While they heave up their mountains wild and high,
  And scoop out their whirlpool graves.

Staggers on the bark in the maddening gale,
  And the tall masts reel and tremble ;
While the hurricane winds give a boding wail,
  And the heart can no more dissemble.

" Now, hard up the helm !   Let her run 'fore the blast ! "
  Comes, as we shuddering wait—
Then the loud trumpet roar : " Cut away the mast ! "
  " We're lost ! " shriek captain and mate.

Lo ! yonder a Light ! a high beacon Light,
  Looms o'er the threatening doom—
'Tis the BETHLEHEM STAR ! and bright, ever bright,
  It guides from an ocean tomb !

We left Tounghoo in January, 1854, and reached England in May in the steamer *Indiana*, spending the summer
mostly in London, Mr. Mason being too ill to see friends.
August was passed in Berlin, with improved health,
studying in the University among Bible translations,
for which purpose we went over.   September we came
to Scotland in the steamer *Petrel*, and were almost
wrecked.   At last we reached Boston, in October, in the
Europa, and re-embarked for India in July, 1856,
arriving at Calcutta in November.   Mr. Mason reached

Tounghoo again in January, and I in April, 1857. This is the only time that my husband ever left India during his "thirty years' war" with heathen darkness.

Now imagine us in the *Jumna*, the graceful *Jumna*, that skims the billows like a light sea-gull, or a stormy petrel on the wing.

We were coming to the close of a stormy voyage. Of course, everybody has seen a hurricane, but a hurricane and a cyclone are just as different as a mountain and Mont Blanc. We were riding at anchor on the Sand Heads, passing congratulations on our arrival, when a pilot brig scudded alongside, trumpeting us off to sea again with all possible speed. Our master paced the deck, looking as if he could bite the wheel off; the first officer bellowed his orders, and Jack went to the anchor with head down as if going to be flogged. It was not very exhilarating to go waltzing back into the deep black waters, especially with the prospect before us of running our bow right into a Bengal hurricane. But off we went, like the poor Rajah who, pressed by land enemies, thrust his head into a rice pot, and rushed into the waters to hide himself.

By the time we were all under way, the winds were blowing very hard, and our vessel close upon a reef. I had heard so much of the dreaded circular hurricanes of the Bengal Bay, that I could think of nothing but fire, so terrifying at sea. I noticed that the lightnings, fierce, hurried, constant, and changing, without thunder, indicated a cyclone, as described by Piddington in his " Law of Storms." The answers of the man at the wheel also indicated a circular motion of the wind. I was, therefore, fearing the worst, when I heard the captain say to the mate in an under tone :—

" The vortex is ahead there."

" It acts like it," replies the officer.

" I know 'tis by the action of the sea."

" Can we do nothing ?"

" Impossible, but I hope she'll outride it ; she ought to ; she's a new, strong ship."

It was true, then, that we were in a cyclone, and rapidly approaching the vortex, the winds every moment increasing, and the barometer rapidly sinking. The sea was lashing itself into mountain waves, or sinking in deep, charcoal-looking gulphs, while its significant seething, gurgling sound was very terrible.

Nothing was heard amid the war of winds and waves but the shrill trumpet orders of the officers, and the sharp, quick, shouting answers of the men.

Suddenly there was a cry, " Ship on the weather-bow !" Up went our helm, out went the trumpets, the captain, officers, and crew, all roaring at the top of their voices. A French barque was staggering right down upon us, apparently in utter bewilderment. At last the intrepid mate posted himself right over the bow, and shook his fists so frightfully, the Frenchman caught a glimpse of them by the lightning, and put about just barely in time to clear us ! Had she struck us then upon our weather-board, probably not one had remained alive.

The hurricane had already raged its twelve hours—six

of them threatening every moment to swallow us—when the joyful announcement was heard that the barometer was at a stand. This was at half-past twelve at night. Fifteen minutes to one o'clock it had begun slightly to rise, and the axes were put by. Five had been prepared to cut away the masts, and orders given to be ready, and had the mercury fallen fifteen minutes longer, they must have gone, or we should have been engulphed. Suddenly again, there was a sort of dying pause in the winds, while the motion of the sea became more alarming, heaving mountains of water upon us, so as almost to capsize the vessel. The lightning chains, too, spanned the heavens in double links, advancing, receding, meeting, chasing. Then we knew we were in the vortex, but not in the centre, for if we had been there, the agitation of the sea had been still more terrific.

We were lying under "bare poles" from eleven o'clock P.M. to four o'clock A.M., waiting to see if the winds would rage again, or change about suddenly and drive us out of our peril. Through the great mercy of the Most High, in answer to prayer, this happened, and the winds came round to the westward. It was a solemn thing to hear the watches called off there in our midnight horrors to see who was alive, and who was gone. It was a solemn thing—the awful stillness of our ship during that fearful pause, when all who knew their danger must have been busy with their hearts and with their God.

140

CHAPTER II.

THE young men of the Tounghoo Karen tribes were now fairly sent out as educators of their own countrymen, and many heathen chiefs had become enlisted as supporters of the scheme, for they were to go wherever they should be called, and depend entirely on the people for support. This plan Mr. Mason had determined to carry out among the preachers also, and make Tounghoo an example to all the regions beyond, as a self-sustaining mission. His excellent helper San Quala favoured it.

"Tell the white brothers," he said to me as we sat two hours conversing about all the interests of the mission before we left, "tell them not to forsake the Karens just yet. We are like children beginning to walk. We toddle, we fall, but we're *trying*."

I had now a great desire to enlist the chiefs in a movement for the young women similar to that of the men, to raise up schoolmistresses who should form elementary classes all over the mountains as fast as little churches could be formed, and thus leave the young men free to go forth as pioneer preachers to the heathen.

Tounghoo was a great country of itself, isolated,

almost excluded from the unhappy influences of seaports.
We thought we might mould it as we would if we began
at once. To make special effort for the men and not the
same for the women, would be doing just what others
have so often done,—confirming the heathen in their prejudices that woman was only a slave to work and bear,
not to speak, or sit with her brothers. But make them
teachers side by side, make the education of young
women just as prominent as that of young men, train
the young mothers, and it would tell upon the race
through eternity. I knew that whatever type of civilization or Christianity was introduced into Tounghoo, it
would be carried up through all the mountains of
Burmah, and perhaps farther still, through Thibet and
Tartary.

While in America I could do very little for the
Tounghoo tribes. As a wife, duty called me first to my
sick husband, then as a mother and *step-mother too*, to
our children, to look after their education, to *try* and in-
cite them to high and holy consecration and activity; as
a daughter and sister, I had to comfort and cheer my
relatives; as a friend of the poor student and schoolmistress, to sympathize with many; and as a housekeeper
with small means and eight in family, to bake, sweep,
and attend to domestic duty. These were my duties
and labours while in the States, but those Tounghoo
women were ever on my heart. What could I do to
begin the work among them? I had no time or means
to go about to interest friends. Then again the public
feeling forbade it. It could make no distinction between

the schools which take in every child at foreign cost, and *aid-schools* which train teachers, and need only help enough to develope native strength. It would have required months to explain this matter, besides a kind, sympathizing helper. One such friend came forward, the Rev. Dr. Beadle, of Hartford, who, with his ladies, raised fifty dollars and a box of clothing and stationery worth fifty more, presented with *sympathy*—more precious still—from a stranger, too, whom I had never met but once! Noble, generous friend! May the Almighty send him sympathizing hearts and helping hands! Undoubtedly, others would have acted as nobly if the subject had been presented to them, but as it was, this, with five dollars from a lady through the Rev. Dr. Westcot, of New York, was all that I had to begin with.

Leaving Boston with so little help for the poor young schoolmasters I had taken up, and with scarcely a ray of encouragement for their sisters begging for instruction, I felt very dejected and desolate.

Many sorrows had encompassed us during our stay at home, deep, piercing, harrowing, but, I thank God, *subduing;* and now, floating once more upon the ocean, I could realize how entirely dependent those poor Tounghoo women were for help on the Arm above. To that Arm—to that Eye—I resolved to look, and to that source alone. Then stole out so soothingly those tender words : " Jesus wept."

Yes, Jesus! Precious Jesus! and it was with *woman* too, and there came another voice : " It is I, be not afraid." Then my soul grew strong again, and calm, and trustful.

It was very strange, but although Mr. Mason made every effort, no passage could be obtained for me and my little boys from Calcutta to Burmah. We even wrote to a chaplain whom we had known when in Burmah, entreating him to intercede for us, and he did, but the troops were being transported to Rangoon, and every steamer and sailing-vessel was full. Mr. Mason, even, was obliged to take a deck passage. Before he left, I obtained his consent to my giving up for a time my personal support from America, in order to make an experiment, and see if the native chiefs could be enlisted in managing and sustaining a girl's school themselves. I had no promises from any living being, for I had not spoken to anyone in India, and no one in America had promised the slightest aid, but I knew that to be successful the school must *belong to the people. I did not withdraw in the least from our mission*; I only proposed to find means where I could, and support myself while doing it, sending reports regularly to the Board, which has been done ever since. Having settled upon this, I wrote out a full account of the plan to the Secretary of the American Baptist Missionary Union, and then shut myself up with my two little boys in a small basement bedroom in Sudder Street.

My first determination was to write something while detained in Calcutta which should create an interest in the Karen people.

I said : " What shall I do, oh, my Saviour ?"

"Ask, ask—if ye ask anything in my name, it shall be done for you." From that day I asked morning, noon, and night, and every day my faith grew stronger.

It happened to be at this time that the great act legalizing the marriage of Hindu widows was brought about, which moved all Calcutta, and, indeed, all India. The papers were full of this wonderful movement, begun by native gentlemen themselves. Of course, I could not help feeling the most intense interest in such a grand reform act, that must usher in light and liberty to captive millions of heathen women, and I could write of nothing else.

Finally, one morning after prayer, something whispered : "Send up your manuscript to Lady Canning." There was no voice, but the thought came like a flash. No idea of addressing Lady Canning had ever entered my mind before. That same day I sent the following note :—

"To the Right Honourable Viscountess Canning,
                    "Government House, Calcutta.

"MADAM,—Feeling assured that every Christian must take a warm interest in the late great movement among the Brahmins in regard to Widow Marriage, I take the liberty, respectfully, to ask if I may be allowed to dedicate the accompanying MSS. to your ladyship ?

"I would also beg the indulgence of explaining why I desire it. My husband, the Rev. Dr. Mason, translator of the Karen Bible, three years ago founded a new mission in the old kingdom of Tounghoo, in Pegu, under the patronage of the American Baptist Foreign Missionary Union. On this undertaking God has been pleased to pour out His Spirit in a most wonderful manner, and the mission now numbers thousands of baptized believers. These converts have erected chapels at their own charges, established some fifty jungle-schools, and support their own teachers. The people are eager for instruction, so that one teacher has four districts in charge at once, spending a day with each in succession.

" Our schools have been greatly blessed of heaven, and during four years that I had the privilege of instructing one in Maulmain, thirty-eight of my pupils were baptized, and write me in their own expressive idiom : ' My heart hits the Lord Jesus Christ exceedingly.'

" For the women of Tounghoo nothing has yet been done, and I am very desirous of opening for them immediately, in Tounghoo city, a National Female Institute, for all the tribes, admitting only such as will devote themselves to the work of instruction. But on account of heavy financial pressure, our American Board is unable at present to aid this object. I have, therefore, resolved to do what I can myself towards making a beginning.

" Therefore, I have asked this favour of your ladyship.

" Hoping that my request may be kindly granted,

" I am, Madam, your humble servant,

" ELLEN H. B. MASON.

" 13, *Sudder Street, Feb. 6th*, 1857."

L

I sent it off, praying, believing that God would arise and plead His own cause.

Weeks passed, weeks of anxiety, yet of humble trust and continued asking. A servant appears at last, and Mrs. C. H. L—— alights at my door.

"I have heard, madam, there is an interesting work in Tounghoo. I should like to hear particulars. I am going to Government House, and would be glad to give Lady Canning some account of it."

I thought—"Truly, this is of the Lord." The next morning I received the following from—

GOVERNMENT HOUSE,
March 14th, 1857.

"MADAM,—I have been very much interested in the account you have given me of the Karens, and should be glad to communicate with you further on the subject.

"If you can call here to-morrow about eleven o'clock, I shall be glad to see you.

"Believe me, sincerely yours,

"C. CANNING."

Five o'clock here is the time for evening drives. Mrs. MacLeod Wylie enters.

"Mrs. Mason! Why are you here all alone?" she exclaims in astonishment. "It was only last night that we learned the fact of your being still in the city."

"I have not been alone, dear Mrs. Wylie."

"No, no, I understand. Now come home with me."

We arrive, and Mr. Wylie, drawing me beside him, asks what are my plans.

I explain to him a general plan.

" How much do you want to begin with ?"

" Two thousand rupees."

" Oh, my dear Mrs. Mason, I am sorry to discourage you, but you won't get it!—but Kitmagar !" he calls, " Bring me pen and ink,"—and down goes at once fifty rupees for himself, and fifty for a friend of his—one-twentieth of all I asked !

" Thanks ! my dear Mr. Wylie. Now may hap I shall get it." And then I told him of my invitation to Government House.

As soon as I could reach my room, and lock the door, I fell before God, and thanked Him that He had sent the two thousand rupees. I could not say the one hundred rupees—I could say nothing but the two thousand.

" I was sure an order had been given for it by the Great Treasurer of missions.

Next day I drove to Government Palace, ascended two flights of stairs into a long corridor, lined on either side with exquisite exotics all in full bloom, and a great number of Hindus, in snow-white drapery, and long white stockings, without sandals or shoes, all touching their palms, and bowing to the floor.

Passing into the drawing-room, the Countess Canning stood before me, arranging some beautiful daisies. She immediately turned, and, smiling graciously, led me to a seat.

" I am glad to see you, Mrs. Mason," she said. " I
was very much interested in the account you gave me.
Pray now tell me something of your Karens. Where
did they come from? What is their religion? Have
they any caste? And how do you work among them so
as to bring about such remarkable results ?"

This opened the way for me to give the Countess a
description of the Karen and Burmese women, and their
want of education.

" And why don't you present your requests to Government, Mrs. Mason ?"

" Surely your ladyship would scarcely advise that—I
a stranger, and a woman too ?" I said.

"Why, yes, I think I would. The Queen, I assure
you, feels a deep interest in the women of her terri-
tories."

I think I sat with her nearly two hours, she repeatedly
refusing admittance to others. Once or twice I attempted to rise, when she gently detained me, saying
she had been much gratified, and should like to hear
more.

On returning home I drew up a brief account and
petition to Government, with the following conclusion :—

*   *   *   *   *   *   *

" If the Government will kindly grant the aids
mentioned to make a beginning, I propose, in order
to make the school permanent, and to enlist the sympathy of all the tribes of Tounghoo, that the land,
buildings, apparatus, furniture, and everything apper-

taining to the institute, shall be held in trust by a Native Board of Managers, chosen at the annual examination."

My friend Mrs. L——, who had called before, kindly undertook to present the petition.

In about a week I received the following reply :—

" *To* Mrs. ELLEN H. B. MASON.

*   *   *   (After quoting the petition)

"As it is understood that the school when once established will be self-supporting, the Governor-General in Council sanctions the grant for the following aids, viz. :—

" 1. A small piece of land with well and fruit-trees.

" 2. One thousand rupees for the erection of buildings.

" 3. Four hundred rupees for furniture and school apparatus."

Just what I had asked for. Who will say this was not from God ? Who can doubt but it was a great answer to prayer ? Among other things, Lady Canning expressed the hope that I would extend my efforts to the Burmese women, and I replied,

" But it is very difficult, madam. They are trained from infancy only to be attractive to strangers, that their mothers may sell them for a high price. Therefore, the mothers will not let them come to us for instruction."

" Then it is a love of money that induces them to fall into such degradation and sin ? "

" Yes, madam. Simply the desire of gain."

" Then why not introduce some attractive accomplish-
ments by which they may earn a handsome livelihood
themselves, such as colouring or embroidery ?"

Her ladyship subsequently sent me two volumes of
engravings and a handsome donation for the school,
adding,—

" I most cordially trust your good work will prosper,
and you have my best wishes."

In my reply, I said,—

" I feel sure that when the Karens come to know that
their chieftess cares for them, it will inspire them with
great zeal to support the school, and they will feel their
honour concerned in the education of their daughters.
They are unlike other Orientals, having a high respect
for woman, and a high sense of honour.   They are, too,
nationally, a grateful people, and be assured, the incense
of prayer will daily ascend from three thousand warm
hearts, scattered upon the mountains of Tounghoo, in
behalf of your Ladyship and the Governor-General.

CHAPTER III.

GATHERING UP THE MANNA.

"A call, ma'am." Mrs. D. She desires me to dine with her. I have passed a delightful evening with a party of Christian friends. The Honourable E. D. is Accountant-General, and he is one of the chief actors in the City Missions, in Foreign Missions, in the Bible Societies, and to my great joy, Mrs. D. takes up a Native Missionary in Tounghoo, whom they have ever since supported generously by a hundred rupees a-year.

"Ma'am, a roll for you," said the Kitmagar, one day on my return from a call. I open it: Two hundred and fifty rupees! Thanks! thanks, my God! I read:

"My dear Mrs. Mason,

"Mrs. M. wished me to hand in this two hundred and fifty rupees, for the support of a native preacher in Tounghoo, under your own and Dr. Mason's care.

"J. M."

I knelt before God with my little boys, and thanked Him for remembering the poor and needy. Dear, good, sympathizing friends! Mr. M. was pastor of the Scotch Free Church in Calcutta.

Another card of invitation from the F's. On this evening I made the acquaintance of one who has power both with God and man—the Rev. Mr. H.; and on returning home, find a roll of one hundred rupees from Hugh F., Esq. "Manna! manna! mother," my little boys say thoughtfully.

Two of the most profitable evenings were spent with the W's. at small dinner parties. The company was very interesting,—the Archbishop, with Mrs. Pratt, including one or two military officers, the dear Milnes, Moncrieffs, and the Rev. Mr. Yates, of the Church of England Mission, who sent me fifty rupees; here also I met Dr. Kay, of Bishop's College, whose sermon on Woman is worth going on pilgrimage to hear.

Mr. W. is emphatically a conversationist. You are sure to find at his table the most talented, brilliant talkers and the most earnest Christians of the land, and I have seen him hold them spell-bound for two hours. It seems to be no effort or intention, but he leads you off so easily, you are not in the least aware of it till you utterly forget you are at the dinner-table; at least I did, and could do nothing in the world but listen.

"Why was not Mr. W. a Missionary?" asked a lady who had heard his inspiring eloquence.

"A Missionary! He's Missionary Extraordinary—a *Nah Khan Do*—Great Ear Chief—a general hearer and helper of all parts and parties.

Mrs. W. is as deeply interested as he is in Missionary work. It was this warm sympathy that induced her to write the "Gospel in Burmah," so graphic in its style, and so correct in its detail.*

These friends usually receive social visits on Thursday evenings, for the study of the Bible, when their large parlours are thrown open ; and when I was with them in 1860, they were soon filled with Government officers, merchants, physicians, and young cadets, with many ladies.   Mr. W. gave out a hymn, which all united in singing ; then prayer was offered, and he read the ninth chapter of Acts, when all made remarks, or asked questions, as they felt disposed.   Mr. W.'s own explanations struck me with a strange power, concerning the Lord's direction to Ananias, to go into the street called "Straight," showing the minute care and knowledge of the Lord concerning even streets and houses.

Among those whose acquaintance I delighted to make was Dr. Duff.   One morning I drove round to Wellesley Square.   The Doctor very courteously led me over the whole of the college.   I was much amused with his geography class.

" What is the world ? "—" A star in the sky."

" How is it kept revolving round the sun ? "—" By two forces."

" What do your Shasters say ? "—" That the earth sits on a tortoise."

" Does it ? "—" No."

---

* This work is republished in New York, and I was told that one Clergyman in the west sent for a hundred copies, saying nothing had ever stirred up such an interest in that region.

"Then your Shasters tell a lie, do they?"—"They do," with a laugh.

"If your Shasters lie about one thing, will they not about others?"—"Yes, Sir."

"Do you believe in the gods about here in Calcutta?"—No, Sir.

Who is God?"—"The Eternal Creator, and Jesus Christ, His Son."

"Do you believe in Jesus Christ?"—"Yes, Sir."

"Have you become Christians?"—"No, Sir."

"Why not?"—"Our parents will not allow us." *

In the evening I took tea with Dr. and Mrs. Duff, and a number of Christian preachers, Hindu gentlemen, and one or two of their wives. I can truly say they were gentlemen in every sense of the word—thorough in the Scriptures, learned in the classics, and seemed to have imbibed much of the Doctor's own spirit—zeal for the holy war. As I looked upon the master and the pupils, and saw how his inspiration was diffused among them, and how they loved him, I could but think how much more blessed it was to give than to receive.

I called on that patriarch, Lacroix, who had been there thirty years at work, yet nobody would have thought him growing old; for he came out with such a beaming eye and elastic step, I could not help wish-

---

* It is a significant fact, that while the Government College has no Bible taught, and is open to all, there are only about a thousand students, while Dr. Duff has all his pupils read the Bible, and preaches Christ to them every day, yet the school numbers fifteen hundred.

ing that some of our woe-begone young pastors, and Missionaries too, could grasp the hand of this then brightening *young* old Missionary soldier.

One of the most successful workers was Mrs. Mullins, now deceased, as well as her sainted father. She had an interesting orphan school, and was a pioneer Bible reader in the Zenanas of Calcutta.

In India it has hitherto been said, the laws of Menu and Confucius say, " Give a woman letters or knowledge, and you give a serpent milk." They know as well as we that "knowledge is power," therefore woman must never possess it. If a little Hindu girl dares to learn books, she will surely become a widow, that is, be cursed of God and man. Little girls are married there when between eight and ten years old. They have nothing to say about the matter. Their fathers trade them off to the one who offers the highest rank or the fullest purse. He may be a very savage in disposition, the father replies : " She's only a girl." Even at birth the degradation of woman commences. A mother forgets all sorrow "for joy that a man is born into the world ; " but, alas ! if a girl, her grief knows no bounds, and she is obliged to remain a week longer in her outdoor den alone.

By and by the infant begins to sit alone. Now, if it is a boy, it is set upon a mat, and bright gilded toys are given it. If a girl, it is set in the dirt, and an old tile is its plaything. So it is through life. Widowhood is only a change of masters ; but then in widowhood, if she has no sons, her husband's brothers are her rulers, and she becomes a slave to the caprice, envy, jealousy, and ill-temper of heathen sisters-in-law.

She must ever after stand in their presence to denote servitude ; when they lie upon a bed, she must lie upon the floor ; when they have their dainty viands, although they too must eat after their husband and out of his sight, yet the poor widow must crouch away even from her sisters, and eat her *one meal a-day* of roots and herbs " boiled," as the law prescribes, "in one pot." She may cook fish for her sons, but never taste it ; she may array her sisters in gay dresses, she must never put off her coarse, widow weeds. She may fit off her favoured sisters for an airing in their vails and polkas, she must never step foot outside of the high picketed wall of her master's enclosure ; she may bring books for her lords, she may never read a letter ; and the more sacred books she may never hear even, lest, alas ! she should obtain some glimmerings of knowledge to solace her lonely spirit. Such is woman's lot now among the helpless millions of India, and much the same throughout a great part of Asia, and this is why the *preseance* of power has been removed from all these eastern nations. They are doomed every one of them, and because they have so degraded woman ; and very likely this is one great reason why the Jews refused the Messiah, for they too had adopted much of heathen philosophy in regard to her position. Even now, in the enlightened United States of America, their women are not allowed to sit with men in the synagogue, or to join in any part of the Hebrew service, not even in the singing.

Yes, God made man a monarch, but gave him a limited monarchy; and whenever he turns it into a despotism, he falls with it. Everywhere and in every department this holds true; the reason we shall come to by and by.

One of the most elevating schools in Calcutta is the School of Arts, where young men are stimulated to emulate each other in drawing, designing, modelling, engraving, and lithography. It is a noble institution, and a beautiful thought; but why should the founders think only of young men? If there was a female department, it might do much to elevate the women of India.

I sent my card to Pundit Vidyasagur, the native gentleman who, with Baboo Vidyarutna, brought about the Widow Marriage Act. He is President of the Sanscrit College, to which he very politely escorted me. On one of the shelves I saw an elegantly-bound volume of the Bible, to which I called attention.

"Yes, madam," the librarian at once replied, "yes, and there is *Hume*," laying his hand on another volume of the same size, and just as elegantly bound, *lying on the top of the Bible*. Government presented the Bible to the college, so they did not dare refuse it, but they covered it with Hume!

Vidyasagur attended me to see a widow whom he had been educating, much to his honour. She was then a respected teacher in a school; a lovely young creature, so inspired with her work, and so inspiring, it did one's heart good to meet her.

I went to see Mrs. Ewart's school for Jewish girls. They had an excellent teacher. It is difficult to instruct these girls, because their parents care very little for sound, useful knowledge, but insist on their being thorough in the geography of the Twelve Tribes. It certainly requires a good store of patience to drill any girls for hours on the localities of Dan, Gad, and Napthali ; however, by perseverance in this particular, Mrs. Ewart has the privilege of teaching them a thousand things about Christ and heaven.

I visited several orphan schools. There is one connected with each Missionary denomination in Calcutta. Dr. and Mrs. Duff have founded a school for the high-caste girls, and have forty or more taught as yet by a heathen pundit, but this is an improvement on the past. The light of Calcutta in female education is the Normal Central Institution, for educating teachers.

The gentlemen in India seem to feel much deeper interest in the elevation of heathen women than our brothers in America do generally. This ought not to be. They may say English officers ought to do more for India. True, but America has its Indians, its negroes, its poor white girls. And then, America is a great country of *educated mothers*, therefore we have a right to expect from her sons some help for these millions of heathen women in Asia.

These first schools are like leaven, and will work, and the Missionaries, with many others in Calcutta, are indefatigable labourers in the cause. But the population is so dense ! Mrs. Wylie says : " In Calcutta alone there are probably *three hundred thousand females*, and within a radius of twenty miles around Calcutta, there are perhaps not less than *a million*. Only a few of all this great multitude can read—only a few have heard of the way of salvation."

What India now needs most is a corps of Bible-reading *women*, of high cultivation, irrepressible zeal, and entire consecration. If the gentlemen would just help these to go as *sappers and miners*, they would next have to prepare quarters for a surrendering enemy.

There is a Sunday-school in Calcutta helping in this work, that interested me deeply. The superintendent is Robert Scott Moncrieff, Esq., and he represents a class of earnest, primitive lay Missionaries scattered all over India. He is a young man just rising, making his own way upward. He rises because he keeps the only sure path—integrity, hard work, perseverance, patience, faith, and trust. But, while toiling unremittingly in a counting-house, with heavy responsibilities, he still finds time to be Sunday-school superintendent, gaol Missionary, and seaman's friend. Heaven reward thee, friend and brother ! " He that soweth bountifully shall reap also bountifully."

One morning the venerable Bishop, good Daniel Wilson, sent for me to breakfast with himself and the Archdeacon. The dear Wylies took me in their carriage.

His expositions of the Scriptures that morning were most clear and impressive, as if the glimpses into their deep treasures grew brighter as he looked over the river, and at the close we all joined with heartfelt earnestness in " Thy kingdom come."

On going to the table he seated me beside himself,

and after breakfast he led me through his library, taking down volume after volume, until he gave me a copy of each of his valuable works, with his autograph in every one. He then showed me the pictures of all his family, and, finally, stepped to his desk and drew a cheque for a hundred rupees, to help me on in my contemplated school. Kind Archdeacon Pratt followed with another fifty, and a nice volume of his own, with his autograph. So I returned home richly laden.

The next day I heard the Bishop preach in the cathedral. His theme was the new birth. He was very feeble, and obliged to lean upon the Archdeacon for support in the pulpit. I could only think of Aaron holding up the hands of Moses, for he seemed to be stepping into the portals of heaven, and very soon after he entered his Father's house of many mansions.

One of the most interesting women I saw in Calcutta was Madam Ellerton, at that time the oldest inhabitant in Calcutta. She had been the friend of Heber, of Carey, of Martyn, and a long line of worthies. She drew me down over her, clasped her withered arms around my neck, and prayed for me till my own tears mingled with hers.

Madam Ellerton had lived with the Bishop many years, and he very tenderly, while I was there, bade her have no anxiety about her burial, for he had seen her tomb prepared by the side of his own in the cathedral!

The native gentlemen who interested me particularly were Lal Beharric Da and Lal Beharric Singh. I heard Lal Beharric Da preach in English to a large audience

in the Scotch Kirk from these words : " Let us go up
and possess the land, for we are able." I thought it
one of the best Missionary sermons I ever heard. It
was glowing with light, and faith, and zeal for his
Master. He is an ordained Missionary, and Professor
in the Duff College. He has recently married a Parsee
wife of great intelligence.

At Beharrie Singh's house I met a party of native
gentlemen, educated pundits and baboos, all of whom
declared their intention to do what they could to change
the degraded condition of their women. Beharrie Singh
gave me a copy of a History of Female Education in
India, written by himself.

During tea I expected that none but the Christians
would eat with me; but at last Vidyasagur took up his
cup, and began to sip his tea. Then the others followed,
and although they declined cake, yet this was perhaps a
nearer approach to eating with a Christian than they
had ever made in their lives.

Mrs. Singh was Mary Sutton. She accompanied
Mrs. Sutton, of the Orissa mission, to America, and
was educated by Baptist ladies in Boston, Mass. She
is a highly intelligent person, pretty, graceful, and a
devoted helper to her husband. When I saw her she
was teaching a little school of Mussulman children, and
it was she who interested one of the donors to the school
to send me a hundred rupees. Mrs. Sutton very kindly
obtained for me a set of Hindu gods, drawn and coloured
by a Hindu painter. The cost was, I believe, a rupee a
piece. They have been very useful to me in explaining

M

Hindu idolatry ; and if Missionaries desire to send home anything from Calcutta, these might awaken more interest than anything else found there.

The interest in the Tounghoo mission increased every day until I left the city. The Wylies, the Moncrieffs, the Milnes, and Mrs. Lushington were pleading the cause of the poor and needy. Everybody I was introduced to helped me in some way or other. Even my hostess, in Sudder street, kind Mrs. Taylor, although taking boarders to help her own children, would accept no payment from me. Her son, too, set about teaching my boys Latin, and would spend hours in giving them instruction, after coming home weary from his day's labours. Why was all this kindness shown to a stranger? For the Master's sake.

Time would fail me to tell of all the friends raised up there, but when I stepped on board the steamer for Rangoon, in March, my soul was running over with love and wonder.

I hastened to my cabin, shut the door, and held up before the Almighty the manna He had given us :—

	RUPEES.
For the Girl's School in Tounghoo	2,231
For the same in Books and Prints from the Calcutta Tract Society	100
For the Preachers and General Purposes . .	614
For printing the Sermon on the Mount in Bghai	100
For personal support, by Mrs. Wylie and Mrs. Moncrieff	300

Besides the grant of land for the school, and a grant from the Calcutta Bible Society for printing several parts of the Bible, under Mr. Mason, in Bghai Karen; altogether in value more than six thousand rupees, or three thousand dollars.

All this, too, without asking for a penny! and given by friends who did not stop to ask if the converts would be of their church, or of any other, but simply if they could be redeemed and elevated to glorify Emmanuel.

I assure you, reader, I felt as if I had just come to the knowledge of what God could do. It seemed too wonderful for me; I could only praise, and lay my head in the dust.

Nor did the great I AM leave the work here. On reaching Rangoon, I simply sent my card to Colonel Phayre, the Commissioner of Pegu, and a plan of the contemplated school to our old Deputy Commissioner of Tounghoo, who had helped me about the slave children. Immediately there came rattling in nearly a hundred rupees from Government officers there.

I called on Mrs. Bell, the wife of the Commander-in-Chief in Burmah, and they invited an interesting circle for prayer, for both General and Mrs. Bell are working Christians. The General himself performs the two-fold part of preacher to his officers, and Missionary to the heathen; and on leaving their hospitable mansion, he sent after me a roll of two hundred rupees!

If these friends, or others there, should happen to see

these pages, they will forgive me, I hope, and will obligingly stand in the Missionary pillory, because I know you do want to see them, reader—those dear, kind friends who so generously pitied the poor Tounghoo women.

CHAPTER IV.

FORMING AN EDUCATION SOCIETY.

On reaching Tounghoo again, who should appear but my old Tutauman. Pointing to the north, south, east, and west, he said,—

" Teacheress, among these hills and valleys there are ninety-six churches, ninety-six chapels, ninety-six Christian schools, and two thousand six hundred baptized converts." The tidings were perfectly bewildering. Men who three years before had never heard of Jesus.

In came the young preachers too, many of them my old pupils, from every point of the compass, with their troops of pupils, and one company bearing palm leaves— a real oriental triumph ! Was it any wonder if I was exhilarated ? I could not help writing back to dear Mrs. Wylie, who had so tenderly sympathized with us : " I assure you I feel half the time as if out of the body. I don't think I could ask any more joy ; for I am sure Emmanuel is with us, and His holy, lovely likeness, in a greater or less degree, is shining all around us."

One day I was saying to one of the young schoolmasters, that it was delightful to teach the people to read, it was so blessed to feed on God's word. " Yes," he answered immediately, "'Blessed are they who do hunger and thirst after righteousness: for they shall be filled.' I read that in the holy book of Matthew."

These converts had already raised seven hundred rupees for books, eight hundred for medicines, besides building nearly a hundred chapels themselves alone, supporting nearly a hundred preachers and schoolmasters; and in the last year they had raised several hundred rupees for a young men's school. How could I, then, expect them to enter upon the new undertaking of supporting schools for girls? Quala, too, on whom I had most relied to further the plan, only said, "As for the food, the Christians can do it." He had heard that the Christians in America looked upon the design with doubt. He supposed it was because men did not approve in America of women teachers. So he would be very wise; he would take no ground at all. He would neither oppose nor help.

Looking over the towering mountains of the land, the scattered hamlets of the people, their drained purses, and many dialects, all new to me, and then this bitter disappointment in one on whom I had counted on as a pillar of strength—shall I confess my weakness? Fear, an indescribable, painful sense of fear, came over me, and, for a time, overpowered every other emotion. I could see no help for all those thousands of Tounghoo women, even after having just witnessed the power of the Almighty arm. I retired at night only to toss from side to side; I arose in the morning only to fear and grieve.

But the Lord gave strength, and it was not long that faith stood so faltering. For a Christian to doubt and fear when his Captain gives the word, " Forward !" is like a soldier stopping under marching orders to inquire about the commissariat supplies. I determined to obey, and leave results to the Master. Peace and joy indescribable followed this determination; and, presently, one of the highest chiefs sent in three young women, very pretty and clever, but not a rupee nor a kernel of rice with them, nor a word about any support. Then arose another trial of faith. If I sent them back, no more would come down ; if I took them and fed them myself, it would be a ruinous precedent. I called the girls, told them every particular, threw the burden of responsibility upon them, explained to them how momentous was the future, how much depended on their stay with us, and then proposed a night of fasting and prayer. We spent it mostly together, pleading with heaven, and before morning those three young women were quite as deeply embued with the spirit of the undertaking as I was myself.

Next evening a chief came in bringing eleven rupees for the young men's school.

"Go and give it to mama for the girls," said Mr. Mason.

" The girls !" he replied, with a side look of disdain.

" Yes, for the girls. They have nothing to eat. They need food as well as the boys."

Very reluctantly the chief came and handed me the eleven rupees.

"Stop, Nah Khan," I said, taking a low stool beside him. "Look at this," spreading out the ground plan of my contemplated building, and explaining to him the whole undertaking. I also told him that I was obliged to give up my own support to do this.

"And how is mama to get her curry and rice?" he asked.

"Ah! Qualay, God's ravens are still in the world," I answered; when he smiled understandingly, and turning to his followers, in an undertone he said,—

"Think we must send mama the great pig!"

Sure enough, a few days afterwards down came the great pig—such a size—laced up in bamboos, borne by seven men, squealing so as to startle the officers all the way through the cantonments. On they came, and laid it an offering at my door, an offering of highland sympathy! The same day my servant went with them to market and sold the squealer for twenty-two rupees. With this, and the eleven rupees, I was enabled to support the girls a whole term.

Seeing I was really in earnest, and had even sold the pig to help, the Nah Khan and his men began also to feel an inspiration about the work. From this time he encouraged and cheered us on. Caleb-like, he said :— "Let the teacheress have no fear. We are able, and we will do all she requires."

Thus God in mercy gave strength and comfort. The story soon spread, and deputations began to pour in desiring to see the *taguau* or plan which I had marked out for the institute. With each company I spent hours in explaining the plan, and the advantage of having the women taught so as to keep the schools, and leave the young men free to go beyond, preaching the Gospel. Some opposed strongly, and I would leave them in a high dispute with one another about the shame of having *women teachers*, and the impropriety of allowing their daughters to learn more than their parents knew. They would become lazy, they would beat out paddy no more, it was argued. They would become proud, and would no longer obey their husbands. Others, however, saw the advantages, and particularly the advantages of having a piece of land of their own, and a large handsome house of their own. The liberal party finally prevailed, and all returned to bring in their pledges and contributions. Each embassy now brought a letter pledging his chief and people to carry on the school, and support it; accompanying the letter with their money, varying from one rupee to thirty rupees.

Next came the search after a building spot. The Deputy Commissioner proposed a ride on horseback; so one morning before breakfast away I went with our mutual friend, the Rev. Mr. Whittaker. The Commissioner was mounted on a cream-coloured pony, with black mane, cut close, and a sweeping black tail. The pretty creature had a fine arching neck, and seemed to know exactly who she carried, for she stepped off as proudly as Bucephalus. My pony, which Mrs. Whittaker had kindly lent me, was also a Shan, but much smaller. I had not been on horseback for twelve years, so that this was an adventure. The Commissioner led the way, and

on we went over all sorts of places, down the river, over
the plains, and at last he came up to a very steep ridge
of table land, which he thought would make a splendid
site for a school.   On the top was a pagoda with a long
graduated ascent of paved steps from the base to the
summit.   Captain D'Oyly rode on, as if there were
nothing to impede us, right up the brick steps.

"Shall I come?" I asked timidly, yet with no
thought in the world but that of implicit obedience.

"Yes, Mrs. Mason, come up," he answered quietly,
turning his head with a grave, careless air.   So on I
went, up, up, up, till I verily thought the pony must
lose his balance and I tumble backwards over his head.
As soon as we reached the summit, he turned to me with
a half-concealed triumphant expression,—

"You're a capital rider, Mrs. Mason, and you are
quite *tractable!*"

Then I saw the mischief in his eye, and understood he
had led me straight up the pagoda just for sport.   We
had a much harder time getting down, and it was not
without some peril.

When I asked the Captain what he played such a ruse
for, he answered with his judicial smile,—

"Oh! I saw you could lead Karens.   I wanted to see
if you could *follow!*"

It was all in vain, however, our scaling the Myugyee
pagoda.   Not a foot of land could we find available, for
the military lines lay far and near, stretching in every
direction.   Once we saw a magnificent old mango near
the river, and galloped off, thinking then we had surely

got beyond their limits ; but lo, to our great vexation, there were twenty or thirty sappers slashing down the reeds and grasses to build an hospital ! Then we turned and galloped as far the other way to a clump of palms standing all alone as much as two miles from the cantonments; but there they were, the forever-present bushmen, putting up a stable. So, after searching in vain till ten o'clock, we gave up and went home.

The next day I started again with Karens, and for five days we scoured the country in every direction, and found nothing. I was resolved to get on to the river, so that the Karens could have the advantages of a river frontage for their boats, bamboos, and produce, as well as water free for themselves and their cattle, besides protection against fires, and a clear way downward, should they be obliged to flee from the Burmese.

Finally, the Nah Khans, the two chief Karens who had been appointed magistrates, suggested that we should go into the jungle on the east side of the Sittang river, opposite to the old fort, on a spot where they said all the Karen paths met. It was a wild jungle, but a particularly convenient place for all the tribes.

" Very well," the Deputy Commissioner replied, " I will go over with you, and we will mark off as much as you want."

Recollecting the pagoda jaunt, I engaged him in an interesting conversation till he quite forgot the land and walk. He suddenly recollected his promise, and stopping short, said,—

" Do you want a *state* here, Mrs. Mason? How far *are* you going ?"

"Only to that old tree; that will make a fine boundary," I answered, pressing on to an ancient banyan that was waving fifty feet over the river.

He looked back in utter amazement at the distance we had gone over, and said something about having it measured. I suggested that he might let us cut down the jungle first, and then it could be-seen how much space there really was.

" Well, call your people, and go to work quickly, but I can't promise you will get all that.

Immediately about fifty came down to clear the land, but applied to me for food. I counted up all they had brought in for the school, and the whole amounted to one hundred rupees. I pointed to my twenty-four pupils, and assured them it would be impossible for me to feed them also. But I handed them twenty-five rupees, telling them they had better appoint two of their number to buy and cook for the whole. The work would then go on much more rapidly.

Two days passed, when they came again, saying the money was all gone. At first I felt disposed to rebuke them, but turned to my closet for an hour, giving the time to prayer and to my dear little help-book, "Remedies against Satan's Devices." In that time God taught me what to do, and strength was given for the day. Having first obtained permission of Mr. Mason, I went out.

"Chiefs, can you build me a house?" I asked.

"Oh! yes; if mama would live in a Karen house."

"How long would it take?"

"We could put one up to-morrow."

"Very well. You go and put me up a house, and I will take the girls all over the river. Then I will buy food in the bazaar, and the girls will do the cooking if you think all would like this?"

"Never could eyes open so wide. They seemed relieved of a tremendous burden, and, springing to their feet, they gave orders to their men, right and left, while I handed them ten rupees more to sustain them while building my house. The next evening I bade adieu to home and all home comforts. They had cleared two spots about forty feet square, and the school-house or shanty they had built me was only twenty feet square, set up two feet above the damp ground, enclosed by reeds and covered with grasses. To this we removed the next evening with our books and twenty-four girls; and here was taught the first girls' school in Tounghoo. At evening we assembled for prayers, and I addressed them kindly, praising them for the efforts they had made, and encouraging them to hope for success if they would let the girls cook for them all. To this several strongly objected, alleging that Bghai food and Paku food were not the same, and their manner of cooking not the same. I then engaged that Bghai girls should cook for Bghais, and Paku girls for Pakus, upon which all sung the doxology most heartily, and every heart beat as strong as Gideon's.

The next day, on the 4th of August, 1857, the chiefs

having arrived, we held a convocation in the little bamboo chapel which they had erected under four ancient mango trees some eighty feet high, and organized the KAREN EDUCATION SOCIETY. Forty chiefs were present, and twenty were represented by letter. The session continued until the 7th. They chose a Board of Managers, consisting of one Paku, one Mauniepaga, one Mopaga, one Bghai, one Pant-Bghai, and one English, besides Captain D'Oyly, who kindly consented to act as president.

One of the first resolutions of the society was to support and carry on themselves the NATIONAL FEMALE INSTITUTE, as they expressed it, " down to remotest generations." The Nah Kahn Qualay stirred up the people to bring in their pledges, and my Tutuaman, Shapau, set off through the Bghai hills for three months, explaining the plan to all the Bghai villages, and soon pledge letters came in from every quarter.

A few of these letters I will give, for I do really think they are curious and interesting documents, considering they are entirely the composition of these wild Karens. These are specimens of more than two hundred letters now beside me, which have been voluntarily sent in by native churches. The first letter was

FROM PWAPAU, THE TEACHER OF KLURLAH.

" DEAR TEACHERESS OF TOUNGHOO,

" Grace, mercy, and peace be with thee for ever ! There are some young women here who do desire to study with mama. We send two of them, who pledge themselves to study hard and become teachers, and the people promise to support them. We send now four rupees eight annas.

"PWAPAU THE TEACHER OF KLURLAH."

The same clan :—

"FROM THE CHIEFS OF HOOMUDUC.

"We are greatly pleased, and we send four girls immediately to study. These we have examined, and they engage to teach school, and do everything they can to build up Christ's kingdom. We send them quick that they may not be behind the others."

From the Mopaga Tribe :—

"TEACHER AND TEACHERESS,

"The plan devised for us we all like much. We will give up our children to study in the great zayat about to be erected, and will furnish them food. All agree perfectly to the Committee of Seven, and we now hope to become acquainted with books. We write this letter that the teachers may know that we agree with glad hearts.

"The doings of the teachers afford us great pleasure.

"May peace and happiness rest on our helpers !

"WRITTEN FOR THE CHURCH OF PANAPOO."

From the Pant-Bghai Tribe :—

"TEACHERESS,

"That which thou hast devised, erecting a building for us, hits the minds of all, both men and women. We agree with great glad hearts, and will send our children and grand-children to study, and we will also furnish them support.

" We will righteously perform the things to which we here agree, both men and women pledging their words ; and in order that mama may know our designs, we have written this letter."

CHAPTER V.

GETTING A TITLE DEED.

" You will surely die there, Mrs. Mason." This was our civil surgeon's belief, and the fear of all our friends; for every one knows how unhealthy it is to live in the midst of new clearings day and night, and especially in a hot climate, where vegetation decomposes so rapidly.

" But, doctor, how do your officers do when bringing your men before an enemy ? "

" Oh ! we go first, of course," he answered, laughing.

" When you know you may get shot first ? "

" Yes."

" Then you see why my husband lets me go and live in the clearings."

There is nothing so important, when labouring to raise up a heathen people, as to let them see that you believe yourself what you teach them. If you would have them trust, you must trust yourself. If you would have them enter into the spirit of that diamond precept, " Seek first the kingdom of God and His righteousness," you must make that kingdom first in the little unnoticeable actions of every-day life, not unnoticed by the heathen. Little things are what they judge by altogether, like little children, and like God too. The minute hand is their guide, not the hour hand. There-

N

fore my dear husband was happy in this arrangement, although, from July, 1857, to July, 1858, I could only have Saturdays for home duties.

Saturday morning two of the school girls would go over, and while taking lessons in sweeping, cleaning, and tasteful arrangement, would put everything "to rights" in Mr. Mason's quarters. In the morning the dhoby always came with the week's washing, and took away for the next week, by which plan everything was changed on Saturday, and all ready for quiet on the Sabbath.* Then the cook's market bill for the week was to be settled, and directions given for the next week, and this had to be done for my husband's table, for my own, for the girls' school, for the young men's school, and for the two Karen hospitals; measuring out, every Saturday, the tea, the coffee, the sugar, the salt, the flour, the curry-powder, the rice, and even the lamp-oil, for every day through the week. By noon the domestic business was completed, and the remainder of the day was a real treat to us both. Then out came my dear husband's letters and scientific papers, with my "woman's plans" to be sifted and turned over by the wisdom and genial heart of one of the most indulgent of husbands, and so these hours were exclusively devoted to each other.

We were greatly favoured in having good servants. Appoo takes care of all my husband's wants, while our

---

* Everybody knows, I suppose, that in hot climates linen has to be changed every day; so that it is always necessary to have one or two dozen changes on hand at once.

friend, the mussulman, keeps all the wardrobes in order.
I have heard of legislators decreeing it the duty of
woman to "smile on her husband and darn his stockings!" Shades of Menu and Fo! Smile, of course, we
will on our husbands; but as for the darning—all non-
sense! old Baboo Hoosim can do it a thousand times
better than I can. He is our family tailor. Every
Saturday morning, at six o'clock, this tall, white-
gowned spectre appears in his Cashmiré turban and
flowing white beard on our verandah. Then out come
the drawers, when everything and anything that wants
repairing is handed over to him. He will find buttons,
and sew them on to all the wristbands, make up shirts
or dresses, trousers or mantles, no matter which; fit up
your bed-room with sheets, pillow-slips, towels, all and
everything, for less money than it would cost you to
furnish materials; because a foreigner always has to
pay a third more for everything than a native. So I
let the servants darn, and I superintend. This latter
must never be left to them, as they soon rattle through
the purse, if you do.

Then little Appoo; he's such a capital fellow! Just
like his master—I mean, he is just as punctilious about
the hours.* His curry is always right, with the whitest

* I have one of the most stereotyped husbands that ever lived.
Up every morning over his tea and toast at six o'clock, then comes
a short walk, then at his translations till prayer time, breakfast at
nine, study till eleven, lie down till twelve, at work again till two,
then a short nap, a bath, dinner, another walk, rest an hour, tea at
eight, translate till eleven. Week after week always the same,
except when broken up by jungle travelling.

rice, everything smoking hot, and just at the hour. At three o'clock precisely, in comes the hot water for master's bath. At seven o'clock precisely comes his unchangeable dinner of curry and rice, or beef steak, fried plantains, and sweet potatoes, with now and then the daintiest little custard "for master," or a nice cup of arrowroot pudding.

With my Yankee notions of housewifery, I for some time endeavoured to tempt my husband to other dishes, which I prepared with great care myself; but, although he would politely taste them and pronounce them excellent, yet I saw he spent no thought on them, and only tasted from mere politeness. So I gave up the cookhouse, much to his satisfaction, and devoted my time to the people. The second year I was able to leave the Karens also on Wednesday nights, and take our boys to join my husband, which afforded us much cause for thankfulness, as the separations of the first year had been to us both long and painful.

Not a little cankering care and anxiety I had in many ways, concerning the land matters and the timber.

The Karens at this time were erecting twelve guardhouses for twelve of the largest villages, in a parallelogram encircling the Institute, and cultivating ground around them. They proposed to make a public road around all, and, perhaps, to take up the jungle beyond and build a small Karen settlement, if the taxes should be satisfactorily arranged, which the Deputy Commissioner negociated for them.

The Acting Commissioner, Captain Hopkinson, stated that he could not, without seeing or visiting the spot himself, or much further information, sanction the grant of land.*

Upon which, Captain D'Oyly wrote the following comforting little note to me :—

" MY DEAR MRS. MASON,

" Do not be downcast. We must have a talk about this, and I hope we may be able to get the Commissioner to change his mind.

" It would never do to let the labour and enthusiasm of the Karens be thrown away. No, indeed ! Be as bold in your present difficulties as you were when you rode up the steps of the Myugyee pagoda, and all will come right. Write yourself, and represent your own case, and I will forward it."

The following letter was therefore forwarded :—

" To Captain H. Hopkinson, Commissioner of Pegu.

" SIR,

" I take the liberty of writing to you, as Captain D'Oyly requests me to do so, concerning the land for which I have applied on account of the Karen Female Institute.

" I would first beg permission to say a word in behalf of these mountain tribes of Tounghoo."

* Colonel Phayre, the Chief Commissioner of Pegu, was then in Italy for his health, and Capt. Hopkinson, Commissioner of Tenasserim, was in charge.

Here followed a brief account of the Karens, and their readiness to receive Christian books.

" From the lowest drunkenness thousands have risen up to sobriety, diligence, and worth. From the lowest ignorance they have become able mathematicians, printers, and teachers. Some of the most eloquent orators I ever heard speak were Karens, and they have been educated almost entirely in their own vernacular tongue. In Tounghoo the work of conversion and education has been most remarkable."

After mentioning the young men's advancement and Quala's devotion, the letter continued :—

" But for the education of the Karen women, very little has been done in Tounghoo, and for the Burmese women nothing at all.

" For many years it has been my earnest desire to establish a school for girls which should embrace all the tribes, bring out and concentrate their energies and philanthropic feelings in the one great object of education, and be to the Christian clans among the natives what Delphi was to the tribes of Greece. God has in the most wonderful manner opened the way for a beginning.

    *   *   *   *   *   *

" You know the grant so graciously given me by Government. It is true I asked only for a ' small piece of land,' but then there was to be a ' well and fruit-trees,' which implies a cultivated piece of ground, and this was what Government expected me to have. But the military and civil lines occupy almost every desirable spot in Tounghoo. I have, therefore, taken an unbroken jungle. The labour of subduing this jungle and keeping the land clear will be very great. Of course, we would not desire to have such a piece of land unless compensation could be made in some way for cultivated ground, 'the well and fruit-trees.' It takes a long time for fruit-trees to grow, and they are invaluable for a school. Therefore it is that I ask for a larger piece of land.

" For a public institution for a hundred girls we require ground sufficient for the school-house, a house for the steward, the teacher, a play-ground, a garden, a grazing-piece, dormitories, out-offices, guard-house, and a spot for a chapel. I would, therefore, earnestly beg you will make us the following grants :—

" 1st.—The whole piece of land, measuring thirty-two and a-half acres.

" 2nd.—Permission to erect twelve guard-houses on the outskirts of this piece for the protection of the school, free of rent, the occupants paying their annual capitation taxes in the districts to which they respectively belong.

" 3rd.—Permission for the Karens, who may take up land beyond the school for cultivation, to pay their capitation taxes in the districts where they belong, for the three years which Government allows to bring the land under cultivation.

4th.—Five hundred rupees towards making the new road required round our land. This is asked because the

road being a public one for all the villages, it seems
hard that we should do the work alone.

"I am, SIR, your humble servant,

"ELLEN B. MASON."

The letter was forwarded by Captain D'Oyly, and
Captain Hopkinson replied in the most gentlemanly
terms, granting, finally, the whole piece of land, permission for the guard-houses free of rent, permission to
make the road around the boundary ; but he said,—
"Mrs. Mason need not make one any better than the
native road that she found on the place." He also
granted all I asked in regard to taxes, and, moreover,
he would give the Karens permission to take up just
as much land as they could cultivate, free of taxes for
ten years.

On the reception of this, the Karens gave ringing
cheers for D'Oyly and Hopkinson !

The next Sunday was appointed as a day of thanksgiving throughout the jungles, and many warm heart-
prayers ascended on that day from the glens and
pinnacles for the rulers who had thus helped us.

Changes, however, prevented the deed from being
made out until the return of Col. Phayre, when I again
laid the subject before him. The following is an extract
from his very kind reply :—

ON THE IRRAWADDY, *April* 12*th*, 1858.
"MY DEAR MRS. MASON,

    "*I fully appreciate the benefit which will result*

*from your determination to educate the Karens as
Christian men, and to make them good agriculturalists.*

" I look forward with great pleasure, in my next visit
to Tounghoo, to seeing your Karen Female School, and
witnessing the assembly of the whole of your Karens
at evening worship. I feel that a great work is going
on, and that it is the duty of all to further it to the
utmost of their ability.

" May I ask you to send me a brief sketch of the
Karen Female School after the close of the present
term,—the number of scholars, what they are taught,
their age, the tribes they belong to, and all particulars
which you think would be interesting. The Government
will, I am sure, be glad to learn all particulars. When
you have scholars of different tribes, do you teach each
in their own dialect?

" Believe me, very sincerely yours,
" A. P. PHAYRE."

My answer was accordingly :—

" The girls are all instructed in two dialects—the
Paku and Bghai. They are making most satisfactory
progress in the study of Christianity, geography, history,
arithmetic, elementary astronomy, letter-writing, the
laws of health, housekeeping, nursing the sick, and
teaching; and are being carefully trained in habits of
order, punctuality, and cleanliness."

It was soon after this that our Deputy Commissioner
was promoted, and a new ruler arrived in Tounghoo.
Directions were immediately given by the Commissioner

for the title deed to be made out, but that deputy a few months after left the commission entirely. Then business fell into the hands of a subordinate officer, and so the saddest delays occurred after the order for the deed had been issued, causing me and the Karens the most intense anxiety for two years, and by circumstances over which the Commissioner had no control. This delay was caused mostly by bad men, who retarded the advancement of female education in the land.

Finally, Colonel Phayre gave with his own hand the Title Deed, as follows :—

TITLE DEED FOR KAREN SCHOOL LAND IN TOUNGHOO.

"UNDER THE AUTHORITY AND SANCTION CONVEYED FROM THE GOVERNOR-GENERAL OF INDIA, IN COUNCIL, IN LETTER No. 1,204, DATED 16TH MARCH, 1857, FROM THE SECRETARY TO THE GOVERNMENT OF INDIA IN THE FOREIGN DEPARTMENT, TO THE ADDRESS OF THE COMMISSIONER OF PEGU, THE SAID COMMISSIONER DOTH HEREBY, AS A SPECIAL CASE, IN ORDER THAT SOUND EDUCATION AND CIVILIZATION MAY BE IMPARTED AND EXTENDED AMONG THE KAREN NATION, GRANT UNTO THE KAREN EDUCATION SOCIETY OF THE DISTRICT OF TOUNGHOO ALL THAT PARCEL OF LAND SITUATED ON THE EAST BANK OF THE RIVER SITTANG, NEAR THE CITY OF TOUNGHOO, NOW IN THE OCCUPATION OF THE SAID EDUCATION SOCIETY, AND CONTAINING ABOUT THIRTY-TWO (32) ACRES, MORE OR LESS ; AND THE SAID LAND SHALL BE HELD IN TRUST BY MRS. ELLEN B. MASON FOR THE SAID EDUCATION SOCIETY, UNTIL HER DECEASE, WHEN IT

MAY BE TAKEN IN CHARGE BY THE KAREN BOARD OF MANAGERS OF THE SAID SOCIETY, IN CONNEXION WITH ANY ONE PERSON WHOM THE SAID MRS. ELLEN B. MASON MAY HAVE APPOINTED TO CO-OPERATE WITH THE SAID SOCIETY OR BOARD OF MANAGERS, AS THEIR TRUSTEE AND AGENT. AND THIS GRANT SHALL CONTINUE AND HAVE EFFECT AS LONG AS THE LAND GRANTED, AND THE BUILDING OR BUILD-INGS THEREON, SHALL BE USED FOR AND DEVOTED TO THE OBJECTS ON ACCOUNT OF WHICH THE GRANT IS MADE; NAMELY, FOR THE ESTABLISHMENT OF FEMALE SCHOOLS AND OTHER INSTITUTIONS, WHEREBY A SOUND EDUCATION MAY BE IMPARTED TO THE KAREN NATION IN THE DISTRICT OF TOUNGHOO, AND THE BLESSINGS OF CIVILIZATION BE EXTENDED TO THEM.

" IN WITNESS WHEREOF, I HAVE HEREUNTO SET MY HAND AND SEAL, AT BASSEIN, ON THE NINTH (9TH) DAY OF JULY, 1859.

"A. P. PHAYRE, COMMISSIONER OF PEGU."

TOUNGHOO, 29th *July*, 1859."

I replied, "Oh how glad are we of this Title Deed ! Every Christian Karen on these mountains will thank our Government for it every day as long as they live." The position was a central one, and approved as of easy access to the great mass of the Karen population.

I think it had cost me to obtain it as many as *fifty* letters. Two years, too, of asking and waiting before the Throne. But God did not forget to be gracious.

" HAPPY IS HE WHO HATH THE GOD OF JACOB FOR HIS HELP."

CHAPTER VI.

THE KAREN CANAAN.

"TEACHERS, I wonder if I love God with all my strength. I am thinking if I *can* do this."

These words were uttered by a very wild chief of the Pant-Bghai tribe. He, with others, felt it a most formidable undertaking, the clearing thirty acres of land, exceedingly formidable for wild Karens. The Nah Khans divided out the whole ground into four wards, giving one to each of the principal clans, so that every one, on going through the jungle, would see "Paku ward," "Mopaga ward," "Bghai ward," and "Mauniepaga ward" posted upon the stakes all along the whole tract.

It is August, and the rains are pouring heavily, but the news spreads like a fire in the jungle. "The Karens have got a Canaan. God has given us a Holy Land!" and mountain echoes to mountain, "Come to the work!" and come they do in troops of five, ten, fifteen, twenty, until two or three hundred cover the jungle. Drenched with rain, down they pour, over crags and snags, through bogs and swollen rivers up to their necks, and not a rag of clothing to change, so poor they are.

"Dahs, dahs, mama! Give us dahs!" (long stout knives) ; for a fourth part of the Bghais bring nothing to work with, so I must buy for them spades and hoes, to the amount of nearly a hundred rupees out of the general fund which the whole supply. These, too, require care, and the men are constantly going and coming, so two of the girls are appointed stewardesses of the tools to give out and receive back, taking the leaders' names in each company. Four others are entrusted with the marketing ; but the rations I give out daily myself to all the companies, so that there shall be no injustice ; besides, I find it much more economical. The girls cook for them with perfect cheerfulness, and all work indeed as Nehemiah's men did building up the wall.

You should have seen the heaps of presents coming to me. On one side, rolls of mats, ten feet high ; on another, long bamboo joints of honey ; on another piles of baskets, and a whole yard full of hens and chickens before the door. You know this is custom a *L'Orient*. On first visiting any superior, they lay before him some token of friendship, or rather of homage.

We let them bring as much as they like, but never take for ourselves a single anna's worth, neither Mr. Mason, nor I, nor our children. We say to them, " It is well, but we will set it all to the school account," and every mat, basket, egg, and fowl, every pound of beeswax or bamboo of honey which we use for ourselves, I pay for at the full market price, and put it into the school funds. This has always been Mr. Mason's custom and my own, and I believe it is far more pleasing to God than it would be to take presents from such poor converts. Both Mr. Mason and Quala, at the close of 1856, reported : " Among the Bghais, things are going back,"—but this new school plan, which brought the tribes to work altogether, seemed to have a mesmeric effect. It made the clans acquainted with each other, drew forth their sympathies, much increased their mutual love, and their interest in one another's welfare ; our Bible studies also greatly aided these desirable results.

It is morning. The girls are at their rice pots. I go to look over the work, advising with the chiefs, and encouraging their men, as I always find that if I have visited any spot in the morning, the men will accomplish double the work there during the day.

But they are still weak—very weak. One morning I find them clearing around the thorn bushes, but have no intention of going into such perilous-looking clumps. A straggling thorn bush runs through the whole tract, which increases very rapidly, and grows into trees all woven and interwoven so as to be quite impenetrable. These the chiefs declare must remain, for not a man will venture into those awful meshes. My two daring boys snatch the dahs from the chiefs' hands, dash in, Saxon-like, slashing right and left, and soon one large clump is laid low. At twilight the torch is applied, and " Away goes one mountain," they shout.

The roots spread far and wide, and in that land will be up again in a week ; so again our boys rush into the work there in the moonlight, and rafts of thorns float down the river. After this, whenever they came to a thicket of thorns, the chiefs would cry out, "Remember the little teachers," when the young men and boys would attack them with a vengeance; but, of course, with bare feet, it was very unenviable work.

The middle of the day I devote to my school, leaving the men to do as they choose; some working, others sleeping, but in the evening comes our Bible-reading. This is deeply interesting. Imagine as follows:—

" I beseech you, therefore, brethren, by the mercies of God, that ye present your bodies a living sacrifice," reads the assistant in Paku.

" I beseech you, therefore, brethren," &c., respond the congregation.

" I beseech you, therefore, brethren," &c., reads the assistant in Bghai.

" I beseech you, therefore, brethren," &c., respond the congregation in Bghai.

" What is it the Apostle wants the heathen converts to do? You may all answer; chiefs, women, young men, young women, tell what you think. What is a *living* sacrifice? How can we make a sacrifice every day, and keep about our work?" Then,

" What about these mercies of God?" &c.

This is something new, and every eye begins to dilate, showing all are in deep and intense thought, till finally the principal chief gives utterance to his views; then another follows, and another, expounding and reasoning, until the room presents a most animated scene of discussion, and all about the Bible. The young women, too, are encouraged to express their thoughts, but this arouses the young preachers.

"Mama, does not the Apostle Paul say, 'I suffer not a woman to teach?' yet you call on the young women here in the presence of the men?"

"Ay, ay, Master Shemoon, but this is *our* Bible lesson. It belongs to the girls' school; and as I, too, am a woman, I fear you will all have to stay away, or let the girls talk." They chose the latter alternative, and these happy Bible-readings were never to be forgotten by either party. The questions usually led to earnest exhortations, which always closed by a hearty application of the text to the business in hand.

Again turning from the assistants to the chiefs, I try to have them feel that, as they are all heads of families and heads of villages, it is eminently desirable that they should understand the Scriptures, so as to instruct their people, and hold up the hands of their teachers, pointing them to Abraham. The question is then put:

"What shall be our subject to-night?"

"Faithfulness," it may be, cries a voice below the platform, and so we take Faithfulness.

"Well, who does God command to be faithful? Does He say anything about it to teachers? Look at 1 Tim. i. 12."

"The Apostle thanks the Lord that He counted him faithful," some one answers.

"See Eph. vi. 21."

"He says Tychicus was faithful," calls out timidly a boy from the corner.

"Is anything said to chiefs? Look at Gal. iii. 9."

"Abraham is called faithful."

"Anything to the Board of Managers? 1 Cor. iv. 2."

"It is required in stewards that a man be found faithful."

"Anything to wives? 1 Tim. iii. 11."

"Wives are commanded to be faithful in all things."

"Anything to children? Titus i. 6."

"Parents are blessed when they have faithful children, not unruly."

"Anything to servants? Matt. xxv. 21."

"Servants are said to have '*well* done' when faithful."

"What does a faithful servant do? Let each one tell."

"A dozen voices respond one by one, all telling some simple thing pertaining to their every-day life.

"What does Christ call those who do whatsoever He commands them?"

"His servants."

"Where does He say they shall be? John xii. 26."

"Where He is."

"I saw a *Daupuwa*, or brother," says one of the Board of Managers; "he said he had come down to work three days. He worked till noon to-day; then he and all his men left for home, so as to reach there to-night. Now, was he faithful?"

"No, no, no," utter a dozen voices of young men and women.

"I heard another say to-night he had worked two

O

days, when to-day at noon he went to the bazaar, and loitered all the rest of the day. Was he faithful ?"

" No, no."

" Tell some other way of being *un*faithful."

" I know," says a young man. " San Yaubu told me, if I didn't dig up the roots of the grass and stumps around the chapel, I should not be faithful."

" And I know," says one of the girls, "if I get tired, and don't teach my class well when mama is out, I'm unfaithful."

And so every one hunts up an answer, and sometimes mingles it with simple confession, showing the power of the sword of the Spirit.

" What is it a faithful witness *will not do*, girls ? Look and see. Prov. xiv. 5."

" Will not lie," answer the girls in low, sweet voices."

" Who was so faithful that none occasion nor fault could be found in him ? Look at Dan. vi. 4."

" Daniel," shout the boys.

Then the heart-searchings would be stayed, and all asked if any one could tell what was promised to him who was faithful in a few things; and then came again their brief, striking applications.

" What will Christ give to the faithful unto death ? Rev. ii. 10."

" A crown of life."

But our five favourite topics were, first, " Thy kingdom come," in the Lord's prayer ; the armour, in Eph. vi. ; the work of tribulation, Rom. v. ; the fruits of the

Spirit, Gal. v.; and the great command, "loving our neighbour as ourselves."

One evening the subject was the first commandment.

" First commandment, 'Thou shalt have no other gods before me,'" calls out the assistant on my right, in Paku.

" Thou shalt have no other gods before me," respond the whole assembly. So he goes through.

" First commandment, 'Thou shalt have no other gods before me,'" takes up the assistant on my left, in the Bghai dialect.

The congregation respond, and so we go through again.

" How can you love the Lord with your *strength?*" it was asked. For some time none could answer. Presently, chief Pwame rose and said,

" I think I understand."

" Well, what is it, chief?" and every eye was fixed on the speaker.

" What is it ?" he replies, towering to his full height. " Why, brethren, if we come here and help mama to build up this school for teachers, and clear this land for a holy place, we are loving Jesus Christ with our *strength*—that's the way, I think."

" Er, er," shouts out chief Poquai with a dozen other voices. And so it goes on, the interest increasing every moment, till ten o'clock, and then no one wants to stop —nor I either.

They always went home talking over the subjects, and they would continue talking them over at midnight, in the morning, in the roads, and in the fields. If any point of difficulty arose and it was referred to me, I never answered them except by quoting other Scripture, or asking questions which should lead them to see the truth, so that when it was reached, all felt that they had got at it themselves. This encouraged them to try, and to drink in with delight the waters that could quench all their thirst.

"SANCTIFY THEM THROUGH THY TRUTH; THY WORD IS TRUTH." This has been ringing in my ears ever since we began this work. It afforded them the greatest pleasure to know that they were to be made holy by the study of God's word. Then they thought that God had given His word as the food for their souls, even as they prepared curry and rice for the body, and they knew if they did not eat their evening meal, they could not possibly dig up roots the next day.

"No," they would exclaim, "and so if we don't feed on God's word every day, we shall never get up the thorns and stumps of sin from our hearts."

The young preachers and schoolmasters were usually about us two or three together, and they always returned with brighter eyes, stronger nerves, and higher aspirations to their work in the hills. This I regarded as one of the greatest blessings that attended on the place— the sparkles of truth and blendings of love would be borne back to the pinnacles of the mountains, and have more or less effect upon hearts, as the teachers were led to personal watchfulness.

I might have talked to these wild men and women

till doomsday, and they would never have made the sacrifices they have made, but for the deep practical truths of the Bible. They loved dearly to have " Cruden's Concordance" talk to them, and would often ask me to take the Holy Figure Book, as they called it, which I always kept on the desk with the Bible.

Subsequently, after a year's teaching, I would ask the chiefs to name a subject for investigation, which they could readily do,—perhaps faith, perhaps love, mercy, or works, visiting the widow and the fatherless, using just weights; indeed, almost every kind of practical subject was taken up in our Bible readings. It was not merely Old Testament stories that we studied, or the miracles or revelations, but Corinthians, Romans, Galatians, Philippians, James, and John. The history of God's dealings with the Israelites was always made prominent, because this seemed to me eminently adapted to lead them to fear God and to trust Him, having always strengthened my own faith. Our favourite parts of the Bible were Exodus, Luke, John, Romans, and Corinthians.

The above are specimens of our manner of studying the word of God every week-day night, men, women, and children, for the last three years, until it seemed as if those who dwelt about the school-grounds grew so fast, we could almost see them grow in a " knowledge of the truth." This was the greatest consolation to us all when we saw them dropping away by cholera. Twenty-five of my Bible class, who had so delighted in studying about the " Light of the World," ascended up in two months' time to bask in that light for ever, and not one murmur, not a single expression of fear, as far as I could learn, escaped the lips of either.

"Are you afraid?" I asked them repeatedly, as I stood beside them and held the hands of those dying saints.

"No, mama. We know Christ will take us." What but the Inspired Oracles could have given such men such faith to die by? such a light through the shadows, such a life-belt for those deep waters?

It was one evening after we had been dwelling on the first and great commandment, that the wild Bghai met me on the steps with the striking remark mentioned at the opening of this chapter :—

"Teacher, I wonder if I can love the Lord with all my strength?"

He wished me to supply his men with rice, and ten men would remain a week and work on the Girls' Place, they buying their own curry. I was obliged to refuse.

Just then a little boy standing behind pulled his tunic, and whispered something low.

"I'll go and talk with my men," he said, hastily.

Half an hour passes. Back comes the chieftain, his little son beside him.

"We've talked it over," he said, "and Poquer says he and the boys will make some baskets and sell for rice."

A week or ten days go by, and looking up the road, a troop of Karens appeared, coming down in Indian file with eight or ten boys, each one's head piled with baskets towering up like little mountains, eight or ten on each head. Without stopping, they forded the river, waist deep, went to the bazaar, sold their baskets, bought their own rice and curry, and came and worked a week in clearing off the land. This is a single example of the practical manner in which these willing hearers applied the Scriptures to their daily lives.

CHAPTER VII.

CIVILIZING MOUNTAIN MEN—GETTING THE PRIEST OFF
THE DINING TABLE.

A COLONEL's wife, soon after she reached Tounghoo, was walking one evening with her husband, when they met a troop of Karens with their loaded baskets upon their backs and bamboo spears in hand.

On coming up the Karens never moved an inch out of the way ; but the leader, confronting the lady, reached out his hand, unwashed as he had come down the mountains. Knowing the English were their deliverers, he could not help giving his hand to any white foreigner he met. Mrs. H. was at first frightened at his wildness ; but the smile and earnest manner, pointing to his native hills, soon convinced her of his friendliness, and she was a lady of too much good sense to refuse : she shook hands with the whole troop, and they went on their way rejoicing, leaving the colonel dreadfully shocked at his wife's soiled gloves.

The colonel, on relating to me the incident, said, " I wish the Karens would learn what water is made for." I trust they are learning, but all the offensive habits of wild savage tribes are not to be altered in one generation.

It was the custom for every disciple to give the hand, but for four years they gave it just covered with earth or lime, any way. For a whole year after commencing the girl's school, I did not dare to speak of it; but when they came to know me so well as their friend, I ventured to suggest, very gently, that if they would lay off their loads and wash in the river before shaking hands, I should like it better. A few walked away, but generally after this they rushed for the river before giving the hand.

So with the pig-pens. Speaking of these, I wrote at that time :—

"One of the Board examines all round the place on Saturdays, and brings me a report. It encourages me not a little to see the pig-pens vanish. Last year the two men who first settled here put up pens right under their doors, according to their custom. I mentioned to the Nah Khan how offensive it was, and that hereafter we could not have them.

"'Oh, mama,' he exclaimed, 'if you do so, not a Karen will live here.'"

So I let it pass, and the pens remained just six months. When they were building new houses, or preparing for it, I mentioned the matter in the chapel. The next evening not one was to be seen under the houses.

The following is a letter from one of the Paku chiefs at this time concerning behaviour at the settlement :—

"I, Khan Poquai, one of the Institute Managers, to the Churches, greeting :

"DEAR BRETHREN,

"Chief Tekalai came to the Girls' Place and stopped two weeks, and went up to worship but two or three times, and two others with him. These three cannot remain on the place. They have brought no letters of introduction, and they go not up to worship.

"My dear brethren, the Teacheress tells us, and very wisely, if any come here to live, they must come with their families and goods, and remain permanently. If they do not this, they had better not come.

"Now, the Teacheress wishes for the good of all the people ; therefore think, I entreat you, of what God says in Matthew, 'If ye take not up the cross and follow me, ye cannot be my disciples.' Now, let us remember this all of us. We who believe, strive to follow Jesus Christ ; every one of us then must bear the cross.

"What is Jesus Christ's cross ? It is obedience to all His commands. Let us remember, brethren, *to do just as He has told us to do.*

"KHAN POQUAI."

The following are specimens of the recommendations brought by all the settlers :—

"Blessing and mercy rest upon the teacher for ever !

"DEAR TEACHERESS,

"I would say a word about our brother Thaboo, who desires to go and live near the Great Schools. Please receive him if he arrives, and instruct him in the truth. He wishes no help, will buy his own house with his own money, and take care of himself, and help build up the kingdom of God.

"TEACHER OF THE CHURCH OF WATHAKO."

"MY VERY DEAR TEACHERESS,

"Now, my brother Hauchu desires to go and live on the Girls' Place, and desires an introduction. He is not a bad man, a liar, or wanderer, or idler, but an honest person. Therefore, please receive him.

"LETTER OF THE CHURCH AT WATHAKO."

"MY DEAR TEACHERESS,

"I will tell you a word about our brother Tatha. Receive him, I pray you, for he is not one that loiters about doing nothing, but is a steady man, and worships, although not yet baptized."

Writing at that time, I remarked,

"The smiles of heaven attend us constantly, and sometimes I feel as if I could do nothing but thank God. If I could take the place of the poor woman who washed her Saviour's feet with tears, and wiped them with the hairs of her head, it seems to me it would be all I could ask. I do think the work here is one living *miracle*. I thought, possibly, after four or five years of toil, we might see Tounghoo teachers able to lead on and work efficiently; and lo, what I was looking away for down the future, we see before us."

The following is from Moung Po, a Shan magistrate:—

" My dear Teacheress,

"I will now tell you a few words about myself. Formerly, I was in great ignorance, and knew not right from wrong; but when I heard the Lord God's commandments from teacher Quala, I believed with all my heart. For two years I have been Nah Khan (private agent) to the Commissioner; but whether I am at home or travelling, I do not forget God.

"I have been out with the Commissioner now three months. He has paid me ninety rupees, and I put my heart in this way. Two months of it I will give to my wife and children to buy food and clothing; the remaining one month, thirty rupees, I will give to the Girls' School to help on the place."

"Can you give so much?" I asked on his coming down, when he replied solemnly,

"Yes, I can. *One-third is not too much for Christ.*"

"Teacher," he continued in his letter, "you tell me to learn Shan again, which I have nearly forgotten. I will do so, and although I follow the Commissioner, I will do all I can to help. I do not seek the riches or honours of this world. Do not think my heart is fastened to the things of this life.

"As my brethren pledge themselves to support the Girls' School, so will I do according to the Scriptures; and this I do with great glad heart, for the mercy and favour of God to me have been very great.

"May heaven bless and prosper the Teacheress."

The Shans came down into Tounghoo in great numbers. The women were pretty and interesting. I hired a Bassein Karen preacher to go among them for six months, and paid him from funds raised there by officers. He met with a good deal of favour.

I then applied to Government for an island lying in the Sittang river, to be set apart to a Shan Mission, and received permission to take a building site for a chapel and residence anywhere on the island. On reaching America, I pleaded for a Bible-reader to go to these Shan women to teach them from the word of God. I found more difficulty than I had expected in securing this. At length it pleased the Lord to remove every hindrance out of the way, and the Shan women have now one Bible-reader of their own in Tounghoo.

Generally the Shans are not willing to be instructed by a Karen. They look up to the Burmese, but down on the Karens. I once found a Burman ready to be taught by a Karen, and a Burman priest, too. We were in Monmogon, on the sea-shore of Tavoy, when a priest from Ava came in inquiring for the white Teacheress.

On my entering, he immediately took his seat upon the dining-table, in order to keep his head above that of a woman. Not quite approving that etiquette, I ordered a nice mat and pillow, which I always kept ready, such as they used at home. Finally, seeing me take a very low stool, and as I was very short, so that his head would still be uppermost, he sat down, though with a most supercilious air.

I handed him the Burman Bible. He desired to have me lay it upon the mat, as he could not receive anything from the hand of a woman, because her touch was defiling to his godship. For the purpose of benefiting his soul, if possible, I submitted, when he read for some two hours, turning from the Gospels to Corinthians, and everywhere, as if no stranger to the book.

"I cannot understand," he said, "this new birth. How should I ? Nobody ever explained it to me." He then allowed my Karen interpreter to explain and exhort, and seemed really to be groping after light. But then this interpreter was a remarkable man, a preacher of God's own making.

In September, 1852, from our sea-bungalow on the Indian ocean, I had written home thus :—"Burmah requires two or three hundred colporteurs—men and *women*—to go with the Bible in their hands and its spirit in their hearts, and thread these streets and mountain-passes, these rivers and nullahs, reading and explaining its sacred truths, and I have no doubt but this would be not only the speediest, but also the *cheapest*, way of converting the nations." Two months afterwards I went on a fortnight's trip up the Tenasserim river, in search of pupils, who would promise to become Bible-readers, both men and women.

"Mong Nong !" called out my head boatman one day, looking off toward the hills. Not a soul was to be seen, and I asked if he was calling the nats.

"No, mama; there is a strange man up here. He ought to preach. He has a big tongue—a very big tongue !"

Soon the wife of the great-tongued man appeared, her

arms full of sugar-cane and bamboo rice-sticks. The natives have a way of preparing rice for their journeys, by roasting it in the small joints of a particular kind of bamboo, which gives a peculiar flavour to the rice. A dozen of these can be stuffed into their wallet, and eaten with *chillie* or red pepper, or with bananas; and it is better than any pound cake, even to my own taste.

He and his wife were attending a great nat feast. Among the Karens the office of priestess is recognised as hereditary, and is held in profound esteem. They have a custom, too, which requires every member of a family to be present at their high festivals. These are family sacrifices, and are conducted with great solemnity. If a single member of the family is absent, or leaves the circle during the celebration of the rite, the charm is broken. Mong Nong and his wife had gone a great distance to attend, but in the midst of it the priestess seemed struck with horror. She threw down the sacrificial·knife, rushed around the room, down the ladder, and into the jungle. All looked on in silent amazement, and Mong Nong, while returning home, began to ask his wife what such a religion could be good for which a single individual could thus destroy. To the Divine Oracles he now resorted daily for several weeks, until fully convinced of the truth. He then led his wife to seek it. Both were converted, both passed through much persecution, and were the means of converting nearly all their families.

His bold, fearless manner, his fine, tall figure, and dignified bearing, made him seem almost like a second

Peter.*   It was this man who seemed to have a magic power over the Ava priest, and I trust Mong Nong will yet bring him to the heavenly world for a gem in his Master's crown.

In the evening Mong Nong was with us at the Bible class. We took up the parable of the talents. His spirit was moved to its depths. I said not a word to him about coming with me, but he began to confess. He said he had buried his talent; he knew he had sinned, and asked if he might accompany me to town as a Bible-reader and preacher ! He went, and for three months, as long as I could find support for him, that man was day and night proclaiming the Gospel among the Bur-mese of Monmogon.

* The man was so much respected, that even the priests would come out of their monasteries and extend their hands as he passed, because they saw he had power with God.

CHAPTER VIII.

"Hurrah ! Hurrah for Commissioner D'Oyly!" is
suddenly shouted from pinnacle to pinnacle, from glen
to glen, from river to river, and all over the Karen plains
of Tounghoo.

"Why is this?"

Because, by one stroke of the pen, Captain D'Oyly
has scattered food, raiment, and love among thirty thousand Highlanders; even two hundred thousand. A
few details will show how this was done.

The Karens had to bring down their loads of baskets,
mats, and pigs, and carry them across the river to the
market, in order to purchase food for themselves while
working on the school-grounds. At these times, the
ferrymen, taking advantage of their necessities, often ex-
torted presents or double fees. The authorized fees were
two annas for a load, or what a man could carry on his
back ; four annas for going and coming, if he remained
over night : no matter if the load was only one mat,
which he would have to sell for four annas, he must
pay the ferryman his two annas. Or suppose he had

P

eight baskets, the usual load, which would bring two
annas each ; these, in all probability, he would have to
spend all the afternoon in selling, then it would be too
late to buy salt and fish until the next morning, so he
must pay two annas for crossing each day, two baskets
out of his eight, or twenty-five per cent. on his barter,
just to cross the river. To this the people submitted all
the first year as of old without complaining ; but as
they were supporting themselves, and working for the
public good, it seemed to me a very hard thing that
those on the place could not take them across.

Finally, I represented the case to the Deputy Commissioner, asking permission to let them cross free in
the school-boat ; but the regulations then existing were
such that it was thought this would be injustice to the
ferryman. However, next April, at the time the ferries
were sold at auction, the Commissioner sent me the
following note :—

"MY DEAR MRS. MASON,

" I send you a copy of the Ferry Regulations. There is
a final clause which will satisfy the Karens, by which you
are permitted to lend your boat *Scot-free to travellers.*
                "GEORGE D'OYLY,
            "Deputy Commissioner, Tounghoo."

The final clause was :

" Parties are not debarred from using boats that may
be lent to them for the purpose of crossing, but no such
boats are to ply for hire."

The ferryman went up to court about it two or three
times, and even now goes up with a troop every time a
new ruler arrives; but it was just to him, as he purchased the ferry with the clause before him. He may
not have received quite so much, but the cause of education in Tounghoo was forwarded thereby by thousands
of rupees.

Upon this happy change, the Karens immediately
brought me in one hundred rupees to help pay the
school-boatman, and from that time all were free to cross
in the school-boats—an invaluable boon; and as the
news spread up the mountains, the very hills clapped
their hands for joy.

Even blessings, however, have their temptations. Not
very long after this favour was granted, one of the school
girls intimated to me that all was not right, but would
on no account tell me what was wrong. I called the
Nah Khan, and asked him to tell me truly, Was he or
the boatman taking hire for ferrying across the mountain Karens? He acknowledged the boatman had taken
trifling things *as presents* for taking them across, as mats,
betel-nuts, baskets, &c., and with his permission, because they came in *such crowds*. I told him I had
obtained the favour for them; the privilege must not be
abused.

Then came a heavy trial. If I screened them, every
one would say the great man can sin, and so can we. If
I exposed the wrong, disgrace must follow to us all, and
probably the Nah Khan would become an enemy to the
Girls' School. I was in deep distress, and knew not

which way to turn, for his power over the people was very great. It produced for a short time a conflict such as no one can realize, unless they can understand what it is to see the object of their heart's desire in imminent peril. But one morning I called the Nah Khan and the boat-master, and told them I must inform against them. They had transgressed against a Government regulation, and the Commissioner must be their judge. I did inform, and they were fined twenty rupees. They paid it, and begged me to forgive them. I told them yes, I could forgive; and as I knew they were not yet fully acquainted with God's law, I should pay them back the fine myself.

"We don't want it, mama; only forgive us," they answered.

I insisted on their taking it; and truly had they been flogged or thrown into jail, I do not believe it could have been half so great a punishment to them as it was for me to pay that fine. I never after heard of any delinquencies, and I believe the Nah Khan went off and put his into the mission box.

Having obtained this boon for the Karens, I proposed to them to establish a Young Men's School on the same land and on the same plan as the Girls' Institute. After much discussion and some fearfulness, they concluded to undertake the support of fifty young men for schoolmasters, the same number as they had insured of girls.

Amidst their shoutings for the Commissioner, they set about this, and soon erected a building a hundred feet in length. They built it entirely themselves, and added out-offices, and a house for the teacher, with a wooden frame.

Dormitories for the girls were also rebuilt, and a large airy school-hall, of course, all of bamboo.

There was, and must be, the most pressing call for the continuation of a Young Men's Normal School in Toun-ghoo. Imagine, reader, that you are looking to the east. You see a range of mountains rising in peaks like the Alps, one above the other, and extending through the whole province two hundred miles.

Now, please think of those numerous pinnacles, all capped with Karen hamlets, and the more distant, for ever making war upon the Christian settlements. On this account the schoolmasters can leave their schools only a few weeks at a time. They come down to study, are perhaps in the middle of Corinthians or Hebrews, and deeply interested. Down comes the chief:

" Teacher, I must have my schoolmaster. The people are beginning to use arrack again, or the enemy is coming. Our teacher must go back immediately."

At such times Mr. Mason always says to the teachers,—

" Go to God. Ask Him. What He tells you, that do." The result is, they immediately return for a week or two, quiet affairs, re-assure the chiefs, and preach to them all they have learned, and the truth, being fresh in their own minds, takes a deeper hold on the people. Then they say,—

" Now, chiefs, we have told you all we know, all that

the teacher has told us. Now we must go and get some more."

By this time the villagers are full of the subject, whatever it is, and they gladly part with the teachers again, and contribute for their support. Tounghoo must have Missionaries who can say,—" Come, brothers," not " Go." They want leaders who can come down and rise up at the same time. Sometimes the young teachers are liable to get high notions, and make the children carry about a stool for them to sit on above the people, as the wife of one did. They turned her out with her husband, and two others with them, men who had been uncommonly well educated, simply because of their city airs, and unwillingness to work with their own hands. They are independent Churches like the Congregational and Baptist Churches of America, and as they support their own preachers, Mr. Mason leaves them free to choose for themselves.

The Tounghoo people will eventually become the chief supporters of the Central College and Theological School in Rangoon ; but it is hoped they will themselves sustain the students they send, and thereby retain the fraternal relationship so desirable between the chiefs and their preachers.

" Tounghoo," Mr. Mason says, " should have the aid of all those who desire the extension of God's kingdom, because, while other missions are surrounded by culti- vated fields, and contain a definite number of persons for whom to labour, this one has no boundary on the north and east but the Great Desert and the Yellow

Sea, which comprise untold races among whom the banner of the Gospel is constantly waved forward.

Besides this region, there are others calling for our labours. The Government Surveyor in Arracan thinks we should reach the hill tribes there sooner than Burmese would, and offers to support two schoolmasters himself among the Kemmees.

The young schoolmasters of Tounghoo make great sacrifices in order to study. Usually they alternate,— the teacher on one pinnacle taking charge of one or two adjacent villages during the absence of their preachers, and they are indefatigable in their studies. Never *once* in that land have I had occasion to urge on either the young men or the young women, for they all seem perfectly *inspired* with a love of books, and really to *thirst* for knowledge.

There was an interesting incident connected with these bamboo school buildings. The chief proposed to cover one large house himself alone, and ordered off two of his men. In about a week we were looking out one day, when we saw something which looked like great bundles of grass winding slowly along the school ground. It proved to be a troop of *women* entirely enveloped in bundles of thatch. Throwing it upon the grass, they all rushed for the river, washed, dressed their hair, and came up to give the hand of friendship. Then they set to work to braid the thatch, and in a few days nearly a thousand leaves were prepared, which in the rains could not be bought of the thatch traders for less than thirty rupees. They had travelled, cut the thatch for themselves, and had brought it *upon their heads for not less than five miles.*

Mr. Mason taught the young men the Bible, mathematics, and preaching. He says, in a note dated October 23rd, 1858: " We went through Matthew, with part of Luke, the Acts, Romans, Hebrews, and First Book of Corinthians. Many learned the first principles of arithmetic, a few land-measuring, and I was surprised to find, at the close of the school, that some who had learned from Mrs. Mason's coloured maps had as good a knowledge of geography as they would have gathered from books in the same time, and could point to the principal countries, seas, cities, mountains, and rivers, as accurately as I could."

Very little praise did those invincibles deserve for all the mountains, seas, and rivers in their memories.

"Go and say over those names! That's a *girl's* study, isn't it?" they would remark.

" Yes, to be sure it is. Of course, men don't need to know the way from Kannee to Jerusalem. To-morrow you needn't come, brothers. Girls, recollect we have closed doors."

Thursday comes. I put up the diagrams and say, " Now we'll learn how the 'tortoise swallows the moon,' " and before the doors are open, the girls' eyes are all dancing with delight over their blackboard eclipses.

Next day, closed doors again. One girl is attempting to explain her tortoise, which makes some sport, when all of a sudden a burst of laughter from behind the mat doors and windows. We all feigned terrible indignation, but the morning after an embassy appears, with this entreaty :

" Won't the Teacheress let the young men come too ?"

There was no need of further urging them on to geography, and I never saw school children more delighted than they all were to learn how it was their feet did not fly off from " that star earth" whirling in the heavens.

We made our own tides too, as the tidal waves do not reach Tounghoo, with gourd worlds and orange zones.

The chiefs brought in money for the young men's board, an hospital was erected, a cook hired for them, and native teachers were appointed by the Board of Managers; but the teachers and schools were both in great want of slates and stationery. I had been seeking for them, and felt very sad when they came to me for such little things as a sheet of paper or a pen, and I could not supply them.

One day I called the pupils of both schools to pray for paper, pens, and slates for the teachers, that God's kingdom might be increased.

The mail comes in—a letter—Mr. Mason hands it to me—and I read—

" I have just forwarded two boxes of slates, containing twelve dozen, with paper, pens, threads, needles, knives, scissors, &c., for your two schools.—M. WYLIE."

Again, we were in great want of means to carry on operations. I called the girls to pray, and asked the

chiefs on the place to pray that God would send money
for the sawyers, so that we might build up the house for
His glory.

In the morning—letters—a draft for two hundred
rupees !

The following acknowledgment was returned to Mrs.
Wylie, of Calcutta :—

" MY VERY DEAR FRIEND,

  " Thanks be to the Most High Name, that you and
your dear husband are still permitted to stand between
India and Burmah.   I cannot say I thank Mr. Wylie—
it speaks too little ; but I will pray Heaven to reward
you all with that *peace* which our Heavenly Watcher
alone can give.   If you are in correspondence with
Major Edwards, or any of the kind friends who have
raised this money, do please tell them how timely their
help was, and the Great Treasurer will not forget their
interest."

The next thing in which we set about instructing
these wild men was making gardens.   In this they
manifested a good deal of zeal and enthusiasm, and
planted some two hundred palms, three or four hundred
betel-nut trees, three hundred plantains, with many
guavas, mangoes, and oranges.

They also planted a great many betel-leaf creepers,
which are very highly valued.   These, I believe, were
all stolen, with about a hundred of the plantains.

The palms all died but two, with many of the mangoes. I had been with them three miles down the river for many of these, standing all day in the rain, returning in the crowded boat at night, and to see our avenue trees die, did indeed cause us grief; but they will, I trust, in the end, succeed in making profitable gardens, and in raising fruit and vegetables enough for the schools.

There was every reason to believe the fruit-trees were killed by the heathen, for there was no end to the trouble they gave us, turning in buffaloes, breaking down fences, cutting off plantains, destroying roads, &c., and in many ways harassing the Karens, and if they attempted to defend their property, they were attacked, and even beaten, by the mongrel Hindu herdmen. At last the Saxon blood bubbled over again. My boys could not stand it, to see the Karens browbeaten and made dogs by heathen; they rose, called out all the boys of the district school, formed a body-guard, and armed them with bamboo swords, staves, whips, and lassos, and then woe to the buffaloes. The moment one showed his head on the place, the guard gave the alarm, when there followed a general chase on the part of the police, and a general stampede on the part of the buffaloes and their keepers.

It was no use now either reviling or pleading. The police generally returned leading up three or four heads of buffaloes, for each of which a fine was demanded of sixpence, and then, to teach them the law of kindness, they often let them off free. This course caused the little fellows days of hard running and weary watching, but it finally tamed the savages, so that they would even

come to them for protection from others, and in the end
they became ashamed of their own meanness. These
herdmen were from the Madras coast, and were calf
worshippers. One morning we found a great calf with
glass eyes set up in our chapel. They thought it a
public place, like a Burman zayat.

We had now seven short streets in our new settlement
around the schools, with elevated roads, usually twenty-
one feet broad, all made and drained, but we could procure neither stone nor bricks for them. Stones there
were none within several miles, and if the settlers attempted to take the most broken bricks from either the
old wall or ruined pagodas, they were driven away with
a vengeance. This brought forth a petition, based on
the fact that almost all our roads were *public*, and made
for the good of the Burmese as well as for the Karens.

The matter was long delayed, owing to the military
authorities possessing the wall. Finally, thus much was
secured to us :

" MEMORANDUM :

" I have given orders that brick from the town wall,
from spots not very near to any of the principal gateways, may be taken by Mrs. Mason for the construction
of a road on the opposite or east bank of this river.

                              " GEORGE D'OYLY.
" TOUNGHOO, *August* 15*th*, 1853.

The old dilapidated parts of the wall were being used
for roads, and had long been a general resource for all
other public purposes.

CHAPTER IX.

SEEKING TIMBER FOR THE INSTITUTE—TEACHING
PERSEVERANCE.

WHILE in Rangoon, before my return to Tounghoo, in
March, 1857, the thought occurred to me to ask Government for timber for the buildings, when Colonel Phayre
immediately gave it his sanction.

As soon as we had organized the Karen Education
Society, having made an estimate, I sent in a petition
to the Superintendent of Forests for two hundred and
twenty-five logs, large and small. This was objected to
as being an unnecessarily large amount, when I had to
write and explain that it was for no ordinary school-
house, but an institution with dormitories, &c. But in
order to get the work begun, I changed my petition,
asking for an immediate grant of fifty large logs, and
added the petition in the form prescribed. This was
allowed, with the promise that I should have more when
needed.

On receiving the grant, the chiefs met to see what
should be done about getting it in—a real Herculean task
to their inexperienced hands. However, they chose
two of their principal chiefs—one for the Bghais and

Mopagas, and one for the Pakus and Mauniepagas, to look out the trees, and see that every village bore its proper share of labour, and if any one failed, the village was to be assessed as the two heads should decide.

They went out by dozens and by twenties, working a month at a time, supplying their own elephants and mostly their own provisions.

Finally, November arrived, the water began to fall, and only four or five logs of timber had reached the school-ground. If the river became very low, it would be impossible to float the logs, and we should be delayed a whole year longer, before anything could be done towards the building.

"Mama! mama!" exclaims Maukie, puffing with all his might.

"What is the matter?"

"Thai Goung"—the Tree Chief—"has taken all our logs!"

"Why so?"

"He says we've cut sixty, ten more than you told us."

"Call up the head men."

"Yes, we have, but they did'nt understand."

"No! Jauque don't know. We've done no such thing." So here was a dispute that ended in the Karens declaring I must go up and see for myself, or they would abandon the work.

The Burmese were annoyed that the Karens should be allowed teak like themselves for school buildings, so the Goung had circulated the report that the Karens were paying no regard to orders, but had felled ten trees

more than the grant allowed. On this plea the Burman
Forest Superintendent seized upon the whole lot, and
confiscated all for Government; precisely as the Burmese
are in the habit of doing in their own territory with
timber merchants and others. A Karen merchant, a
friend of mine, thinking he could make money faster,
went up into Burmah, had an audience with the King
himself, (so he declared,) and contracted for a large teak
forest, or the privilege of working it for five years. The
King gave him a golden umbrella and the title of Chief
Forest Goung, supplied him with elephants, and greatly
honoured him. Of course, the ruse took, foresters flocked
to the golden *Tee*, and great numbers joined in the
enterprise. The Chief Forester borrowed money largely
to support his men, and at last the timber was all down
to the water's edge, several thousand logs of beautiful
teak.

"Ho, stop there!" halloos a red-sashed peon, riding
up in great haste, armed and frowning.

"What is it?"

"The King forbids the removal of his timber."

Of course, all work comes at once to a dead stop.
Dismay is pictured on every face.

Off rides the golden Umbrella, several days' journey
up to court. The King doesn't know him; no audience.
The Sandozain sends him with his petition to the Sandegan. The Sandegan thinks there must be a mistake.
It is the Nah Khangyee he wants. This functionary
can take no note of the matter. It does not belong
to him. He had better go to the Minister of the In-

terior.　All this time work is at a stand-still, and debts increasing.

Bribes, bribes are wanting.　He must bribe, and that largely too, from the Woongyee down to the lowest peon. The Karen found these largesses would amount to more than half the value of the timber, the costs of working, felling, and transportation to the other half, and he was penniless.　The timber was still on the shore, and the poor fellow in a Burman jail, when I left the country.

This is simply a specimen of the Burmese system of extortion.　So our Kannee Timber Goung no doubt intended to build himself a snug little house out of the Karens' teak.　Convictions to this effect are expressed to the Deputy Commissioner—that it is all a Burman trick.　He does not believe it, but writes :

" MY DEAR MRS. MASON,

" Bring in the logs at once by all means.　I will send an order to the Goung of the district that he is to let them go when your men come for them.　You know that fining you (I had begged him to fine me,.if they had done wrong, and not punish them) would be fining myself and all others interested in your labours.　The Superintendent of Forests must be the judge.　In the meantime, use the fifty logs."

Now the matter had to be investigated.　Burmese Reporters would all go with the Goung.　Karen chiefs were too careless, and too easily browbeaten by their enemies.　None had strength and zeal combined enough for the work.　Therefore, in order to save the character of the Karen Christians from destruction, I undertook, with my husband's consent, to go over the forest, and count every log myself.

The following is my journal forwarded to him :—

"I betook myself to the boat, and had just started when the clouds began to thicken, and it soon came pouring down, and rained incessantly for twenty-four hours. At night we found lodgings in the verandah of a semi-Burman house, for the woman refused to give us any other quarters. Everything was wet through, over-dress and all, except my pillows. We spread them out, took a supper of cold fowl and bread, talked a long time with the family concerning the Christian religion, sung a hymn, had prayers, and sat down to write, but fell asleep at the fifth word. I had been asleep perhaps half an hour, when, 'Bow wow! wow!' sounded close to my ears. I aroused up, and found I had companions in two jackall-looking dogs, which had crept up there to escape the rain, as I had myself.

"The second morning the rain was still pouring. The river, the boatmen said, was so swollen, it would be impossible to stem the current. We could reach the timber-camp by noon on foot, but we had not proceeded twenty steps before I was just as wet as a drowned chicken, and speedily returned to the boat.

"They were heathen boatmen, and thought, as I was a woman, my standing in the rain was of no conse-quence. The river was a real mad river; deep, and scooped out as if it had dug graves for every careless passer-by. But the bottom was covered with white pebbles, and the water so clear, we could see every little fish on the bottom, just what he was about.

" There are no lofty mountains flanking the stream here, but the forest is very old, and its beautiful trees have their leaves of every possible form, and of every shade of green.

" Then there came the rope-plants—the nymphs of the forest, so gracefully looping up the creepers all along the shore, studded with blue, yellow, and purple blossoms.

" The poor boatmen had to be half the time in the water when we reached the rocky bed of the stream, urging the boat from side to side, from snag to snag, waist deep, and often pulling us right under a clump of knife-edged fan-palms, or, still worse, under the long, ponderous cables of the rope-trees that grated over our heads, to the imminent risk of turning us all into the water.

" As soon as we reached the camp, I started with one of our Karen Board of Managers on an elephant, crossed the river, and began to climb ; and climb we did indeed, for nearly an hour,—now down through a deep ravine, then up again, until we reached the summit of a mountain far distant.

" ' Dear me ! not far enough yet ?' I asked.

" ' No, mama.' So down we plunged again into a deep, deep gorge, and there, between two almost perpendicular ridges, lay one of the monster logs that had been such a trouble to them. Around this three or four more, all too large to be ever pulled up the mountain, or through the gorge. The Karens have tried to hire the Burmese to saw them in two, but they demand four rupees each, so they are putting forth their own skill; and they wanted me to see their management.

" I don't much enjoy tramping over these jungles myself, or having the Karens do it, for I half expect a tiger-leap at every turn. Still we are going in another direction to-morrow, where I am told a few trees have been felled, a whole day's journey there and back. Good night. I'm going to read Deut. xii. 7; will you please tell the boys to read Luke xiii. 19 ?"

Mr. Mason writes in reply :

" Teacher Kouk-kay has written a letter for the Karen *Star*, in which he says : ' Mama Mason makes exceeding strenuous efforts for Tounghoo. In order that the people may get wisdom, she is planning the erection of a large building for girls to study in. The teacheress has now gone into the jungles to exhort the people to bring down the timber quickly. Moreover, the Commissioner desires us to learn, and to this end HE helps her.' So you see your labours are *not unappreciated by the natives*."

This I repeat, reader, not because God favoured me, but the *work*, and, therefore, it came like a little olive-leaf to my weary heart; indeed, I could not help regarding it as an answer to prayer, for this young preacher was one who had opposed the Girls' School. Indeed, he had been the strongest opposer, lest they should fall under woman's government.

Those Kannee Wide Awakes ! With a shout and a

rush they mustered on the sand-beds in the Kannee creek, in the moonlight, and formed themselves into small companies of tens and twenties, chose their own leaders, and filed off in ranks right and left, ready for action.

" Do you, officers, agree to command, each of you, the men under you ?"

" We do."

" And do you, soldiers, agree to *obey* your captains ?"

" Er, er. We will obey."

This questioning was the duty assigned to me, for mama must review the company.

The scene was to them extremely exciting, and to me very cheering.

For two months the Karens had been at work trying to get in the timber for the school-house, yet not half the roads had been cut, nor half the logs even found.

They were so undisciplined. Each set of men would obey only its own chiefs, and if their own chiefs were absent, they would obey nobody. So the chiefs, being each independent, had no idea of yielding to one another ; consequently, the works progressed very slowly.

As soon as I reached the jungles, I suggested this military kind of order, and from that time the work went on so rapidly, they were astonished at themselves, but they needed instruction in almost every department. Mechanics they had no idea of, and I found they invariably attempted to drag logs up high mountains the small end upwards, and it was not without a good deal of reasoning that I could induce them to change.

As concerned roads, too, the idea of cutting a smooth path for a mile or two more for two or three logs seemed an intolerable burden, so they tugged against snags and crags. Sometimes I would find them on a high mountain, just in time to save elephant and rider from certain destruction, as in one instance when they barely escaped. They had reached a part of the road, lying immediately over a precipice of seventy feet or more, and the road just sloping enough to give the log a cant downwards, when nothing could have saved them. A mere boy was on the elephant's neck, who knew nothing more than to trudge on straight before his eyes. I advised the captains to appoint one of the cleverest men to attend each elephant, with two clearers to watch and repair the roads.

The consequence was, they were able to drag as many logs in a day as they had been before in a week.

CHAPTER X.

LIFE IN THE WOODS—HOW TO MAKE BRAVE MEN.

THE following conversational letters to the President of the Karen Education Society of Tounghoo give glimpses of life in Kannee at this time :—

"KANNEE JUNGLE.

"MY DEAR MR. PRESIDENT,

"I almost think you will break the tenth commandment, and covet my rural pleasures. Yesterday I determined to show the Karens that perseverance would conquer all difficulties, so started with a guide, six or eight Karens, and three elephants, to find some fifteen logs which have been felled in the depths of the forest, several miles inland, and which, report said, '*would not move.*'

"After crossing streams three or four times, then a deep miry plot, where at every step the elephants sunk up to their bodies, we resorted to a wood road, and thankfully enough, for I was greatly frightened lest we should sink entirely. On the wood road we travelled some two hours, then turned into a deep, thorny jungle, and wandered on for two hours more, cutting our way at every step, till at last our guide cried out,—

" ' Hai mat—lost ! ' and finally acknowledged that he
had never been to the place. It was then twelve or one
o'clock ; I sent a party forward to reconnoitre, while we
tethered the elephants to browse. After two hours the
party returned, with the report that they had found five
logs, but not the slightest path, and so far in, we could
not possibly cut our way to them and return that night.
Seeing in their looks a strange dislike to proceeding, I
thought it better to take Franklin's advice.

" ' Stoop, stoop,' so told the men to do quickly just
what they pleased. Of course, the elephants were turned
back, and I sunk down in the houdah, thinking what
could be the design of such a lesson of disappointment,
and finally concluded that neither the Karens nor their
teacher had yet wreathed their brows with Job's laurel,
when suddenly down shot a ponderous creeper from its
airy swing upon my head. As soon as I could collect
my scattered senses, out stole two or three long thorny
fingers and caught my hat, and, when I resisted, clung
with all seeming malice at my fingers.

" The Karens compassionated my head, but I begged
them not to pity my head, but my heart—that I was so
ashamed to go back with three elephants, and without a
single log. To attempt to do a thing and not do it !
Upon this, every head drooped, and all were silent for
some time. Finally, the chief said,

" ' Let not mama be sad. Monday night there shall
be a good straight road every step of the way through to
the timber.'

" ' Yes,' responds another. ' And we 'll come and

sleep here till every log is in.' And they kept their word, dragging down triumphantly every log felled.

"But I was going to tell you of our Sabbath in the wilderness, when we all 'went up into the mountain to pray.'

"Last Sabbath morning we assembled on the top of a hill, in a bamboo grove, over-arching so as to form a most lovely pavilion. There we spread our mats, and sung our Karen psalms, making the hills and glens echo to native airs. I took up the parable of the feast in the fourteenth of Luke, explaining to them how the Gospel was first preached to the Burmese, but they, having neglected it, had caused the Missionaries to turn to the Karens. Then directed their thoughts four years back, to the first time they ever heard the name of Jesus. Again to the subject of the evening before. 'Seek ye first the kingdom of God and His righteousness, *and all these things shall be added unto you*,' making them tell over themselves the various ways in which God had shown them that He knew their need, and had provided for it. I assure you there was not a dull eye or a vacant expression among the whole audience. Then attention was called to the remainder of the parable, showing that it was their duty now to go after the savage Bghais, and 'compel them to come in.'

"'Aye, but the preachers must do that,' they answered. 'The Lord commanded His servants, the little teachers.'

"Then they had to learn how the order was for all, and how *they* were doing it by building a house in which

to educate teachers just as much as the teachers themselves. I even impressed upon them that every log of
teak or iron-wood post they secured was calling just
so many of the halt and blind. They came down the
hill greatly animated, the young men saying one to
another,—

"'I didn't understand all that was said, but I shall
try and call two of the blind ones to-morrow'—that is,
obtain two logs for the school-house.

"'And I shall try and get three.' And so on, and
so on ; and the next day they did work, as if their very
lives depended upon it.

"I mention these little things that you may know
your people, and the power that will move them ; while
flogging would only crush and wither every upspringing
of self-respect. *Flog* Christian soldiers! I was so indignant to hear it suggested to you. If I could have
my wish, that degrading punishment should be banished
from military life, from sailor life, and from all civilized
bodies.

"A short time before, they had asked if we shouldn't
give up, and not try to find the logs.

"'Englishmen never give up,' I answered, which
created a smile, but nothing moved them to a firm resolution, until the appeal to their own self-respect. So
you see what material you have for *soldiers*. Forcing
might have pressed them on for a time, but would not
have accomplished this work ; while a single appeal that
touched their hearts brought every log. The Karens
will never make soldiers good for anything, unless their

leaders are men of *moral power*.   Order and discipline
belong to school-boy lands.   Of course, we ought not to
expect it here among men just redeemed from barbarism ;
but when I look around upon one and another, whom I
know to be as noble, self-sacrificing men as ever lived,
fasting all day themselves and giving their food to
others, of which they are capable, in order that a Christian school might be established,—when I think of this,
and then remember how these men looked and spoke the
first time they came to visit us, I cannot express my
joy.

" *Thursday.*

" Oh, me ! if it would not tire the patience of Job, to
sit here on the ground hour after hour, and watch a
dozen men hack, hack, hack, on a single log, with a
single axe, just big enough to cut off a squirrel's ear.
They won't use a bigger one, although I have bought
three for them.

" But I was going to give you a chapter for your
history of Tounghoo, and will begin with my beautiful
glen.   You should have been here this morning to see a
Kannee sunrise ! so lovely, grand, and exhilarating !

" Just picture yourself on a bluff forty or fifty feet
high, standing under a lofty canopy of arching branches
interlocked, from which run down rafters, and beams,
and pillars of long woody creepers.

" Then there are such Swiss-looking windows, cur-
tained with green leaves, here and there looped up on
one side by a twisted gray cord-plant and tassel, while

the other side is thrown open. Our front is an arched portico about fifteen feet high, of heavy cord-plant spanning clear over the cliff. Now we see away down the bluff large overhanging acacias, tasseled with a thousand pendants, looking into the sweet little Wechaduc creek all buried in shadow. Then, turning to the left, we have a deep winding gorge, brimfull of sunshine, gushing along the sides of the rocks, now glancing over the waters, anon dancing around them as if held by the spell of their murmuring music, as they warble along round the base, while other beams shoot out, colouring whole showers of golden leaves, across the glen or the trembling foliage upon the opposite mountain. Now cast your eye along the lofty forest, striped with white-barked lagerstrœmias, and you lose the stream for a moment, then catch it again winding lazily down, and going to sleep in a cove overhung with bowering fan-palms.

"In the fore-ground, right over a jutting point below the cliff, where the little creek falls into the Kannce river, stands my lodge in the wilderness. It is a booth ten feet square, covered with wild plantain leaves, and enclosed with nature's own palisade of reeds and grasses.

"We want a moon, and then the night view would be picturesque enough ; for on the opposite shore stand four large, wild gipsy-looking huts full of mountaineers, boiling their chatties, roasting fish, lounging, and singing over their camp-fires in all manner of classical attitudes ; while torch-lights are streaming up on to their brown faces and happy eyes, their striped kilts

and red turbans; and meanwhile the pebbly creek goes
ripple, ripple,

> 'Faint and low, faint and low,
> To and fro, to and fro ; '

till all thought of teak, hills, and tigers dies away in its
mesmerizing lullaby."

" To MY DARLING BOYS :

" You can't think what a nice, cozy nest I have,
encamped on one side of a crooked little brook under a
few plantain leaves.

" My house is quite sumptuous, I think, for Kannee !
I divide it—that is, in imagination—into bed-room,
bath and receiving-rooms, for you must know, I hold a
levee here every morning. Then during the day it is
Kannee Court-house. What would the Commissioner
say to this ? Don't you think he would be looking
after the Stars or the Eagle's beak ?

" At evening my hall transmutes itself into a chapel,
and so ends the day. The brook is murmuring its
little psalm. The peacocks are screaming out like
muezzins in the mountains, and all else is still.

" This is just the most coaxing little brook I ever
heard. It reminds me of one that used to go singing
past my bed-room window away under the old birches of
Vermont, when I was a wee thing, ten years old—the
very brook in which I was baptized. I have always
loved that brooklet ; its sound goes with me like a thread
of silver, soft and soothing through my life.

" Do you know, boys, I have some other music here

—a Kannee band of frog screnaders ? One would think
the creck full of bassettos, tenors, and altos, calling and
answering from shore to shore. I should think the
cicadas might join in for sopranos. Now, if you don't
know these big words, look in the dictionary."

"Little things again!" Yes, friend reader, don't
you like little things ? I do. Life is made joyous or
painful by little things. Its little pauses are more to us
than its great capitals. The delicate turn, the unseen
glance, the sympathetic smile, a single strain from some
old song, affects us more than the grandest orations and
ovations.

It was the most painful part of my work for the
Karens that I was obliged to be so much away from my
husband. But here again God cares for us ; for he was
kept in better health than he had enjoyed for *fifteen*
years !

" My DEAREST HUSBAND,

" When you can spare the boys, I wish you would let
them shoulder their bags, and come over here with the
Karens. They can march it, and reach here at night.
Tell them to put up one suit each, with one loaf of
bread each, and two pounds of roast beef, for the journey, with two bundles of plantains, a little salt, and
their umbrella. They would have a world of enjoyment,
and never forget it. Tell them to keep *between* the
Karens, not before or behind, lest the tigers eat
them up.

"I have some most valuable men here—self-sacrificing souls as ever lived, who will do anything to get the logs. Our work is going on beautifully now, and I hope will come to an end next week, Saturday, but that is uncertain. We can only drag three logs a-day, with the best possible will, they are so far away ; and you know we had *fifty teak* to get, and *seventy-four ironwood.* Don't go away before I come back."

The following letter reached me at Kannee from the Pant-Bghai country.

"MY DEAR TEACHBRESS WHO LOVES US,

"That which I wished for exceedingly you have sent me—books, pens, and paper—things which I love best. When I saw them, I held them up in the presence of all, and the children rejoiced with me ; the elders were also very glad, and their faith increased.

"The people of this village come every day to worship God, although they have no chapel ; but they are much afraid, and keep themselves armed, lest their enemies should try to kill them while at worship. Therefore, pray that love may increase among this people, who are still pagans. One of the villagers has been to the girls' place and seen the work, and heard of the plans for the Karens, and has come back and told us a great deal, until the hearts of all the villagers are very hot. When I heard about it, I raised my heart to God thus :—' Oh God, stretch out thine arm, and help mama to complete her undertakings speedily, I beseech thee.' "

San Quala at this time sent me his kind remembrance :

" MY DEAR FRIEND MAMA,

" May the great love and peace of the Almighty God rest upon you and your pupils—girls and boys—for ever !

" Teacheress, I know you do not forget us. Do you think I have forgotten you ? I have not—not for a moment. I learn everything about your schools and doings. Your power of doing is very great. I cannot forget, I remember you always, and as God blesses your work, my heart is exceedingly happy.

" You have increased our strength with bread, sugar, and cocoa-nuts, which we have received—a very great gift—besides the ten rupees to buy a goat for our babe. Do not feel anxious about us in the least. Everything I need the Christians supply with a free will. There is nothing in this world that I want, except that I may go and preach Christ, so that souls may be saved—this is on my heart continually. But my wife and child are sick all the time, and this shuts me up at home and makes my heart very sad. Because it is the judgment of heaven, I try to endure it. Pray for me, dear Teacheress.

" QUALA."

This I received as a great answer to prayer. Mr. Mason had told me if Quala opposed the girls becoming schoolmistresses, he did not think it would be of any use to try, as he would not be likely to change his mind when once determined. Thanks to the Almighty, who can turn *all* hearts, he did change from a state of indifference to feel a lively interest in the work, and subsequently did all in his power to help us on. I believe that God will yet influence many others to follow his example.

CHAPTER XI.

HUNTING FOR IRON WOOD POSTS—CONQUERING DIFFICULTIES.

"Qua au! Qua au!" Look out! Look out! cry the Karens one to another. "Tigers in this jungle."

Scarcely are the words spoken, when :—

"Ka! Ka!" Tiger! tiger! screams the forester at the head of our little party.

I had wandered all the day before, and found only five suitable trees. Again we had started on foot through streams and thickets, morasses and thorns, and up at last on to a high ridge of table-land. I walked, as it saved them the trouble of cutting the way for an elephant, whose houdah is so high. We were ascending, tired, and slowly, yet another last hill, dreaming of our solitary work, when all came to a dead stop with this dread scream. It was not a tiger, but a leopard, right in our path. The Karens set up a tremendous whoop, and the beast trotted off very deliberately. A day or two after I saw a small one, as I was upon the elephant. It was walking leisurely along the valley, a few rods distant from me, and looking up as if doubtful whether to notice our intrusion.

R

There was a beautiful teak log, larger than could be drawn away, seven and a-half feet in girth, on the side of a hill ; so one of the managers dug out a little saw-pit, and contrived by his own wit to get the log over it, and saw it through *lengthwise;* this was the first time he ever sawed a foot, and, of course, I had to go and encourage him. Another time I taught them the use of the wedge, by which they saved two other fine logs.

Floating the timber was the next great task ; for the Karens had not one of them learned to swim, and never floated a log before in their lives. They often lost their turbans, and were nearly losing themselves too, but they would not have a Burman to help them. Their self-respect was aroused, and they were determined to show that they could perform great deeds as well as Burmese. An instance of this national pride occurred once near our door. The bank of the river caved in, burying a very valuable teak boat ; several Karens attempted to raise it, but failed, so I sent for a Burman. Poquai, the Paku member of the Board, hearing this, hastened over with a picked number of Karens, asking,—

" Shall God's men call for heathen to help them in such a little thing ? "

I paid the Burman, and dismissed him. In about two hours Poquai brought up the boat, when all looked at me with such laudable triumph and satisfaction, that I felt really proud of them. The very next night the boat for which we had paid forty rupees was missing, and we never heard of it again. Probably the Burman knew where it went to. This makes the *fourth* that has been taken from us, or been lost, since commencing these schools.

Our fifty teak logs, when spread out on the school land, were worth one thousand rupees, and the Burmans could not help regarding them with covetous eyes. So when the timber Goung came to make his report to Government, he seemed determined to make out that the Karens had exceeded the number granted to them. I measured every foot of the logs with him, and pointed out where one had been cut into two parts. Still he sent in his report, counting the sawed and split logs *as two*. This led to a report on behalf of the Karens.

I wrote thus to Captain D'Oyly :—

"*14th July*, 1858.

" Sir,

" I shall feel greatly obliged if you will do me the favour to express to Government my most sincere thanks for this gift to the Institute, and to all who have aided me in obtaining it. In answer to the kind inquiry how much more will be required, I would say, the timber already granted will not be nearly enough for the school-house alone, without dormitories. I would, therefore, beg you kindly to recommend a further grant, *provided* that the Government will allow us to defray the cost of felling, and floating into town, from the amount of timber granted. Without this permission the grant would now be quite useless to me, as I could not command the means to pay for its transportation, and the Karens, having lost two of their elephants,

R 2

would not feel able at present to make any further effort. Owing in part to their inexperience, the Kannee timber was pointed out in the most difficult places possible, in the deepest gorges, and on the tops of the highest pinnacles, so that it cost us severe labour, and many months of time, with three elephants and a hundred men, to obtain it; and then nearly one-half of the logs had to be cut or sawed in pieces. I would, therefore, ask if a further grant be made, that it should be given in localities accessible in the dry season by water, and that the Goung be ordered to give us *sound* timber.

"I am, Sir,
"Your humble servant,
"Ellen B. Mason."

The following was Col. Phayre's immediate reply, ordering the Goung to give us *standing trees*, which would ensure good timber.

"D. Brandis Esquire,
To the Superintendent of Forests in Pegu, Rangoon.
"Sir,
"With reference to Mrs. Mason's request, in a letter dated 14th July, 1858, for a further grant of one hundred and twenty-five logs of teak timber, for the purpose of completing the Karen Female Institute, and your remarks thereon in your proceedings, dated 14th instant, I have the honour to inform you that, under the special circumstances of the case, the Commissioner has

been pleased to accede to Mrs. Mason's request, and desires that the timber may be made over to her as required.

"*9th Oct.*, 1858."

Besides the teak, we had to get in a hundred iron-wood posts. The heads of tribes reported them all felled, each village having felled its share, some twenty, some forty logs; but all they brought in were as crooked as serpents, and they could do no better, they said, unless I went with them. It was in February, and very hot; but again I walked twelve miles, over mountains and gulfs, and not a single straight log could be found. I went into my hut too tired to speak, threw myself on the mat, and poured out my despair to God. The Karens saw without a word that I was distressed, and that made them wretched. With heavy hearts we assembled that night.

I tried to be cheerful, but dwelt on the loss of respect-ability which would follow to the Karen chiefs, and the triumph the Burmese would feel, on comparing the posts of Jesus Christ's kyoung with theirs. I avoided, how-ever, asking them to cut any more posts. I had not spoken long, when the two head chiefs stepped forth and harangued the people with so much effect, they all voted to fell a *hundred* more, on condition that I would select them!

No small task this to go over all these mountains again, and find a hundred straight *iron-wood* trees. The next morning I set out, though as with a leaden weight upon my heart, with a large company impatient for the work.

I soon found three beautiful trees as straight as a plumb-line, but from four to five feet in girth around the base.

"Oh, mama, our people could *never* hew down *iron-wood trees!*" the chiefs exclaimed in dismay. Iron-wood is the hardest timber known, and so hard, it is seldom used except for house posts. At last they found that in no other way could they get them long enough or large enough for such a building, and they determined *to try*. Guess at the task—*eight men* had to work *three hours*, relieving one another, before they got down a single one of these trees. Then it took twenty men *two days* to hew it down at the base to the required size. In this way I passed over the ridges where iron-wood was found, leaving five and six to battle with each tree, as far as I could persuade them to join the battle at all. So we continued for two weeks before we counted up the whole number.

The Mopagas and Bghais were on the point of giving up, and some did; but the Pakus and Mauniepagas persevered, exhorting their weaker brethren with great gentleness, and at last the tremendous task was accomplished. Then came the dragging or hauling, almost the hardest work of all, for some of the best logs we had found were in the most inaccessible places. Four of them were fifty feet long without the slightest crookedness, and one day we sent for one of these far into the deep forest. Through ignorance or carelessness, when I was not with them, they had felled this one so as to let the top fall up the cliff, leaving the large end downwards, on the side of a mountain and over a tremendous gorge. After a long consultation, it was resolved to hitch the elephant to the large end, and try and turn it half round, so as to bring it to lie horizontally across the mountain, instead of perpendicularly, that we might drag it off, ascending circuitously. Not knowing in the least what men of sense would do in such a dilemma, I allowed them to try this ; but no sooner had the elephant moved the log, than it began to slide, pulling the beast down after it, and we stood horror stricken, thinking it must be dashed over the precipice, rider and all, when it was stopped by a large clump of bamboos. The rider, a brave boy, had succeeded in leaping off, and as soon as possible the tackling was cut, and the poor elephant released. But it was so frightened, it could never be made to pull any heavy weights afterwards.

The next day we started again with two elephants, two large iron chains, and provisions for two days, deter-mined still to have the log ; so they put up a wigwam of bamboo branches, and by my continual urging and calling, I succeeded in getting all up from the gorges, with their water jars and fire-wood, before dark, for tigers, we knew, roamed over all that forest. The most diffi-cult to get in was old Kargau. He had dug out one of those pretty, flesh-coloured bandicots as large as a kitten, broken its legs, and stuffed it into his wallet, to suffer all day till it should be spitted alive.

I sent my assistant to kill it. The mountaineer

thrust him roughly away. I persisted, and it was at last put out of its misery, but the owner never forgave it. They tell me it is the practice everywhere either to keep their small game alive or strangle it, so as to retain the blood.

Perhaps the Apostles found it as hard to train the Antioch Christians. As we assembled that evening under the bamboo arches upon the mountain, I called the assistant to read Acts xv. 20, and we had quite a warm discussion on the subject. All agreed with me that it was wrong, except old Kargau, who had the bandicot. He would not give up. Perhaps the others would not if they had found any game, but it so happened that he was the only one that caught a bandicot that day.

Toads and frogs they serve in the same manner, and toad-hunting is very common. The toads are beat up by scraping the bare foot over the grass, when the toad will hop or croak, and the hunters pounce upon it at once, or give chase, break its legs, and clap it alive into their bags. Snakes, too, skinned alive, they stuff wriggling into their bags for supper; and I really think it has cost me more labour to change these cruel practices than it ever did to learn a new language.

Tired and nervous, but not discouraged, my boys and I spread our mats and lay down, praying earnestly that God would teach me, that I might teach them how to obtain the log. Then we made another trial. We took two very strong elephants, placed them above two large deep-rooted trees, and hitched two long chains;

then some twenty men shouted to the beasts with such vehemence, they gave a tremendous pull, and, being goaded on, up came the prize, stretched horizontally across the hill, right above the great teaks, entirely clear from the fearful abyss beneath. When the Karens saw the elephants were safe, and the log positively secured, they gave one long mountain shout of joy, after which we all knelt and gave thanks to God. The same day we hauled it up the mountain, and the next day into the water.

The Burmese, when they saw it, said such a log could not be bought for a hundred rupees, that it could not be found, and no Burman ever did or ever could get such a log, or would even make the attempt.

The poor elephant that was frightened belonged to the Girls' School, and cost me four hundred rupees. Her name was Poma, and she was so gentle, we could always ride on her with safety. She knew my voice like a child, and would put her trunk into my boys' bedroom window every morning for a plantain. They could do anything with her. She would kneel down at their bidding, put out her leg for them to climb up, or hand them water when they were thirsty, and she delighted in carrying them across the river on her neck ; of course, they were very fond of *Poma*, and were always making up nice bits of barks or tamarinds and salt for her, but one day she was brought home sick. She laid her trunk on the ground, and tears positively ran down her face ! The boys and girls were very sad. I sent for a Burman doctor, and took her to our own yard.

Finally, she seemed better, and was taken off to browse among young bamboos, of which they are so fond. But a few days had passed when they sent to me in haste, saying Poma had fallen down, and was too weak to get up. I went to her some two miles. As soon as she heard my voice, she stretched out her trunk towards me, and moaned as if asking for sympathy. The Karens brought two stout elephants to raise her up; but she could not stand, though she took food and drink from my hands, and from the girls and boys, while she would take from no others; but, alas, she could not swallow, and as soon as we were gone, she rolled it all out upon the ground, having taken it from simple attachment, so I begged the men to shoot her. Her tusks brought forty rupees, but they often sell for eighty rupees.

After five different encampments, absorbing six weeks of time, we succeeded in getting all the logs, with bamboos and ratans to raft them down to the mouth of the Karen river.

I had delayed until nearly dark superintending matters, and then found the elephant left for me was an ugly brute that I did not dare mount. There was but one chief remaining behind, but he and his two men set to work and made me a bamboo raft three feet wide. On this they poled me down that wild, mad river, about six miles to our own camp. The following is a letter written to my friend Mrs. Wylie at this time :—

"I have felt very sad about spending time in the jungles, traversing pathless mountains and glens in search of timber, but now I see the hand of God leading me onward, for in no other way could I have come so near the hearts of the people, or been made acquainted with their individual characters. Now I know whom to trust, and how each can be made useful.

"I am thankful that I was able to be with them, for it cheered them not a little, taught them to think and reason more correctly, and through God's mercy prevented sickness. During the last week many came in here to see the logs and look upon them with great delight and satisfaction. No doubt it will be far better for the people that they have had to work hard for the timber, for had I purchased it, they never would have valued it half so much. Now they are pouring down to settle round the Institute.

"It was one of the most interesting nights I ever spent, when we encamped at the mouth of the Kannee river after more than three months of hard toil, six weeks of which I had spent with them ; now there lay the logs, strung to bamboos, filling the river.

"A hundred Karens were stretched around six or eight camp-fires, covering the sand-bank just below my booth of grasses perched on the overhanging cliff.

"The full moon was rising behind the trees, its soft light shimmering upon the waters and lighting up the faces of the Karens, as they stood in dripping garments, some drying themselves around the camp-fires, others tending their chatties or their cooking vessels.

"We all knelt down and poured out our hearts in grateful praise, and, after singing a hymn, which sounded far over the waters, coming back in echoes from the mountains, I got into my little boat, made our way through the foaming surf, and rowed down to the city, reaching home at midnight."

CHAPTER XII.

THE RAISING—THE PIC-NIC.

A GRAND festival was that of ours! I mean the "raising."

It had cost us from two and a-half to three rupees each to bring the iron-wood logs to an equal size, and plane them.

Finally, a day was appointed for planting the posts of the Institute, and an exciting time we had of it. About two hundred workmen came in, but at first they had no idea but of merely raising the posts.

I called the Board, and explained to them how necessary it was to level the ground and to brick under and around the posts, and they said it should be done; but the other chiefs opposed, thinking it a useless waste of time. Finally, I was obliged to appear and address the crowd, which was so silent, that I spoke only in my usual voice, which always seemed to have a strange effect upon them; probably the great contrast between my voice and their own high key was the secret of it; but I always recognised on such occasions the immediate presence of the Almighty God. Seeing by their eyes that all were ready, Chief Ledda of Baugalay seized upon the moment, struck an electric cord which brought out roars of laughter, and all rushed to the work ; some to the ground, others in troops, shouldering their spades and pick-axes, for digging out bricks.

They found this under preparation a pretty formidable work, but after three or four days of hard labour it was accomplished. Several thousands of bricks had been dug out of the old town wall, backed a quarter of a mile, boated across the river, and seventy tall, smooth, iron-wood posts were firmly planted six feet deep, enclosed in brick. In one of the posts was deposited a small lead box, in which we had a Government plan of the grounds, the history of the Karen Education Society, with a photograph of their President, a letter from Colonel Phayre, an account of the schools, a notice of the Karen Bible, a few letters from the head girls, and a few coins. The opening was then so closed up, that no one probably could ever find it.

Connected with this was a Sunday-school celebration, the first one ever witnessed by the Karens in Tounghoo. The long beautiful lawn between the Institute and Young Men's School had been prepared with seats, and a platform for strangers. Settees had been placed for the chiefs and elders, who arose one after another and addressed the assembly in their own native languages, but with an eloquence perfectly irresistible.

Several English officers and ladies were present, who also addressed the congregation, Mr. Mason interpreting. The children then sung the " Happy Land," in Karen.

Mr. Mason pronounced the benediction, and they were left to enjoy the repast.

Refreshments had been provided by our kind friend and helper, Captain Bond, Commander of the Artillery, and native food by Mr. Mason. Little eyes were very big with expectation on that day, for the long tables on the lawn were loaded with boiled fowls, rice, sugar-cane, plantains, corn-balls, Shan and Burman sweetmeats, and English cakes; the eating stands were wreathed with flowers, and the orphans all appeared in their new dresses, given them by Mr. Mason.

No sooner had we left than down rushed the wild Bghais, pouncing like bears over all the tables.

"Children fed, and grown people hungry!" they muttered with scorn. "No good, no good." So one seized a fowl by the neck, another turned a whole dish of rice into his turban, and another filled his wallet with cakes, and off they leaped, the ducks and hens dangling, and one old man very deliberately munching two corn-balls, first one and then the other.

The children went home in great disappointment. The next day I assembled the whole concourse, and read to them Luke xiv. 13. "When thou makest a feast, call the poor, the maimed, the lame, the blind: Ye shall not afflict my fatherless child;" and again, "Pure religion is to visit the fatherless," &c. "The stranger, the fatherless, and the widow, shall come and eat," and asked them if they did not some of them break God's law the night before. The Board of Managers immediately took up the matter, and gave them such a sermon, they all cried out,—" Stop, brother, stop! We'll pay! We'll pay!" and immediately laid down ten rupees to buy again for the children. One chief sent off at once to the mountains and brought down his fatted pig, and all vied in giving the poor one good dinner.

But the young preachers now came down upon me with great earnestness, thinking I could not possibly have the least authority for making any festival at all.

Pic-nics, Sunday-school celebrations, gatherings for the poor, all alike were " devil feasts" to them. It might do for a Christian land, but not among demon worshippers, they said. I told them, if it wounded their consciences to see the poor little children get a good dinner, they need not come, but such as approved might come and make addresses. For my own part, I believed the Bible was written for all countries alike, and that said, " *When* ye make a feast, call the halt and the blind."

The care of the young preachers, however, shows a beautiful love for Bible truth, which is their great safe-guard, and will, in time, regulate all their intercourse. It is of no use to talk to these people, unless you can *prove* from the Bible it is right. The following letter from Mr. Mason shows their earnest desire for truth :—

" No feature of the work among the Karens appears so full of promise as the eagerness with which the young preachers seek for instruction on Biblical subjects. During the three or four weeks spent with our Associations, whenever I sat down to eat, there were always a number of young men around me seeking information on difficult subjects; and when I strolled into the forest, a long peripatetic train questioned me at every step. Sometimes I would seat myself to rest on a granite rock, overlooking the plains thousands of feet below, when all would quickly surround me,—a crowd of young men with their open Testaments, each one eager to ask concerning some passage or other that he found it difficult to comprehend. One would desire me to explain Paul's assertion, ' For me to live is Christ, and to die is gain.' Another, the expression : ' I am crucified to the world, and the world is crucified unto me.' · A third finds it difficult to understand, ' I could wish myself accursed from Christ.' A fourth could not comprehend our Lord's language in relation to John the Baptist ; while still another was perplexed with Peter's statement, that ' David had not ascended into heaven.' ' David, the good man who wrote the Psalms, has surely gone to heaven. Were there two Davids ?' Some had chronological difficulties to settle ; others asked for historical information, and still others had numerous inquiries to make on the natural productions mentioned in the Bible ; while not a few had questions to ask which Gabriel himself could not answer. Thus a single lecture would be diversified like mosaic, with theology and botany, exegesis and zoology, metaphysics and lightning wires, history, sacred and profane, geography, ancient and modern, with a sprinkling of almost every other subject of the past, the present, and the future.

s

After lying down to sleep, I often heard the younger teachers inquiring of their seniors the signification of various passages, and asking information on numerous topics on which they had been instructed. In this way the knowledge communicated to one is passed on to tens, twenties, and thirties, making my school of theology as wide as the province, and its pupils as numerous as the ministry within its borders; and it is an undeniable fact, that when we need a man to go to a station where there is real self-denial to be endured, it is one of this irregular corps who volunteers. They are the cream of the churches, rising by the law of moral power, a law as immutable as the law of gravitation."*

It was while in the Kannee jungles that I made a trip into the ancient Mopaga country in the north.

We started with one elephant, but found the road so very steep and rough, I sent it back.

The path led over three sharp alpine peaks, and through as many deep glens; then out gushed broad sunlight over an immense paddy field, with here and there a wee bit of a shanty, and I began to congratulate myself on finding a resting spot again, when I chanced to look forward, and lo, there were the boys who carried my little *bundle*, away on the tip-top of another cliff, as far as the eye could reach. I had been quite ill the night before with fever, and was far too weak for such

* Mr. Mason means that no school can make the man, but he would also say that no man can be made without the school, or without *letters*. No man can be a warrior without his arms.

a jaunt, but it was useless to look back when once started; and, besides, we could not look downward without clinging to the bamboos, as we should have gone to the very deeps. So we went plodding on, and even after reaching the narrow opening in the sky, by clinging to the roots, rocks, and whatever could help us, still no house appeared, nor the slightest vestige of any village; but, following our guide, we wound along on the side of the hill, down, down, down, and were about to step off into a gorge as black as night, when a dozen hands were raised, and a whole flood of mountain music burst up the ravine, and held us spell-bound!

It was the little congregation of Wechaduc, yet far distant, at prayer, and singing,

"Rock of Ages, cleft for me,"

in their own native tongue.

I stayed my steps, and listened with emotions indescribable, glancing over the whole history of the past four years in as many minutes, until lost in bewildering joy, for well did I recollect the first visit of those *taubeahs* to our house. The leader was the minstrel who came to inquire if God's Son had come from heaven. Now he came smiling down the glen to meet me, his babe in a blanket upon his back for me to bless! And on reaching the house, all the mothers, to the number of a hundred, I should think, brought forth their infants for me to lay my hand upon their heads. I knew not what to do, whether to gratify them or not, for it seemed fearful to think of standing in the place of our

s 2

Blessed Redeemer. However, I patted their little heads, and shook hands with some four hundred, then went into the chapel, and explained to them who alone could bless their little ones.

The whole village consisted of only one house, besides the chapel and teacher's residence.

Imagine a building four hundred feet long and thirty wide, divided into some thirty rooms; then another house parallel, just separated by a verandah three feet broad; then still another parallel, separated by a verandah just the same, and all three alike, except the central row, which is perhaps ten feet shorter at each end, leaving an open court in front and a work-yard behind. This central row belongs to the chief and his relations, and he holds his court in the first hall. Each compartment has its little bedrooms, just long enough to stretch one's-self in, with cooking-box and all manner of jungle apparatus strewn on bamboos above; while beneath is a pigsty, walled up with bamboos to the floor, which is about six or eight feet from the ground, with little trap-doors in the floor, so that they may feed the pigs without going out! There are three separate roofs to the building, and under the eaves extend long bamboo spouts. This constitutes the village of Wechaduc, one of the largest of the Mopaga tribe.

I found forty children in this village who could read very well and repeat the Catechism by heart. Several of them had been baptized. This school was taught by Nau Tejau, one of the Bghai head girls of the Institute.

The rains are pouring hard. The sawyers have all

run away—will not work in the rain—demand higher wages. I am in distress; have no means to go on with the work. I call in the chiefs and girls, lay the case before them, and entreat them to ask God for money to complete the building for His glory. All bow in prayer. Eight o'clock,—nine o'clock—ten o'clock, and still we plead there upon our faces:

"O Lord, if this undertaking pleaseth thee, 'Establish thou the work of our hands.'"

In the morning I go out, and look over the half-sawed logs. Saws all still—not a soul comes. I cannot raise wages—I have no money. Oh Lord, do not suffer thy servants to be put to shame! Oh Lord, the heathen are rejoicing. They revile thy name—they cry, "Aha! aha! where is now your God?" Oh Lord, make haste to deliver us.

At two o'clock comes the mail—there is a letter, and I read:—

"CALCUTTA, *August 8th*, 1859.

"MY DEAR MRS. MASON,

"You will see, by my letter to your husband, that I have had the pleasure to receive from a friend a donation of eight hundred rupees for your school. It is from a friend who has lately gone to England.

"MACLEOD WYLIE."

Thanks, oh thanks, to the Almighty Jehovah! Now "Let the heathen rage and imagine vain things," but we will acknowledge *the Lord our deliverer*.

CHAPTER XIII.

THE KAREN NATIONAL BANNER.

" Why cannot the Karens have a banner—a national banner—now that such numbers of them are coming out of heathenism ? " This question was asked among the chiefs of Tounghoo, after a visit to the cantonments, where they had examined with great delight the English standard.

The Institute being set up, the question of banners arose, and it was decided that every Karen clan which joined the Education Society, and helped to support the Girls' School, should be allowed to put up a banner on the building. Six clans raised theirs at once, taking for their distinctive flags the clan-emblems embroidered on their tunics. These are seen on the front posts or iron-wood pillars of the Institute. They represent the Sgaus, Pakus, Maunicpagas, Mopagas, Bghais, and Pant-Bghais, who have joined the enterprise. This excited a great deal of enthusiasm, and the village maidens all vied with one another in weaving and embroidering the most beautiful flags.

It was after erecting these banners for the tribes that the question came up concerning a national emblem or a Union standard for all. Quala took up the subject with earnestness, and sent an epistle to the churches in Tounghoo. He then chose a device for them, which was a Bible with a sword across it. This banner has recently been presented to the nation. The following is an account of its presentation extracted from the *New York World*, of August 8th, 1860 :—

" In the Mariners' church, in New York, last Sabbath evening, a national banner was presented by one of the largest Bible societies in America to the most interesting and hopeful nation in all Asia, the Karens.

" This strange, wild people are being rapidly Christianized, and they have sent to America for a national flag to commemorate their exodus out of heathenism,— the most remarkable and exhilarating request that we have ever heard of from a new nation.

" The following remarkable letter was read from the principal native teacher :—

" LETTER OF QUALA, THE SECOND KAREN APOSTLE.

" ' To all the churches in Tavoy, Maulmain, Rangoon, Bassein, Shwagyn, Tounghoo, and Prome, greeting !

" ' To the great teachers, small teachers, men and women, young women, young men, deacons, elders, old and young, one and all, greeting !

" ' I, a son of Tavoy, Teacher Quala, trust you all know and understand the word of God, and can speak of the things pertaining to the truth and light which God has given us. In order that we may be able to

conquer our enemies, and escape from every evil hand,
God has given us a weapon. What is it? What kind
of a weapon is it?

"'Behold! The children of Judah, when they
escaped out of the hands of the Egyptians, in order that
their children might understand how they were delivered
out of their hands, erected banners with emblems of the
hawk, the lion, the bear, and ox.

"' Again, the ENGLISH nation, when they escaped out
of the hands of the idolatrous Romans, erected a standard of the cross as a national emblem; and when their
king went to rescue Jerusalem from the Moslem invaders,
took back Judah's lion, so that future generations might ,
understand. Again, the AMERICANS, when they declared
independence, erected a national emblem of the eagle,
with stars and stripes. This was to inform every nation
that they would rise heavenward, over every enemy.

"'Therefore, my brethren, young and old, mothers
and fathers, grandmothers and grandfathers, nieces and
nephews, uncles and aunts, cousins and friends, children
and grandchildren, we, the uncivilized, the children of
the forest, barbarians, without books or understanding,
without a king or a name in the earth, we, the nation
in thick darkness, whom God has compassionated and
sent His own Son Jesus Christ to save out of our darkness and bondage;—we, in the year of the world five
thousand eight hundred and thirty-two, received books
from the hands of the teachers—the children of America.
We received the HOLY BIBLE, the words of God, and
the ten commandments which He gave to His people, the

children of Israel, by the hand of Moses. This was a
treasure more precious than all the books of the earth—
the best above all books ; the CHIEF among books.

" ' We, the Karens, were like wild beasts of the
mountains—like the wild speckled fowl of the jungles.
We had no knowledge, no understanding, no power.
But now we have received instruction indeed. Now to
us Karens God has given books and teachers, and now
we, too, have schools and school-houses all our own.
Therefore it is well if we rejoice with exceeding great
joy ; and now let us erect a National Banner, as other
Book nations have done. Let us erect it over our school-
houses, and let us choose for our emblem, not a lion or
any beast, but the weapon which God hath given us by
which to subdue our enemies—even the " WORD OF
GOD, WHICH IS THE SWORD OF THE SPIRIT."

" ' Now, teachers and teacheresses, friends, the children
of God among the Karens everywhere—what think you?
Will this be good, or will you differ from me ? Instruct
me, I pray you, if there is a better way. Dear friends,
let us think of what our mothers taught us. " Dogs go
in troops ; they catch the deer. Villages united conquer
enemies." This is what I have to say : " If many work
together, much the reward, and the greater their
strength."

" ' Dear friends, let us look at Luke xii. 15. I have
seen a letter—Karen teachers asking support of the
foreign teachers, and I was greatly ashamed. Brethren,
teachers, churches, all, consider, I pray you. The white
foreign teachers were like our father and mother ; first,

they had to be instructed by others, but they did not lean on their instructors for their curry and rice. They did not ask their teachers to feed them. Let us follow the white foreigners, and learn of them till we can make clocks, and glass, and swords, and cannon, and tele-scopes, and fire-carriages—till we know the earth's boundaries, all nations and medicines; but let us sup-port our own schoolmasters and preachers.

" ' The white foreigners do not ask the Burmese to feed their teachers. The Burmese have teachers, and they do not ask the white men to feed theirs. There-fore there is no place for us to ask—not in the least.

" ' Do we not know ? Do we not understand ? Birds build nests ; the young ones learn. Fathers die ; sons take their seats. Mothers die ; daughters take the mothers' places ; and think, I pray you, of King Solo-mon's words : " A wise son is the joy of his father, but a foolish son is the grief of his mother."

" ' Let us not seek for ourselves alone, but seek, plan, and devise for our posterity down to the remotest gene-ration. Therefore let us erect a banner for our whole nation, and glorify God, that the surrounding nations may know that we have come out from heathenism, and are determined to be a Christian people.

" ' QUALA.'

" This is a literal translation of Quala's Karen letter, published in the *Star*, a monthly paper printed in the Karen language. At the time of presentation, the Secretary of the American and Foreign Bible Society, the Rev. F. Haynes, preached a very able sermon. The Rev. Mr. Stewart then made over the flag to the BIBLE SOCIETY, remarking that his congregation had given till he had to tell them to stop giving; and Mr. Haynes, on receiving it, made some stirring remarks in relation to the Mariners' Church, especially in connexion with a member going out from it who had been the first source of the great Swedish reformation in Europe.*

" The flag has a blue ground, with the device of a Bible and sword in colours, and a motto : ' THE SWORD OF THE SPIRIT, WHICH IS THE WORD OF GOD.' The motto is in the Karen language, in large white letters.

" At the close of the sermon, Mr. Haynes presented the flag on behalf of the American and Foreign Bible Society. Mrs. Mason received it in place of her husband, now in Burmah, on behalf of the nation. Mrs. Mason then replied as follows :—

* In 1834, F. O. Nilsson, a converted Swedish sailor, was baptized by the Rev. Mr. Stewart, of the Mariners' Church, N. Y. In 1839, he returned to his native land to preach the Gospel to his countrymen and kindred. After labouring several years amid persecutions, fines, and imprisonment, he was finally banished from the kingdom, leaving fifty-six baptized believers scattered in different districts.

In 1855, the American Baptist Publication Society adopted a system of Colportage for Sweden, and on the 8th of September, the Rev. A. Wiberg, as Superintendent of Colportage, sailed for Stockholm, where he arrived on the 7th of November. Some fifteen Colporteurs were appointed, and soon all Sweden was traversed by this devoted band. As the result, there are now upwards of one hundred Baptist Churches, with a membership of between five and six thousand.

" 'I beg to thank the American and Foreign Bible Society for this Karen National Banner. I thank you, Sir, in behalf of the twenty-five thousand Karen converts of Burmah, enlightened by the Bible which your Society has so liberally given them, in their own language.

" 'I thank you in behalf of my husband, the translator of the Bible for the Karen nation. I thank you in behalf of the four hundred young preachers and teachers of the Karen nation; in behalf of the four hundred district schools of the nation; in behalf of the four hundred Sunday-schools of the nation; in behalf of the seventy-five thousand Karens who have determined to come out from heathenism, and to receive Christian books.

" 'It may be known to you that many believe that a hundred years hence the Karens will be the ruling power in India, and the Missionary nation to all Asia, the right-hand of the English nation, because they so generally receive the Bible, while so many of the nations reject it. Therefore I thank you, Sir, in behalf of all the hundreds of thousands of Christianized, civilized Karens who shall tell of this gift to their children, and wave this national banner; and especially I would thank you in behalf of the *women* of the Karen nation.' "

CHAPTER XIV.

HELP FROM ENGLAND.

It was on my way to Tounghoo that I wrote an account of my school plans to my kind friend, Robert Scott Moncrieff, Esq., of Calcutta. His brother, the Rev. W. Scott Moncrieff, of London, took the letter immediately to Miss Webb, Secretary of the " Society for Promoting Female Education in the East." I had then never heard of that Society.

And as if God would say, " There shall be no failure when I undertake," he had previously sent the Rev. W. Hazeldine to see Miss Webb. Mr. Hazeldine was Chaplain at Tounghoo, and had been out on a tour among the Karens, where he took the jungle fever, which had compelled him to return to England; but he had carried with him there a world of sympathy for the Karens. Now, I beg to ask if any Christian man, woman, or child, can doubt for one moment that there was in all this a most remarkable answer to prayer.

The Society for Female Education in the East has been in existence twenty-eight years; has sent out, according to the Report for 1862, one hundred and three female teachers; had then raised £53,355; had sent out work for sale to the amount of £31,830; and rendered aid in various ways to Girls' Schools, superintended by Missionaries' wives, and by private individuals. Two hundred and fourteen of these schools are, at present, in connexion with the Society; yet what are these among so many? They have NATIVE as well as EUROPEAN teachers in the field, and are labouring in China, Burmah, the Punjaub, Calcutta, Benares, Lucknow, Madras, Tinnevelly, Bombay, and many other parts of India, Ceylon, Mauritius, South Africa, West Africa, the Levant, and Egypt. Yet this Society began with nothing in 1834, and has been carried on entirely by ladies, and ladies of different denominations, working in union for one single object, the glory of God in the salvation of heathen women.

Its Report for 1860 closes with this striking, and in America almost forgotten, command :—

"And bring my *daughters* from the ends of the earth."

On hearing of my undertaking for the women of Tounghoo, Miss Webb, the Secretary, immediately opened communication with me, and very kindly made inquiries—offering to help us. This drew forth the following letter :—

"TOUNGHOO, *August 22nd*, 1858.

"My DEAR FRIEND,

"I feel myself under great obligations to your Society for taking an interest in Burmah. I thank you, espe-

cially, for thinking of our dear Karens, and in so friendly
a manner offering me aid. I recognise in this fact a
clear answer to my prayers. I see as striking evidences
that the Lord is working among these Karen mountains
as if a voice from heaven should proclaim, ' This is
God's work in the land of the Bghais.'

" Our second term and three days' examination are
just over. The girls have been more successful in learning than I have ever seen girls in my native country in
the same time. They have now a tolerably exact knowledge of the Gospel of Matthew, the Acts, the history of
the Old Testament, the geography of Asia, Europe,
North and South America, and a good understanding
of the solar system. The latter has been particularly
interesting to them, because they have always been
taught that in an eclipse of the sun or the moon a demon
devours the heavenly bodies.

" Our Girls' School numbered, the last term, sixty
members, all from the best families of the Pakus, Mopagas, Bghais, and Pant-Bghais. They have not in a
single instance appeared in soiled apparel. They have
washed and cooked for themselves, and brought their
own food from the market. One was expelled from the
institution for theft ; but severe measures were required
in only one or two instances. One of these was the case
of a chief's daughter, who, for neglect of duty, was sent
out of school, or rather for a week was not allowed to
recite her lessons. This was a great trial to her, as she
had been the first in the school. Still I saw no mani-
festation of anger ; on the contrary, all that she said

was to beg for forgiveness, and she returned a humble and polite girl.

"The other case gave me great anxiety. We had a rule that every pupil should have her hair put up in a decent and orderly manner when she came into the school-room in the morning. One day almost half of the girls had neglected this duty. I sent them back to their rooms; and when I called them, not one appeared. There was evidently an opposition to the rule. They were all forbidden to enter the school or come into my room for three days. This was a great trial to them, though they had their meals as usual. On the second day, three of them declared their resolution to return home, and they would have done so, if others had been willing to follow them. I feared and prayed. But I sent them only this word, that if they went away, they would show to all the churches that they could not humble their hearts, and all the headmen would rejoice that they did not need them for teachers. That was enough. Not one of them left, and I had no further trouble in respect to cleanliness. Often during this period I would see their sparkling eyes peeping through the bamboos during the hour of recitation; that was a favourite hour with all, for I had introduced the custom of allowing them to examine me, instead of my examining them.

"I have for the Female Department one paid male teacher, two assistants, one Paku, and one Bghai; then two other sub-assistants, one for the sick and one for the bazaar business. These are permanent. Under these are six heads for the boarding department, two for house-work, two for sewing, two for the ground around and under the houses, and one for the sick. Besides these, we have ten monitors chosen monthly; the other heads are chosen weekly. The monitors see that all bathe and dress their hair properly, keep their places in the classes, and recite correctly.

" In the Young Men's School I have the superinten-dence of two general teachers, one cook, two hospital-heads, two house-heads, and two heads for the grounds ; these heads, too, are all chosen weekly, the monitors monthly.

" Every Wednesday morning all assemble together, young men and young women, to take lessons in good manners, and in keeping a day-book.* So everything goes on in an orderly manner, whether I am present or not. No one receives the least pay, except an arithmetic-book or the money to purchase one.

" By having two schools at the same time, I find many opportunities to instruct the young men as to their behaviour to the other sex. For example, it was a rule that six of the girls entrusted with the marketing and six of the men should purchase all their vegetables at the bazaar, and bring them home. I soon discovered that while the girls came home with heavy baskets on their backs, the young gentlemen tripped on before with

---

* In this day-book we made a record of every rod of land which they cleared, every foot of road they made, and every stump they dug up, which excited great emulation among them, and saved the school much sickness in term time.

T

a very light bag or bundle under the arm. I took great pains to change this custom, in which, however, I did not entirely succeed, because the young men were not in the least ashamed of it, and the girls were disposed to boast of the burdens they carried. One of the teachers said to me—

" ' Mama, if our wives work much and carry heavy burdens, we love them ; if not, we hate them.' That is the prevailing feeling among the unbelievers. In time, I think I shall succeed in bringing the young men to be ashamed of such things ; but it takes more than one term to change heathen customs.

" At the public examination I desired the best of the young students to examine the girls in the presence of the assembled chiefs ; but I did not venture fully to unfold their attainments, lest I should awaken opposition to the school. In fact, a teacher has already come out openly, and declared to the chiefs that they would yet come under woman's government. Pray for me! Oh, pray for *us* in this exigency ; for here lies our great danger. Many were at the outset opposed to a girls' school, because, they said, the girls would become indolent and useless ; but, in fact, they feared lest they should acquire knowledge. To obviate this objection, the girls have willingly taken their spades and worked in the garden two hours daily, labouring as zealously as the men.

" The men settlers around our place have a good school-house, and support a teacher for all the children in the village. My two boys examine this school every

Saturday, and teach the children Bible history from pictures, requiring the scholars to read everything in the Karen Bible. They repeat what has been learned before the whole assembly at the close of the Sabbath-school, which embraces all the colonists, male and female together, with both the schools.

" As these people live around me, I have a good opportunity to accustom them to cleanliness, order, morality, uprightness, love of children, and sympathy with the sick and bereaved, all duties which they deeply need to be taught ; so that even in this respect a school is formed in which I esteem it a precious privilege to give instruction.

" In regard to all that God, the Almighty God, and not man, has done here, I can say, Behold, God is my salvation. I will trust and not be afraid, for Jehovah the Lord is my strength. He whose throne is in Heaven—who sends His word upon earth, and His word runs very swiftly, He will rule from sea to sea, and from the river to the end of the earth. They who dwell in the wilderness shall bow before Him ; for He will save the poor when he crieth, and the needy, and *him that hath no helper.* He is God, the faithful God, who keeps covenant and faithfulness,—the Almighty. During the last year I have learned the meaning of that name, the ALMIGHTY, for no one can pray, ' Give us this day our daily bread,' like one who has no bread.

" When I first resolved to attempt this self-sustaining school, I promised my husband that I would write to some Society in England or Scotland, and endeavour to obtain help for myself. But my duties were so pressing, that for six months I could not find time to do it. During this period God had sent me so much, I could not find the heart to do it. It seemed to me a thing forbidden. It appeared as if God had called me to trust, and to lift up my eyes to the hills from whence all my help came. I did so without fear or doubt, and now He has sent your Society to aid me further.

"I think I shall let the Karen girls of the highest class enter the Ornamental department. Because they are so diligent, Mr. Mason thinks they have a good claim to this privilege, and they take great pleasure in drawing, embroidering, and music. Even our old chieftains looked on the drawing-books of the girls with visible pride, having a taste for art and brilliant colours. I will give an instance to show their love of the beautiful. After the posts of the house, sixty in number, were well set, I said to a member of the building committee that they would look very pretty if they were painted and lackered. The very next week the Pakus and Maunies brought one hundred and thirteen rupees for this object. One or two days afterwards, a Mopaga head-man visited us, and wished to learn how everything was to be done. I mentioned this, and asked him if he had heard what the Pakus were doing. He knew nothing of it, and said not a word, but after three days he came again with two other aged head-men, and counted out *ninety-three* rupees as a contribution from two villages only, for the purchase of paint for the posts!

" The land, building apparatus, furniture, and everything indeed appertaining to the School, is made over legally to the KAREN EDUCATION SOCIETY, that Society engaging to support and carry it on perpetually from 'generation to generation.' So that no Foreign Society, or individual, can have any claim upon the property of the Institute, or any control over it, it being left wholly to their own Board of Managers to control for themselves. With this knowledge before your Society, could you help me ?

" If you would undertake the *permanent* support of a principal and a native female assistant, you would relieve me of much anxiety. The support of a single lady would amount to about £72 sterling per year. The support of an assistant for the Karen department would be £10 sterling, and for the Burmese, £18. As to myself, I have no fears. I only wish that the existence of the school may be made as secure as possible.

(Signed) " ELLEN B. MASON."

The Report of the Society for 1860 gives the following result :—

" There are few fields of Missionary effort upon which the eye of the Christian rests with more adoring wonder and gratitude than upon Burmah. The deep interest which the Committee anticipated would be felt by their friends in connecting themselves with this work, as announced in the last report, has not been disappointed, and the ' Special Fund for Burmah ' has almost met the demands upon it. Of Mrs. Mason's Training School for Karen girls at Tounghoo, the Committee have received heart-stirring accounts, and they have rejoiced in being able to support this labourer in her arduous yet delightful work. The large supplies of school apparatus, which the liberality of their friends placed at their disposal for her, have arrived safely.

" The Committee have this year undertaken also the maintenance of a native female teacher for a school for Burmese Karen girls at *Kemendine*, under the superintendence of Mrs. INGALLS. To those who are acquainted with the history of that mission which ' Judson prayed into existence,' her name needs no introduction ; and much gratification has been felt at this opportunity of sustaining her self-denying and zealous efforts for the benefit of the heathen females amongst whom she has taken up her abode."

Thus wonderfully did God open the minds and hearts of English Christians to see the utility of the work, and to sympathize in my undertaking, when I had almost said, My father and my mother had forsaken me ; then the Lord took me up.

And now I sing,

" I love the Lord, because He hath heard my voice and my supplication, because He hath inclined His ear unto me ; *therefore will I call upon Him as long as I live.*"

CHAPTER XV.

COLONEL PHAYRE'S REPORT—THE TABERNACLE IN THE
MOUNTAINS.

I AM in the mountain village of Baumuduc;—a chief
enters in high spirits.

" We've seen the Perdo ! the Perdo !"

" Well, what did he say ?"

" Oh, he's God's Commissioner !"—rubbing his hands
—" he's God's Commissioner !"

" Why, how do you know ?"

" Oh, he shook hands with the *children !* I know he
loves us !"

The Commissioner of Pegu had just made Tounghoo
a visit, and attended the Paku Association. He gave
his hand to every one, old and young, and would even
stop his great horse, and reach down for the wee babies
which the mothers held up, by which he greatly won
the confidence of the Karens. They were much delighted with his kind acts in helping them to teak
for their chapels, and in appointing for them their own
magistrates. In many other ways he also won for himself golden tablets in their memories.

Mountain is here piled over mountain, but after two

days we espied an opening leading to what appeared to
be an old inhabited country, with a pinnacle some six
hundred feet high, looming up before us perpendicularly,
crested with a cluster of gigantic bamboos. Just under
this cluster, upon one side of the summit, stretched the
tabernacle along the ridge; a most picturesque sight,
but I think I was full three hours in reaching the place
after the scene burst upon us. News had gone before,
and on reaching the base of the pinnacle, the path was
bordered on either side by disciples all the way to the
door of the chapel, waiting to hail the Commissioner as
their benefactor.

Colonel Phayre remained five days, attending every
service, and listening to all the speeches, which were
partially interpreted to him as they were spoken. He
gave us resolutions and speeches on educational pur-
suits, on supporting the schools, on caring for teachers,
—true Missionary orations, equal to any in London or
Boston. Sgaus, Pakus, Maunicpagas, Mopagas, Bghais,
and Pant-Bghais, also addressed the assembly, and the
scene was perfectly exhilarating. One esteemed deacon
rose to speak in a soiled dress, when another told him
to sit down, and let the clean folks talk, but generally
there was an evident striving to be tidy and respectable.
Each village had its booth encircling the great tabernacle,
so that I fancied myself in the feast of tabernacles
among the cedars of Lebanon.

After our Association closed, we made an excursion
over the top of the mountain, down to sweet Wathako—
a charming spot in a basin of the mountain, where we

found a new teak chapel, very neatly built as far as it was completed, which had already cost the little church a thousand rupees. The one in the village where the Association met had cost them fifteen hundred rupees, all paid by themselves.

The village was swept clean, and we all went into the old chapel and had a pic-nic. Everything looked civilized and advancing, and the children were well trained in school.

Encircling this village in the mountains were groves of many hundred betel-nut trees. A betel or Areca-nut grove is one of the most agreeable objects the eye rests on in Burmah. Imagine two hundred trees with trunks as large as hop-poles, forty feet high, without a single branch or leaf except at top, the fronds, of the freshest green, then floating out in loveliness and grace, while the whole ground is made a chess-board of tiny brooks to water the trees.

It was at this place that they had made an attempt to overcome two boys, when the Gospel was first preached there. One man entreated Pwapau to remain, and declared he himself would become his pupil whether others did or not. But the young men began to come in, and he soon had a school of forty scholars. After awhile, the father of two of the lads sent to call them home, to keep a feast to the nats. The boys sternly refused to go, or to perform any more heathen rites. The next day over came the men of the village, thirty or forty, stoutly armed, and surrounded the school-house. One of the boys was caught, and compelled to march off to the feast; but the other, Talaoo, leaped out of the back of the house, dashed into the jungle, and escaped. This young man made a glowing speech on the Bible at the Association, and the chief who led the armed band was there too, and made a speech. He is now a deacon of the church.

The following is the Commissioner's Report :—

" *To* CECIL BEADON, ESQUIRE,
      " *Secretary to the Government of India,*
                        " CALCUTTA.

" SIR,

" 1. Having lately returned to the station of Toung-hoo, from a short tour among the Karen mountain tribes dwelling to the east of the Sittang river, I have the honour to submit, for the information of His Excellency the Governor-General in Council, a brief report of what I have observed among that interesting race of people.

" 2. The mountainous country of the Tounghoo district, in which the Karen tribes reside, extends over an area of about two thousand square miles. It is bounded by the line of the British frontier, with Burmah on the north, along the parallel of 19° 29' north latitude, on the south by the river Youkthwa, which divides it from the Martaban province, on the east by the country of the independent Red Karens, and on the west by the lowlands skirting the Sittang river. Within the above tract of country dwell the several tribes distinguished by the Burmese under the general name of Karen.

These tribes, though acknowledging a relationship to each other in race, yet bear separate distinctive names for themselves. Their dialects, in some instances, differ from each other, so as to render communication between the tribes nearly as difficult as if the languages were altogether distinct. The following are the names of the several tribes or clans within the above tract of country :—

" 1. Paku.   2. Maunicpaga.   3. Bghai, divided into two sections.   4. Wewau.   5. Sgau.   6. Mopaga, and one or two more not yet satisfactorily ascertained.

" 3. It is impossible to give an accurate return of the numbers of these people, but they may be stated generally to be about fifty thousand, of whom more than twenty thousand souls are either professed Christians or under Christian instruction and influence. They are scattered over mountains which rise five thousand feet above the sea. Their villages seldom contain more than thirty or forty houses. Their cultivation, like that of all the Indo-Chinese mountaineers, is carried on, not by terracing the hills, but by cutting down the forest on the mountain sides, burning the whole mass of timber and grass, and then sowing the seed in the ground among the ashes.

" As the next rain washes away the fertile vegetable soil, a crop cannot again be raised on the same spot for some ten or fifteen years. Each village, therefore, requires a wide extent of mountain land in order to have a rotation of cultivatable spots. This method of cultivation acts as a barrier to the progress of the people, since they are engaged in a constant struggle against the forest.

" 4. Up to the year 1853, the several tribes, and it may even be said the different villages of the same tribe, lived in a state of enmity and actual warfare with each other. By open force or by stealthy manœuvre, they would capture women and children, and sell them as slaves to other tribes; while they generally put to death all grown-up men who fell into their power. These predatory habits still exist, more or less, among those tribes who have not accepted Christianity.

" 5. In my annual administration report I have narrated how, by the unwearied labours of the Rev. Dr. and Mrs. Mason, of San Quala, and other Christian Karen teachers from the Tenasserim provinces, Christianity has been introduced among these tribes; how their languages have been mastered and reduced to writing, and how religion and education have simultaneously wrought a vast change in the habits, the feelings, and the hearts of these wild mountaineers.

" 6. The Government has been pleased in past years to make grants of money to Dr. and Mrs. Mason for the translation of books, and for the building of the school for Karen females at Tounghoo. Having now been present at the meeting in a central mountain village of a considerable number of people from all the tribes—an annual gathering held to recount their past proceedings, to compare their progress, and to animate each other to future effort—having witnessed this deeply-interesting meeting, I deem it my duty to report, for the information of his Excellency the Governor-General in Council, the result so far of the work which has been going on among these tribes.

"7. Their educational institutions are closely connected with their village or clan system. Each village community constitutes a church or congregation in itself. Among the Sgau, Maunepaga, Paku, and Wewau tribes, there are fifty-eight stations or churches. At each village there is a teacher and a school. The teachers are generally young men of the tribe who have been selected and instructed under the care of the Rev. Dr. Mason. The village teacher is not in all cases an ordained Minister, but he it is who conducts the public worship, and is also the schoolmaster. In each village a church is erected, and the school is held in the same building. At those villages which I have visited, these mountain places of worship were neat wooden buildings, with a house adjoining for the Minister or Teacher. All are built at the expense of the people, and the Teacher is entirely supported by the same means. I need hardly add, that it is a completely voluntary system. A bamboo fence, put round the church and the Teacher's or Minister's dwelling, separates them from the rest of the village.

"8. Among the other tribes, namely, the Bghai and Mopaga, there are sixty-two stations, or parishes, as they may be termed, which I am informed are provided for in every respect as above described.

"9. In January, 1859, the Paku Association of all the churches belonging to that and some adjoining tribes held a meeting, at which I was present. It was at a village named Baugalay, situated on a fine commanding position, at some three thousand feet elevation, with forest-clad mountains all round. There were about seven hundred or eight hundred people present, men, women, and children. The Rev. Dr. Mason, with several Karen Ministers and Teachers, occupied a central platform of bamboos, slightly raised above the ground. Around the platform, under the shade of a temporary shed of bamboo, were the Karens, seated according to their tribes and families, clad in their picturesque national dress, and with intelligence and deep interest in the objects for which they had met beaming in their faces.

" 10. The business of the meeting commenced with a hymn and with prayer, both in the Karen language. The Karens have naturally a taste for melody, and the soft sounds of their language are well adapted to vocal music. Several of the young Karen Ministers and Teachers successively addressed the assembly in earnest language, exhorting the people to make increased exertions to educate their children, to support religion, to procure Bibles, and to be careful of them when they had them. One read a paper containing a brief account of the illness and death of a brother pastor, who had lately died. Several of the chiefs also briefly addressed the meeting, exhorting the people. Finally, it was announced that the Associated Churches had subscribed over five hundred rupees towards the support of the central schools at the town of Tounghoo, where both boys and girls are educated more highly than can be done in the village schools. They are trained as teachers for the other schools.

" 11. It was a wonderful sight thus to behold in the midst of an assembly of tribes so lately savage, and without written language, the evidence of a people appreciating the benefit of religion and of education, supporting pastors and schools, listening to speeches on social improvement and religious duties, delivered by men of their own race in their own tongue, abandoning their evil habits and their cruel wars, and living as quiet, industrious mountaineers, anxious for improvement. I was surprised at the youth of some of the teachers, and more at the respect and attention shown them by many of the chiefs. This is the rather remarkable, as we might almost have looked for jealousy from the latter at their own influence being impaired. It is not so, however. Dr. Mason has found, as was to be expected, that young people were more readily impressed with new ideas than those advanced in life, and has employed young men as teachers, while their education ensures them respect and influence among both chiefs and people.

" 12. Though the people support their village teachers and schools, and will, and do, also support those youths who go to study at the Normal School in town, yet it is beyond their means to defray all the expenses of the latter institution. I was present at an examination of the Female Institute at Tounghoo, by Mrs. Mason. Fifty were present. They appeared to acquit themselves creditably in geography, arithmetic, and other branches of knowledge. To show what a change education has wrought in the opinions of these people generally, I may mention that, in the absence of regular teachers in the more remote villages, some of the chiefs have applied for young women from the Institute to instruct the children of their tribe. This fact, showing a disregard for their previous prejudices—for they heretofore considered women only as useful drudges to ' the lords of creation'—evinces the wonderful change effected in their habits of thought.

" 13. I have entered into these details of the progress made among these tribes, in order to lay clearly before the Governor-General in Council my reasons for making application for further grants towards supporting and extending education among them. On this subject I beg to annex copies of two letters to my address, one from Mrs. Mason, dated the 13th of January, 1859, and one from the Rev. Dr. Mason, dated the 21st. Both ask for assistance for the Normal School for Karen young men, established at the town of Toimghoo.

" 14. Hitherto the Government has contributed as follows towards education among the mountain Karen tribes : two thousand rupees for the translation and printing of useful works in the Bghai and Maunicpaga dialects, and fourteen hundred rupees for books, apparatus, &c., for the Karen Female Institute ; a grant of land at Tounghoo has also been made for erecting the building.

" 15. With reference to the present application by Dr. and Mrs. Mason, I beg earnestly to recommend that the Honourable the President in Council will be pleased to sanction a grant toward the Young Men's Normal School,—a school which is to fulfil the important object of furnishing instructors to the various tribes scattered over the mountains. The great importance of aiding the Rev. Dr. and Mrs. Mason in affording these young men a liberal education, through whose agency these tribes may be raised from the depths of ignorance and barbarism to hold hereafter, it is hoped, a prominent place among Asiatic races, the great importance of aiding in this noble object, requires not a word from me to recommend it. I shall content myself, therefore, with stating that many tribes still remain to be recovered from barbarism, and with recommending as follows :—

. " 1st. That the sum of three thousand rupees be granted towards the building of a school-house for the Karen young men at Tounghoo. This school is proposed to be of brick, and one hundred pupils are to be educated therein.

" 2nd. That I be authorized to procure for the said school the following instruments :—

" 1. A telescope, on stand, of sufficient power to observe the eclipse of Jupiter's satellites.

" 2. A sextant and artificial horizon.

" 3. A pair of globes, one foot in diameter.

" 4. A prismatic compass and chain, complete.

" 5. A set of school maps.

U

" I have not the means of making an estimate of the expense that will be incurred in procuring instruments, but I believe that twelve hundred rupees will be the outside.

    " I have the honour to be, SIR,
       " Your most obedient servant,
            " A. P. PHAYRE.
" *February 3rd*, 1859."

I have felt very thankful to our Commissioner for writing this report, as it reaches a class of men who seldom or never read Missionary publications.

Colonel Phayre, too, being Agent to the Governor-General of India and for Her Majesty, can speak with a power which no other person can wield in Burmah.

It is a day or two before the Bghai Association. I am distressed and sad. I cannot go out to my husband —have no money to pay the workmen—the Chinaman is urgent for wages—doors and windows half done—I seek to the Lord : " Oh Lord, may I go to the Bghai mountains ? If it please thee that I go, do thou graciously send me some money ; thou art the *mighty God of Jacob*."

I begin to prepare some cake to take up to my husband, for I am sure I shall go.

It is morning ; the door opens, and a servant enters.

" A roll ma'am, from the General." He opens it out on the table, counts two hundred and fifty rupees, and hands a note. I read :—

" My dear Mrs. Mason,

" I am very sorry for your having to leave so unexpectedly, as I have been planning to accompany you to the school on the other side of the river, but must hope for another meeting at some future time. Wishing you and Dr. Mason every blessing and success in your undertaking, with kindest regards,

" Believe me, yours, very sincerely,

" J. Bell.

" P.S. The two hundred and fifty rupees I send to help on your work."

General Bell was commander of the British forces in Burmah ; he has aided us to the amount of five hundred rupees, and has often cheered us with his kind notes. I regarded his help at this time as a special answer to prayer. " Blessed be the Lord God of Israel, who *only doeth wondrous things.*"

It was about a month after the excursion to the Paku hills that I went up to the Bghai country, and wrote from thence to my dear friend, Miss Webb.

" The vacation of my schools is now begun, and I am enjoying rest on the very tip-top of the loftiest Bghai mountains, writing on a divan of slender bamboos, raised five or six feet above the ground. A line of brown figures lies stretched on one side in their close Highland-looking blankets—a very tableau of mummies, Israelitish enough to be brothers to the pyramid-builders. Above us stretches a dome of the purest blue, while the stars are looking right down into our faces.

u 2

"Among the bamboos around us, are eight or ten more Karens circling their camp fires; some with crimson turbans and dark-bordered tunics, grasping their boar-tusked spears, with long black locks streaming over their shoulders. The torch-lights, glimmering through the feathery bamboos, make our pinnacle pavilion a perfect Alhambra. The moon is just rising from under the mountains, and sends up streams of silver light; there again they come, softening, soothing, stealing around those dark shadowy forms, just as the light of truth is now stealing around the darkness of their heathen minds. From a deep abyss on the left is heard the cry of the peacock, which arouses the fear that tigers may be our near neighbours. Strange that these two inhabitants of the jungle should have such an affinity for each other.

"Four days ago, upon a sister pinnacle, there lay stretched before us one of the grandest views amongst mountain grandeurs. We had been travelling two days, climbing ridge upon ridge and peak upon peak, when suddenly a cry of joy burst from our bearers, 'Ta Opo, Ta Opo!' (the Tabernacle. All exclaimed in one breath, 'Where? Can you see the village?' 'Er, er,' (Yes, yes,) was the electrical reply shouted from lip to lip, clear over the mountains.

"Truly it was a bewildering scene, where beauties new and wild seemed to meet the eye at every angle. Just at our feet there opened out one of the wide Toung-hoo farms, extending over hill and dale, just felled and burned, ready for clearing. The seared bamboos, strewed over every inch of ground, gave it the appearance of a ripened corn-field, and contrasted strongly with the lively verdure of the young foliage beyond, and this again came into bold relief against the dark green of the ancient forest, walled behind with purple pinnacles. On the left loomed Mount Gazeko, far above his brethren. He bears the reputation of having been conquered by a famous mountain on the south, when he had his head cleft asunder; but now both repose in peace, surrounded by Christian settlements.

" The cynosure of every eye was Mount Magadoo on our right, on the very summit of which could be distinctly seen a long colossal Tabernacle, which, being constructed of split bamboos, glistened in the sunlight as if its walls had been of brass, reminding one instantly, in its position—encircled by hills—and by its colour, of Jerusalem's Temple. At our feet lay a narrow defile, the beginning of that path which, now winding tortuously across the glen, now around the base of the mountains, now lost in a gorge, and now re-appearing, winds up, up, up the long ascent to the Tabernacle.

" It was perhaps four o'clock when we espied the scene of the great Convocation, and it was not until after four hours of hard travelling that we neared the place. We then found the path widened, and swept, and lined on either side with young men and old men, come to bear me on. The way was still over two mountains, and very steep, but the Bghai Christians would not for a moment leave their post. At length we reached the last peak, and found the path crowded with

women and children, each of whom was determined to
have a grasp of my hand. My pupils formed the fore-
ground, and went before as a body-guard, compelling
the crowd to file out right and left, while I walked
up until the throng became so dense, that the chief
of the village, fearing I should be smothered, came and
carried me away over their heads to the chapel, where I
took a stand on the steps, and shook hands with
about two thousand Abrahams and Sarahs, Deborahs,
and Dorcases, and their babies.

"The next morning all assembled in the Tabernacle,
which was one hundred and fifty feet long by seventy-
five broad, built right over the crest of the mountain,
which had been cut off one cubit in depth, to make
a level space for the pulpit, that being placed in the
centre, enclosed by a bamboo trellis, with a writing-
desk on one side, and a preaching-desk on the other,
around which were seated four ordained Karen preachers,
and about one hundred young preachers and schoolmasters; my school-girls were arranged on the left
hand. It was the annual session of the Bghai Christian
Association, and one of the most interesting meetings
I ever attended. Committees were formed, and resolutions passed, and speeches made, full of burning zeal,
ON THE STUDY OF THE BIBLE, AND ITS DISTRIBUTION,
on the support of the District Schools, on the importance of holy living, on female education, and on
brethren settling their own difficulties.

"At the close of the last speech on the latter subject,
every one rose and pledged himself NOT TO GO TO WAR

WITH HIS BROTHER. Oh, the infinite power of the Gospel of Christ! To see one thousand clear-eyed, high-browed, strong-armed men, who, from their childhood, had hated each other, kidnapped and speared each other whenever they could, now exchanging the clasp of peace, and publicly pledging themselves to help and love their neighbours as themselves!

"When I looked over the dense mass of heads, and saw at least three-fourths in clean new tunics, jackets, and turbans, and the women, at least all the younger portion, well dressed, I felt that a great and mighty work had been done in the Bghai country since 1853. Truly the deaf have heard the words of the BOOK, and the eyes of the blind have seen out of obscurity; they also that erred in spirit have come to understanding, and they that murmured have learned doctrine.

"The letters read from the churches of this Association showed that twenty-seven Bghai villages had come over to Christianity within the year, had built school-houses, supported schoolmasters, and established, in the place of their mythical *Mosha*, the worship of Jehovah: there are only forty-four *heathen* Bghai villages remaining. The Mopagas are all brought in except three villages, and *ten* new ones were numbered this last year with the Paku Christian communities.

"At this assembly the chiefs and teachers enacted three rules, which ought to be on every church door, or, perhaps better, on every closet door.

"1st. *That they will not marry heathen companions.*

"2nd. *That they will aid in supporting their teachers.*

" 3rd. *That they will do all they can to enlighten the heathen.*

" The girls of the Institute were arranged along one side of the platform, tastefully dressed in their own costume, of their own manufacture ; and at the close of the convocation they all rose and sung in Karen that inspiring piece—

> ' Hark ! ten thousand harps and voices
> Sound the note of praise above :
> Jesus reigns and heaven rejoices ;
> Jesus reigns the God of love.'

" The effect was perfectly inspiring, and as the strains of music floated away over the hills, and down the glens, we could hear it echoed back from the neighbouring pinnacles, as if choral voices were answering down from the heavenly plains."

CHAPTER XVI.

THE MIGHTY HAND IN THE MOUNTAINS.

IT is the last day of the Association upon the Karen mountains. The moderator rises, and reads off fifteen names of schoolmistresses now ready for service, and the congregation is informed that any who desire a schoolmistress can apply to the Karen Board of Managers at the close of the session. The girls pull their turbans over their faces in bashful modesty, as the eyes of the assembly fall admiringly on the seat beside me. The Association adjourns ; a score of chiefs crowd forward saying,—

" Give us a schoolmistress. Give us a schoolmistress." Here is a report from the first Paku who went out, the principal head-teacher in the school. The chief who called her had been a notorious robber, and I felt afraid to let her go.

" Teacheress, that chief will never become a Christian if she does not go. Our young men have been there, and no one can remain. If he gives his word, she is safe."

This the chiefs all agreed in, and I left it entirely to her. Nau Tsah went, and God kept her, like

Daniel in the lions' den. After some weeks she wrote back :—

" MY LOVED TEACHERESS,

" As God has given me a place, I strive to do His work. After two days many left the school, and returned to their play and work. When the chief returned with the maps, I said,—

" ' Chief, I came here to instruct your children. Put them into my hands.'

" 'I did put them into your hands,' he replied, ' but they like to run about. They cannot sit still.'

" ' Chief,' I answered, ' give them into my hands entirely, and if they do not learn, I will be responsible.' Then the chief said,—' It shall be as you say.' So now there are twenty-nine learning very nicely, and nineteen are new ones who never learned before. This is God's power. Mama, I am a young girl : I have many fears lest I should not do well. I entreat that you will pray for me, that I may increase in wisdom and ability.

" NAU TSAH."

Again she says,—

" Everything you taught us I tell to the people here, to the women, and to the men also, if they ask me. I am not ashamed of the Gospel of Christ. Just as you divided the classes and the time at the Institute, so I do here, and read the Scriptures in the presence of all ; but the young men on Sabbath did not come to worship. Then I sent and entreated, and they came, but I saw they had been asleep, so I said to them,—' Brothers, is it good to sleep on God's holy day ? Ought we not to get strength for the soul from God's Word ?' After this all came to study the Bible in the school-house.

" Mama, dear, I am very happy. Pray that God's Spirit may help me."

When it was time for the next term at the Institute, the chief heard of it, and immediately placed a guard over my brave girl to keep her from leaving them! Nau Tsah wrote to me that she could not get away, but that all were so good to her, it made her weep, because she was unworthy, and she knew God was there.

Finally, I had to send to the chief that if he did so, the managers would not dare let him have another schoolmistress. So he gave in, and, coming up to Nau Tsah, he said,—" Teacheress, my people all love you. Promise me you will go to no other village." She promised ; then he appointed an escort to attend her down, and as he bade her good by—

" Here, teacheress," he said, " here is a rupee, an umbrella, and a dress. Don't forget us."

Nau Tsah burst into tears on telling me of it. " Why," she said, " mama, God is too good to me : I did'nt expect anything." All had gone out freely, asking nothing, expecting nothing, but feeling amply paid in having the *privilege* of working, as they expressed it, in God's vineyard. Their mothers, too, noble sister spirits, toiled day and night to spin and weave their dresses, while they were teaching gratuitously, because they felt they were doing it for Christ. Surely for the sake of this work of love God will establish this school.

The girls had made it a subject of prayer with me for the whole year that God would open the hearts of the chiefs to receive their services. Then all doors opened at once, through the mountain region, at every point of the compass, as if Jehovah had spoken : " Behold, and see if I will not open the windows of heaven, and pour you out a blessing!" "I say unto you, *All things* whatsoever ye shall ask in prayer, BELIEVING, *ye shall receive.*"

"Mama," said a preacher's wife very eagerly, during this Bghai Association, "shall not Nau Meu go to our village? I am so anxious to learn of her. Do compel her to go."

"What shall I do?" said Nau Meu, in a low tone, as soon as she could speak to me alone. " They call me *five* ways."

"Don't you know who can tell you, Nau Meu?"

"Oh, yes, yes," she replied, and was soon out of sight. The result showed with what spirit she left the altar. Many villages had called her where she could have had every comfort, but she turned from all to a most filthy, repelling-looking people, in a Bghai village, where she knew she must deny herself betel-nut, to them a very great sacrifice, and many things to which she was accustomed, and which it would be hard to do without. The following are her letters to Mrs. Dalton, of Edinburgh, and myself, from the jungles, translated literally :—

"DEAR FRIENDS WHO LOVE THE KARENS,

"I, Nau Meu, one of the girl teachers, wish to say a word.

"I am now teaching in the Bghai country. I have *seventy* pupils, and they are trying very hard to learn. I can now speak their language, for which I thank God exceedingly. They are all very kind to me, and I entreat you will pray for me, that I may do them good.

"NAU MEU."

The result was most satisfactory and cheering. The chief soon came down with ten rupees for the school, for which he had never given anything before. He came with his men also, and cleared his portion of the ground, the first and best of any village in the mountains. His people, too, began to come in more tidy; and when I asked after Nau Meu, their eyes always glistened with delight.

The result was what it often is in Christian lands: Nau Meu soon had an offer of marriage from the cleverest young man of the place, and the whole village beset her to accept it!

The following is from the same teacher to Mrs. Dalton:—

"DEAR MAMA,

"I long greatly that God's kingdom may increase. I will tell you a word of my country. It is now four years since we first heard of the Eternal God, and eighty-eight have become disciples in my village. When we were in the hands of Satan, my elder brother had the small-pox, and my uncle caught it of him, and another person caught it of my uncle. This person then kidnapped my uncle, as all the Karens used to do if they caught a disease of any one. Then my uncle caused persons to waylay my brother, and catch him, and would have sold him to the Burmese, but my poor mother wept continually, and at last borrowed money enough to buy him back. She gave two gongs which cost sixty rupees each, and a large one which cost two hundred and fifty rupees.

" When my uncle became a disciple, he gave back the large gong to my brother. My wicked uncle has changed. He has built a house on the Girls' Place, and we love each other much. The Tounghoo people, who are not disciples, do after this manner continually, and are very wicked. Now the school is dismissed that we may all reap paddy, but all of us love the school with a great love."

The following, in Karen, was sent in by the schoolmistresses of the Institute without any suggestion from me, with a handsome suit of Karen clothes, asking if they might give them to Captain D'Oyly when he was leaving for Prome. It is translated literally :—

" To the Great Commissioner whom God Blesses.
" Dear Sir,
" Since you ruled over Tounghoo, it has pleased you to help us poor Karen people, so that we rejoiced

greatly under your rule, and now, when we hear you are going to another country, we feel that our hearts will go after you exceedingly, even as the deer thirsts for the water-brooks.

" We pray that the great King of Heaven may bless you during life, even as He blessed Mordecai and Queen Esther. For this reason, we, poor people, before we received the Eternal God's commands, knew nothing at all of books. Now the English Commissioners have come to Tounghoo, and a place has risen for us to study in.

" This is God's great mercy, and we rejoice and praise Him, and the name of Jesus Christ, continually."

I might tell many stories about the Mighty Hand in the mountains, but I will stop for only one more. One day a Bghai chief, who had not been baptized, came down almost in a rage to know what had become of his teacher. He had opened his village to books only about three months before.

" Mama, has my teacher gone with teacher Mason ?" he asked, with some appearance of impatience.

" Yes, brother, he has gone on a tour to the red Karens, but he will be back, we hope, in two months."

" Two months ! I must have another."

" Suppose you take one of the girls, chief ?" I suggested.

" *A girl*," he repeated, towering up in scorn, and I could see every lip of his attendants curled with disdain.

" Oh, never mind," I answered, gently. " If you

don't like, you needn't have one, but just come in and hear them recite." Out of politeness, merely, he and his men entered the school-room. I called up the principal Bghai mistress to examine the school, briefly, in reading Bghai, in the Bible, in arithmetic, and geography. She was going over the large outline maps, and the school intensely interested, when the chief rose and walked along in a bending posture to the front of the platform, followed by his men. All sat down in profound respect, but very soon their eyes began to peer open, as if they would roll out; their hands fell down, their mouths opened, and there they sat, their heads stretched far forward. Finally, the chief said in a low tone,—

"I'll have that one—that one," pointing to the mistress who was questioning the others.

"Er, er," all his men joined in. "We'll have that one." Nau Lanui hid her face for shame, and the whole school was on tiptoe. After some persuasion, Nau Lanui ventured to go with them, and then came the real triumph of knowledge, for every one of those young men stepped forward, offering to carry something. One took her slate, another her hymn-book, and even one grasped her little basket of clothes, a thing those men could not before have been hired to do, for with them nothing is so defiling as to touch a woman's dress, and nothing so degrading as to carry burdens for her.

However, all forgot these prejudices in their delight, and hope of acquiring wisdom. The girls vied with one another in helping them off; for, as we did not like one to go alone, they offered to support two, and two went with them the same day fifteen or twenty miles into the mountains, which is as much as a hundred in a country of roads and carriages. On the way they met another troop on a similar errand.

"We've got the best teacher there," the men called out.

"Then she shall go with us," the others retorted, and they came near, bearing her off in spite of them.

"Let her alone! Go to the school and get another. Haven't you got feet?" shouted the men with their prize, and pushed on.

The adventure proved an entire success, and this girl has ever since been regarded as a kind of sybil or oracle among the tribe.

The plan of the school in Tounghoo was an *experiment*, but no experiment ever succeeded more perfectly, for it has united these wild clans under one banner, and awakened a spirit of enterprise and energy, such as they never before felt or knew. The Karen Education Society at first numbered only sixty chiefs, but it has increased to two hundred and sixty, and thus far they have been more than faithful to their promise. Since the school was opened in 1857, the chiefs have contributed 10,000 rupees.

In Burmah, no appeal to self-interest will move to action, if it touches the native sense of honour. The poorest Burman will walk off and forego his supper rather than endure a single word wounding to his self-respect. So with Karens. You appeal in vain to their

X

sense of fear or love of gain. Say to them,—" If you do not thus, the Commissioner will not help you," and they would look down from their soul-pinnacles with unutterable contempt. But just say, " GOD expects this of KARENS," or, " Your brothers are watching your feet," and you touch a chord that will vibrate through every glen of Tounghoo. Therefore, in proposing a school to the Mountain Chiefs of the land, I appealed to this innate self-respect—simply telling them they would have the honour before all the surrounding nations of educating their women like the greatest nation in the world, and they should have the honour of doing it themselves in institutions of their own, and under managers of their own, only Government would help them to begin ; AND ABOVE ALL IT WOULD PLEASE YUAH.

And now this Karen Female Institute will be cherished as the Delphi of their tribes, to which they will continually resort, and from which they cannot return without carrying to their mountain homes some glimmerings from the light of science, and a clearer knowledge of the True God.

PART III.

CHAPTER I.

SETTLING A COLONY—KAREN RESOURCES.

I KNEW it would be in vain to build a school-house, unless the Karens would some of them live near enough to protect it, for the heathen would carry off every board, one by one. Besides, a *girls'* school could not be main-tained without protectors, and these must be *Karen* protectors. Karens could not live there without *support*, and they could not find support without *land*. To settle only two or three families around us would be useless. So I applied to Government for a tract of land on which experiments might be made, a tract large enough for all the tribes near Tounghoo.

There were other good reasons for trying to bring the Karens down to the plains. Their mode of cultivating the hill land, as described in Colonel Phayre's letter, leads them to be always migrating, so that it is very difficult to keep up their mountain schools with any regularity; the same cause keeps them poor, and renders it exceedingly difficult to support their families and teachers. They have nothing against times of distress, so that if there comes a drought, or if armies of rats destroy their rice-fields, numbers die of starvation.

Considering all this, Mr. Mason thought no one could do a greater good to the tribes in Tounghoo, than help them to begin lowland paddy cultivation.

The Karens want *instruction.* Their forests abound in valuables, but they know not how to make them available. In the first place, they want good rice land on the plains, and to be taught the cultivation of cotton.

Colonel Phayre once sent the South American cotton seed to experiment with in Tounghoo. I left before hearing the full result of that experiment, but I heard that planted around the schools, on rich soil, it grew too luxuriously, and yielded only a small basket, but what there was of it had long silken fibres, and the seeds fell out at once, to the great delight and amazement of the Karens. I imagine that soil was too rich, as it went mostly to leaves, and on the sand hills it seemed to lack nourishment, but probably if the forest were cleared half a mile inland, cotton would grow well in Tounghoo. The Karens would enter into its cultivation, I think, with spirit, and this would encourage the rice cultivators. But they would need to have instruction at first in adapting the soils, in seeking out suitable localities, and to have a machine for cleaning the cotton. Secondly, they require instruction in working iron and lead. They have both in Tounghoo, and loadstone. They would soon learn to make plows and other agricultural implements for themselves, axes, and carpenter's tools.

They need instruction in preparing leather and making good strong shoes, which their people would buy all over the hills. Pegged shoes, if introduced, might be the means of raising up large villages in the mountains, for the manufacture of pegs alone, as I have seen in New Hampshire.

Their buffalo and cow hides, deer and goat skins, might then be of use to them. Preparing leather would bring them to work their limestone, and their rock salt, which is also found in the hills of Tounghoo. Valuable barks, nuts, oils, and catechu trees, abound likewise, and careya, and mangrove trees, on the coast would supply tannic acid.

They need masters in wood-work of all kinds ; their mountains abound in beautiful woods, and they might learn to make wooden wares for themselves, instead of using bamboo troughs. Their red wood is almost equal to mahogany, the hopea, and a kind of turminalia, which they call "bitter wood," because the teredos will not eat it, might be very useful for drawers and chests. They have sassafras, too, and ebony is so abundant, they make their great pestles, six feet long, of it. They have matchlock-wood and lance wood, and a soft white wood that might answer instead of pine. Wicker-work they would excel in, and the ratans wreathe their gorges all through the mountains. I have seen them thirty feet in length. Their forests, too, abound in cordage plants, and they already understand a curious kind of rope-braiding in Tounghoo, that far excels that made by any of the other tribes, and they braid thatch in a very superior style, which lasts twice as long as Burman thatch.

If they could have instruction from a practical bota-

nist, their forests would yield medicinal plants largely
for export. They have abundance of gamboge, liquid
amber, the camphor plant, (Blumea,) a kind of native
cinnamon, ipecacuanha, manna, clove, cassia-bark, citron,
bhang, nux vomica, castor-oil, cutch, turmeric, betel-
leaf, leea, sessamum, cardamum, ivy, sarsaparilla, heart-
seek, garlic, and gum-arabic—not the true, but the gum
of the cashew tree, which is quite as good. The true arrowroot, (Maranta,) also, is beginning to be cultivated, and
might be to any extent. They have a pine from which
tar and pitch might be manufactured in abundance, and
the wood-oil, I am sure, might be put to some economic
purpose, besides supplying torches.

They have the best of dye-plants, the cashew, mela-
stoma, shoe-flower, ebony, and physic-nut, for black dye;
ruellia and asclepias, for blue; sappan, tamarind, mo-
rinda, log-wood, for red; safflower, gamboge, butea,
turmeric, and jack, for yellow; and they make a fine
green with turmeric and soap-acacia. They have four
or five indigenous trees producing excellent varnish, but
all goes to waste.

(If you ask how I know these things are there, I
answer, my husband says so, and he's my Cyclopedia.
See his book on "BURMAH." Phinney, Blakeman, &
Mason, New York.)

To redeem these riches of earth, or to elevate the
Karens, it needs the help of Government, and the help
of philanthropists. Especially are these aids and en-
couragements needed for the women of these nations,
for does not woman educate the farmer, the soldier, the

teacher, and the Legislature? When the Prince of Wales was in New York, I presented the subject to him, particularly in regard to Female Education in India, taking the opportunity to give some particulars, through Colonel Bruce, concerning the Karens, and the Girls' School in Tounghoo. The Prince answered very kindly, and I hope may not wholly forget either the school, or those who have so kindly aided us.

An application being made for land to the Duputy Commissioner of Tounghoo, he wrote back the following note, in the latter part of 1857 :—

" MY DEAR MRS. MASON,

" If your mountain friends will only clear the land and cultivate it, I will give them as much as their hearts desire.

" GEORGE D'OYLY."

Captain D'Oyly gave orders that the Burman Thugyee should accompany me and the Karen chiefs, to select the land, and that he should give them good fields in the vicinity of the Institution, and on the strength of this we started together.

Fancy us mounted on two great elephants—I on one, and the Burman head-man on the other, each of us with a score of followers. The Nah Khan and several Karen chiefs are of the party, and two of our best assistants are behind.

On we go, over logs and bogs—now on a wide open prairie, the sun burning into our very brains, and anon the elephant sinks up to his body in a broad marsh, sinks, sinks, so fearfully, that our hair almost stands on end, lest we should never again emerge.

" There, Thugyee, there 's a nice field. It stretches up a long way, too."

" Yes, but this I gave yesterday to a couple of Burmese."

We wander—farther and farther.

" Come, Thugyee. Here are fields."

" But the Burmese yonder, pointing half a mile off, will want this to enlarge their fields."

" And this ?" Coming to another tract of wild land that might have been cultivated thirty years before.

" Oh, this is grass land. I couldn't give this to the Karens."

" Karens want grass land as well as Burmese, and the Commissioner said that you must give them good land."

So we travel, two whole days, over an area of nearly fifty miles, always receiving the same answers. At last I stopped short.

" Thugyee, listen ! The Commissioner ordered you to give the Karens land—good land—and near the school. We 've travelled long enough. Give us the land !"

Upon this the Thugyee rode off hastily to a long jungle skirting the river.

" There," he says, " take this."

" This !" the Karens exclaimed in dismay. " We can never clear off these great trees. It will be useless.

Why cannot he give us grass land as he does the Burmese ?"

" Wait brothers, be patient—see what rich soil. Look at those paddy stalks as large as your little fingers," pointing to the fields adjoining. " Let us get this if we can, for he does not mean to give you anything." Then turning to the Burman,—

" We can have this, you say ; but then we must have the whole jungle, as far as we choose."

" Yes, except where the Burmese have commenced clearing."

There were many obstacles to the cultivation of this tract, which were almost insurmountable to the Karens. The strip of good land was very narrow, the trees thick and large, the Burmese fields close adjoining, and there was a public road running through all.

We could only persuade fourteen men to attempt the business the first year. They succeeded in clearing and planting each a pretty good piece of land, and with great pride they watched it. One morning, when the rice was about two feet high, they all came running down to me with fear and wretchedness depicted on every face.

" What is the matter ?" I inquired.

" Gone ! gone !"

" What is gone ?"

" The paddy. The Burman buffalos have destroyed the whole."

" How did it happen ? Had you not good fences ?"

" Yes, we had fenced every lot carefully ; they must have been turned in." None but those who have gone through what we have in securing land—in persuading wild men to make an attempt at civilization, and in supporting them while doing it—can understand our grief on that morning. The men went to the Thugyee for redress.

"You must catch the buffalos," he told them. So they watched day and night, and at last succeeded in catching two. They received for all their loss *five rupees !*

Upon this they were utterly discouraged, and all but two returned to the jungles.

So the matter rested for several months, when the Thugyee came to me to know if the Karens were going to cultivate that land any more. "The Karens cannot cultivate lowland," he said; "the Burmese can, and it must not lie waste."

We told him the land would be occupied, when he left with a very dark brow.

I called the Karen women and explained to them how fruitless all my efforts for a permanent school would prove without protectors, and endeavoured to arouse their philanthrophy and love for Christ's kingdom. It was not, however, until after several days of prayer and exhortation that they could be persuaded to go up and live in the rice fields. Finally, six families volunteered, and I engaged to advance them rice for six months. To cheer and strengthen them I went up every week, helped them to plan the little settlement, and encouraged them to persevere. The first week on my reaching the camp, they all came out and grasped my hand with tears, so

like my own children had they become. I found them
all huddled into one circular hut, built of brush and
reeds, and a little bedroom for the night-guard in the
top of a tree.

The second week they gave me a happy surprise and
led me up into a neat little chapel, where a boy teacher,
about fourteen, sat by a pretty bamboo table, surrounded
by twenty little children in school, learning to read.

The Commissioner had liberally invited the Karens
down to the plains, promising them land and protection.
This had greatly encouraged the chiefs, and they mustered several new families for the work. How should
they get buffalos was the next question, and two or
three resolved to sell their fruit gardens. I was one day
speaking of their great want to Colonel Phayre, when
he said,—

" I 'll make them a loan for buffalos."

" You will ?" I asked in surprise. " Are you in
earnest ? Would you *dare* to trust them ?"

" I will," he answered with a quiet smile, and to our
great joy ordered the loans, sending this kind note to
Mr. Mason :—

" I request you will have the goodness to inform the
Karens, to whom this advance is made, that I do not
name any particular time for repayment of this advance,
but that I expect them to repay when, with ordinary
exertion, they can do so. They have my best wishes."

This, too, we recognised as a special answer to prayer,
for which we thanked God and took courage.

CHAPTER II.

SECURING FISH PONDS—SKETCHES OF KAREN CHARACTER—LITTLE FRANK.

" HALLOO ! there, you Karen dog. Pay me half a rupee !"

Seeing the women and children running, I inquired what had happened, but before they could answer, a stout, hard-looking Burman came leading a Karen up to the chapel, declaring he would take him to court. On inquiring I found one of the new settlers had stepped into a pond, and with his axe had caught two fishes for his supper. The pond had been rented by the Burman, and there was no way but to pay the fine, which I did, for the offender was very poor and hungry.

On the east side of the Sittang river there are fifteen or more large ponds full of fish. These are annually rented out by the Government, and bring in a little revenue. But the poor always suffered on account of the heavy fees demanded by these pond-holders.

One time when I was in the jungles, a villager complained to me, and begged me to intercede for him. They had made a small trap by the shore, trying to get a few fish for their suppers. The goung came round, ordered it to be destroyed, abused the poor man, and imposed a fine, which forced him to sell his pig to pay. All this was contrary to Government rules, for Colonel Phayre, on purpose to protect the poor, had made a provision, that no river or creek should be taxed at all, or hand-nets anywhere, or any kind of small traps. Moreover, the ponds were to be rented to the settlers *around them*. But this was all Greek to Captain Rock, then Deputy Assistant in charge; consequently, I sent up the following petition :—

" As the present monopoly of one man over all the ponds in Kannee makes it exceedingly hard for the Karens here to procure any fish for daily use, I would beg the privilege of taking one pond for them in the immediate vicinity of the Karen paddy field, during this present year."

The answer was contrary to the printed law before him,—that Government could recognise but one pond-owner in that region.

" Apply for the whole," says Mr. Mason, which I did at once, for two hundred rupees, the same as the Burmese had paid. No excuse could be found for refusing, so I took them for one year. This caused universal joy among the poor of all classes : great numbers were about to enter into the fish trade, when the cholera scattered them. I had intended to let the Burmans have one-half, but I sold thirteen ponds to the Burmese for just what I gave, reserving two of the best free for the Karens and other friendless persons. So the Karens, Shans, and poor Burmese, were liberated from their oppressors, and supplied with fish in abundance for the taking. The ponds and the buffalos had a most happy effect, and many now came down to join the colony, until my hands were doubly full.

" Mama, will you buy me a pair of buffalos ?" " And me ?" " And me ?" came from twenty at once.

But who was competent to buy, was the perplexing question. The Karens were no judges of buffalos—the Burmese would either cheat or rob them. Just at this time a Shan was introduced to our camp, an old herds-man. So he was sent out with the bravest Karen there, to make the purchase of one pair of buffalos and a cart. On returning, the Karen only came to me with the change. At that moment the Shan made a motion behind the Karen, indicating that all was not right, but on questioning, I could obtain no satisfaction. Imme-diately I called two Karens, and sent secretly to inquire the sum for which the buffalos had been sold. My messengers had ten miles to walk ; but I felt sure there was dishonesty, and as we had many buffalos to buy, it was an important matter. The Paku member of our Board also came to my aid, and so cross-questioned the two during the night, that he drew forth a confession, and early next morning sent Thatug to me with ten rupees more.

The thief came on his knees begging forgiveness, and promising solemnly to steal no more. We forgave him, but his history was a sad one.

His place flourished above all others. He was far more industrious, and kept his garden in better order, and was always ready to help anywhere and everywhere; besides, he was so fearless, he was really a great acquisition to our new settlement. But one day I was called to see his wife, who lay nearly senseless, the blood streaming down her face. He had struck her with a club, and nearly killed her, then fled to the woods. Upon this I learned that he was a murderer, feared by all. He had speared a man in his rage, and had sold one wife to the Red Karens, and whether she was living or dead no one knew. I immediately gave notice to the Acting Commissioner, who sent his peons, and cast him into prison. Some thought it served him right; others beheld with trembling a brother of the church in gaol; and, altogether, I scarcely knew what to do. It was true he had sold his wife and killed a neighbour, but then it was before he heard God's commands. Others in the church had been either robbers or kidnappers. If God and the church had forgiven him, those things ought not to influence in this case. These thoughts, with his humble pleading, troubled me not a little, for he made no plea, only, " O Lord, I am a great sinner; I have an awful temper; I cannot govern it: it will send me to hell. Oh, God! oh, God!"

" Who maketh thee to differ?" whispered a still, small voice within. Mr. Mason was in the hills, but I could not rest; so I sent to the gaol the same night, paid his fine of fifteen rupees, and set him at liberty. He came to me directly, fell upon his face, and implored

Y

me not to send him off from the place. We took his
garden for the fine, and gave him five rupees, with a
new piece of land outside the school lot, to begin anew.
But one morning the neighbours came leading Thatug
again. They had suspected him, had set a watch, and
caught him stealing young trees and plantains from his
old garden. So then it was the general voice that he
must be expelled; and he was, on condition, however,
that if he conducted himself well for one year, he should
again be restored. For a time he tried and did pretty
well, but before six months were gone, he was caught
again stealing a goat in the night, which he carried to a
poor man, and they killed and ate it together. So he
was brought down once more, led by a cord around his
body, and the man who ate with him was brought as a
witness.

"Do you not know the partaker is as bad as the
thief?" I asked.

"No, we never heard of such a law."

"Well, if they take him up to court, he would just
witness himself into gaol with Thatug, and I don't see
why he should not be there too."

"No, no," they cried, "he is not a bad man, and
never did anything of the kind before. He shall not go
up at all." The case ended in giving Thatug six
months of hard labour on the roads; yet, strange as it
may seem, I believe this man will be found at last with
the forgiven thief in paradise! He has gone back now
to the new settlement a changed man, and will yet, I
have no doubt, be one of the most upright and faithful.

I assure you, reader, we do not know the strength of temptation till we encounter it *under the same circumstances* with our brothers.

I had another hard thing to meet in those days. Nah Khan Qualay, the man who had been first to take up the work and help it forward, on whom I relied more than upon all the other chiefs together, came, when we were assembled, dressed in sackcloth, standing under the house pleading for forgiveness. In amazement, I inquired what that meant, when he confessed that he had two wives! It appeared that his real wife was very sickly, and that she had no children. He saw a pretty slave girl and bought her, provided for her and all her family at a distance from his home, and had joined the church without letting this fact be known. Some did know of it, but it is a rule with Karens not to inform. He had been a member of the church three years, and all this time had been transgressing the law of God.

Seldom did I ever suffer such mental distress as then. For three days I could only groan. The slave wife had now a little son, and, of course, the truth must be told, so that all confidence in the man's integrity vanished like the dew. The report spread far and wide over the hills, and hundreds came down to see the humility of the greatest Khan in the jungles. Qualay sat on the ground in soiled garments, the very picture of despair, confessing to every one, and begging forgiveness of every one, offering, too, to put away the young wife, and never look on his boy again.

I could not help pitying the culprit, whose great

desire was to have an heir to his title and his property. Still such deception and transgression could not be lightly passed by. He had built himself a handsome house on the girls' place, so as to hear petty causes there, which would have been a convenience to the Bghai tribes, and have tended to bring the heathen Karens around us where they could hear of God, and see the schools. I was hoping for great good from this arrangement; but this sudden disclosure dashed all our plans, and crushed all our hopes.

Mr. Mason and San Quala both agreed that he must be excluded from the church, and then came the question, Could he have a court-house on the school land? I referred the case to the settlers, and told them they must decide the matter, simply exhorting them to do it in the fear of God. Their decision was, that his house must be pulled down and removed from the school land, and that he should no more visit the place until restored to the church. I had not quite expected this, and for a week my strength left me. It seemed to me impossible to go on in our arduous work without the aid of this chieftain.

The Board of Managers all felt so too, and had everything at stake, but the law of God glittered above their heads like a two-edged sword, and they dared not shield the Chief. He is the greatest man, they said. Every eye is on us. Nobody believes we shall dare speak out. Finally, I suggested that we call the Nah Khan, and let him judge himself. We did so in the presence of all the Board of Managers and the principal chiefs. We laid the whole case before him, the injury he had done the cause, the unhappy influence on the minds of all the tribes coming and going, and cast the whole burden of deciding the matter upon his own conscience. Then appeared the true Christian shining out over all his transgressions.

" I have laid a stone of stumbling," he said ; " I will do all I can to remove it." This was his answer, coming up from under the floor, for he utterly refused to enter the chapel while the stain was upon him. Immediately that man went to work with his own hands, solitary and alone ; he took off the boards and the roof from his house, the big tears dropping over all, which so excited the commisseration of the crowd, that they all stepped back in awe, except the principal chiefs, who, with great deference, offered their aid. When they got to the posts, the crowd was called, and in a few hours the beautiful house that had cost months of labour, and was a great ornament to our grounds, was gone, and the Nah Khan, who had been as *my brother*, had gone too.

Here, again, were visible the footsteps of the Almighty, for instead of the people fainting, as I had feared, they were ten times stronger than ever before, so that the wildest Bghais came pouring down, having confidence in the law of God. Singular, too, it was, a short time after this, a large teak monastery, south of our school, was burned down, and the lighted thatch falling on it, a small house just below where this had stood was burned. Had that building been there then, probably nothing could have saved the INSTITUTE, as the south wind blows very strong. Truly, God is *Almighty*. I feel happy to say the Nah Khan kept his promise, never visited his boy, and only once or twice had it brought to him. After two years of exclusion, he was restored to the church, and now, having buried his poor invalid wife, he has been lawfully married to the mother of his boy. But I fear that boy will be to him an Absalom.

The next attempt at purchasing buffalos ended in buying a sick one that died in two days, and another old one that "would not draw." But perseverance! nobody can tell what that will do! After a while the Karens learned to trade better, and every day the buffalo regiment had to be paraded up before the Institute, and I was obliged to go out and review it. What constituted a good buffalo I had not the slightest idea, except that it ought to have sound hoofs, a clean tongue, and ears that "would stand." This I learned as they did, by the sick one being minus all these good qualities. Practice, however, makes perfect, so we persevered in the study of buffalos till we all learned that long horns were obstinates, big bones would not fatten, and very small hoofs would break and run. In the end, the Burmese acknowledged the Karen buffalo herd to be the handsomest and best of all in the region. We had the same experience with carts. At first the Karens were sure to come home with some broken-backed cart, which the Burmese had put off to them for twelve rupees, while they might have bought a new one for sixteen. I did not tell them they had been deceived. There's nothing like learning one's self. I advised them to go immediately and get a load of paddy. They went off in high spirits, but coming home, over went the whole load upon the ground in the middle of a broad prairie. There were only two men. One had to go five miles for a new axletree, and as soon as he was gone, the crows and vultures pounced down upon the load, and, in spite of the carman, appropriated a good share of it to themselves. "Amai! this old rickety cart wasn't worth two rupees," I heard them telling the others on their return. They never mentioned it to me, they were so much ashamed. Ever after they took care to buy good carts.

Rice is the staple food of this place instead of bread. The Karens have no money to lay up in advance, and they were quite at the mercy of the traders in the rains. I resolved to build a store-house, and store for them one thousand bushels of paddy; then they could buy of me at cost price when the paddy rose; for the Burmese raised the price from thirty to seventy rupees the hundred baskets, or from four annas to a rupee the bushel for unbeaten rice. The Burmese traders were shrewd enough to see what I was doing, so they kept up the price, and I had to pay forty-five and fifty rupees the hundred, and in the same proportion the Karens had to pay for all eatables.

Their ploughs, yokes, everything indeed, I was obliged to look after. These obtained, I must then go up and divide the land, and this was the hardest of all. No new cultivator would raise his axe till I apportioned off his lot. It was of no use for me at first to delegate this business to another. Mama must say herself what should be theirs. So I submitted, knowing they would after awhile learn to trust the assistant, who always accompanied me, which they now do; but for many weeks at first I had to go out twice and three times the week nearly the whole length of the land, five miles in extent, dividing off their lots to arrange for their school-houses, and their dwellings; to prescribe for their sick, to cheer them on, and instruct them in the Scriptures. Their Bible studies they missed more than anything else. They had been for more than a year constant attendants at our Bible class, and were so deeply interested, they could repeat a great deal by heart, and I never visited them without a Bible meeting; but these field labours were really much harder than all my teaching in the house, although there I had no help except natives and our own boys.

One day, on returning, I was met by the girls, saying my little Frank was sick. Without a moment's delay I hastened to him. This was on Monday. On Wednesday evening, I had no little Frank in this world. When I saw he must die, I bent down and told him the worst, just as I had always done when giving them medicine. " You are going to Jesus, darling," I said: " you are not afraid to go?" He looked up, at first startled, but instantly signified that he was not afraid, and that look was so loving in the midst of his agony.

The dear brothers were parted—our little circle broken, and so suddenly—so unexpectedly—by a death so in-

expressibly painful, I had scarcely strength to lay him
in the grave. His papa was in the hills, and could not
reach us, so I buried him alone, with our kind friend,
Captain Bond, and the Karens. I heard a Minister
once remark in the pulpit : " Some people under bereavement go about their business, and you scarcely see any
difference, while others are entirely overcome. This
is owing to finer and more acute feelings in the one than
the other." So a lady once said to me when my heart
was breaking,—" Why, you look just as usual !" I
think the Master Himself taught us on this subject.
He bore about with Him the heaviest bereavement, and
yet worked on with cheerfulness.

My angel boy was a dear little missionary, and taught
a Sunday-school of little Karen orphans for two years
before he died. The children and girls of the school
were inconsolable.

He was a great reader ; he had laid by story books at
my request, and taken to graver studies. He was well
acquainted with Humboldt and Layard, and Buchanan,
and the Pilgrim's Progress was his daily companion.

The stroke was indeed heavy, and tears were my
nightly companions, yet I trust tears of submission.
His own mother died when he was only three months
old, and kind Mrs. Bennett, now of Maulmain, became
a dear and tender mother to him, until I went and
claimed him, which was before he could walk much.
There were only three months' difference between him
and my own little boy, so they were like twins, and
until the last week of his life, my pet lambs would jump

into my arms at once. His name was Francis, but when he came to me I named him *Meus*. He was a daring, restless boy, and it was very hard for him to keep from cutting the benches and spoiling the inkstands in school. One time I had to pay quite a bill for this, but I only gave it him to pay, telling him I would have to go without my dinner that day. His little lip quivered, and he could not possibly swallow his own dinner. He would often come, after we returned to Burmah, twine his arms around me, laying his sweet face close to mine, and whisper, " I am so glad you didn't leave me in America, for then I should have been a *bad* boy. You know I couldn't *be still*, mama," leaving tears of tender gratitude upon my cheek ; and truly I was afraid to leave him, lest he should be treated with severity for his restlessness, and so become stubborn.

My dear boys at one time bore a heavy weight upon their hearts for months ; at last they came to me and made a full confession of all their heart-sins, and poured out their long pent-up sorrows. After this they were very happy, and tried to live in the fear of God. They had sinful hearts, but they struggled hard and obtained the victory, so that I recollect only a single instance where a wicked nature betrayed itself, and then but for a moment, during all the last year of Frank's life. From being restless he became quiet, from being careless he became exceedingly watchful, and from being hard he became as tender as an infant in all his emotions. The change was remarkable and striking, and I doubt if boys ever enjoyed more of Christ together.

They studied everything together, reciting to one another; with my examining them on Saturdays, they got on so as to enter the High School Latin Class in Newton Centre, Mass., after reaching home when seven years old, and they went through arithmetic alone. They generally kept their study-hours very regularly, knowing that an exhaustless fund of amusement was ready for them as soon as the lessons were well learned. They had their own little Burman high-backed saddles, their own pony, and their own boat. At four o'clock, they donned their Highland costume, and steered with all speed over the river to the orphans, who knew just when to expect them, and were always ready on the beach; and these poor children miss them now.

They taught all the boys in the settlement how to swim, and girls to row a boat, and to ride. My Frank was a fine rider, and could manage any pony that was brought in to our village. He was thrown two or three times, so was his brother; but they both rode so that they would gallop up and down the roads at the swiftest possible speed, without saddle or bridle. Boating was a source of great amusement to both the boys, and this, too, they taught the Karen students, having first learned themselves, for the young men coming from the mountains were extremely fearful of water. One time, Frank was rowing me across the river, when there arose a sudden squall, which came near capsizing the boat. We had a dozen Karens in the boat, and all too much frightened to give the slightest assistance. "Bail out!" he cried, "and sit still. We'll go it." This re-assured

the Karens, and he landed us all safely. It was a very
wild scene, and one of great peril. The wind was blowing a gale, and the whole river in commotion, the breakers
all around us, and the white crested waves every moment
dashing over us. Edwin had rowed his boat across, and
stood ready to strike out if we went over. And over we
must have gone but for my brave little pilot, who stood
up amidst the wild waters, and gave his orders loud
above the roaring winds, and in a tone so calm and self-
possessed, it inspired every one present, so that each one
did the very best thing possible, and we all reached
shore without harm. It was really a great feat, and
he, dear boy, was amply paid by seeing that his papa
and I appreciated his skill.

With all their play and study, one would think they
could not have been of much service to me, but oh !
they were, and when gone, I missed my darling on
every rock, every wave, and in every corner of the
house. All the time I was in the jungles after timber,
Frank and Edwin were our accountants and apothe-
caries, selling, during that time, four hundred rupees'
worth of medicines and books to the Karens. Every
ounce of this and every book they had set down in
perfect order, and rendered the account to their papa,
with all the money received in. Frank, also, kept my
bazaar account for me, and servants' bills, and everything expended in the family.

Soon after this parting, I was brought very low with
fever for three weeks ; and in the rains I wrote to my
daughter :—

"I have scarcely done anything for many months but nurse and doctor the sick. Cholera has been raging all around ; and out of our little settlement, thirty-four are now at rest. I have taken four very severe cases of cholera into our own house, and, by God's blessing, they are now well : the last was Quala, whose wife had just died with cholera in the jungles. Twenty-five orphans are with us, all made so within three months. On the mountains they all flee and leave the sick to die alone, and remain unburied until the wild beasts enter the house and devour them."

CHAPTER III.

THE "KING OF TOUNGHOO."

OUR sufferings were thought to have been caused by cholera. If I thought otherwise, it was not wise to think it aloud ; but scarcely had we recovered, when Captain Rock, the "King of Tounghoo," as he crowned himself, called on us with a train of Burmese.

"Mrs. Mason, these Burmese have come with a petition for some land. You see I know nothing about the matter—nothing at all," he said. I begged to explain that the Burman Thuygee had given the land to the Karens by order of the former Deputy Commissioner. "But you bring no documents," said the King. "I can deal only with *documents*. You had better write immediately to the Commissioner for documents."

"The Commissioner knows all about the matter, and has given orders that we should not be molested."

"Aye ! Is that your school-house over the river?"

"It is the *People's* house."

"Oh, ay, but I've not much opinion of this mission work. Missionaries, no doubt, *mean* well ; but it's all useless—there's no changing savages. You'll never succeed."

"The Commissioner thinks we *have* succeeded."

"Well, but, Mrs. Mason, what shall we do about this matter? It's very unpleasant—particularly unpleasant."

"There is nothing to be done. The Commissioner of Pegu gave the Thuygee orders commanding him what to do."

"The Thuygee! How? what? where is it?" in apparent amazement, whereupon the Thuygee was obliged to produce the order which commanded him not to trouble the Karens, and not to give the jungle to any other party till the boundary should be settled.

"Yes, I see; but, Mrs. Mason, these people say they want to enlarge their fields. I know nothing about it—nothing at all. It's very bad—very bad, indeed, this mingling of races."

Two weeks after this boding interview, I went up into the rice fields, and, to my dismay, found the Burmese had began to clear the Karen land. We were entirely at the mercy of Captain Rock, so I wrote up to him. He replied that he had ordered all work to cease, and had appointed a Burman to go out and investigate the subject. Commissioned a hostile Burman, and that, too, directly contrary to official orders! I entreated that the subject might be left where the Commissioner himself had left it.

"That cannot be," he answered. "It is clearly my duty to prevent all trespassing. I shall to-morrow re-issue my order to the Goung to take up any Karens whom he may find trespassing upon the land in dispute."

Entreaties were again employed. No reply: the work

was all stopped, the Karens in great distress, the Burmese rejoicing, declaring that Captain Rock has determined all Karens should go back to the hills. One Burman comes riding into the fields with an elephant to trample down the Karens—their houses are pulled down —they are terribly threatened and frightened, and we flee to prayer, and are all of us found in the chapel till twelve o'clock.

In the morning arrives the Rangoon mail, and I read,—

"*To* ——, Esq., Collector of Customs, Tounghoo.

"Sir,

"I herewith enclose to you a copy of a letter dated the 8th of February last, which I addressed to Captain D., directing him to make over to the mountain Karens some vacant jungle land in the circle of Kannee. As this has not been done, I herewith invest you with special powers to proceed and do so.

"When completed, I request you will send me a copy, showing the exact boundaries given to the Karens.

"Any Burmese settlers on land within that which the Karens applied for, who have entered since the date of the application, will be directed to quit.

"I have, &c., &c.,

"A. P. Phayre,

"*Com. Pegu, Agent to the Gov.-General.*"

By the same mail the following came to me from Colonel Phayre:—

" As soon as the papers reach me, I will endeavour to make everything satisfactory. I consider it a great object to induce the mountain Karens to come down to the plains. You may be sure I will do all I can to encourage them."

The order had been issued previous to Captain ——'s order, and had been ten days or more on the way, so it was very singular that it should reach us just at this time, as if God, foreseeing the distress that would come upon us, had so arranged it on purpose to comfort us, and to grant *special* answer to prayer. Truly, " It is not in man that walketh to direct his steps." I immediately telegraphed to the Commissioner :—

" Thank you ! *Thank you !*" Heb. vi. 10 ; and took for our subject, in the Bible class that evening, 1 John v. 14, " And this is the confidence that we have in Him, *if we ask anything according to His will, He heareth us.*"

This arrangement sent the Karens for a time back to their paddy fields. But the result of this officer's investigations will be seen in Mr. Mason's official letter to Government :—

" TOUNGHOO, *June* 12*th,* 1859.

" *To* COLONEL PHAYRE, COMMISSIONER OF PEGU.
" SIR,

" I have the honour to acknowledge the reception of your letter, dated May 18th, 1859, making inquiries relative to the Kannee lands now in cultivation by the

Karens. To make the matter as plain as possible, a map of those lands, accompanying this letter, will be found reduced from the Surveyors' map, made by the Superintendent of Customs. According to a statement in one of your notes to Mrs. Mason, that ' No interference or occupation of the land, after the date of the application, could be allowed,' Mrs. Mason pledged her word to the Karens, who were very fearful lest they should lose their labour, that the land they cleared should be their own, and fifty-five men have been at work in the forest, more or less, for the last five or six months. The Superintendent, making his boundary, has cut off *twelve* of the *best* paddy fields cleared by the Karens, running along the watercourses where the water is a cubit deep, leaving them only a narrow strip, where the water is but ankle deep. These fields, on which they had worked for some six months, he has given to the Burmese, whose broad, rich fields already stretched as far as the eye could scan.

" He admits that the Karens are wronged by the arrangement he proposes, because he recommends *remuneration* to be made. He writes me, ' The Commissioner will, I doubt not, consent to a moderate pecuniary indemnification being made to them.' Now, if the Karens have commenced their cultivation illegally, they are not entitled to ' pecuniary indemnification ; ' but Mr. —— says they *are* entitled to it, therefore they have commenced cultivating their lands *legally*, Mr. —— being judge ; and all we ask is to have this legal occupancy confirmed to them. Money is not the article wanted, *but the land*, and Mr. ——'s special powers were to make over the land applied for; and by refusing to do this, and recommending that the Karens shall be driven off the land for a pecuniary indemnification, he seems to me to have travelled out of the docket, and assumed 'special powers' not granted him. Instead of making over the land as directed, he goes into a lengthened statement of reasons for taking it from the Karens, and giving it to the Burmese; the main one of which is, that the Burmese are rich!

" The whole space of good paddy land is very small for a large number of people. The remainder is either too sandy or too dry for paddy, and will answer only for temporary cultivation or for gardens."

The Superintendent of Customs was not a man that feared God, and was overawed by Captain ——. He was soon after removed to another post, and again the work fell back into Captain ——'s own hands, who had long hoped to be appointed Deputy Commissioner of Tounghoo, but hearing that the vacancy was otherwise filled, he was like a wild elephant, ready to trample nations, Government, and all into the ground, so he sent Mr. Mason another note :—

" Tounghoo, *25th July*, 1850.
'" My dear Sir,
" A few days ago two Burmese came and complained to me of your Karens, as I prognosticated would be the case. I ordered the Kannee Thugyee to investigate

z 2

into the matter, and to report to me.   He is here now,
and may I beg you to attend and hear the case further
investigated."

On his departure from Tounghoo, the Superintendent
of Customs had issued an order, permitting the Karens
to resume their work again, and had commanded that
no one should interfere with them, being compelled to
do so by Colonel Phayre.   This order Mr. Mason sent
up to the court.

Captain —— replied, " I must issue a fresh order,
and *insist* upon the land being *vacated by the Karens
till the decision of the boundary comes from the Commissioner.*"

This threw the Karens and myself once more into the
deepest distress.   I again telegraphed to Colonel Phayre,
and soon this note came from Captain —— :—

" August 3rd, 1859.

" DEAR SIR,

" I beg leave to send you the accompanying telegram.
Your people are to reap the *one* crop that they have *now
cultivated.*   I will issue the necessary order."

" Now, let us show the Burmese what Christianity is.
We 'll not utter a word of triumph as they did to us,
but we 'll only speak kindly," says the principal cultivator, in which all the others join.   Praising God and
giving thanks, they proceed again to their fields.   Two
or three days pass.   In comes the Thugyee with another

paper, utterly forbidding the Karens to proceed. We again remonstrate, and the following is received from Captain ——— :—

" I told the Thugyee explicitly to let them alone, as far as the *crop sown* by them was concerned, which it is most clearly understood they are to have, but I don't understand that they are to *continue* further cultivation."

They were in the midst of ploughing and sowing their fields, in the greatest haste, as the right season for it was rapidly passing.

More entreaties follow, telling Captain ——— that the Karens cleared the fields themselves, that they would have no rice for the whole year, that they had already suffered extremely by cholera, and that they and their little ones were starving.

Answer :—

" I shall certainly adhere to my resolution, and not allow either party to reap any benefit from the land ;" and the Thugyee ordered every one to leave the fields with their families and buffalos. Difficult as it was to write to such a wicked man, I did again, stating that, if compelled to drive away their buffalos, the Karens would never be able to repay the Government loan, and he alone must be responsible for the money. Upon this he permitted the Karens to remain in their homes and tend their buffalos, *provided they would not raise a hand to work on the land in question*, but threatening that if they did that, and were brought before him for trespass, their fine should exceed all the value of their anticipated crops.

Picture, reader, forty or fifty families, in as many
different houses, scattered up through the fields. All
of a sudden there appear red-belted peons all along,
hooting out Government orders to stop all work. The
plough is arrested in its furrow—the sower's arm is
caught back with its handful of seed—the uplifted axe
is jerked from the hand of the forester—the poor mother
bending over her potato patch is ordered into the hut,
and the armful of faggots is knocked from the arms of
the little child.

Weeks pass, and Captain D'Oyly, as a special favour,
comes from Prome,—Captain D'Oyly, the benevolent
Commissioner, who gave them the land; a man remarkable for deep penetration, for skill in dealing with
the different classes of nations; a man noted, too, for
his sympathy and fear of God. To him the Commissioner of Pegu writes :—

"I consider it of great importance that the mountain Karen tribes should be induced to settle in the
plains, and cultivate land. I feel assured you will also
see the importance of the case in that respect, and also
of the question generally being settled satisfactorily and
justly for both parties."

Four days pass, and Captain D'Oyly is laid on a sick
bed—one week, and he dies. A pall! a pall! Alas,
for the Karens! Captain —— again takes the field,
and the Karens are scattered.

Two Karen chiefs, who were leaders in this undertaking, had also died very suddenly. It was said by
cholera, but I held their hands when they died, and

was no more sure of that than the officers were with
Captain D'Oyly's horses. He had four or five, one
pair of beautiful iron greys, which were great pets.
First a common one died, then another, then one
of the greys. Captain D'Oyly was in the jungles
upon official business, and seeing all his ponies going,
his friend, Captain Bond, roused up, and examinations
were made again and again, still the ponies died, until
every one was gone! The natives cried *snakes!* Captain D'Oyly was a Christian Commissioner, and sought
earnestly to honour the law, human and divine. He
detected a Burman of high rank in harbouring robbers,
and sharing the booty, for which he fearlessly cast him
into prison. It was soon after this that all his ponies
died; and since we commenced the paddy cultivation,
the Karens have had four elephants die, two of which
cost seven hundred rupees each.

I confess I feel that my own life, and that of every
one who attempts to work for God's kingdom in Tounghoo, is in jeopardy, as well as the school-buildings.

I sent a text to the Commissioner of Pegu :—

"*For we wrestle not against flesh and blood, but
against principalities, against powers, against the rulers
of the darkness of this world, against spiritual wicked-
ness in high places.*"

As the Karens were driven away in the midst of their
ploughing, when too late to make mountain fields,
seventeen families had not a kernel of rice for the year.
These suffered greatly, having been reduced a part of
the time almost to starvation, and must have come to

still greater suffering if the others and ourselves had not helped them by sharing their sufferings. Thirteen families had only from twenty to forty baskets, when they had cleared land enough for one hundred baskets each, and more. Out of six Bghai villages commenced, only *one* man was allowed to cultivate at all, and he had only thirty or forty baskets, when he and the other Bghais had cleared land enough for a good crop. Thirty-eight families had been so alarmed by the threatenings of Captain ——, that they fled for ever, it is supposed. But the continued perseverance of the others amidst such heavy oppression proves, that, if rightly cared for, the Karens will yet greatly remunerate Government for any aid it may render them.

You will ask why it was that so many should harrass the Karens. I can only answer, Satan was let loose for a little season, for some wise purpose, perhaps to drive them into the sure tower and rock of defence.

CHAPTER IV.

KAREN SOLDIERS.

COLONEL PHAYRE, finding the independent Karens a
pretty formidable host to deal with, resolved to form a
mountain police of reliable Christian men, who should
be able to protect their own schools, chapels, and homes.
Upon this I petitioned that fifty might be enlisted from
the paddy cultivators on the plains ; I thought it would
help them to pay for their buffalos.

Among them would be found the fittest and *strongest*
men now, for after a year spent in the neighbourhood of
the schools, they could walk twice as far, carry twice as
much, and accomplish more by *contrivance* than the rest.
They would be the most *obedient*. It would inspire the
men on the mountains, to see a body of soldiers prac-
tising on their own parade ground. They would feel more
secure, because the Institute Guard acts as the pulse of
the nation, holding immediate and daily communication
in a direct line with every village and hamlet, from
Shwagyn to the Burmese territory on the north, and to
the Red Karen kingdom on the east. Then it was of
importance to protect this post, as here would be grouped
their most costly buildings, libraries, and school appa-

ratus, and schools, too, in constant operation. But above all these considerations, the Kannee Pass led right through their paddy settlement, and this was the key to the city from the north-east. Colonel Phayre was very willing to allow the arrangement, provided it did not too much weaken the guard on the hills. The new officer was empowered to organize the Karen police, but when he called for the men, they hesitated.

" Is Captain —— going to organize us ?" the Karen chiefs inquired in dismay. " Teacher, we are afraid." They remembered the sacked villagers had obtained no redress ; they remembered the rice land was not yet given, and when he sent for them, only a very few would come at all. Colonel Phayre's plan was to form two companies in the mountains, supply them with arms, and a certain quantity of ammunition monthly, and let them learn to use them themselves in the jungles, paying them a mere nominal sum, just enough to make the hill men recognise them as soldiers. This he and Mr. Mason had arranged, as the cheapest, wisest, and best for the people, and it pleased the Karens far better than to come to town at full pay.

Captain ——'s judgment was to make them barrack soldiers, and have them thoroughly drilled. Mr. Mason doubted the expediency of doing this, and did not like to meddle with it ; besides, he had no time. Then Captain —— turned to me :—

" Come," he said, " Mrs. Mason, they will do anything you tell them. Call them down and encourage them to enlist."

Mr. Mason, under the circumstances, thought I had better do it. So the Board of Managers was called. They immediately telegraphed to every pinnacle and glen by their runners, and in two days nearly two hundred chiefs and men stood before Captain ——, the Deputy.

" Great Chief, greeting," they said, as all appeared in highland garb and dignity ; but they noticed he did not give his hand to them as Colonel Phayre and Captain D'Oyly had done.

" Tell them," said the Captain, " I will enroll two companies, with two captains, two lieutenants, eight sergeants, and one hundred and sixty men."

" Th'kyen," they replied, " we are afraid. We are ignorant men. We do not understand white men's customs."

" Never mind ; I 'll send a man over here to teach you."

" Suppose your man drinks, he will spoil all our young men. Suppose he flogs, our people will all run away."

" He shall not do either. I know a good man who never drinks. I 'll send for him."

" Would he be patient ? We cannot learn quickly. We don't know Burmese talk."

" He shall neither flog nor drink. He shall be patient. I want you to remain on the plains until you have learned thoroughly."

" Th'kyen, we are chiefs. We have the care of our villages and of God's work on the mountains. We cannot remain constantly."

" But I will pay your captains forty rupees the month, the lieutenants twenty-five, the sergeants sixteen, and the sepoys eight."

" Th'kyen, let the great Governor keep his money. Give us arms, powder, shot, and *land*. We will learn to shoot; we will defend our villages and chapels."

" But I cannot give you these, unless you come and learn soldiers' business."

" How long must we stay away from our homes ?"

" Till you have learned to be soldiers."

" Shall we then go back ?"

" You shall."

" We cannot learn with the Burmans. They do not worship God. They drink and swear. Our young men would follow in their ways, and be ruined. We cannot drill with heathen."

" You need not. You may have Karen barracks in your own village, and be drilled here."

" How can we learn here, Th'kyen."

" I will send men to teach you. You shall be entirely separate from the Burmese, and have nothing to do with them."

" Shall we not have Burman officers ?"

" No. I will make Karen officers."

" Shall we certainly be taught in our own village, and not be called over to learn with the Burmese ?"

" You shall."

" Th'kyen, our men cannot support their families on soldiers' pay. Give them less money and some land."

"You shall have the land as I told you, every bit of it" (impatiently).

"Mama, we are afraid. If he means true, why does he not pity our starving brothers? Why does he not let us have the land *now*, and why does he not bring back the captives? Teacheress, we fear this Government man. Do you advise us to enlist?"

"I cannot advise. He appears truthful. You will get no arms unless you do enlist."

"Teacheress, pledge your word with this Governor's, then we will enlist."

"Captain ――, they are afraid," turning to him. "They fear Government will ensnare them. They will not enlist unless I give my word with you."

"Pray give it, Mrs. Mason. I will deal honourably with them." And so I gave my word that the promises made them shall be sacredly kept, and they gave in their names, the best chiefs being appointed officers.

It is the Sabbath—the chiefs and men are assembled for worship. Hark! What are they listening to? Why do the young men look at the chiefs, the chiefs at one another, and all at me so questioningly? Drive, drive! clack, clack! go the hammers—up—up go the rafters all through that holy day. Captain ――'s workmen building him a new house. Nothing is said.

It is Monday morning—the chiefs are on the verandah.

"Teacher, I want my name taken off from the list of *Bos*" (officers). "And mine," "And mine," said one after another.

"Why, what's the matter now?"

" Oh, this ruler *does not know the Ten Commandments !*"   As usual, I go to Mr. Mason.

" You had better return," he said, "and reason the
matter.   Tell them they will probably encounter many
temptations, but on the other hand, if they do not enlist,
Government will give them no arms, and there will be no
protection for them against their enemies."

I find them all assembled in the Institute.

" Then what shall we do ?" they cry all at once,
greatly excited.

" Don't you know what the Bible says ?"

" Er, er," answered Poquai.   " ' Let him that lacks
wisdom ask of me.' "   I leave them to prayer and consultation.   Again the chiefs appear on the verandah.

" We have determined what to do," and they hold out
a list of resolutions :—

" 1st. *We will not work on God's holy day.*"

" 2nd. We will not drink arrack, or toddy, or brandy,
or allow our men to use these drinks."

" 3rd. We will take care only of our own country."

" 4th. We will have permission to leave our business
honourably, if we dislike it."

" Oh, oh ! Captain —— won't sign any such paper,"
I said, taking it in to Mr. Mason.

" Then we may *not enlist*," was the determined reply

" Why do you name the third ?" Mr. Mason asks
just then stepping out of his study.

" Because, teacher, this Governor *does not know the
Ten Commandments.* So whether he will be good or
bad, we do not know. Supposing he is bad, then he gets

angry with us ignorant Karens. He says, I'll punish 'em, so he may send us away over to the west and leave our homes unprotected; then an enemy may come immediately, destroy our villages, and break up our schools."

"This is correct reasoning, but why the fourth resolution? That is contrary to all military usage."

"Teacher, we know our people. If a Karen does not like a thing, he'll run away. No officer, no money, no Government can keep him. Then we are made ashamed before the Great Governor, and our name is injured before our brethren in America." I begged them, if determined, yet to soften the matter down a little and be polite, which they tried to be, and then went up, asking for Captain ——'s signature and the Government stamp.

"Oh yes, yes; I'll sign it. Come with me to court." Immediately there comes a Burman goung, and pours down fifteen hundred rupees upon the floor before the Karen officers. Then another follows:—

"What's your name?"

"Chief Ledie."

"And yours?"

"Chief J'Que." So he goes round, and takes the names of all the officers in his book.

"Done! Take your money and be off!" gruffly, with a haughty toss of the head.

"Give us the paper, Th'kyen," entreat the chiefs.

"Go—go. I can't attend to you; I am full of business," says Captain —— in displeasure.

" We wait, Th'kyen," and there they sat until noon, when two came over to me.

" What *shall* we do, mama?" they asked in great distress.

" Have you signed any receipt?"

" No."

" Are you sure?"

" Yes."

" Have they not taken your names?"

" A Burman set down our names, but we have not touched the money."

" But you have given your names, and without the paper!"

" We gave nothing. The Burman *took* our names." I referred the matter again to Mr. Mason, and he decided that they were under no obligation to take the money, without the signature promised to their resolutions, as they had told him they could not serve without it.

" We will not touch it!" they cried resolutely, and again took their seats to await his convenience. Two o'clock comes, three o'clock, and no indication of the signature; four o'clock, and Captain —— leaves the court.

" We go, Th'kyen," say the chiefs, rising.

" Take the rupees."

" Give us the paper, Th'kyen!"

" The Mengyee will give no paper. Take the money and be gone."

" We leave it here, Th'kyen."

" You *dare not* leave it. It is yours, and you are responsible."

" We *will not* have it, Th'kyen, without the paper."

A secret messenger is despatched to Captain ——. He re-appears, throws them a letter in Burmese, ordering them away gruffly. They desire to have the paper read, but are peremptorily ordered out that the doors may be closed. So they take up the money, and being half-famished, having sat there all day, they go immediately over to their Karen settlement, and send the assistant with the paper to Mr. Mason. Mr. Mason reads :—

" You are to obey me and the officer whom I place over you !"

" That all ?" he asks in dismay.

" That is all."

Terrible indignation we knew would rise in every breast, that evening, among the Karens ; and long we sat deliberating on what course to pursue ; until Mr. Mason became alarmed.

" Go over," he says, " and try to soften their anger, and help them to arrange for guarding the money through the night, for they will surely be robbed."

Ten o'clock rings—Shemoop is called—I jump into my little boat, and reach the landing. The gong is rung, and in a few minutes nearly two hundred men in their Highland tunics, with dahs in hand, and in great excitement, are hovering close around me in the moon-light.

" Come, brothers, let us go in and talk over this matter. Now speak, each one. Say just what you choose," for I thought it safer to let them exhaust their pent-up feelings first. And they did speak, one after

2 A

another, and poured forth their indignation upon the
English Government, until every eye gleamed and many
leaped to their feet, snatching their dahs and war-clubs
in one wild clamour.

"Gently, gently, brothers."

"Sit down!" shout the captains. "Let mama speak."
Instantly every voice is hushed, every form has dropped
upon the floor, and every eye is fixed to hear if I can
say a word in extenuation. Very gently, in a low voice,
I ask :—

"Are there not kidnappers in your nation ?"

"Yes."

"Would you like Commissioner Phayre to declare
you *all* kidnappers ?"

"No—no—we understand."

"You saw the Great Commissioner at Klurlae. Did
he ever tell you a falsehood ?"

"The Great Commissioner tell a lie! No—no—he
couldn't tell a lie! He knows the Ten Commandments."

"Then do not put this sin upon the English Government."

"No—no—we must not."

"Then again, did you not say this man knows not
the Ten Commandments ?"

"Er—er. So we have reason to fear."

"Then, ought you to call all Englishmen bad ?"

"No—no, but why does he not learn ? He knows
books. He is a disciple."

"*Is* he a disciple ? What does the Bible say is the
beginning of wisdom ?"

" The fear of God," answers Pwama, again.

" Without the beginning, can there be progress? Ought we not to pity rather than be angry with him ?"

" Er, er, the teacheress is right; but we'll carry it back," exclaim the Captains, in one breath.

" May be he'll put you in gaol."

" Let him put us in gaol—let him cut off our heads— we can bear it," thundered the Captains, towering up. " Brothers," they cry, turning to the sepoys, " you have not taken one anna of this money. You are free. Go home if you choose. To-morrow we carry all back and pour it at the Governor's feet. *We won't eat Government money.*" In half an hour, scores of these men, who had enlisted as soldiers at my earnest entreaty, were tramping off up the mountains, as hard as they could go, declaring they would never again come down at the call of Government. The next morning the Captains went up once more to Captain —— with Nah Khan Qualay, and begged for the right paper.

" I can never sign such a paper," he replied. " No Government officer would agree to such propositions."

" If the paper does not please the Governor, let him not sign it; but let him dismiss his humble servants to their homes."

" I shall not dismiss you. You have enlisted."

" We go, Th'kyen," rising, bowing themselves out.

" Go where ?"

" For the money, my lord." And so he allowed them to depart; but on their reaching the river, a messenger was despatched to call them back. They went and stood at the foot of the steps, half expecting to see an execution.

"Hear," says Captain —— "here's your paper," and gave them the veritable document, just what they had asked, stamped with the Government seal. With joyful eyes they brought it to Mr. Mason, and desired us to write a note of thanks to Captain ——, which was done, assuring him that blessings would fall upon him from every pinnacle of the mountains, when he sent us the following kind reply :—

"It gives me much pleasure to think that in carrying out the signing of the Karen petition, I should, at the same time, have afforded you so much satisfaction ; and I trust, with your valuable assistance, to be able to show that the Karens, if properly cared for, will prove as able settlers of the country as the tribes around them. I was much amused yesterday to see the Karens sit so utterly regardless of the rupees before them. I supposed they would grasp them like Burmese and Shans ; *but I see they are not to be bought over from the service of the great God whom you have so wonderfully introduced among them.*"

"Now let us thank God," said Poquai, one of the Lieutenants, and in humble awe and love they bowed there at once, and sent up their warm heart-breathings to the Almighty, whose own right arm had wrought their deliverance.

It was then thought that Captain —— had only

been trying these Christian officers to see what they really were; but, however it was, we knew the answer was from the Lord; and that night we took for our text in the Bible class, "I will sing of the mercies of the Lord for ever; with my mouth will I make known thy faithfulness to all generations."

One day a messenger came in out of breath, saying, the Bogyee Brigand, who had sacked the village mentioned, was pouring down his men towards the Christians again. The Deputy Commissioner sent up an embassy with a written message, threatening this Rob Roy of the north, if he didn't behave himself, he would set a thousand rupees upon his head. His ambassadors went as far towards the hostile region as they dared, to put up the message on a stake in the path, and hastened back to court as hard as they could go. The pickets soon found the missive, and hastened to send it to their leader. In a few days a letter from the daring brigand was found much nearer home, bidding defiance to the Government, and telling the Deputy to beware, or he would come and spear him and burn his town. The marauders came on, gathering strength at every step. Again he reached the plundered chief's village, which now lay powerless before him, for his force was said to be several thousand strong.

"See," he says, "what do you gain from these white Colahs? What have they done for you? Resist me now, and I'll burn your village; join me, and I will redress your wrongs in a different way." The plundered chief was entirely at his mercy; he had no power

to resist the demands of such a sweeping force, and, of
course, gave him food and shelter. Some said his
people joined the warriors. If they did, it is not strange,
though I think it was untrue; but the Border leader
pushed on, coercing and persuading. and under the magic
name of Menlong, he carried all before him.

The Deputy Commissioner is sleeping quietly in his
own house—one nearest the invader's route. What
dreams he of danger at that midnight hour? But hark!
a knocking at the door. What is it?

" Th'kyen! Th'kyen! Menlong! Menlong!"

Captain —— starts up — the English forces are
called in haste to the battle—meet the brigand, who
flies into the forest—Captain —— with six Englishmen give chase—the friendly Karens see the Commissioner's danger—rush to the conflict—the robber is
overborne, but he sells his life dearly—three brave
Karens lie slaughtered at his feet—the prisoner is taken
down to the spot which he had reached nearest to town,
and is there hung.

Tounghoo is saved—but was it saved by foreigners?
No, indeed! It was saved by the Karen police of native
Christians, who gave the warning, and who so boldly
risked their lives for their ruler.

CHAPTER V.

CONCLUSION—DEDUCTIONS—THE PAST OF THE KAREN NATION.

THUS far does Mrs. Mason describe this true "Romance of Missions:" we should not perhaps venture to use a word that commonly appertains to the kingdoms of the unreal, but that we have the authority of Dr. Mason, her grave and sober husband, for it, in his appendix to his little book called "THE KAREN APOSTLE," which has been often re-published both in England and America, a fourth edition of which lately reached us by the hand of Mrs. Ranney, a sister Missionary, just fresh from Rangoon. "The history of the introduction of Christianity among the Karens," Dr. Mason says, "is too full of 'truth stranger than fiction,' to be believed by those afar off from us, and yet the brightest colours of these scenes of surpassing interest are perhaps never seen at home."

"The days most interesting to myself," he writes in 1862, "during more than thirty years of Missionary life, are those spent at the Association Anniversaries. These people must be seen on their native mountains to be appreciated and understood. Between one and two thousand persons, encamped in booths covered with green branches, are gathered around a large central bamboo building erected for the occasion, in which they assemble four times a-day.

" It is their annual holiday, and dressed in their best, the large proportion in new clothes, more especially the women and children, their appearance in the varied garments of a dozen different tribes and clans is most picturesque. Standing in their midst, surrounded by the wild scenery of their wild hills, with their unbroken ponies dashing to and fro, they seem wilder than the Bedouin of the desert ; but what a contrast to the Arab who has been deluded by his False Book ! When the gong brings the people to worship, the scene appears to change by enchantment. The young men arise to address the congregation by turns from the Word of the true God; and we could believe ourselves again at home, listening to the eloquent discourses of our popular preachers.

" The Karens are a remarkable people, and a remarkable change has come over them—like the change of the lion to the lamb. The most astonishing feature of the whole work, to my mind, is the number and talent of the NATIVE PREACHERS that God has raised up among them."

In 1860, Mrs. Mason again left Burmah for America, to invite, by personal intercourse and description, the aid of American and English ladies in her sphere of labour. She passed by way of London, and, during her then short visit, was introduced to the details of the " Missing Link" Mission among our HOME HEATHEN, and became confirmed in her ideas that very similar plans will be found useful in Tounghoo, the Bible-readers, however, being necessarily of a different age.

"Before I left home," she says, " Mr. Mason had often spoken on the subject of Bible-readers in Tounghoo, and the desirableness of setting forth a company of NATIVE FEMALES, with this object, to go from house to house, and from hamlet to hamlet, to read and explain the Scriptures directly to the women."

Mrs. Mason was detained in America, first by much personal affliction. She caught the small-pox during the summer, and recovered from that sad disease only to nurse her young daughter-in-law through rapid consumption, and then to lay her in an early grave. She was further occupied in sending forward her own daughter, Miss Bullard, to take the care of the Karen Institute, while she should yet be detained in America by the publication of her book ; thus hoping to elicit further help for the mission, and also to persuade assistant teachers to accompany her on her return, securing THEIR support in England and America.

Miss Bullard arrived safely, and did good service for many months, but she has since married and accompanied her husband to India. " She was remarkably successful while she remained in the school," says Dr. Mason, "and especially helped us in teaching the Karens music. We must not now ask any one to take her place who does not possess this accomplishment. Five or six of her pupils are out on the hills, and one of them writes that she has fifty-eight pupils. More than six hundred fresh converts have been baptized during the year, and nearly fifteen hundred rupees are brought in for the support of the pupils of the two Institutes. More female teachers and Bible-readers have to be continually raised up here," adds the Doctor. " Mrs. Mason made a good beginning, and Ella made a good mark, but that would soon be washed away, unless others shall follow, to add ' line upon line, and precept upon precept.' "

We hope very soon to hear that Mrs. Mason is once more arrived at Tounghoo. She left England in February, and has been heard of from Rangoon. Her chief ambition for the present little book is, that it may be made the means of raising funds for the KAREN and BURMESE Missions to Women.

She hopes it will have proved various things, and she has written not without an idea of alluring some of the lighter class of readers who do not in general read Missionary books,—of disarming their prejudice and attracting a new circle of friends.

She trusts that from these pictorial records may spring a conviction,—

1. Of the faithfulness of JEHOVAH to His promises.

2. Of the power of HIS HOLY WORD.

3. That the foundation of successful Missions is their aim from the first, to raise up NATIVE TEACHERS.

4. That it is necessary to enter into the *secular* affairs of the people, in an attempt to Christianize them, for such is the example of Jesus.

5. That *sympathy* with those we want to teach, in things great and small, is the gift of heaven.

6. That the importance of FEMALE education in heathen lands cannot be over estimated, and that all obstacles must be overcome to attain it, because of the great influence on whole nations of their women and girls.

7. She further wishes it to be observed that the reason why the Karens are so especially accessible to the efforts of Bible-readers, and the reason they are so much more ready to receive Christ than the surrounding heathen, is, because they recognise in HIM the ancient " YUAH " of their traditions, even the same as our " JEHOVAH."

As we ourselves in LONDON have arrived simultaneously at six at least of these conclusions, having picked them up from experience in dingy courts and alleys, it has been very refreshing to learn them anew among the jungles and the pinnacles of old Tounghoo.

God speed to our Missionary sister in resuming her work of love! It is very sweet to think that she takes out with her the support for seven girl Bible-readers—one for each Karen Clan, for one year, from the friends of the " Missing Links " in our country. American ladies charge themselves with the provision of training teachers to prepare and superintend these readers.

Mrs. Mason was so pleased with the large pictorial diagrams, on calico, printed and coloured by the WORKING MEN'S EDUCATIONAL UNION, in illustration of " THE BOOK AND ITS STORY," and of " THE BOOK

AND ITS MISSION," as means of teaching to the Karens the history of the Bible in other countries, that she took out three sets of each, *i. e.*, three sets of thirty pictures. They will probably soon learn to design similar ones.

The subjects of the above double series are as follows :—

Stone Books.

PICTURE WRITING, at Karnak, Thebes.
WRITING ON STONE : the Rosetta Stone.

The Manuscript Ages.

ANCIENT MANUSCRIPTS AND WRITING MATERIALS.
MULTIPLICATION OF COPIES : the Scriptorium and Scribe.
THE DEATH OF THE VENERABLE BEDE.
WYCLIF CITED BEFORE ARCHBISHOP COURTENAY.

Bible Translators.

THE BIBLE CHAINED.
LUTHER FINDING THE BIBLE.
LUTHER TRANSLATING THE BIBLE INTO GERMAN.

The New Era.

MULTIPLICATION OF COPIES : the Printing Press.

Enmity to the Bible.

THE BURNT ROLL ; or, the Scriptures Destroyed.
SEARCH FOR NEW TESTAMENTS at Oxford and Cambridge.
BIBLE BURNING AT PAUL'S CROSS.

The Bible Free.

ST. PAUL'S CATHEDRAL ; the Jubilee Sermon.
THE BIBLE HOUSE AND WAREHOUSE.

Of " THE BOOK AND ITS MISSION," the vols. for 1856 and 1857 are illustrated. The subjects are as follows :—

Lands without the Divine Book.—Heathen.

TIBET, THE LAND WHERE THERE IS AS YET NO BIBLE.

BURMAH.—THE MISSIONARY JUDSON COME TO PRESENT A PORTION OF THE BURMESE BIBLE TO THE HAUGHTY EMPEROR.

THE ROCK OF BEHISTUN.—Key to Nineveh Characters.

DAGON AND NEBO.—"GODS OF THE KINGS OF ASSYRIA."

Lands of the False Book.

SKETCH OF CONSTANTINOPLE.—Bible Colporteur on the Bridge.

THE COLPORTEUR AMORGA AT BAGHCHEJUK crying "Holy Book" in the Market Place.

Lands where the Teachers have hidden and burned the Book, but where it is now finding Entrance.

THE BURNING OF HEBREW MANUSCRIPTS IN SPAIN.—Scene: The Stone Fire-place near Seville.

THE SWISS COLPORTEUR IN THE ALPS.

Ancient Churches which first possessed the Book.

SKETCH OF MONT CASTELLUZZO.—"Bible among the Vaudois."

NIGHT CLASS IN POITOU FOR SCRIPTURE READING.

THE NESTORIAN CHRISTIANS.—Scene: Salt Lake Oroomiah.

Protestant Countries.

SALE OF SCRIPTURES BY SUNDAY SCHOLARS OF MANCHESTER.

LIEUTENANT GRAYDON AND HIS BIBLE VAN TURNED INTO A STALL AT A FAIR AT LAUSANNE.

THE BIBLE-READERS IN OLD ST. GILES'S.—A Thicket by Night.

"PARTY OF MODERN BIBLE-READERS IN ST. GILES'S."—Scene: A Mothers' Class. On the other side of the Picture the entrance to "Church Lane."

N.B. Each picture is provided with frame and eyelets for convenient suspension.

Note.—The address of the Working Men's Educational Union is 25, King William Street, West Strand, London, W.C.

Everything that concerns the BOOK OF GOD has immense value in the eyes of this remarkable people.

But the Karens have no book, or fragment of a book, to which they can trace their oral traditions handed down diligently from father to son in their songs. When Dr. Judson entered the country, they had not even a written alphabet, but their fathers had told them that once they possessed the word of the eternal God, which gave them histories of the Fall and of the Flood, and bade them never worship idols. They say that the Prophet who had the charge of this book was reading it one day beneath a tree and he fell asleep, when a dog came and tore it to pieces. Then God was angry, and gave them up to the evil spirits, or " Nats," of whom they are ever since in fear. This rendering is slightly different from that given in page 103, but is accounted for by the variations in oral tradition.

They have many beliefs evidently derived from the Old Testament, and some very remarkable ones, originating perhaps in other sources. They say that men had at first one father and mother ; but because they did not love one another they separated, and their languages became diverse, that

> " The KAREN was the elder brother,
> And obtained all the words of God.
> God formerly loved the Karen nation above all others,
> But because of their transgressions, He cursed them,
> And now they have no books.
> Yet He will again have mercy on them,
> And love them above all others.

> " God departed with our younger brother,
> The white foreigner.
> He conducted God away to the West.

God gave them power to cross waters and reach lands,
And to have rulers from among themselves.
Then God went up to heaven.
But He made the white foreigners
More skilful than all other nations.

" When God had departed,
The Karens became slaves to the Burmans,
Became sons of the forest and children of poverty ;
Were scattered everywhere.
The Burmans made them labour bitterly,
Till many dropped down dead in the jungle,
Or they twisted their arms behind them,
Beat them with stripes, and pounded them with the elbow,
Days without end.

" In the midst of their sufferings,
They remembered the ancient sayings of the elders,
That God would yet save them,
That a Karen king would yet appear.
The Talien kings have had their season ;
The Burman kings have had their season ;
The Siamese kings have had their season ;
And the foreign kings will have their season ;
But the Karen king will yet appear.
When he arrives, there will be but one monarch,
And there will be neither rich nor poor.
Everything will be happy,
And even lions and leopards will lose their savageness.

" Hence in their deep afflictions they prayed,
If God will save us,
Let Him save speedily !
We can endure these sufferings no longer.
Alas ! where is God ?
Our ancestors said that when our younger brothers came back,
The white foreigners
Who were able to keep company with God,
The Karens will be happy.

" Our ancestors charged us thus—
  'Children and grandchildren,
  If the thing come by land—weep
  If by water—laugh.
  It will not come in our days,
  But it will in yours.'
  Hence the Karens longed for those
  Who were to come by water."

Another remarkable tradition among the people was as follows :—The elders said, " When the Karens have cleared the Horn-bill city* three times, happiness will arrive, so when the Burman rulers made them clear it the last time, they said among themselves, 'Now we may suppose happiness is coming, for this completes the third time of clearing the Horn-bill city;'" and true enough, for before they had finished, they heard THAT THE WHITE FOREIGNERS HAD TAKEN RANGOON.

Dr. Judson had lived fourteen years in Rangoon, preaching the eternal God, in whom none would believe, while the poor unnoticed KARENS were continually passing his door, and singing the same truth by the way—

" God is eternal, His life is long ;
  One Kulpa, He dies not ;
  Two Kulpas, He dies not ;
  Kulpas on Kulpas, He dies not."

The first Karen who attracted the Missionary's attention was Ko-thahbyu, a slave, whom he took into the mission family as a free man, and after instructing him in the Gospel, baptized him. Ko-thahbyu then became

---

* The site of an old city near Tavoy, which the Karens were called on to clear occasionally, when the trees grew up over it.

a remarkable pioneer preacher to his countrymen, in one village after another, for thirteen years, and raised up other NATIVE preachers. The above astonishing traditional beliefs had caused these wild tribes to move among the haughty Burmans, unimpressed by their gorgeous temples, their gay processions, and their glittering festivals. In sorrow and subjection, they bore their heavy burdens, and " waited for the Book."

The beloved Judson spent twenty years of his devoted life in preparing the Bible for the Burmese. The best translation in India is admitted to be that of the Burmese Scriptures by Dr. Judson. It is as Luther's Bible to Protestant Germany. He prayed only that he might live to see a hundred converts in Burmah, after he had given to the people the word of God in their own tongue. He lived to see many more than this even in his own church at Rangoon ; and what he saw besides among the despised Karens surpassed his hopes.

But it was for Dr. Judson's noble successors—and it was more especially for Mr. Wade and Dr. Mason—to have the high privilege of GIVING THE BIBLE TO THE KARENS. " With the aid of two Karens who understood Burmese," says Mr. Wade, " I analyzed and classified the Karen sounds, and adopted a system of representing them which embraced all the syllables occurring in their language." The system adopted by Mr. Wade is so admirably conceived, that a person ignorant of a single letter can learn to read Karen with ease in a few weeks ; whereas, Dr. Judson says, that after two *years'* diligent study of the Burmese, he had

2 B

made less progress than he had in two *months* in the
study of the *French* language. This fact marked the
open path for the Missionary of the Book, and how
wonderful it was to find that it was for nothing else
these people were waiting. " HAVE YOU BROUGHT GOD'S
BOOK ?" said the simple, timid villagers of Dong-Yhan
to Mr. Wade;—the very first question they asked the
white foreigner;—and when the answer was, to show
them the treasure, though in ENGLISH, and to tell
them that parts were already translated for the Burmans, then came the immediate reply, " But you must
do it for us also."

Mr. Wade adopted the Burman alphabet, for the
simple reason that the Burman type only was at hand
at the time, and when it proved inadequate to express
the fifty-four vowel-sounds of the Karen, (itself having
only ten,) a few new letters met the difficulty. When
the translation of the New Testament was accomplished,
however, no attempt was made at printing it for several
years for want of pecuniary means, and each book was
copied and circulated as fast as completed in manuscript. The Karens soon learned to write as easily as
to read their language, which they had never before
supposed was capable of being represented by signs.
They are now vaulting day by day from a state of down-
trodden slavery into a claim upon the title-deeds of their
old nobility in the scale of nations. Mr. Mason affirms
that the alphabetical powers of the Karen alphabet are
of Arabic or Hebrew origin.

From the time of their expectations being realized,

and of their receiving the book in their own tongue, this people have delighted to be ruled by its precepts, as all the foregoing narratives evince, and this particular circumstance irresistibly points us back to their *origin.* They *must* have received their traditions from God's chosen people, the JEWS, and many of their habits and observances lead to the conclusion that they are themselves, as they say, of the race to whom, and to whom alone, were committed the keeping of the holy oracles in old time.

There are no traces among them of NEW TESTAMENT light, which forbids the idea that they could have derived their knowledge from the Nestorian Missionaries, who were so widely scattered over Central and Eastern Asia from the seventh to the thirteenth century.

There is testimony that there were Jews in China as early as B.C. 258, (see " Edin. Cycl.," vol. vi., p. 95,) and there is no reason for concluding that they were the first visitors of their race. May not the merchant princes of Tyre have had dealings with the Chinese ? and would not the ships of Solomon, sailing from the Red Sea, and spending three years on their voyage, (1 Kings ix. 26 ; 2 Chron. ix. 21,) have possibly met the same people at some of the ports of trade ?

It appears, from a paper read at the meeting of the British.Association, in Oxford, in 1860, by Dr. Macgowan, concerning his personal researches in China, that he found evidence of the existence of a numerous and wealthy colony of Jews existing about a century before the birth of Christ in the city of CHINTU, the capital of the province of Sz-chuen. A magnificent temple which they had erected was destroyed, and they suddenly disappeared from Chinese territory. As this occurred about the time of the expulsion of the Huns from China, and as that city was near its western border, Dr. Mac-gowan supposes that some of these Chinese Jews found their way to the adjoining mountains dividing China from Burmah, and that they were either the progenitors of the Karens, or that through them this remarkable people obtained their Old Testament traditions, which, preserved among them for so many ages, appear thus wonderfully to have prepared them for the reception of the Gospel.

The same authority describes the MIAUTSE Aborigines, or hill-tribes of China, as having many resemblances to the Karens, and dwelling on the confines of their country.

"The Karens regard themselves," says Dr. Mason, "as wanderers from the north, and one of their traditions states that a party of them came across 'the river of running sand' on an exploring tour. It is [regarded as having been an arduous work, to cross this immense quicksand with the sands in motion like the waters of a river. The tradition was quite unintelligible to me, until I read the Journal of Fa-hian, the Chinese pilgrim who visited India about the fifth century, which threw a sunbeam on the subject. He constantly designates the great desert north of Burmah, and between China and Tibet, as ' the river of sand.' " *

---

* The Desert of the Great Gobi, that wide "sea of sand and salt" often blown into ridges by fierce winds, and stretching away north of the table-lands of Tibet, to the great wall of CHINA eastward.

In Deut. xxviii. 64, it was said to ISRAEL, " The Lord shall scatter thee among all nations, from one end of the earth to the other ;" and many think that the excellence of some of the Chinese rules of morality may thus be explained. Confucius was but the prince of compilers ; he does not pretend to originality ; and he may very probably have held communication with some of those heaven-taught wanderers, who always brought with them the law of God, and occasionally, at least, must have "called it to mind among the nations whither the Lord their God had driven them."—Deut. xxx. 1.

There is a new colony of modern Jews at Kaifung, the capital of Honan, in CHINA. Wherever they have colonized, they have, as we know, remained as a peculiar race in the midst of those around them, and are distinguished, at least, by Jacob's distinction, " the race that plucks out the sinew." Some of the Kaifung Jews have been honourable in literature, several of them governors of provinces and Ministers of State ; but at present they are few in number, degraded in condition, and the wisest men very ignorant of their own religion. Some Hebrew Scripture MSS. were purchased from them, which do not, however, appear to have been of more ancient character than those already possessed in Europe.

It is very remarkable that from the Missionary seminaries of the New World, at Massachusetts and

in Pennsylvania, about a generation since, there went
forth the young men,—now grey-haired,—to different
points of the East, whose loving labour was in the
course of time to bring to light such wondrous things,
particularly concerning the Book, and the Book-peoples.
We refer to Dr. Mason and Dr. Perkins, of the Nestorian Mission, at Oroomiah.

We have seen Dr. Mason preparing the Bible for that
obscure and probable portion of the ten tribes, who may
be said to have thirsted for it during its loss more than
all the others, and who may, perhaps, therefore, be privi-
leged to proclaim it to all their kindred. They are
receiving Christian ideas more rapidly than any people
in the world,—unscathed, like the Affghans, by Moham-
medanism, and but slightly by the surrounding super-
stition of Budhh. It is daily developed that they are
neither a scanty nor a scattered people, but extend
at intervals over at least twelve degrees of latitude,
and ten of longitude, and they are calculated to be in
number at least five millions. The study of their
derivation will probably throw further light on the
OUTCAST ISRAEL of the Old Testament.*

The Missions of the Book of the present day are
unravelling the tangled threads of Scripture history in
a manner least expected. "It is only in the Bible," says
Dr. Moore, "that we find a bond of connexion between
man and man, through all his kindreds, from the

---

* See a most interesting work, entitled, "The Lost Tribes ; or,
the Saxons of the East and West." By Dr. Moore, of Hastings.
Longman & Co., 1861.

beginning to the present, and to the end." This author, in his charming volume, points especially to the Hebrews, who, while "swallowed up" among the nations, (Hosea viii. 8,) have yet influenced those nations, quite distinctly from the eight or nine millions of men still recognised as JEWS. He treats of the Tribes who never returned to the Land of Promise, and yet who remained not in Assyria, the land of their exile, but overflowed among the Scythians, or *Sacæ*, (derivation I-*saac*,) into the land of the Tartars, and thence into all parts of the habitable globe.

In Amos vii. 9, the word "Isaac" is synonymous with "Israel." The prophet speaks of the "house of Isaac," not long before Israel's banishment, and after they had separated themselves from the house of David. It is very remarkable that the name of *Sacæ* is not applied by any classic historians or geographers to any tribe of the Scythians until some time subsequent to the exile of the house of Isaac. For the research into the links of connexion between the *Sacæ* and ourselves, the *Saxons*, we must refer our readers to further particulars in the above-named volume, and then to the wondrous 37th chapter of Ezekiel,—the "joining of the stick of Judah and of Ephraim," over which a light will then begin to dawn, which may soon increase to full daylight.

But Dr. Perkins, and Grant, and Stoddard, and others in the bright roll of American names, had their mission to the NESTORIAN CHRISTIANS, to the descendants of that remnant of Israel who remained in Assyria

—the "remnant according to the election of grace"—
spoken of by Paul in the 11th of the Romans, to whom
he alludes as connected with the rest of his people, in
his defence before King Agrippa in Acts xxvi. 7, "Unto
which promise our twelve tribes, instantly serving God
day and night, hope to come;" and to whom the Epistle
of James is addressed: "To the twelve tribes which
are scattered abroad, greeting." They are greeted as
brethren, and their *faith in Christ* is commended; therefore they must have become Christians in the first century. James, the Bishop of Jerusalem, addresses many
of these Jewish converts as having backslidden, and
dedicates to them his practical Epistle.

The Nestorian Christians inhabit the same district of
Adiabene as was occupied by converted Israel; and
Nestorian churches and prelates have flourished in an
uninterrupted succession in the same places where they
were founded by the Apostles among these Israelites.
The Jews assert very positively that the Nestorians
were converted from Judaism to Christianity immediately after the death of Christ, and the marvellous
history of the NESTORIAN MISSIONS IN THE EAST, commencing with that of the Apostle Thomas to India
and to China,* continuing through thirteen centuries,
testifies to the same fact, although their extent has been
very indistinctly appreciated, because lost in the subsequent clouds of Romanist Missionary efforts, and we
may also add their fables.

* That he visited these regions is the constant tradition of the
Syrian Church.

The tablet of Seg-nan-foo* dug up in 1625, relit the torch of history on this point ; and for a generation past, as we have said, America's chosen sons, with our English language, but acquiring for their Missionary purpose the ancient and modern Syriac,—the former being the language used by our Lord Himself,—have opened the old conduits, like Mr. Layard among the rock sculptures of Bavian, and restored to this ancient of ancients, among the churches, the refreshing stream of the " water of life," in a tongue that its children would understand.

They had not, like the Karens, lost their book utterly. They had no printed books ; but they possessed, says Dr. Perkins, a few rare manuscripts of almost all the Bible, rolled up and hid away in secret places in their churches, to keep them from the ravages of the Mohammedans. Some of the copies are very venerable, written with the nicest care on parchment, and dating back to the period of England's Magna Charta. They are mostly found among the wild mountains, from which some tribes of the Nestorians descended three centuries since to the more genial plains of Oroomiah.

From those original districts, where they still abide as the *Protestants of Asia*, they sent forth their missions to the East and North, the traces of which remain to this day. They were doubtless undertaken to China and India from the knowledge that people of their own kindred were known to be in those countries, though they never reached the Karens, or they would have

* In the province of Shensi. See " Book and its Story," cheap edition, "China," page 385. Also, "The Nestorian Church," page 431.

told them of Jesus; and now their self-sacrificing devotion in past ages is richly repaid in the outpouring of the Holy Spirit on their children. Scarcely a score of the priests could read their own MSS. when Dr. Perkins reached them, and *not one woman*. Now there are 3,000 intelligent readers of the Bible, and every reader, child or adult, is an independent lamp in his dark village, neighbourhood, or household.

The thought of making the children who are educated in Bible knowledge "lamps" in the heathen villages, is fraught with instruction. Let us remember the happy Missionary Karen girls, and make similar use of our own English girls in country villages. There are girls connected with every Bible class and mothers' class in London, who might be Bible-readers. Mrs. Porter, who has long been engaged in Missionary schools at Cuddapah, Madras, assures us that allured by the singing of a child, in its own village, of some part of "The sweet Story of Old," and then by its reading of the New Testament, a native woman came forty miles to hear. Perhaps the girls in our village schools would be very different when they leave them, had they been *so taught in the Scriptures that they could teach again*, for the word of the Lord would never return unto Him void, but shall prosper in the thing whereto He sent it.

Immediately that the NESTORIANS, like the KARENS, had received in their own tongue the wonderful words of God,—ever sacred in their memories,—they, too, rose in the scale of nations. "When I commenced," says Dr. Perkins, "reducing the language of the Nestorians to writing, I early observed that there were no words in that language for *wife*, and *home*. Why not? Because the things signified did not exist among the people. *Woman* and *house* were the nearest approximations."

" In all their social and domestic usages, woman was the down-trodden slave, and man the tyrant lord. Mothers and sisters, among these fallen Christians, were not accustomed to eat with their husbands and brothers when we first went among them ; they must serve and then take the remnants, if any there were; but the revival of pure Christianity has elevated woman to her proper dignity and place."

The girls return from the Missionary Schools to their mountain homes in Tyari to teach and bless their kindred. "We have enjoyed," says the same Missionary, " seasons of most affecting interest in giving instructions to those young brethren and sisters on sending them forth to their distant posts of toil and self-sacrifice—as we had ourselves left the endearments of America to come to dark and far-off Persia.

" I now recall one such young married couple, who have long been located in a deep gorge of those central mountains which are the home of thousands of Nestorians, where the lofty encircling ranges limit the rising and setting of the sun to ten o'clock A.M. and two P.M. most of the year; where the towering cones of solid rock, like peering Gothic spires, cast their pointed shadows from the moonbeams on the sky, as on a canvas, nay, rear their summits against that canopy which seems to rest on them as pillars ; and where, in

winter, men must creep around the steep and lofty cliffs
with whispers, lest the sound of their voices by an echo
bring down upon them the terrific avalanche ever ready
to quit its bed at the summons of the slightest jar."

There are many such secluded spots among the lofty
mountains of Koordistan ; and here it is that our intelligent, cultivated young helpers plant themselves as
spiritual watchmen.   The most rugged districts of these
mountains are the most populous, as they offer the safest
asylums to the long-persecuted Christians.

Even these secluded districts were, seventeen years
ago, the scene of the massacre of thousands of Nestorians by the ruthless Koords ; and yet now the valleys
thus desolated are again quite as thickly populated as
before.   The dreadful barbarities of the Koords, who
tossed infants on their spears, led to their subjugation
and punishment by the Turks, and drove forth the
trembling survivors from their native cliffs and gorges
to come in contact with the people of other nations,
breaking up their entire isolation from the rest of Christendom in regions where they had clung, as for their
life, to their rare parchment copies of the New Testament in an ancient unknown tongue, locked up in their
venerable old churches.

The Missionary work among the Nestorians has been
eminently God's work,—" the excellency of the power"
has been very clearly seen to be of God, and not of men.
" Now," says Dr. Perkins, " we have been permitted
to meet at the communion table with hundreds of Nestorian brothers and sisters in Christ at the same time ;

and never, till admitted to the marriage supper of the Lamb, do I expect to sit in such heavenly places in Christ Jesus as at these Nestorian communions."

To "Israel" converted of old, and to "Israel" hidden among the heathen, what if at these two points AMERICA has been honoured to carry the message which is to make them blossom and bud, and fill the face of the world with fruit? "Behold, these shall come from far : and, lo, these from the north and from the west ; and these from the land of Sinim."—Isa. xlix. 12. It is no light thing "to be God's servant to raise up the tribes of Jacob, and to restore the preserved of Israel." The 49th of Isaiah is a wondrous prophecy, as relating to their gathering together.

To return in conclusion to the KARENS, as Mrs. Mason would have us. The Institute for 50 girls, as her frontispiece will show, is finished, and finished at a cost of upwards of 11,000 rupees ; a self-supporting normal school for 50 young men is also erected, and there are 140 self-supporting Jungle schools in Toung-hoo ; but foreign help is still needed in many ways, to the provision of which it is hoped the reading of this little book will conduce. If native preachers, school teachers, and Bible-readers are to be sent forth, their support of £10 a-year must at first be guaranteed ; and help, as we have seen, must often be afforded to them and their families in times of distress, famine, and sickness. Teachers go out hitherto without any stated salary, taking just what the people can give them.

Mrs. Mason's visit to America issued in the estab-

lishment at Philadelphia of a WOMAN'S UNION MIS-
SIONARY SOCIETY FOR HEATHEN LANDS, whose object it
is to send out and sustain single ladies to raise up and
superintend native Bible-women and School Teachers.
They have already raised £400 for this purpose.

Of the fund for Mrs. Mason's use, entrusted to the
Secretary of the London Bible and Domestic Female
Missions, she took with her on her return £70, as
the salary for one year of seven Karen Bible-woman,
and £52 likewise was placed at her disposal for inci-
dental expenses and appliances in starting the missions.
She writes that the idea has already taken effect, and
that she found four Bible-women at work in Rangoon
under fit superintendence, but needing pecuniary help;
and she adds, " I am daily asking God for means to supply the native Schoolmasters and Schoolmistresses each
with a new Karen Bible (cost 6s.), which they are long-
ing for more than meat and drink. Will not England
do this for the Karens, and increase and multiply the
Bible-readers both for the Burmese and the Shans."

" The Shans are even a more interesting race than
the Burmese. They are the merchant princes (like the
Armenians) of Burmah. They come down to its seaports every year from the mountains, bringing precious
stones, Chinese cloths, nice lacquered boxes, silver-
hafted knives, sugar, stick lac, and spades. No Missionary ever dwelt among them; once a Karen teacher
visited for about six months, among the hundreds who
pitch their tents in Tounghoo, and they have, ever
since, inquired for their friend ' Sahya.'

"I once met a large company of them on the plains. I thought the women exceedingly beautiful. They are a broken nation like the Karens, no longer having a king of their own, but paying tribute to foreigners, and they seem to feel their degradation deeply. In the cities they are Buddhists, but Buddhism is not their native religion. The women might probably first be willing to receive the Gospel, for among the Karens they have generally been the first to come forward—first to receive the teachers—and first to renounce their superstitions.

"Woman is the educator of Burmah, and, strange to say, she carries on the chief business and trade of the country. It is she who, at present, tramples on the 'white book,' and gives her son the palm-leaf; who teaches the toddling child to tug its dress full of sand up hill every night to the pagoda. She also excites discord, fans rebellion, and overturns dynasties. She *can* and she *will* rise. Teach her to rise towards God, and let us do it ere it is too late. An aged Burmese said to me, 'Don't tell me; I can't learn your prayer; I'm too old. Your Jesus doesn't know me. I've worshipped Guadama. I've done good. I've fed the priests. I've built a kyoung. If I take another religion now, I shall fall between the two. No, no; let me alone. I'm an old woman; if I'm lost, I'm lost. Had I heard when I was young, I might have believed, but *Loonbie Loonbie*, too late, too late."

"'All is dark,' murmured another citron woman; 'we know nothing; we are lost in the jungle.'

" After reading to her, for a third time, a tract to which she seemed to give ear, we thought she appeared indifferent. Feeling sad, I arose, and inquired if she desired Christians to visit her no more.

" ' No teacheress,' she exclaimed, with emphasis ; ' *I am thinking!* '

" Oh, how often have these words brought comfort ! When the cold ' Go !' has met us—when the laugh of derision has rung after us—when traversing mountains and burning sands, with blistered feet—when we have sunk weary on the threshold of home, then it has echoed in our ear, ' Burmah is THINKING !' and when, in Christian lands, we have met the nerveless hand, the cold eye, the heartless tone, then came again the echo— ' BURMAH is *thinking!* '

Christian friends! England MUST help Burmah and her Karen mountaineers.

Subscriptions in favour of Mrs. Mason's general work will be received for her at Messrs. Ransom's, Bankers, 2, Pall Mall, and by Messrs. Nisbet, Berners Street. Those intended especially for her SCHOOLS can be remitted to Miss Webb, Secretary of the Female Education Society, 15, Shaftesbury Crescent, Pimlico, S. W. ; and those for BIBLES and BIBLE-WOMEN FOR TOUNGHOO, to Mrs. Ranyard, 13, Hunter Street, Brunswick Square, W. C.

Printed by M. S. Rickerby, Hand Court, Upper Thames Street. E. C.

RECENTLY PUBLISHED.

THE MISSING LINK; or, Bible-Women in the Homes of the London Poor.

By L. N. R.   Small crown 8vo., 3s. 6d. cloth.   Also, a cheaper Edition, 1s. 6d. cloth limp.

"This little Book of which upwards of 40,000 copies have now been circulated in this country, is the illustrative exponent of a Mission commenced in London five years since, showing how we may TAKE OF THE PEOPLE TO MEND THEMSELVES, as well as HELP THEM TO HELP THEMSELVES. Surprising as it may seem, it has been proved that as an instrument of civilization—an instrument for working out domestic and social reform, THERE IS NOTHING LIKE THE BIBLE."

LIFE-WORK; or, The Link and the Rivet.

By L. N. R.   Crown 8vo., 3s. 6d. cloth.

☞ A volume, supplementary to 'THE MISSING LINK,' has just been published, under the title of 'LIFE-WORK,' which, if possible, surpasses its predecessor in interest, as showing the further and successful working of the system described. We trust both volumes will find their place in the library and in the heart of every lady in the land."

THE BOOK AND ITS STORY.

By L. N. R.   Post 8vo., 4s.   84th Thousand.

"A book which all lovers of the Bible ought to read."
"We should like to hear of this most instructive volume finding its way into every family where the Bible is a household book. The numerous facts recorded are of the most animating character, and are all calculated to increase the confidence of Christian men in the simple reading of God's HOLY WORD, as a direct and powerful instrument of human salvation"

THE BOOK AND ITS MISSION.

"This Magazine, price 3d monthly, is the organ of 'THE LONDON BIBLE AND DOMESTIC FEMALE MISSION,' [See the 'MISSING LINK,' and 'LIFE-WORK,'] and keeps its subscribers acquainted with their current affairs. It is, therefore, strongly recommended to those who are following out the principles of these Missions in town or country. The Missions of the Book ABROAD are included in its pages, as well as those AT HOME."

2 c

MEMORIALS OF JOHN BOWEN, D.C.L., late Bishop of Sierra Leone.

Compiled from his Letters and Journal by his SISTER. Post 8vo., 9s. cloth.

THE LIFE OF THE REV. RICHARD KNILL, of St. Petersburg.

By C. M. BIRRELL. With a Review of his character by the late Rev. JOHN ANGELL JAMES. With Portrait. Crown 8vo., 4s. 6d. cloth. Cheap Edition, 2s. 6d. cloth limp.

"Mr. Birrell has discharged his work with fair ability and good judgment. .... Mr. James's review is an elaborate, discriminating, and suggestive performance."—*Daily News.*

BRIEF MEMORIALS OF THE REV. ALPHONSE FRANCOIS LACROIX, Missionary of the London Missionary Society in Calcutta.

By his Son-in-Law, Rev. JOSEPH MULLENS, Missionary of the same Society. Crown 8vo., 5s. cloth.

"These memorials are among the most interesting records of Missionary life and labour that have ever been written."—*News of the Churches.*

THE LIFE OF ARTHUR VANDELEUR, Major Royal Artillery.

By the Author of "Memorials of Captain Hedley Vicars," "English Hearts and English Hands." Crown 8vo., 3s. 6d. cloth.

"It would be difficult to imagine a more beautiful and touching story than the simple and not unusually eventful life of Major Vandeleur.'—*Morning Post.*

THE BASUTOS; or, Twenty-three Years in South Africa.

By the Rev. E. CASALIS, late Missionary Director. Post 8vo., 6s. cloth.

"The work gives a capital insight into the life of a powerful African tribe, and as such is a valuable contribution to ethnological science."—*Athenæum.*

COAST MISSIONS: a Memoir of the Rev. Thomas Rosie.

By the Rev. JAMES DODDS, Dunbar. Crown 8vo., 3s. 6d. cloth.

"This volume is highly valuable. The incidents of Mr Rosie's brief life are full of romantic interest."—*British and Foreign Evangelical Review.*

ANNALS OF THE RESCUED.

By the Author of " Haste to the Rescue ; or, Work while it is Day." With a Preface by the Rev. C. E. L. WIGHT-MAN. Crown 8vo., 3s. 6d. cloth.

" This is a deeply interesting volume. It is a book of similar character to ' English Hearts and English Hands,' and !shows what may be effected by well-directed and individual efforts."—*Watchman.*

MEMOIR of the LIFE and BRIEF MINISTRY of the REV. DAVID SANDEMAN, Missionary to CHINA.

By the Rev. ANDREW A. BONAR, Author of the " Memoir of Rev. R. M. M'Cheyne," &c., &c. Crown 8vo., 5s. cloth.

" .... No reader can peruse this brief Memoir without both pleasure and much profit."—*The Dial.*

HELP HEAVENWARD : Words of Strength and Heart-cheer to Zion's Travellers.

By the Rev. OCTAVIUS WINSLOW, D.D. 18mo., 2s. 6d. cloth.

" It is replete with sound, searching, practical remark, conveyed in winning and affectionate spirit, and with luxuriant richness of phraseology." —*Scottish Guardian.*

RAGGED HOMES, AND HOW TO MEND THEM.

By Mrs. BAYLY. Small crown 8vo., 3s. 6d. cloth. Also, a Cheaper Edition, 1s. 6d. cloth limp.

" We scarcely know which to praise most highly, the matter or the manner of this work. Her style is as attractive as her subject. Mrs. Bayly has wrought with an artist's eye and spirit."—*Daily News.*

EVENINGS WITH JOHN BUNYAN; or, The Dream Interpreted.

By JAMES LARGE. Crown 8vo., 4s. 6d. cloth.

" The volume abounds in most valuable matter, eminently calculated to Instruct and to edify. It is replete with interesting facts."—*British Standard.*

MISSIONARY SKETCHES IN NORTHERN INDIA ; with some Reference to recent Events.

By Mrs. WEITBRECHT. Crown 8vo., 5s. cloth.

" An Interesting account, partly historical, partly from personal recollections, and partly contemporary correspondence and publications of the results of Missionary exertions in North India."—*Daily News.*

GOD'S WAY OF PEACE: a Book for the Anxious.

By HORATIUS BONAR, D.D. 18mo., 2s. cloth.

" The name of Dr Bonar carries with it such weight, that it is almost enough for any book to be inscribed with it. The present, although one of his smallest volumes, will probably turn out to be one of the most useful."—*British Standard.*

"THE OMNIPOTENCE OF LOVING-KIND-NESS:" being a Narrative of the Results of a Lady's Seven Months' Work among the Fallen in Glasgow.

Crown 8vo., 3s. 6d. cloth.

" We have been exceedingly interested with this volume. Many of the histories we have read are very touching. We heartily wish this book in the hand of every British Christian matron."—*Church of England Magazine.*

CONFERENCE ON MISSIONS HELD IN 1860 at Liverpool.

Including the Papers read and the Conclusions reached ; with a comprehensive Index showing the various matters brought under review. Edited by the Secretaries to the Conference. 440 pp. demy 8vo., 2s. 6d. cloth.

" The volume presents the ablest manual on the great question of missions to the heathen that has ever come under our notice."—*British Quarterly.*

THE ROMANCE OF NATURAL HISTORY.

By PHILIP HENRY GOSSE, F.R.S. With Illustrations by WOLF. Two Series, each post 8vo., 7s. 6d. cloth.

" This is a charming book. . . . This romance of natural history will be one of the best gift-books which can be procured."—*Daily News.*

A SECOND SERIES OF HYMNS OF FAITH AND HOPE.

By HORATIUS BONAR, D.D. Fcap. 8vo., 5s. cloth. Also, a Pocket Edition of the First Series, 32mo., 1s. 6d. cloth.

" There is a freshness and vigour, an earnestness and a piety in these compositions We have much pleasure in recommending the volume to our readers."—*Evangelical Christendom.*

THE WANDERINGS OF THE CHILDREN OF ISRAEL.

By the late Rev. GEORGE WAGNER, Author of " Sermons on the Book of Job." Crown 8vo., 6s. cloth.

" These are very interesting productions. The sermons are excellent." —*Clerical Journal.*